THE DARK NIGHT OF THE SOUL

Mal Stevens

THE DARK NIGHT OF THE SOUL

This is a work of fiction. Names, characters, places, and incidents are products of the author's imagination or are used fictitiously. Any resemblance to actual persons, living or dead, events, or locales is coincidental.

Disclaimer

This work of fiction explores themes of grief, loss, emotional abuse, and psychological distress. These elements are woven into a story of healing and resilience; however, some readers may find certain passages emotionally challenging. Reader discretion is advised.

ISBN 978-0-6456803-5-5 (paperback)
ISBN 978-0-6456803-6-2 (ebook)

Published by Mal Stevens.
First published 2008. Revised edition 2026.

www.malstevens.com.au

Dedications

For **Marinda, Aimee, Steven and Lily,**
…the LOVES of my life…

For **Silla**…
…you're UP there too mate…

For **Muzzy**…
…always…

The Dark Night of the Soul is akin to a spiritual depression. It is a period in your life after you wake up to your true divinity that everything will seemingly go wrong. It is not uncommon for friendships/relationships to break down, to lose jobs, and to experience some of the hardest things you ever have (internally and externally). This is part of the process. It wakes you up to your shadow self, shows you what to work on in yourself, and it also makes you extremely resilient. Trust the process. The bad is being cleared out to make room for the magic to happen - Unknown

~*~

To anybody who has ever suffered through grief, shattered beyond repair, through loss, disbelief and devastation, may you find peace x

condemnant quo non intellegunt

Table of Contents

Prologue

The woman at the Roebuck servo eyes my little Mazda like it's a joke. Her hand pauses mid-swipe of the counter, her gaze flicking from the dust on my car to the horizon behind me, that endless Kimberley sky that can turn from blue to bruise in a heartbeat.

"And where are you going in that?" she says, her tone caught somewhere between disbelief and concern.

"Home," I answer. "Perth, if the road isn't already closed." I say it in a voice I learned from my grandmother, the one that makes a dare of ordinary words, that says *don't test me, love, I've weathered worse.*

Poppy slides back into the passenger seat with a bag of chips and that look that means she's reading me better than I'm reading myself. She doesn't speak, just opens the packet with that delicate crinkle that sounds far too normal for a day that feels like the end of the world.

We join the highway and meet the water before the highway remembers it's a road. Brown. Fast. A moving skin. The horizon folds in on itself as the rain stitches the distance shut.

I brake without thinking, the bonnet dipping toward the flood like a bow. For a moment the wipers can't keep up, and the world becomes nothing but motion, sky and river trying to trade places.

Then a white 4WD pulls alongside. The driver is the man from the next bowser - sun-cracked face, towbar scuffed, eyes the colour of tin. He leans across, hand a small wave. "Follow me," he mouths. "Close."

I don't even nod. I just do it.

The flood lifts us. The engine light coughs yellow, then mean orange. The steering wheel loosens under my palms the way a hand slips from yours when someone is dying. The water slaps. The bonnet shudders. My pulse is a drum in my ears.

Poppy's breath goes small beside me, and I hear her father's voice again, the way he always finds us when we need him the most. *"Carry them,"* he says.

"I can't," I say, out loud or maybe not. "You do it."

We rise. Or the road does. The engine catches. We break the surface and the whole car exhales, that shuddering sigh machines make when they've decided to keep believing in you a little longer.

On the other side I roll my window down and shout "Thank you!" into the wind, but the man has already U-turned, going back the way he came. Angels don't collect thank-yous. They collect repetitions.

There are three more crossings. Each one tests a different part of me, the part that trusts, the part that listens, and the part that refuses to quit. We borrow the courage of strangers like its fuel, an old couple's Land Cruiser, a young family in a Prado, and then, God help me, no one at all.

The last water is high enough to lick the bottom of the windscreen. The Mazda coughs again. The light flashes. Poppy puts her hand over my fist on the gear stick and squeezes.

"Dad's carrying us," I tell her. "Angels are carrying us. God is carrying us."

I say it to talk my heart down from its ledge, but the cabin warms, not like heat, like hands. The air thickens with something unseen yet deeply known. We float. We crawl. We make it.

On the far bank Poppy starts to cry, quiet and clean, and I let her. There's nothing left in either of us that isn't gratitude or exhaustion.

Hedland is rain and no reception and the kind of silence that means everyone we love is terrified. We leave again. The tyres hum a hymn for the living.

In the dark, grief makes a joke of my sense of direction, and I drive two and a half hours the wrong way. By the time we stop at Auski Roadhouse I can taste the metal of shame. It's a dry taste, like coins and memory.

We turn around. We take the unsealed road, the road that humbles you into paying attention. Every corrugation is a sermon. Every pothole, a question: *Are you awake now?*

At midnight in Cue we sleep inside the car, two women folded into the same small miracle. The rain slows. The stars peer out like shy witnesses.

At dawn, the Great Northern remembers itself. The country opens like a chest unstitching. We arrive home at half past twelve with the sun high and feathers of salt on our cheeks.

I make tea. My hands won't stop shaking, so I let them shake.

Poppy leans against the kitchen bench and tells me I drove like a legend, and I tell her legends are just mothers who refuse to die before their daughters grow up.

Later, when the house is quiet and I'm not, I understand something simple and enormous - I have been letting other people choose whether I live fully or not.

The flood doesn't care if I am lovable. The flood doesn't care who texted last. The flood cares whether you keep the wheels moving and your eyes on the line and whether you ask for help while you can still be heard.

I boil the kettle again.

I stand in the doorway and look at the strip of sky the same way I used to look at men, and I ask, *Will you be kind to me?* The sky doesn't answer. It keeps being sky. It keeps being blue in a way that isn't about me, and somehow that's kinder than anything.

Tomorrow, I will plant gerberas. Today, I will write. We were carried. Now we learn to walk.

Chapter One

Before something breaks, it rehearses the sound of breaking.

They say when your life is about to change forever, you don't always notice the warning signs. Sometimes they arrive quietly, dressed in ordinary clothes, disguised as a day like any other.

In September of my forty-first year, the day looked perfect. Sunlight pooled on the kitchen tiles and the kettle stuttered to a boil. Birds outside repeated their old, rehearsed lines as if nothing new would ever happen to anyone. The sky wore its best blue. The jacaranda shook loose a handful of purple confetti. Even the breeze pretended it had nowhere urgent to be.

From the outside, it could have been any morning. But inside me, a different weather had gathered, low, electric, waiting. I stood at the sink with my coffee cooling in my hand and felt the kind of silence you don't make on purpose. Not the soft, restful kind. The watchful kind. The kind that presses a palm over your mouth and says, *listen.*

For years I'd been moving through life like glass, transparent, careful, easily shattered. My marriage of twenty-two years had sanded me down to a dull edge. Alcohol. Violence. Infidelity. Lies. A family with barbed wire in their mouths. We once tied white ribbons around our promises and called them forever. Over time each ribbon rotted into string, then thread, then nothing.

I slept beside betrayal and woke to it wearing my breakfast smile. Told myself this was love. Told myself I was lucky. Told myself a thousand small stories so I could keep living the big one.

I was stubborn though. Stubborn enough to keep putting

one foot in front of the other. Stubborn enough to choose lipstick over truth on most mornings. Stubborn enough to mistake endurance for devotion. Even as the bruises faded into that sickly yellow and his words rang in my bones - *you're useless, you're nothing, you'll never be anyone* - I clung to scraps of meaning like a woman clutching fabric on a windy cliff.

Back then I still believed that commonsense would save me. That if I made the lists, paid the bills, smiled at the neighbours, folded the towels just so, the universe would notice my effort and reward it with peace. I didn't understand yet that commonsense has no jurisdiction over chaos.

That September morning I didn't know it, but I was about to lose even that small illusion.

The warning didn't come how you might imagine. No thunder, no omen. Just light. It was the way the sun hit the garden path, clean, hard, and honest. In that brightness something inside me cracked and spilled a picture across my mind, my body thrown at a wrong angle, skull split against brick, blood thin as watercolour.

It happened in a heartbeat, sudden, complete, and it didn't feel imagined. It felt like memory. Like I'd already done it. Like I was already gone.

And the strangest part? For that sliver of time, it was beautiful.

No performance. No fear. No waking up to the same argument inside a different day. Just silence. Like stepping out of a costume that had grown heavy as iron. Like slipping into water and not needing air. It wasn't dramatic in my mind, it was simple, cool, inevitable. The thought rested against me with the tenderness of a hand on a fevered forehead.

Then the world snapped back. The kettle shrieked. The dog scratched at the laundry door. Somewhere, a lawnmower argued with the morning. I breathed, shaky, guilty, and set the coffee down untouched.

Life, I reminded myself, doesn't let you leave just because you're tired.

I put on my shoes, the jacket with the loose button I kept promising to fix, picked up my handbag and keys like a woman who knew where she was going and why. It was the performance I'd mastered, the one where my body moved the right way while my mind lagged behind in the shadows.

The radio chattered as I drove. A voice selling insurance. A song I used to love before loving it became impossible. Every red light felt too long, every green too short. The world carried on as if my life wasn't cracking at the edges. Mothers pushed prams, a man washed his ute, school children crossed with backpacks bouncing against their spines, all of them breathing the same ordinary air that suddenly felt foreign in my lungs.

I had an interview. The kind you attend because people who love you insist you must be doing something about things. A fresh start, they said. A new chapter. Words for greeting cards from people who've never had to rebuild from splinters.

The building was small and square, smelling faintly of toner and stale carpet. "Take a seat, Lena," the receptionist said, smiling with her mouth but not her eyes.

The leather chair tried to be kind to my back. I tucked my hands together so they couldn't betray the tremor in them. The clock on the wall ticked with the smug patience of bureaucracy.

The man who arrived to interview me was small and balding in the precise way of men who love their pen collections. He asked about experience, strengths, goals. My mouth shaped passable sentences. My knee juddered under the desk, so I gently pressed it down with my palm.

"Is something the matter?" he asked, voice clipped with a Monday's impatience.

Yes, I wanted to say. *Everything. The whole of it. There's a fault line running through the floor and it's humming.*

But I shrugged instead, and it looked like indifference.

He studied me the way people study a recipe they don't trust. "If you don't want to be here, you're free to go."

So I did the least sensible thing and stood up. Left my empty smile on his desk between the stapler and the neat fan of post-its. Walked through reception with my head down, feeling the fluorescent lights turn my skin to paper. No one stopped me. Why would they? To them I was just another woman in a neat jacket and cheap heels, someone's wife or mother, sliding through a life as ordinary as office carpet.

Outside, the air hit my face like clarity. I got into the car and sat for a long time, engine off, hands slack on the wheel. I thought about calling someone, anyone, but who do you call when you don't yet know what's ending?

I don't remember turning the key, only the sudden sound of the indicator clicking like a heartbeat. The world moved around me, and I followed because stopping felt too loud.

I drove without direction with the suburbs peeling past me in slices, school zones, shopping strips, and driveways glossed with sprinkler water.

At one intersection, an old man with a walking stick waited for the green light, and for some reason the sight of him undid me. The tenderness of his slowness. The patience. I wondered if he had once loved someone the way I had, hard enough to lose himself in the effort of it.

By the time I reached the coast road, the sea was that bruised blue it gets when it's thinking about rain. I pulled over, let the wind slap my face, and watched waves muscle the shore. The horizon looked like something you could step across if you wanted it badly enough. I thought about the image from that morning, my body, the brick, the blood, and wondered how many women had stood in this exact place rehearsing their exit in silence. The world wouldn't even notice, I thought. The tide would carry me away as gently as a rumour.

Then the wind changed. A burst of sea spray, cold and stinging, smacked me full across the face, and something primitive inside me barked, *No. Not yet.*

So I turned inland.

The car seemed to know where to go when I didn't. It took me to the kind of pub that exists at the edge of every town, the one that smells of fryer oil and defeat. I walked in because it was easier than turning around.

The bartender gave me a nod that meant I won't ask. There were four other people scattered along the bar - men in work boots staring into their schooners like the answers might be floating at the bottom. The TV murmured a muted horse race. Somewhere in the corner, a jukebox blinked like it couldn't remember what decade it was.

The first sip bit. The second eased. The third made promises it would never keep.

The glass in my hand was blessedly honest, cold, heavy, and unpretending. It didn't love me, but it also didn't lie. I liked that about it.

I thought about how many times I'd sat across from Marko in pubs like this one, watching him charm a room, buy another round, and tell stories that made people forget he was dangerous when the night turned. I used to love that part of him, the way he could light up a crowd. It took me years to see that the light he gave off wasn't warmth, it was fire. And I was the thing left smouldering at the end when it went out.

The bartender slid another drink my way without being asked. "On the house," he said. I nodded, too tired to decline, too polite to refuse comfort when it came disguised as habit.

By the time I left, the day had dissolved into a bruise-coloured evening. The car park shimmered with heat that had nowhere to go. I sat behind the wheel and stared at my reflection in the rearview mirror, eyes swollen, mascara gone rogue, and a woman rehearsing calm.

"Commonsense," I said aloud, testing the word like it belonged to someone else. "You'd think I'd have more of it."

The voice that answered was my own, but quieter: *You had survival, love. That's not the same thing.*

The drive home was a blur stitched together by taillights and denial. I don't remember traffic lights or songs, only the way the steering wheel felt, hot, slick, and foreign under my hands.

My jacket slid off the passenger seat in a tired slump. Somewhere between the highway and the driveway, I lost the thread that held me upright. I turned into the street too fast, braked too late, and the car stopped a metre short of the garage door.

I sat there a long time, engine humming, breath coming shallow and quick. The house glowed with that false warmth of lights left on to pretend someone cares.

When I finally made myself move, my legs didn't want to

hold me. I tripped on the first step, palms out, catching nothing, and went down hard on the coarse mat. My knuckles split. The sting was a mercy. It reminded me I was still here.

I knocked, gentle and foolish.

The porch light flicked on and the door yawned open like a lesson.

Marko stood there. His eyes were wide and red, the skin beneath them bagged from nights that hadn't known sleep. There were bags at his feet - two cheap duffels and the suitcase we'd taken to Bali the summer we pretended sunsets could fix us.

"I-" I started, but my voice cracked on the smallest word in the language.

He stepped around me.

The sound our wedding ring made against the doorframe as he brushed past was so soft I almost imagined it.

I grabbed his ankle, absurd, desperate, and childish. My cheek pressed to the cool tile, humiliation burning its way down my spine. No word I could think of would make this moment smaller. None could enlarge me enough to fill the space between us.

He shook me off like you shake off a dog you don't want to kick. Then he carried the bags to the car.

I watched him drive away through the blur of my breath on the glass. Stood there long after the taillights sank into the road's black mouth, and the empty street steadied its face for the neighbours.

There's a kind of quiet that follows a door closing like that. It isn't silence, it's the sound of a life that has just realised its shape.

The house held its breath. Every object seemed to lean away from me, the photo frames, the couch cushions, even the dog's empty bowl.

I walked through the rooms like a stranger touring the ruins of her own home. The kitchen smelled faintly of lemon cleaner and loss. A single plate sat on the counter beside an untouched sandwich, its edges curled.

I poured a glass of water and didn't drink it. I lit a candle without knowing why. I thought about calling my sister, but what would I say? *He's gone again, but this time it feels permanent?* She'd heard it all before.

So, I sat on the floor, knees drawn up, and stared at the small flame until my eyes blurred. The wax pooled like a wound, and I thought, absurdly, that even candles know how to bleed gracefully.

When sleep came, it was jagged and brief, the kind that forgets to be merciful. I dreamt of the sea again, of waves closing over me, cool and heavy and kind.

When morning came, it came without mercy. The light was too clean, too honest. It didn't care that my eyes were swollen or that my mouth still tasted of last night's salt. The house looked both smaller and emptier, as though grief had already started eating through the walls.

I moved through it like a trespasser. The kettle, obedient as ever, clicked on, and the sound seemed obscene. I poured coffee I didn't drink. The dog nosed my leg, confused by the rearrangement of loyalty in the air.

Outside, the jacaranda had dropped half its flowers overnight, small purple casualties scattered across the path. I thought of the sun the day before, the way it had cut across the tiles, that clean slice of light that showed me my own end. Maybe that had been the warning. Maybe every woman knows when the story's about to change but doesn't have the language for it yet.

The clock on the wall coughed its seconds. The fridge hummed. Somewhere, a truck reversed, beeping like a machine learning to apologise.

I should have cried, but I didn't. I was too tired for performance, even my own. Instead, I just stood there, breathing in, breathing out, and tried to remember the last time I'd felt uncomplicated joy. The memory wouldn't come.

By mid-morning, the phone began to ring. It was my sister first, then a friend, then silence again. I didn't answer. What would I say? *He's gone, but I can't tell if that's a tragedy or a reprieve?*

The dog barked once at nothing, a small defiance. I almost thanked him for it.

I thought about cleaning. Cleaning is what women do when language fails. We polish, wipe, fold, stack, as if order can replace meaning. I started with the kitchen bench, moving things that didn't need moving, aligning the canisters, refolding the tea towels, trying to trick the universe into symmetry.

But the air stayed wrong. Every sound had an echo. Every shadow a memory.

I sat at the table and stared at the phone. The part of me that still believed in reconciliation whispered, *He'll call. He always calls.* But the part of me that had been paying attention knew better.

It wasn't rage I felt because rage would have meant energy. It was something quieter, the hollow thud of finality.

Hours passed in their strange elastic way. I must have stood. I must have moved from one room to another. The sky outside shifted from white to pewter. A storm was coming. The kind that makes you believe the earth is capable of weeping.

I lit another candle because I couldn't stand the overhead light, it was too clinical, too witness-like. The flame wavered, small and sincere.

That was when I heard it.

Three small knocks against the wood. Polite. Too polite.

For a second I thought maybe it was him, maybe he'd forgotten something, maybe regret had turned the car around.

But even before I opened the door, I knew.

The silence behind it had a weight. A heaviness that waited with folded hands and didn't care if I was ready.

Chapter Two

Some truths arrive on tiptoe and still split the floorboards.

That night after he left, I didn't sleep. I sat at the kitchen table, tracing the grain in the wood as if it were a map that could tell me how to get back to the woman I used to be. The house hummed its small, loyal noises; the clock ticking, the dog shifting in her sleep, the faint hum of the refrigerator keeping time. Outside, the sky was thick with silence.

Something in me already knew. It wasn't a thought or a fear. It was a knowing that lived lower, deeper, in the bones. The air itself had weight, a density that made every breath deliberate. I kept telling myself I'd apologise in the morning, that it was just another fight, another bruise on a wall already painted with them. I'd call. He'd answer. We'd say words that pretended to fix things.

But beneath those promises, something waited. The quiet before the storm that doesn't just pass over you, it becomes you.

The knock was polite. Too polite.

Three small taps against the wood, the kind you'd expect from a neighbour borrowing sugar.

Two officers stood on the porch, their uniforms sharp, their hats tucked just so. Faces practised into that symmetry of solemnity they must rehearse in mirrors. Compassion shaped into straight lines.

"Mrs -?" one asked.

I nodded, though the name felt foreign in my bones.

"There's been an accident," the other said, his voice low, deliberate. The words arranged themselves in the air like a small, cautious hurricane.

Time fractured.

I didn't hear the prepositions or the adjectives. Just the nouns. Accident. Vehicle. Husband. Dead.

The floor slipped out from under me, though my body stayed standing. I gripped the frame with both hands as though it could keep me tethered to the world.

They kept talking, their voices careful, factual, trained. Single vehicle. High speed. Alcohol involved. Next of kin. Time of death.

The words fell like stones into me, sinking deeper than breath could reach.

I didn't ask the usual questions - When? Where? How? I only whispered the three words that came like an exhale from my ribs. "I love you."

The officers exchanged a look. They weren't trained for this part, the part where a widow answered death with a confession.

My knees buckled. I sank to the floor, cheek against the tile that still held the night's cool. I didn't sob at first. I made no sound at all. Just lay there while their solemn voices hovered above me like distant radio static.

They offered me a chair. I chose the floor. It felt like the only honest place.

"He was upset," one of them added gently, as if I might not grasp that part.

"I know," I said, though the words scraped my throat. "He was upset because of me."

Silence. That was another skill they'd been taught. To hold it without flinching.

"He was drinking because of me."

They looked at the carpet.

"Dead because of me."

The sentence tasted like coins. Heavy, metallic, and bitter.

When they finally left, their condolences clung to the air like stale perfume. The door shut behind them, and the house exhaled into a silence so vast it screamed.

I folded in on myself. My body heaved, sobs cracking their way out of me in guttural bursts I didn't recognise as mine. I clawed at the carpet as if I could find an exit in the fibres.

The world outside was obscenely normal. A lawnmower droned down the street. Birds argued with the morning. Somewhere, a child laughed. How dare they, I thought. How dare life keep on going when mine had just been obliterated.

Hours passed. Or maybe minutes. Time had slipped its leash. The house filled with fragments.

The kettle whistled though I hadn't turned it on. The dog pawed at the laundry door, whining, confused. The phone rang, then rang again, then gave up.

Neighbours arrived like moths drawn to a flame, carrying flowers and casseroles wrapped in foil, the universal language of people who don't know what to say. I nodded, thanked them, and then set the dishes on the counter. As if grief could be absorbed through pasta bake and chicken pie.

The food went cold. I couldn't taste anything.

At night I lay in bed, waiting for headlights that would never sweep across the curtains. Waiting for a car that would never pull into the driveway. Waiting for the sound of his key in the lock.

Sleep finally dragged me into dreams where he was still alive, still close enough to touch. I woke with my arms stretched across the sheets, clutching air.

The guilt arrived like an occupying army.

He was dead because he had been drinking.

He had been drinking because he was upset.

He was upset because of me.

The logic was circular, relentless, and unbreakable.

I wore it like a second skin, heavier than grief. It clung to every thought, every breath, and every corner of the house.

The pub replayed itself in my mind on a cruel loop, the glass sweating in my hand, sparkling like it was the only honest thing in the world. The comfort I had chosen over him.

The memory of his face at the door, swollen eyes, wordless, carrying bags that weren't just luggage but verdicts.

The taillights bleeding red into the road's black mouth. The final punctuation mark to our unravelled story.

And the whisper in my head that repeated without mercy: This is your fault.

At the morgue, denial cracked into dust.

They were expecting me. Voices hushed, footsteps echoing in that hollow space where grief is stacked like paperwork.

My feet dragged across the sterile tiles until I reached the cold table.

And there he was.

Not the man who laughed, or shouted, or bruised, or cried. Not the man who kissed my neck in crowded kitchens, or who left socks balled in corners, or who ruined holidays with his temper.

Just a body.

Still. Pale.

No fights in his silence. No betrayals in his closed eyes. No cruelty in his folded hands. Just a man who had once been mine and wasn't anymore.

I wanted to touch him, but I couldn't. My arms hung frozen

at my sides. If I reached for him, I feared I might fall into that coldness and never climb out.

The sob that tore from my chest startled even me. It was not just pain, it was recognition. That everything I thought I knew about love, about marriage, about endurance, had been shattered.

In that sterile room, one truth cut through the fog, and that truth was that my life would never, ever be the same again.

Grief isn't tidy. It doesn't move in straight lines or offer neat closure.

It's jagged. Non-linear. Some days I was flattened, barely able to stand. Others I was incandescent with fury, at him, at myself, and at the universe for its obscene indifference.

And then there were days of nothing. A hollow blankness more terrifying than pain.

I haunted the house like a ghost, touching objects that no longer belonged to anyone, his shirts sagging in the wardrobe, the dent in his pillow, and the jar of peanut butter he always left unsealed.

The ordinariness of it broke me more than death itself. How could life look unchanged when everything had collapsed?

The mirror began to frighten me. I would catch glimpses of myself and look away quickly, as though grief had made me see-through. The house itself seemed to tilt, heavy on one side, as if its bones too were learning to live without him.

There were nights I thought I heard his boots on the verandah, or the jangle of his keys. I would hold my breath, heart pounding with hope and dread, until the quiet made a fool of me again.

Then came the funeral.

It arrived like a wave I couldn't stop. People filled the church with their well-meant sorrow, the scent of lilies, the scrape of chairs, the murmur of hymns I didn't believe in. I sat in the front pew, hands folded, face composed, heart unrecognisable.

I wanted to stand up and tell them everything. That he wasn't just a good man. That he was complicated, cruel, brilliant, broken. That love and pain had lived side by side in us for so long they were indistinguishable.

But I stayed silent. Because funerals aren't for truth. They're for mercy.

Afterward, someone hugged me too tightly and whispered, "At least he's at peace now."

I wanted to laugh. Peace was never his language.

When the crowd thinned, I stayed behind. The sunlight streamed through stained glass and broke across the coffin in fractured colour. I pressed my palm to the wood and whispered the words I hadn't said enough when he was alive. "I forgive you."

Then, quieter still, "Forgive me, too."

The sound of my own voice echoed like a secret prayer. Somewhere, deep in the timber, I imagined it was received.

The church emptied slowly, like lungs deflating. Outside, the world had the audacity to shine. People lingered in small clusters beside cars, balancing plates of finger food, whispering condolences that evaporated before they reached the heart. I stood there, half-watching, half-drifting. Someone pressed a paper cup of water into my hand, and I stared at it as though it were an alien object. The liquid trembled with the same small, nervous energy that lived beneath my skin.

Later, when everyone had gone, I drove home through streets I barely recognised. The world had grown too bright, the colours too sharp. The jacarandas that had been blooming only weeks before were thinning, their purple rain turning brown on the footpaths. Every corner held a ghost of us, the café where he'd laughed too loud, the servo where we'd argued, and the park bench where we once sat in silence and called it love.

Back home, the house waited, unchanged, unbothered, cruelly intact. The dog barked once, then quieted, as if recognising the new order. I closed the door behind me and felt the sound of the latch echo through every empty room.

That night, I didn't turn on any lights. The dark was kinder. I moved through the rooms by memory, tracing the walls with my fingertips, learning the shape of absence. His scent lingered in pockets, the faint bite of aftershave, the ghost of smoke on a jacket he'd never hang up properly. It clung to me, that smell, until it became both comfort and punishment.

I slept on the couch because the bed was too loud with memory. Every indentation, every crease in the sheet, screamed that he had existed. I wrapped myself in a blanket that smelled of rain and exhaustion, and for the first time in days, I dreamed of nothing.

When morning came, it brought no mercy. Grief is greedy, it devours every corner of your life and still asks for more. I moved through the rituals of the living like a marionette, feed the dog, make coffee, and then stare at it until it went cold. The smallest actions felt monumental. Lifting a spoon. Turning a tap. Breathing.

There were moments when I forgot. Fleeting, merciful lapses. I'd see something on the television and think, I have to tell him that. And then the remembering came, swift and violent. Like falling down the same flight of stairs, again and again, knowing every step but unable to stop the descent.

Days folded into weeks. The casseroles stopped arriving. The neighbours stopped checking in. The phone went from ringing too often to not at all. I became invisible, which was both a relief, and a kind of death in itself.

It was then I began to speak to him aloud. Quietly at first, embarrassed even in my solitude. "You missed the bills again," I'd mutter when I opened the mail. Or, "The dog's off her food, you'd know what to do." Over time, the conversations grew longer. I told him about the way the garden had gone wild, about how the moon seemed closer these nights, about how the world kept spinning despite my protests.

Once, during a storm, I stood barefoot on the back step, rain streaming down my face, and shouted into the dark sky, "Are you happy now?" The thunder answered, low and distant. I took it as yes. Or maybe no. It didn't matter.

Grief taught me strange things. How time can expand and collapse in the same breath. How laughter can slip out of you like a betrayal. How the world, in its endless ordinariness, keeps offering itself to you even when you've sworn not to take it.

One afternoon, weeks later, I found myself in the supermarket staring at the shelf where his favourite cereal used to sit. Without thinking, I reached for it. My hand froze halfway. The absurdity of it broke something open. I laughed, sharp, ugly, too loud, and then cried right there between the Weet-Bix and the canned peaches. People stared. I let them.

That night, I wrote in a notebook for the first time since it happened. Just a single sentence. He died, and the world didn't. I stared at it until the words blurred. Then, below it, I wrote another. Neither did I.

It wasn't hope. Not yet. It was simply fact.

The weeks rolled on, slow as syrup. Every day I woke,

expecting to feel less, but grief doesn't dilute, it ferments. It changes shape, sharpens edges, and then softens again. It sneaks up in small ambushes, the smell of petrol, the hum of a particular song, the way the light hit the kitchen bench at 3 p.m.

I learned to live around it. To cook enough for just Poppy and I. To fold only our clothes. To leave his mug in the cupboard instead of by the sink. These were tiny rebellions against the past, acts of reluctant acceptance. And yet, sometimes, I'd still catch myself waiting. Listening for a sound that would never come.

One morning, while sorting through a drawer, I found the note, the one he'd written long ago, scrawled on the back of a receipt. "Common sense things," the heading read, his handwriting slanted and impatient.

1. Don't forget to fill the tank before long trips.
2. Always hang the washing out early before the sun hits.
3. Be kind, even when you're tired.
4. Love doesn't fix everything, but it's still worth trying.

I read it again and again until the ink blurred, tears smudging his words into ghosts. Common sense, he'd called it. But there was nothing common about survival.

Some nights, the house still feels like it's holding its breath. I lie awake listening for the shift in the dark that tells me I'm not alone, not haunted, exactly, but witnessed. There's a softness that settles in those hours before dawn, a sense that maybe he's there, just beyond the edge of the light.

The voice inside me, the one that began as a whisper, has grown steadier. It doesn't tell me to move on. It tells me to stay. To stay in this body, this breath, this strange half-life that's learning how to become whole again.

Grief, I've realised, is both a tomb and a teacher. It shows you every fracture you've ignored, every truth you've buried beneath routine and reason. It demands that you rebuild yourself from the inside out, bone by bone, breath by breath.

Two people died that night. One on the road. The other standing upright in a house that had grown twenty sizes too large.

But the sick, stubborn truth of grief is this, it doesn't let you die with your dead.

It demands that you catalogue the wreckage.

Answer the phone.

Accept the casseroles.

Sign the paperwork.

Listen to sympathy spoken like passwords.

It forces you to walk barefoot across the fragments until your feet are bloodied and blistered and still moving.

And that is how the bottom fell out.

Not with a bang, but with a thousand small collapses.

That was the day my dark night began.

The day I lost him.

The day I lost myself.

And the day, without knowing it, I began the long, brutal climb back.

Because when the bottom finally falls out, there is only one direction left to go.

Up.

Tomorrow the practical grief will begin, the calls, the clothes, the telling and the retelling in past tense. The sky will keep being blue in a way that isn't about me, and I will learn to breathe inside it. But that is another chapter.

Chapter Three

Time folded strangely after the officers left. Days bled into one another, each one replaying fragments of the last. I don't remember what order things came in, the phone calls, the viewing, the funeral. It all felt like one long day that refused to end. But the news didn't stop at my door. It never does.

Grief has a way of spilling, leaking through walls, sliding under doors, carried on the tongues of people who don't know what to say but say it anyway. By the time the officers' car pulled away from the curb, the story had already begun its slow crawl through the town. Phones rang. Whispers spread. Pity grew legs and walked itself into every kitchen and every shopfront. By nightfall, people I hadn't spoken to in years seemed to know, their voices landing in my voicemail box with the same tired script: *I'm so sorry. Please call if you need anything.* But I didn't need anything. Not food, not flowers, not advice. Poppy and I needed time to collapse without being watched. We needed silence that didn't choke us. We needed permission to not yet be strong. None of those could be delivered in a casserole dish.

The morning after, my sister appeared without warning. She carried her grief in her body, eyes red and swollen, lips bitten raw, movements too sharp, as though still trying to outrun the news.

"Oh, Lena," she whispered, pulling me into her arms before I could step back. Lavender soap, cigarette smoke, supermarket perfume. Her scent undid me in ways I hadn't expected. I collapsed against her, but even in her arms, I felt brittle. Like glass wrapped in newspaper. If she pressed too hard, I would splinter. She didn't cry much in front of me. Instead, she filled the kitchen with the busyness of survival like tidying counters that didn't need tidying, boiling the kettle, and rearranging the flowers into cleaner vases. Movement was her shield, her way of fighting what had already won. I let her. I didn't have the strength to argue.

At one point she turned, mug trembling slightly in her hand, and asked, "Do you want me to stay the night?"

I shook my head. "No. I just need… quiet."

She nodded, but her eyes said she didn't trust me with my own solitude. She lingered until dusk anyway, hovering in doorways, half-afraid to leave me alone with the ghosts.

By afternoon, the neighbours had started arriving. One by one, they appeared on my doorstep, carrying sorrow like baskets of bread. Some knocked gently. Others shuffled awkwardly, holding foil-wrapped casseroles with too much cheese. A few hugged me too long, their pity thick enough to suffocate. Their words blurred into a chorus, *We're so sorry… He'll be missed… If there's anything you need…* Each phrase struck me as both kindness and cruelty. Kind because they cared, cruel because none of it could bring him back. I thanked them anyway, because refusing kindness when offered feels like another sin. But inside I was screaming, *stop looking at me like that. Stop pitying me. Stop making me the main character in a tragedy I never auditioned for.* When they left, the kitchen was crowded with offerings. Lasagnas stacked like bricks. Soup in Tupperware tubs. Bread still warm from ovens. The house smelled of garlic, grief, and pity. I hadn't eaten in two days. I couldn't bring myself to start now.

Instead, I stood at the sink, staring out at the yard where his boots still sat by the back steps. Mud dried in the treads. Half an imprint of him, stubborn as the life he'd left behind. The funeral home called next. Their voice was clipped, professional, the tone of someone who dealt with loss by treating it as paperwork. "We'll need to confirm arrangements, Mrs -. Viewing, service, burial or cremation…"

I stared at the phone, my mind splitting under the absurdity of it. My husband had been alive less than forty-eight hours ago, and now strangers were asking me to choose between boxes and flames.

"I -" My throat broke. "I can't."

"You'll need to," the woman replied, not unkindly, but with the patience of someone who had walked widows through this conversation a hundred times before.

I hung up. The phone rang again later. I let it ring until it died. That night, I dreamt of rooms full of coffins, each one whispering my name.

The family descended soon after. Aunts with loud voices. Cousins whispering in corners. My mother pacing, sharp-eyed, scanning the house for signs of how bad things had really been. "She looks terrible," one of them murmured. "She should have seen this coming," another said under their breath. The words reached me anyway, each syllable landing like a stone in my chest. I wanted to stand up and scream at them, to tell them they hadn't been there for the bruises, the broken promises, the nights when silence was more violent than shouting. But shame sealed my mouth. It's a strange thing, shame. It doesn't just live in your chest. It climbs your throat, clamps your jaw, forces you into muteness while the world speaks over you. So I stood in my own living room, surrounded by people who claimed to know me, and felt lonelier than if I'd been alone. That evening, when they finally left, the house seemed to sigh in relief. I sat on the floor among the flowers, petals already wilting in their vases, and realised that death makes everything expire faster, the blooms, the milk, and the lies we used to live on.

The viewing nearly broke me. I didn't want to go. Every part of me screamed to stay home, to keep him alive in my mind, to refuse the finality of seeing his body laid out like an object. But the family insisted. Closure, they called it, as if closure were a gift you could unwrap in a cold room. He lay there, dressed in a suit he hadn't worn since weddings and job interviews. His face was pale, waxen, unnervingly calm.

"Doesn't he look peaceful?" someone whispered.

No. He didn't. He looked gone.

I stayed at the edge of the room, my legs refusing to carry me forward. My hands ached to reach out, to touch his hand, to prove to myself he was real. But fear rooted me where I stood, the fear of cold flesh, of permanence, of confirming that all the years of love, betrayal, violence, and hope had been reduced to this, silence. Others filed past, touching him, murmuring prayers. None of them knew him like I had. None of them knew the weight of his hands, the cruelty hidden in his tenderness, the secrets we had carried in the dark. I turned my face away, because in that moment, grief and relief tangled too closely, and I didn't want anyone to see. Outside, the air tasted of disinfectant and rain. I leaned against the brick wall until the tremor left my legs. A cigarette butt smouldered near the drain. I remember thinking even smoke knew how to leave better than I did.

The funeral was worse. The church was crowded with faces I hadn't seen in years. Some came for him. Some came for the story. Some came because small towns teach you to show up whether you mean it or not. The service was stiff, rehearsed, the words of the priest landing like stones, *ashes to ashes, dust to dust.* People sniffled at the right moments. A choir sang hymns that had once comforted me and now felt hollow. When they looked at me, I couldn't meet their eyes. Their pity was unbearable. Their whispers louder than any sermon. *She let him leave. They'd been fighting. He was drinking. She should have stopped him.*

I became both victim and culprit, widow and suspect. And the cruellest part? Some small part of me believed them. After the service, the coffin disappeared into the ground like a swallowed word. The thud of soil against wood was the loudest sound I'd ever heard. I didn't cry then. I just stood there, frozen in the rain, until someone, maybe my sister, led me back to the car.

That night I lay awake, listening for him. The creak of the house, the sigh of the fridge, the shuffle of the dog, all of it disguised itself as his return. But he never came. Instead, shame visited me. It sat at the end of the bed, whispering that I had failed. That I hadn't loved enough, hadn't forgiven enough, hadn't fought hard enough. It told me that his death was my fault, and I believed it, because grief makes you gullible to lies that sound like truth. I pressed my face into the pillow and whispered, "I love you." The words tasted like blood. Too late. Always too late.

Days wore the same face. Grief didn't kill me. It hollowed me out and forced me to keep breathing. It made me live in the wreckage, walking barefoot across shards of my old life, bleeding with every step. Nights bled into mornings, indistinguishable. I would wake gasping, my body jerking as though falling from some invisible height. Dreams of headlights, of impact, of silence. I'd reach for him instinctively, only to find the cold impression of absence. Sometimes I thought I heard his voice, half asleep, between breaths, a whisper just behind the curtain of reality. It wasn't words, only presence. A shift in the air. A memory masquerading as sound. I'd whisper back anyway: *I'm still here.* The dog slept closer now, as if guarding me from something she didn't understand. She'd lift her head in the dark, ears twitching, waiting for a step that never came. We were both haunted by habit.

Days took on a strange texture, heavy and translucent, like being underwater. The world was muted, every sound arriving through distance, the kettle's hiss, the soft whine of a fly, or the slow tick of the clock. Even colour seemed to fade. The sky dulled to ash, the jacarandas wilted into bruised purple, the garden went wild and indifferent. One afternoon, I opened his wardrobe. The smell of him struck me first, earth and sweat, faint traces of engine oil. His shirts hung obediently, shoulders sagging as if waiting for orders. I pressed my face into one and breathed until I couldn't tell where I ended and the memory began. Then anger came, sudden and white-hot. I tore one sleeve, then another, until the fabric gave way with a sound like heartbreak. I wanted to destroy the proof of him, to scatter him so he couldn't haunt me anymore. But grief is circular, it punishes you for every attempt to escape. By the time I stopped, the floor was littered with cotton and buttons, and I was shaking so violently I could barely stand. I sank to the floor, clutching a torn cuff in my fist, and whispered, *You left me with everything and nothing.*

The world expected function. Bills still arrived. The dog still needed walking. The washing still needed doing. The banality of it enraged me. How could life demand chores when my heart was rubble? I learned to move through those days as if underwater. People mistook it for composure. They didn't see the undertow. At the supermarket, strangers I barely knew stopped me mid-aisle. "I heard about Marko," they'd murmur, voices syruped with sympathy. "You poor thing." Their eyes scanned me like a headline they'd already read. I became a story told in fragments, passed between checkouts and cafés. Once, I overheard someone say, "Such a shame. But you know, they weren't happy." I left my basket right there in the aisle and walked out, the fluorescent lights chasing me into the sun. I sat in the car and laughed, a raw, disbelieving sound that cracked in the middle. It wasn't funny, but the absurdity of it all demanded laughter or madness. Maybe both.

In the weeks that followed, I started walking at night. The dark felt safer than daylight, and it didn't ask questions. I walked through the backstreets, past sleeping houses and lemon trees shedding their fruit. The air smelled of dust and sea-salt. Sometimes I ended up at the edge of town, near the railway where trains passed without stopping. The vibration in the ground comforted me, it was proof that something still moved, even if I couldn't. I'd stand there until the last carriage disappeared, wind pressing tears from my eyes. One night, I found myself whispering into the rails, *Where are you now?* The metal stayed cold. The stars above blinked, indifferent. But a breeze rose then, lifting my hair, and brushing my cheek with a softness that felt deliberate. I took it as an answer. Maybe the only one I'd ever get.

The phone calls slowed, then stopped. The casseroles spoiled in the freezer. The flowers browned at the edges. People moved on, as people do. I didn't blame them, they all had lives to return to. I just didn't know how to return to mine. Loneliness isn't quiet, it hums. It fills every corner of the room until you start talking back to it. I spoke to the house, to the dog, to the shadows on the wall. Sometimes I caught my reflection mid-sentence and startled myself. The widow talking to ghosts. But even that was living. A fractured kind of living, yes, but breath was breath, however uneven.

The first real morning came weeks later. I woke before dawn, the air still silver with sleep. Outside, the world was hushed and waiting. For once, I didn't dread the light. I opened the door, stepped onto the porch, and felt the chill sting my skin awake. Somewhere, a magpie began to sing, clear, defiant. I closed my eyes and let the sound pierce through me. The song wasn't for me, but it reached me anyway. *Tomorrow*, I told myself, *I will try to eat. Tomorrow, I will answer one phone call. Tomorrow, I will live just enough to see if living still fits.* And in that fragile promise, I felt something like the smallest flicker of forgiveness, not from him, not from God, but from the piece of me that still wanted to survive.

Exile isn't always about leaving a place. Sometimes it's about being cast out of the life you thought was yours. That's where I found myself next, banished into a world that no longer felt like mine. But maybe exile is also where rebirth begins. The shattering news had come and gone, leaving wreckage in its wake. The headlines had faded. The calls had stopped. The casseroles had cooled. But somewhere beneath the ruins, a pulse remained, weak, steady, insistent. By the time the sun went down, the world had already rearranged itself without asking my permission. The phone had gone quiet. The food had cooled. Even the air had stopped holding its breath for me. I stood at the kitchen window and watched the sky fold itself into night, blue becoming black, black becoming something quieter. The flood had come and gone. The wreckage was mine to catalogue.

Tomorrow would bring a new kind of cruelty, the kind measured in forms and signatures, in tidy lines that insist on endings. But tonight there was only this, a house that still breathed, a dog that would not leave my side, and a pulse in my wrist that kept saying the same impossible thing - *keep breathing.*

Chapter Four

Some silences arrive dressed as peace, but underneath they hum with unfinished sentences.

The paperwork arrived next, fat envelopes stamped URGENT in red, as if grief obeyed deadlines. I opened them one by one, pages fluttering like white flags. Death certificates, insurance forms, bank closures, motor registration, each requiring my signature, each demanding that I acknowledge in ink what my heart refused to believe. Every line of his name felt like an incision. *Marko - deceased.* I wrote the words so many times they stopped belonging to language. They became soundless scratches on paper, a ritual of erasure.

The woman at the post office recognised me when I came to lodge the documents. "I'm so sorry, love," she said, lowering her voice to that tone people use for the newly broken. "You're being very brave." Brave. The word struck like a slap. There was nothing brave about survival. It was just breathing that refused to stop.

On the way home I pulled over near the lake, where the reeds bent low and the water licked the stones. For the longest time I just sat there, hands limp on the steering wheel. A dragonfly skimmed across the surface and vanished. Somewhere, children laughed. The sound was almost unbearable in its innocence. I wanted to shout, *don't you know someone just died?* But the world kept spinning, unashamed. A duck shook water from its back and carried on. The lake kept the secret, as lakes do.

Back at the kitchen table, I lined the forms in miserly rows, chasing a straightness the world no longer offered. The kettle clicked and I forgot to pour. The pen left a groove where a signature should be, as if even ink had grown tired of telling the truth. When I finally scrawled my name, it looked forged, a stranger claiming to be me.

Days didn't collapse anymore. They thinned.

Grief stopped arriving as a wave and became a climate, something I lived inside, something that altered how everything else behaved. I learned its weather patterns. The dull pressure behind the eyes. The way time stretched and slackened, hours sagging like wet clothes on a line. I wasn't drowning anymore. I was treading, endlessly, in water that never warmed.

Sleep became unreliable. I would drift off only to surface moments later, heart racing, convinced I'd forgotten something essential, my child, a door, a breath. The house felt altered at night, as if it were holding its own breath. Floorboards creaked with unfamiliar authority. The fridge clicked on and off like a nervous companion. I started leaving lamps on, not because I was afraid of the dark, but because darkness felt too much like agreement.

Sometimes, in that half-waking space, I sensed him, not as a vision, not even a thought, but as pressure. A displacement. As if the room remembered him better than I did. I never heard words. Just the sense of being observed by something that had once known me intimately. I stopped questioning it. Grief has its own logic, and arguing with it only made me tired.

The dog adjusted before I did. She followed me from room to room, nails clicking softly behind me like punctuation. She slept pressed against my legs, her warmth a quiet insistence that I was still anchored to the living. If I stood too long staring into nothing, she nudged my knee with her nose, impatient, practical. Her needs were inconvenient and therefore necessary.

The world beyond the house continued with offensive enthusiasm. Mornings arrived whether I participated or not. Rubbish trucks roared past. Neighbours trimmed hedges. Someone nearby practised the same piano piece every afternoon, always stopping in the same wrong place. I wanted to knock on their door and beg them to finish the song, just once.

I began to understand how grief makes people invisible. Not erased, just misaligned. Conversations slid past me without landing. Instructions had to be repeated. I nodded a lot. People mistook this for resilience. I let them. It was easier than explaining that I was conserving energy the way injured animals do.

One afternoon, I found myself standing in the hallway without knowing why I'd gone there. I stood long enough for the sensation to become embarrassing, even though no one was watching. That was when it occurred to me, grief had taken my sense of sequence. Cause and effect had loosened. I did things because they were next, not because they mattered.

And yet, beneath the numbness, something remained alert.

Anger, mostly. Not the sharp kind, but a slow-burning resentment toward a world that kept asking me to adapt. Toward people who wanted closure, progress, neat sentences. Toward the phrase "at least," which should have been outlawed in mourning. At least you had time. At least you knew. At least -.

There is no "at least" in absence.

The smallest interactions carried surprising weight. A cashier asking how my day was. A friend pausing too long before my name. A stranger's curiosity disguised as kindness. I learned how quickly grief turns you into public property. Everyone felt entitled to a version of my story that made them comfortable.

I didn't correct them. Correction required belief in a stable narrative, and mine had dissolved.

What I did instead was endure. I moved carefully through the days, as if the ground might still give way without warning. I learned where I could stand without breaking open. I learned when to retreat. This wasn't healing. It was reconnaissance.

And somewhere in that slow, unremarkable survival, something inside me began, not to mend, but to hold.

That night, laughter turned into sobbing, the kind that folds your body in half. I let it. Grief, I was learning, had no manners.

Weeks slid into one another like unmarked pages. I measured time by the height of the grass, the pile of unopened mail, the way my tea cooled before I remembered to drink it. The world kept offering itself, ordinary and unstoppable. I couldn't meet its gaze. I started writing lists, small, desperate ones: take dog out; feed yourself something green; try to sleep before 3 a.m. Half the time, I lost the paper before I could tick anything off. But the lists became proof I still wanted to keep track of a life, even if I couldn't live it properly. On a better day I added wash pillowcases and felt almost triumphant when the wet cotton clung to my wrists like a quiet applause.

One night, I found myself walking again, barefoot this time, down to the old park where the swing set squeaked in the wind. I sat on one, the chains cold against my palms. The moon hung low and indifferent. Across the oval, sprinklers hissed to life. Their rhythm reminded me of his breathing when he used to fall asleep beside me, the small catch before the exhale. The memory landed sharp as glass.

"Are you anywhere," I asked the dark, "or is this it?" The answer was the same as always, silence, stretching endlessly but somehow holding me up. I pushed off with my toes and let the swing give me a small, borrowed flight, a child's defiance that didn't fix a thing and still loosened something that needed loosening.

I stopped walking when dawn broke. The horizon blushed with a light that didn't care who I was or what I'd lost. The air was cool, honest. For a long while I just stood there, barefoot in the dew, feeling the earth pulse faintly beneath my skin. It was the first time I'd noticed that life still had a rhythm, and that my body, despite everything, was keeping time with it. When a magpie carolled, the sound threaded through me like a needle pulling skin together from the inside.

The days that followed were slow resurrections. I began to notice the small things again, how steam curled from a cup, how sunlight dripped through the blinds, and how the dog's tail thumped once, softly, when I said her name. It wasn't joy, not yet, it was participation. Sometimes I'd catch myself humming. Not songs I knew, just sounds. Fragments of being alive. They startled me at first because I thought maybe I was going mad. But then I realised madness and healing sometimes look the same from the outside. I started sitting in the garden each morning with my tea, the same one he used to make too strong. The grass was overgrown, a tangle of green stubbornness. Weeds pushed through cracks in the path, unapologetic. I admired them for it. The living never ask permission to exist. A bee shouldered into a lavender spike and came away powdered with its small victory. I watched as if it were a lesson.

Letters continued to arrive, condolences written in cursive loops, charity pamphlets promising peace for a monthly donation, envelopes marked *To the Estate of Marko*. Each one landed like a tiny death. I stopped opening them. One afternoon, I took the whole pile to the backyard and set them alight in the firepit. The flames caught quickly, paper curling inward on itself like a fist. Smoke rose, sweet and acrid. I watched until the names turned to ash and the ash turned to nothing. It wasn't an act of anger, it was an act of release. A private funeral for all the unfinished conversations, for the versions of us that never learned how to stay. As the last ember dimmed, I whispered, "Go if you must, but take the ghosts with you."

The air stilled, as if listening. Then a breeze lifted the ashes and scattered them toward the jacarandas. Tiny grey petals against bruised purple bloom. It felt, absurdly, like a blessing.

Evenings became survivable. I cooked again, though half the time I forgot to eat. I left the radio on low, filling the house with other people's voices. Sometimes I danced barefoot in the kitchen, slow, clumsy, the kind of movement meant only for ghosts. I kept expecting sorrow to object, to slam the door and demand I stay faithful to pain. But it didn't. Grief, I learned, isn't jealous. It just wants to be acknowledged. Once you stop pretending it's gone, it sits quietly beside you, companionable in its way. I began to write. Nothing profound, just notes, fragments, single words that felt like breath: empty, river, carry, light. I didn't know it yet, but I was building a bridge back to myself, one word at a time.

The town kept its distance, the way people do when they've exhausted their sympathy. The world moved on, but I had slowed. There was a strange freedom in that, the permission to exist outside the clock. Sometimes I'd drive without destination, the road humming beneath the tyres, long and straight and mercifully empty. I'd talk to him then. Tell him about the weather, about the dog, and about the way the sky sometimes looked like forgiveness. I never heard answers, but I felt less alone in the asking. Other nights I stayed home and let the silence stretch wide. I learned to stop fearing it. Silence, I realised, isn't absence, it's space. Space for something new to enter.

The first storm of the season came without warning. Rain hit the roof in wild, percussive bursts, wind shaking the windows. I stood by the door and watched the garden bend. For the first time in months, I didn't close the curtains. I let the storm come in. Lightning split the horizon, and for a heartbeat the entire yard glowed white. In that flash, I saw everything, the broken branches, the water pooling in footprints, and the ragged beauty of chaos. It didn't scare me. It looked like truth. After, the air smelled of eucalyptus and wet dust, the scent of endings and beginnings intertwined. I stepped outside barefoot, rain soaking through my clothes. The earth was soft, forgiving. I tilted my face upward and let the sky baptise me. It wasn't a cleansing. It was an acknowledgment. The storm wasn't mine, but it understood me.

In the weeks after the rain, small things began to grow where I hadn't planted them, tiny green shoots in the cracks of the patio, a volunteer sunflower by the fence. The kind of growth that doesn't ask permission. I started leaving the back door open in the mornings, letting the air wander in. The dog lay at the threshold, half inside, half out, like she couldn't choose which world we belonged to. Neither could I. But each sunrise pulled me closer to the one that would become mine again. I wiped the kitchen bench with a slow, circular grace, as if polishing a coin I might one day spend on hope.

I went to the lake one evening, the same one where I had once shouted at the sky. The water was calm, rippling gold beneath the setting sun. I threw a small stone and watched the circles spread outward, wider and wider, until they disappeared into the distance.

That's what grief had become, ripples. Softer now, but endless. I whispered, "I forgive you." And then, after a pause that felt like breath itself, "I forgive me, too." The wind shifted. I could have sworn I heard laughter, light, familiar, impossible. Maybe it was memory. Maybe mercy. Maybe the same thing.

As the sun dipped, I noticed something at the edge of the reeds, a faint shimmer, like light bending through heat. It pulsed once, twice, and vanished. But in that brief flicker, something in me stirred. A feeling I hadn't known since before the darkness. Not joy, not hope, something quieter. Curiosity. The faint spark of wanting to see what might come next. I turned toward home with wet cuffs and a heartbeat that felt newly my own.

That night, as I lay in bed, a thought rose unbidden, glowing faintly like a coal that refuses to die, what if this pain is not the end, but the preparation? I didn't try to answer it. I just let it burn. Outside, the storm clouds had cleared. The sky stretched black and wide, and the stars pricked through like tiny windows into another world. In that vast silence, I whispered one last thing before sleep took me, *If there's a next beginning, let me be brave enough to meet it.*

Morning arrived without fanfare, and still it felt like an arrival. I opened the back door and stood in the frame, the yard wearing last night's dew like a borrowed veil. The lemon tree sulked in its usual way, a single bead of water that clung to a thorn and refused to fall. Somewhere down the street a radio tried on an old love song and found the key a little higher than it remembered. The dog nudged my calf and waited for instructions I didn't yet have the authority to give. "Soon," I told her. "Soon." She believed me, the way animals do when they mistake patience for prophecy.

By late afternoon the light let itself down over the fence pickets and everything wore a thin halo as if the day were pretending to be gentler than it was. I moved through the rooms without destination and ended up at the back door again, palm resting on the flywire, forgetting to open it. The house behind me kept its wild, polite quiet, whilst the yard ahead of me held its ragged invitation. I stepped out and felt the concrete's stored heat return my weight back to me as if to say *Yes, you are here.* Birds stitched gossip into the lemon tree. The peppermint leaves nodded in a language I was only just beginning to relearn.

I didn't know it then, but exile was loosening its grip, not because the distance had shortened, but because I had learned the shape of it. The world had not come back to me, I had inched toward it, barefoot. The air carried a faint scent I couldn't place, dust, eucalyptus, and the idea of smoke before smoke becomes fact. It was nothing. It was everything. Some part of me heard a summons older than language, a calling that wasn't a word so much as a warmth.

Tomorrow, something will call my name. Not the voice of the dead, not memory, but something older, something that sounds like fire and feels like awakening. I don't know it yet, but it will come. And when it does, I will follow, barefoot into the yard, into whatever burns without burning me up, and the next chapter will begin.

Chapter Five

Some fires don't come to destroy, they arrive to show you what in you cannot burn.

By late afternoon the sky had dropped its mask of blue and put on its burnished gold, the kind of light that pretends everything is gentle. Sun slid down the fence palings and turned the dead bougainvillea to copper wire. The lawn, such as it was, wore last summer's grief like a bad haircut. A wind lifted and set the day down again, the way a mother might move a feverish child from one hip to the other.

I stood at the back door with my hand on the flywire and forgot to open it. The house behind me was all echo and casserole foil, and a silence that never quite behaved. It was the third week of strangers' kindnesses, their hand-written cards in careful, round letters: thinking of you, in our prayers, here if you need. Bless them. Bless their need to make shape out of the shapeless. Bless the way their sentences shook at the edges like fawns on new legs.

But the day was too shiny for sorrow. It was indecent, almost. As if the world had rinsed itself and refused to keep my stains. Even the birds were busy with their old gossip, stitching bits of sound into the lemon tree. I wanted to stamp my foot at the sky and tell it to darken properly. I wanted thunder that knew my name.

Instead, I slipped off my shoes and stepped outside.

The concrete was sun-warmed and human, the way skin holds summer long after the water has gone. I stepped onto the cracked path, toes finding tiny constellations of grit, and moved into the back yard like someone entering a chapel she did not belong to anymore. The jacaranda had thrown down fresh purple, the petals stuck in the uneven places, bruises against the grey. The air smelled of dust and eucalyptus and a sweetness I could not locate.

He loved this time of day. The thought arrived before I could stop it. He would've leaned against the post with his beer in its stubby holder, sunglasses still on, making some remark about the Freo Doctor coming in late. And I, because performance had once been my religion, would have laughed at the right moment and helped turn the sausages so they didn't blacken on the outside and stay raw at the heart.

The heart, I thought, is the only part we never learned to cook properly.

I crossed to the shed. The key on its string tapped the door with that friendly clink I'd known since Poppy was little. He'd hung tools like museum pieces, spanners by size, the post-hole digger with its bite polished deep, jars of screws and nails he'd labelled with a level of care he never turned on me. Everything had its place here. Order did not raise its voice.

My fingers found the latch without asking permission.

The rifle lay where he'd left it last winter after foxes got bold with bin night. I had never touched it other than to pass it across or complain about the smell of oil. He'd shown me how the safety worked, once, and I'd said, I don't want to know, because marriage had been a ledger, what I knew I might be made responsible for.

I took it up now because I needed a thing that was heavier than grief.

It surprised me, the intimacy of the weight. How the butt tucked into that soft space between shoulder and chest as if it had been carved out of me on purpose. How my hands remembered what my mind had refused to file: click, breathe, don't jerk the trigger. The wood was warm from the shed, and I could smell oil, old rain, and a trace of cordite. Two sparrows flew in at the sound, scolding, then flew out again because my breath disturbed their dust.

"This is mad," I said to no one, and my voice sounded like it had learned to crawl.

I stood in the doorway and looked up into the huge, indifferent blue. The sun had started its slow confession behind the gum. My arms lifted without asking me first, the way you lift your arms in a dream and find yourself flying. I thought of the prophet in a story I used to half believe, barefoot before a bush that burned but did not burn up. Take off your shoes, the voice had said to him. You are standing on holy ground.

Barefoot, I thought, and looked down at my stained feet.

"So is this holy?" I asked the air. "Or just stupid?"

The air kept its counsel. Somewhere over the fence a neighbour's radio tried on a love song from 1999 and decided it still fit. A dog barked like a joke told too often. A plane threaded a white stitch across the top of the day, and for a heartbeat I wanted to be on it, tiny and contained, tray table up, the pilot's voice smooth with certainty: Ladies and gentlemen, we will be touching down in the kind of life you can trust.

"Liar," I told the sky. "There's no landing."

The rifle's barrel drew a black line through the gold. I breathed in and the day breathed out. All those verses I'd grown up with came flooding back, unwanted and inevitable, cast your cares, be still, fear not, and to my own surprise I found myself answering in that little voice I'd only just learned to hear again, the one I call by many names because naming it correctly seems to matter less than listening: I am here. Don't tidy this. Let it burn.

"What if it burns me up?" I asked.

Then we will find what can't be burned.

I had become a woman who argued with the air. But maybe grief is the oldest prayer, the one where you don't have any words, and also too many.

I didn't want to shoot the sky. I wanted to wound it the way it had wounded me, to make it flinch, to see it bleed dusk. But even in my fury I could tell the difference between what would satisfy and what would save me. Both were small. Both were dangerous. Only one would let me wake up tomorrow and recognise my own mouth in the mirror.

I lowered the rifle.

"Coward," I told myself, and then corrected: "Alive."

The wind came thin and high through the peppermint tree, and the leaves answered it like sequins. Heat pressed a hand into the small of my back and held me steady. A dragonfly hovered at my eye level as if the day had manufactured a jewelled comma just to keep the sentence of me from ending in the wrong place.

He would've laughed at that thought, the way I make poems out of anything if it stands still long enough. He'd hated how I spoke in images when he wanted facts: Did you pay the gas? Why are you crying? Where did you put the socket set? He didn't understand that metaphors were the only tool I owned that didn't break in my hands. What else can you use on a life this stubborn?

I set the rifle on the threshold and walked out into the yard with my palms open as if I were surrendering at last to an enemy who had been kinder than I'd let on.

"Alright," I said. "If there's a fire to be had, let it be the right kind."

A gust pushed hard enough to clang the wind chime in that old, out-of-tune way. The gum leaned and murmured and, mad as it sounds, I had the sudden sense that the whole yard exhaled. As if the place had been holding its breath with me, waiting to see whether I would choose to burn down or burn through.

I walked the path to the far corner where the ground always felt more honest. The soil there remembered winter, remembered mud on children's shins and the ritual of pegging sheets so they made small white hills between the lines. I pressed my heel into the dirt, and it took my weight without argument. Holy ground, I thought. Not because it's winning, but because it keeps taking us.

It was then that I noticed the heat wasn't all in my head.

Beyond the back fence, on that strip of nothing land the council pretended to care about, a ribbon of smoke had lifted. Someone's careless butt, someone's bad luck. It wasn't a roar yet, just the sort of small fire that thinks highly of itself. Dry grass went to flame the way gossip goes to town. The wind toyed with it, spreading its red handwriting in quick, clever loops.

I stood perfectly still, astonished, and also not astonished at all. "Of course," I said to the universe, weary and almost laughing. "Of course you'd send me an actual burning bush."

Not a bush, a run of thatch and weed, a mat of tinder framing the base of a half-dead wattle that caught with a greedy lick. The flames were too close for comfort, not close enough to be danger yet. Fire has a sound we forget until it is in our ears, soft, busy, like silk being ripped in a polite room. You can smell its appetite, and you can feel its certainty.

I went back to the shed without thinking. Found the old hose in a coil like a sleeping snake, dragged it out, discovered the kinks in it were just stubbornness, not fate. The brass tap coughed, shuddered, and finally agreed to be a river. I climbed the fence with the same gracelessness I use on everything I've had to survive and dropped into the council strip like a woman sneaking into her own life.

"Not today," I told the fire. "Not my house. Not my neighbour's dog. Not my stupid lemon tree that won't fruit."

I sprayed in a low arc, the way my father taught me from some old bushie he respected his whole life: wet the edge, drown the ambition, don't waste pressure on the part that's already confessing. Steam rose up like a choir. My toes sank into the mud I made. The hose rattled in my hands with a joy that had no business showing up just then.

I worked until the little run of savagery sighed and fell in on itself, until all that moved was smoke pretending it still knew how to be a flame. Bits of blackened grass clung to my legs, and ash went soft in the air and made tiny moons on my shins. I turned off the tap, and the sudden quiet was a kindness I hadn't earned.

When I climbed back over the fence, hose slung wild across my shoulder like some ridiculous sash, I realised I was shaking, not with fear, but with the simple fact that my body had done a thing it could be proud of.

In the quiet that followed, I put the hose away, coiled it in a circle as neat as I could manage, and set the rifle back where I'd found it. A magpie watched from the clothesline, head cocked as if to say, *Well, are you finished with the theatrics?* I bowed to it, half mad, wholly alive.

The sky had given up on gold and moved to ember, the colour days earn when they have gone through something. The first star came out, far too early and perfectly on time. I remembered wishing on stars as a child. I remembered how I'd stopped when I learned the sky did not bargain.

Still, I whispered my wish into the yard as if it were a kind animal that might lean close enough to hear.

"Let it burn the right things," I said. "The lies. The pretending. The part of me that keeps looking for approval like a thirsty dog."

A breeze lifted my hair and set it down again like a blessing. Or maybe that's the wrong word. Maybe, agreement.

Inside, the house smelled of lemon dish soap and the flowers my sister kept bringing although I told her to stop because their dying felt like additional work. I left the back door open, and the evening came in soft, moth by moth. I ran water in the sink and watched it become warm, then hot, then just right. My hands turned pink, and the dirt lifted from beneath my nails and swirled away like a story that had finally lost interest.

Grief, I decided, is a fire that pretends to be a flood. It will drown you and scorch you depending on the day, and some days you cannot tell the difference. But if there's anything true in the oldest stories, it is this, the voice we need most often hides in flame, and when you get close enough to hear it you think you will die from the heat, but you do not. You come away singed, smelling of smoke, a little ridiculous, and somehow changed.

The kettle clicked off with its agreeable certainty. I poured the water over a teabag and watched the cloud of brown spread like an idea. A moth came to investigate the steam and decided against it. The floor under my feet remembered the afternoon sun and kept a little of it for me.

I could feel the fight in me changing temperature.

Rage had been hot and wild and exquisitely unproductive. It

had burned in all directions, especially toward people who did not deserve it, including myself. But out there on the council strip I had made a smaller fire mind me, and now something inside had turned its head like a horse being asked to go where it has never gone. The anger was not gone, but it had found a task. Not burn down. Burn through.

I stood at the bench with the mug in my hands and said it aloud to the empty house, to the moths, to the bit of universe that seemed to be listening now that I had stopped shouting.

"I am not going to kill the sky," I said. "I am not going to kill myself. I am going to let this burn what it needs to, and I am going to see what's left."

The sentence didn't feel brave. It felt practical, the way a woman looks at her pantry and decides how to make a meal out of the last tins and an onion. You don't publish that decision, you just do it, and hope that it tastes like enough.

Later, much later, when sleep came the way a stray cat finally does, circling, suspicious, then curling into that warm place at the back of the knees, I dreamed the yard was full of lanterns. Not the paper kind, and not electric, something older, small fires held inside glass. They hung from the gum and the Hills hoist, and they floated at eye level the way dragonflies do. In the dream I walked among them with my hands tucked into my sleeves because I did not trust myself not to touch the flame and claim it. The air smelled of rain that had not arrived yet.

A voice, my voice, and not, spoke as if from inside my ribs.

You do not have to perform your way out of this.

You do not have to hate your way out either.

Tend. That is your way. Tend the small light.

I woke to the house answering back with its familiar clicks

and sighs. For a second I could not find my body. Then the day found me. I stretched the way you stretch when you haven't earned rest and it has come anyway. The first bruise sky of morning pressed its face to the window. Somewhere a bin truck announced itself like royalty. The dog in number twelve told the bin truck what he thought of it and felt better immediately.

I padded to the back door. The patch of council strip beyond the fence was a smear of black and silver, that pretty, ugly aftermath. The wattle was charred at its base but had kept its crown, stubborn, ridiculous, alive. A single wisp of smoke lifted like a prayer that didn't know it was finished.

"Same," I told it, and almost laughed.

I made coffee and drank it this time. The first sip brought the world into focus, the second made it bearable, and the third taught me to breathe in ordinary air like it was a kindness. Across the sink, my face in the window was not the one I used to make before work when I believed mascara was a sacrament. This face was plainer, and truer, and carried a little soot in its eyes that would not wash out soon. I did not dislike her.

I wrote a list I had no intention of completing:

- Call the insurer.

- Cancel the… (I did not write the word funeral because we had already done that practical horror).

- Put the rifle back behind the tarp and tell Eliza to nag me about a gun safe again.

- Buy lemons from the market until mine learn how to grow.

- Ask the doctor about sleep.

- Water the bit of yard that is brave enough to try again.

I pinned the list with a magnet and decided to do the last one first because it was the only one that did not require speech.

Out in the yard the hose gave me that small obedience again. The water made a dark run in the dirt, and everything smelled of promise and old rot. The lemon tree took a drink in its grudging way. The peppermint leaves glittered with temporary jewels. I turned the nozzle and made rain for myself, because why not, and for one minute I stood like a child and let the spray freckle my skin. The water traced the collarbone I'd forgotten I had. When I stopped, drops clung to me like punctuation.

There was a ring at the front, one polite ping I would have missed if not for the house's new habit of carrying sound.

I found a parcel on the mat, brown paper and twine and my name in my sister's knockabout handwriting. Inside, wrapped in tissue, was a small ceramic bowl the colour of smoke. For ashes, her note said, then added in brackets, not the sad kind, the kind you grow things in.

I pressed the bowl to my chest with both hands and felt ridiculous for crying over something so small and containing so much. I could see it already on the windowsill with basil seeds whispering their stupid hope into the dirt. I could see my fingers learning to be gentle again.

The phone buzzed. I looked at his name in my contacts and surprised myself by not deleting it. He was gone, and also not gone, and both had to be true for a while. Grief is a room where contradictions are allowed to sit without debate.

I made another coffee for the simple fact that I could. The house held the smell the way a person holds a found kitten, unsure where to put it but unwilling to let it go. I stood at the bench and watched the street settle into the business of acting like everything was ordinary. The postman did his daily rehearsal. The sky squinted at its to-do list and decided on blue again.

"You're relentless," I told it, and for once I did not mean it as an accusation.

I don't know when a chapter ends in real life. But standing there with wet hair and a smoke-coloured bowl against my ribs and the memory of a little fire I had told no, I felt the page turn, not because I made it, but because it was ready. The next part did not promise to be kinder. It promised to be real, and sometimes I think real is the only kindness we can trust.

Behind that feeling came the thought I had been avoiding, the one with its own weight and temperature, covenants. The agreements you make, the ones that save you and the ones that strangle you, the lines you sign with your best pen and the ones you half-sign in blood. Marriage had been one. Family myths had been another. The quiet oath I'd made to keep the peace at any cost. The contract I'd written in invisible ink that said my comfort mattered less than his.

The hose dripped onto my toes like a priest with bad aim, and I laughed in spite of myself.

"Alright," I said to the empty kitchen, the moths, the sky that wouldn't stop being itself. "If the bush has burned and the voice has spoken, then let the next work be the work of broken covenants."

The word didn't frighten me the way it once would have. It felt accurate more than dangerous. Because that's the thing about fire, once it has shown you what survives, you don't waste as much time begging the kindling to behave like oak.

I set Eliza's bowl on the sill. I opened the back door wide. The yard, rinsed and ridiculous and dearer to me than it had any right to be, breathed in. I breathed out. Somewhere over the fence the radio moved on to another forgotten hit, and the magpie threw in a line of its own, a black-and-white amen.

The day did not become holy because I said so.

The day was holy because it was still here. Because I was. Because something had burned and had not burned me up. Because I could feel, faint, steady, the ember that refused to die, and knew, with a kind of tired gratitude, that it was mine to tend.

And that is how I walked from the yard into the next hard mercy, out of flame, carrying only what would not turn to ash, toward the long, blunt undoing of the promises that had been killing me.

I did not know their names yet, the vows I'd swallowed whole, the small treaties I'd signed against myself, but I could feel them loosening, thread by stubborn thread. Tomorrow, I will lay them on the table, the spoken and the secret, the ones I made to please, the ones I made to survive. I will hold each up to the light that did not ask my permission to arrive. And then, with steady hands, I will begin the work that fire taught me, to break what was never holy, and to keep what is.

Chapter Six

Some promises crack quietly, like ice underfoot, long before you hear the break.

The notebook lay open on the table, its blank page staring at me like an accusation. My hand trembled as I drew two uneven columns down the middle of the paper. On the left I scrawled a single word: Vows. On the right, another: Reality.

It felt childish, almost petty, to make a list. But my chest was too full and my mind too scattered. Sometimes grief is too heavy to hold in silence, it needs to be pinned down in ink before it crushes you entirely.

I pressed the pen so hard the tip tore the page.

Vows: Love and cherish.

Reality: Bruises hidden under foundation.

Vows: Honour.

Reality: Words slung like stones: useless, nothing, unworthy.

Vows: Forsaking all others.

Reality: Messages on his phone at 2 a.m. from numbers I didn't recognise.

Vows: Until death do us part.

Reality: The death came early. The parting too late.

I stopped. The paper blurred. My hand hovered above the page, caught between fury and collapse.

The word covenant came to me unbidden. It wasn't a word I used often, but it rose up like smoke from some deep place in memory. A covenant wasn't just a promise. It was something sacred, binding, eternal. And mine had shattered like cheap glass.

I pushed the notebook aside and opened the bottom drawer where dust kept its own ledgers. Between warranty cards and old school photos lay the wedding booklet the church had made for us, cream cardstock, embossed vines, our names printed with a flourish that looked expensive because it was meant to. When I slid the ribbon off, a scent lifted, faint and powdery, like a dress box that hadn't been opened since a different weather. I saw myself again, hair sprayed into stormproof obedience, white fabric biting under the arms, a smile I had stitched to my face so hard it might have drawn blood if joy hadn't blinded me to the thread. The church organ had swelled. My father's hand had been strangely light under my fingers, as if he feared he might bruise me. We were led to the altar by words older than our grandparents, and I repeated after the minister with a tremor I thought was holiness. Later, when the confetti stuck to the sweat behind my knees, I told myself that the small unease in my gut was hunger, not warning. I bit into cake and promised to never forget this feeling. I kept that promise longer than was good for me.

That night, I dreamt of a courtroom.

The walls stretched high, carved with shadows, as if judgment itself had built the place. I stood in the witness box, barefoot, clutching the hem of my dress. My heart slammed so hard I thought my ribs would splinter.

Across the room, my husband sat, his wedding ring glinting like a weapon. His eyes were red-rimmed but hard, the way they had been the night he left.

The judge's voice boomed from somewhere above the rafters, "You swore before God and man. You swore. And yet here you are, dragging the broken pieces."

My throat burned. "He broke them first," I whispered,

though it sounded feeble even to me.

A lawyer I didn't know stood, his robes whispering as he moved. He opened a book I recognised instantly, our wedding vows, printed neatly, black on white. He read them out loud, line by line.

"To love and to cherish -"

"Objection!" I cried, my voice cracking. "There was no cherishing. There was bruising and silence."

"To honour -."

"He honoured bottles, not me."

"To forsake all others -."

I felt my chest collapse inward. I saw the late-night phone calls, the half-hidden receipts, the lies so thin they could barely hold themselves up.

"To death do us part -." I screamed then, raw, guttural. "Death has already come! He's gone. And I'm the one left standing in the wreckage!"

The gavel slammed. The sound cracked the dream in two, and I jolted awake, soaked in sweat, my breath clawing the air.

The notebook was still open beside me. The pen lay across the page, accusing. I closed it with shaking fingers, but the words inside burned like fresh wounds.

Morning brought the smaller courts, the kitchen bench where I ruled on whether tea counted as nourishment, the inbox that cross-examined me with overdue notices and condolences, and the hallway mirror that asked who I thought I was living as now. I avoided verdicts, made toast I didn't eat, and tied my hair with the elastic I'd found around a bunch of drooping lilies. Even grief needs a hair tie.

In waking life, the trial was quieter but no less brutal.

The mornings stretched long, filled with paperwork, signatures, and phone calls. Widow, they called me now, as if the word could contain everything I had lost. Strangers asked for certificates, for proof, for forms filled in black ink. Each document was a reminder, not only had the man I married died, but the vows we once whispered were nothing more than broken contracts now, dissolved in bureaucracy and soil.

One afternoon, sorting through his belongings, I found the box.

A shoe box, scuffed and taped at the corners. Inside, scraps of our beginning. Wedding photos, folded letters, a pressed flower from the day he had asked me to dance in the garden. My throat closed as I touched each relic.

There we were, two children dressed up as adults, holding hands before an altar, promising forever. His eyes had shone that day. I remember believing his every word.

I slammed the lid shut and shoved the box under the bed.

How do you reconcile the man who held your hand with trembling reverence, with the man who spat insults like venom? How do you hold in the same body the boy who kissed you in moonlight and the husband who broke your ribs with silence and rage?

I couldn't. So, I tried to split them, to tell myself they were two different men. But memory is cruel. It doesn't separate cleanly. It tangles love and betrayal together until you bleed from both at once.

Money had its own liturgy. Joint account. Joint debt. Joint signatures that had once felt like a duet now sounded like a trap. I sat at the bank with a numbered ticket that glowed red, waiting to be called to the desk where a young man with an unnervingly tender voice said, "Let's take care of the practicalities." Practicalities, a word that eats romance for breakfast and calls it balance. He slid papers across to me and I slid my name back, over and over, until the syllables stopped meaning me. When he asked if I wanted to keep the account name or change it, I said I didn't know. He nodded with professional mercy and clicked his mouse like a metronome. There are covenants written in blood, and others in BSB numbers.

The women at church told me to forgive.

One leaned close, perfume thick, and said, "Forgiveness is your path to peace, dear."

Her voice was syrupy, but her eyes were sharp. Forgiveness, to her, was neat and final, like sweeping dust under a rug.

I wanted to scream at her. To ask if she had ever felt fists through words. To ask if she had ever held her breath so her daughter wouldn't hear her crying through the walls.

Instead, I smiled that small brittle smile I'd perfected and whispered, "Yes, I'll pray on it."

But forgiveness wasn't neat. It wasn't final. It wasn't even close.

Forgiveness, for me, was a jagged thing. Some mornings it looked possible. Other mornings it felt like another chain around my neck.

Maybe forgiveness wasn't the point. Maybe survival was.

My mother called and asked if I'd considered "reaffirming my vows privately," as if a second ceremony could glue a broken cup. "We all make sacrifices," she said, which in our family was code for women swallowing themselves without leaving teeth marks. I let the words pass over me like weather. After we hung up, I sat on the laundry floor between the washing basket and the ironing board and cried until the dog pressed her forehead to mine and reminded me that love can also arrive with bad breath and perfect timing.

One evening, I sat outside under a bruised sky. The jacaranda dropped its purple confetti around me, soft as regret. I lit a candle on the table, the small flame shivering in the wind.

I stared at it, thinking vows are like candles. Beautiful in their promise, fragile in their keeping. If tended, they burn warm and steady. If neglected, the flame sputters, smokes, and dies.

Ours had died long before his body did. That was the secret I carried, the one no casserole-bearing neighbour wanted to hear. He had died to me years earlier. The man who left the house that final night was already a ghost.

And yet, I mourned him. The boy I had first loved. The life we might have had if promises had been more than paper. The family I thought we were building. I mourned not just the man but the myth of him.

Sometimes I spoke to him.

Late at night, lying awake, I whispered into the dark, *"Why?"* *"Was any of it true?"* *"Did you ever love me, or just the idea of me?"*

Silence answered. Silence, and the faint hum of a fridge in the kitchen, and the dog sighing in her sleep.

Once, half-asleep, I thought I heard him answer. I tried.

It wasn't enough. But it was something.

On the third Thursday, Eliza stormed in with groceries and the kind of concern that wears boots. "You need a doctor to help with sleep," she said, emptying spinach and a stubbornly cheerful punnet of tomatoes into the fridge. At the clinic, the GP asked gentle questions and did not look away when I didn't. He wrote a script, gave me a pamphlet with a blue cover that promised steadier nights, and asked if anyone at home could stay if the dark got heavy. "I have a dog," I said, and he smiled as if I'd said an angel. In the car I read the side effects and decided to start with tea and breath, then see. I kept the script in my wallet beside the photo of us on Malus Island, our faces windblown and falsely simple.

The ring had become its own court case. Some mornings it felt like armour, other mornings like evidence. I wore it to the sink and took it off to sleep, then swapped those rules because I was tired of obeying objects. Finally, I placed it in Eliza's smoke-coloured bowl on the windowsill with the basil seeds that had not yet decided whether to be brave. "For now," I told it, as if a circle of gold could accept a postponement clause. The bowl made no promises and that, unusually, felt kind.

The dreams kept coming.

In one, I stood at an altar again, except this time I was alone. The pews were filled with shadows, faceless, watching. My dress was torn at the hem, my bouquet wilted. The priest held out a book, but when I opened it, the pages were all blank.

"What do you vow now?" he asked.

I looked around, panicked. My hands shook. I didn't know.

And then the strangest thing happened, the shadows began to whisper. Not cruelly, but insistently. Vow to yourself.

It was absurd. It was impossible. But in the dream, I lifted my chin and said the only promise I could manage: "I vow to stay."

The gavel slammed again, and I woke with tears on my cheeks.

The following week I sat in a community hall that smelled of instant coffee and scuffed hope. A circle of chairs, a plate of biscuits untouched like a test. No one asked for the long version. A woman with inked vines on her wrist said, "I'm Clare," and the room breathed as if it had been holding its chest for years. When it was my turn, I said, "I'm Lena," and the ceiling didn't fall. We spoke in first-draft sentences, not polished, not for publication, good enough to keep us breathing. On the drive home I didn't turn on the radio. The silence felt less like absence and more like space I had earned.

In real life, staying was messy.

I drank too much on some nights. I screamed into pillows. I drove aimlessly until the tank was nearly empty, music blaring loud enough to drown out thought.

But I also started small rituals. Lighting a candle at dusk. Writing in that cursed notebook. Breathing slowly, deliberately, as if air itself was a vow I could still keep.

And slowly, I began to understand broken covenants are not just about what you've lost. They're about what you have left.

On a wet Saturday I pulled every sheet and towel from the cupboard and built a small mountain on the lounge room floor. It felt like a fort and a bonfire at once. I sorted, folded, refolded, talked to myself out loud the way you do when you are both the witness and the clerk. "Keep," I said to the thick blue blanket we bought that winter we couldn't stop apologising. "Donate," I said to the guest towels no one we loved had ever used. The house listened without interrupting, the way a good friend does when you're finally telling the truth.

The last entry in the notebook that week was simple:

Vows: To myself.

Reality: To live.

I stared at the words until they blurred. For the first time, the columns didn't feel like enemies. They felt like a bridge.

A covenant had been shattered, yes. But maybe a new one

could be born, quiet and private, written not on paper but on skin and breath.

When people asked how I was doing, I lied, as usual. "Fine," I'd say. But inside, the truth was sharper, I was walking barefoot across broken vows, bleeding with every step, but still walking.

And maybe that was enough.

For now.

That night I opened the notebook again and wrote another column where the margin should have been. Not Vows. Not Reality. Something smaller and far more dangerous: Practice. Under it, I listed what the body could keep when the heart failed audits, water before coffee, shoes by the door so the dog believes in tomorrow, the window cracked an inch at night, so the air doesn't go stale with unsaid things. I added one more line, hands steady for the first time in months. Speak to myself like I am worth keeping.

I didn't sign it with my name. I signed it with a date and a quiet amen. And when the kettle clicked off, a small, domestic gavel, something in me stood, was sworn in, and told the truth out loud, I will not keep the promises that require my disappearance.

Chapter Seven

Between the vow I rewrote and the life that hadn't caught up yet, I moved like a ghost refusing to leave.

The morning after the notebook, I woke to the sound of the bin truck heaving itself down the street, that metallic roar like something swallowing its own tail. It took me a confused minute to realise why the noise felt wrong. He used to drag the bins out, shirtless, yawning, scratching the back of his neck like a cliché. The memory moved across my mind like a shadow of an old bird on a new wall. I lay still and watched it pass. The house smelled like other people's flowers. Lilies loud as trumpets lined the hallway, roses hunched in their glass prisons, shedding petals like silence. Everywhere I turned, grief had a fragrance. When I opened a window, the wind hesitated before entering, as if it, too, wasn't sure I was still here.

The dog followed me room to room, toenails ticking a nervous morse code on the floorboards: you okay you okay you okay. I wasn't, but I put my palm on her head and lied on purpose. "Yeah, mate. We're… here." Alive felt too ambitious. Here would have to do. I made coffee and forgot it on the bench. When I remembered, it had skinned over, that thin sour film you have to break to sip. I tipped it into the sink and watched the brown spiral disappear. The drain made a polite throat-clearing sound. I envied it, how simply it let go of things.

A text pinged. MUM: You need anything today? I can come. I stared at the screen until the letters lost their shape. ME: No. Please don't fuss. Three dots. Then nothing. A mercy.

I dressed in whatever my hand found first, black leggings with a scuff on the knee, his faded t-shirt with the stretched collar. It still held a breath of his smell , detergent, salt, the ghost of a cologne he'd liked when things were good. I pressed my mouth to the shoulder and then hated myself for it. The dog looked at the leash. I clipped it on and we went. Outside, the world was doing its reckless ordinary. Two kids shot down the hill on scooters. The postman did his theatrical whistling. A man jogged past me, sweat already bright like varnish on his temples. No one slowed. No one looked twice. I was both grateful and offended by their indifference. It confirmed my suspicion, I had become negative space, a cut-out where someone used to be.

I walked to the oval and stood by the fence. A woman from the school committee spotted me and did that quick double-take people do when they're trying to remember the correct face for a particular kind of tragedy. She approached as if I might bolt. "Lena," she said, her voice dressed in sympathy. "We heard." Her eyes flicked to the dog, then to my shoes, then back to my face. People scan for data when they don't know what else to do. "We're so sorry." Her perfume smelled like peaches. For a second, I wanted to lay my head on her shoulder and be five years old again. Instead, I tucked a strand of hair behind my ear and offered the phrase I was learning by rote. "Thank you."

"If there's anything -."

"I know."

We looked at the oval. A magpie scolded the air. Far off, someone's laughter broke into pieces and fell. She cleared her throat. "The committee can organise some meals. A roster, maybe? Just while you -."

"Please don't," I said. "I can't keep up with the containers."

"Oh," she said, startled by the specificity.

We stood a moment longer in the shallow pool of our awkwardness. Then she reached out and squeezed my forearm with two fingers, as if checking my temperature. "Take care," she said, and left.

I wondered what care even meant, now. Showering felt like an achievement worthy of a ribbon. Eating was negotiation. Sleep was a thief that came when it wanted and took what it could carry. On the way home, the dog found a scrap of someone's sandwich near the bin enclosure and looked at me, guilty. "Go on," I said. Even she needed an easy win. Back inside, the answering machine blinked in hysterical red. I pressed play and listened to a chorus of very kind people saying very kind things I could not hold. Then a message from my sister, that particular brand of tough love only sisters can get away with: "Call me, you mule. I don't care if you cry. I can do crying." I smiled without showing my teeth and didn't call.

I tried to do a normal task, a foolish, ordinary thing to prove my body could still follow instructions. The pantry had become a cupboard of ghost-objects, cereal he liked (untouched), the peanut butter jar he never closed properly, tins with labels equal parts optimism and lie. I pulled everything out, wiped the shelves, lined the jars up in parade formation. It looked like achievement and felt like moving sand. When I finished, I noticed my hands had been shaking the whole time. It was fascinating, in a grim way, to watch the nervous system do its stubborn work. The body insists. Even when the mind is stuck in a room with no doors, the body keeps knocking on the walls.

The doorbell startled me into the present. I wasn't expecting anyone. The lilies in the hall turned their pale faces toward the sound, as if they, too, were curious who would dare. It was the neighbour, the one with the immaculate lawn and the husband who always waved like he was signalling a small plane. She held a Tupperware container with the lid slightly fogged. "Lasagne," she announced, meaning I did the only thing I knew. "It freezes."

"Thank you," I said again, that phrase my sole currency. "I… this is kind."

She rocked on her heels. "We… uh… we were here the day the police came. We saw the police car. We didn't want to intrude." I nodded, because there was nothing else to do with a sentence like that. "If you need someone to mow. Or… well. If you need." She didn't finish the thought, which I appreciated. There are needs you cannot speak in daylight.

After she left, I put the lasagne in the fridge beside someone else's pie and a bottle of wine I had promised myself not to open before noon. The fridge hummed, self-satisfied, full of other people's efforts. I sat on the kitchen floor and let my back rest against the cabinet. The cool of the tiles came up through me. The dog lay down with a sigh, her head on my knee in that loyal way that could wring tears from a rock. From this angle, I could see the underside of the table, a constellation of gum Poppy had hidden there during the long dinner that became a fight that became a door slammed. The sight made me tender and furious at once.

I pulled my phone from my pocket and opened the note I'd started after the notebook: Things That Prove I'm Still Here. It read, exactly as I typed it then: Dog's head is heavy. Coffee goes skin if you leave it. Tiles are cold through leggings. Lilies smell like hospitals and weddings at once. Sister calls me mule and means stay. The wind hesitates but comes in when asked. I added, Lasagne fogs under its own lid. It felt both profound and stupid.

Maybe that was what life was now.

In the afternoon, I tried to nap and instead fell into that half-sleep where dreams graft themselves onto reality. I was in our old bedroom, the one from the rental where the windows stuck in summer and the carpet had a permanent stain we covered with a chair. He sat on the edge of the bed, elbows on knees, the posture of a man who has used up all his sentences. "I didn't mean to," he said. "Which part?" I asked. "The leaving? The drinking? The dying?" He flinched like words could bruise. "Any of it." "Which means all of it," I said. The dream was unusually clear, I could see the little scar on his chin from the time he'd tried to jump the fence in thongs and lost. He closed his eyes. "You were always so… much." "Alive?" I offered. He shook his head. "Bright." I laughed, mean. "You preferred me dim." He looked at me with the face he used when he wanted to be forgiven. "I preferred you quiet." I woke with my heart thudding. The room was empty but pulsing, like it had a heartbeat separate from mine.

Adrenaline had a taste, and it sat at the back of my tongue like pennies. I went to the bathroom and splashed water on my face. The woman in the mirror looked like a b-side version of me, all the clarity gone. I rested my forehead on the cool glass. "You're not crazy," I told her. "You're grieving." She blinked, unconvinced.

The next day I had to go to the bank. There's a particular humiliation in standing in a public place and saying your husband is dead to a stranger across a desk. You watch them reach for the laminated checklist they keep for women like you. You provide proof, as if grief were a claim you might be exaggerating. You sign where they point.

Any changes to your address?" the woman asked, typing with

nails that made little pink clacks on the keyboard.

"No," I said. "Not yet."

"Employment status?"

I wanted to say living dead and see what box she'd tick. Instead, I said the words that had once belonged to the version of me who knew how to answer such questions. "Casual. Between contracts."

"Okay," she said brightly, as if I had ordered a salad.

Leaving the bank, I ran into a friend I hadn't seen in months. Our last conversation had been about paint colours; I could almost see the swatch book in her hands.

"Oh, Lena," she said, and the oh carried everything. Her eyes filled before mine could. She took my hands. "I didn't want to text. It felt... cheap."

"Thank you," I said. (How many times could a phrase earn its keep?)

She glanced at the bank doors, at the street, at my face. "Do you want to get a tea?"

I didn't want tea. I wanted to sleep for a year and wake in a different body. But I nodded, almost grateful to be told what to do for an hour. We sat by the window. People passed, their reflections sliding over our faces like weather. She didn't ask the bad questions (Did you see him? Was he drunk?). She asked the good ones. "How's your breath?"

"What?"

"Are you breathing?"

I tried. A shaky in, a jagged out. "Sometimes."

"Okay," she said. "Sometimes is something."

We talked about nothing on purpose, the barista's tattoo, the way the shop across the road changed names every six months. I realised she was building a bridge of trivialities so I could cross the room without falling through it. When it was time to go, she hugged me the way I like, firm, not lingering into pity.

"I'll text you the weather. Not the feelings," she said. "Every morning. Just the weather." And she did: Sunny. Overcast. Wind picking up from the west. It anchored me more than she could have known.

Nights were the hardest, as if darkness cancelled my ability to pretend. I lay on the mattress and counted backwards from a hundred, the way I'd read in an article about sleep I didn't believe. Ninety-six, ninety-five… the numbers were too tidy for my mind to hold, and soon I was counting leaves on the jacaranda instead, the ones visible in the streetlight, the ones not. It was an unfair system the unseen will always win. On the fourth night after the viewing, rage came for me like weather breaking. No warning, just a sky split. I found myself in the laundry, of all places, throwing a basket of his shirts against the wall. They thudded, humiliatingly soft. I wanted smash, crash, shatter. Destiny gave me cotton. I grabbed the bottle of his old aftershave from the shelf and threw that instead. It hit the tiles and exploded, the smell leaping up at once, sharp, male, a memory with teeth. I slid to the floor, palms on my knees, and breathed it like poison or sacrament, I couldn't tell which. "Why," I said to the room, to the bottle shards, to the man whose absence could still make me stupid. "Why did you put the barrel of your anger in your mouth and pull the trigger at forty-two with a car?" (I knew how melodramatic it sounded. I didn't care. Grief turns us all into bad poets.) The dog's nose nudged my shoulder, a reminder that there still existed living things that were not me. I buried my face in her fur. "I'm sorry," I said, and didn't know to whom. I expected to feel better after breaking something.

I didn't.

The rage didn't leave, it crouched, alert, waiting for the next reason to stand. If grief was a sea, rage was the rip current. I made a note in my phone: Ask someone about anger, and then immediately deleted it. I didn't want to be anyone asking anything yet. Not the counsellor. Not the priest. Not the universe I was still not sure I believed in or, worse, suspected might be watching with exquisite indifference.

Days braided into each other. I kept a ritual of small survivals. At dawn, I opened the back door and let the morning air make its first decision about me. I stood barefoot on the deck and let the cold bully me awake. I watered the pot plant I had previously ignored into resilience. I circled the block with the dog and said hello to the old man who trimmed his roses like a mission statement. He told the dog she was handsome and told me the name of a cloud. I forgot it immediately and decided that was okay.

In the quiet hours, I organised drawers no one would ever see. I threw out the socks with nobody's partner. I wrote letters I didn't send. I apologised to the girl I had been, the one who stayed too long at a table where the food looked like love and ate like shame. I thanked the woman who had dragged me out of that house with the stubbornness of a mule and a prayer, though prayer was too church for what I meant. Maybe asking was the word. I was learning to ask life to keep me.

One afternoon, I went back to the notebook and opened to a clean page. The crease down the middle had become a habit. On the left, I wrote The Living Dead. On the right, Proof of Life. Then I set them down as simply as they arrived, laughing at nothing and then feeling guilty for the sound, moving through rooms like a rumour, nodding while people talk and hearing none of it, eating standing up, not to be a person who eats, but to keep from falling. And then, against it, the kettle shrieks and I answer it, my friend texts the weather and I look up, the dog thumps her tail when I say her name, and the plant grows despite me. I felt ridiculous and tender at once. You can be both. The heart is an untidy backpack; it can hold everything at once if you stop trying to fold it.

That night, I slept. Not deeply, not mercifully, but enough to make morning look possible. In the dream, I walked through our old house, the one from before even the rental with the stain. Every door I opened led to a room I had left and a version of me I had abandoned. In the last room, a girl stood by the window. She was maybe twenty-seven and sunburnt, her shoulders peeled from a day that had seemed like a good idea at noon. She was holding a bouquet of jacaranda flowers like a promise she didn't know how to keep. I sat beside her on the garden bench. We watched birds. We didn't speak. I woke with the sense we had decided something together, though I couldn't have told you what.

The next morning, when I took the bins out, the neighbour with the pilot wave was mowing. He cut the engine as I passed. "Hey, Len," he said, using a nickname only people from the old life could get away with. "How you holding up?"

"Like an IKEA chair missing a bolt," I said before I could stop myself.

He laughed, a surprised bark. "We've all got a wobble." He nodded at the bins. "Need a hand?"

"I've got it," I said, meaning please let me lift something I can actually carry.

He lifted a hand - pilot wave - and revved the mower back into its tidy roar. I watched the neat lines he made in the grass. There was a certain obscene pleasure in order. I understood it now more than ever.

Back inside, I stood in the hallway between two rooms and felt the exact moment when my breath turned into a blade. I pressed my palm flat against the wall and counted to ten. At seven, the blade dulled. At ten, it was just air again. I realised with something like awe that I had not thought of the garden path all morning. No cinematic fall, no white shock of surrender. The picture that had once come to me with the tenderness of a hand on a fevered forehead was taking a step back. Not far, just one step. It was enough to notice. *"I see you,"* I told it in my mind. *"I don't choose you."* The sentence didn't feel brave. It felt bored. Oddly, that seemed like progress.

That evening, I lit a single candle on the kitchen table. I didn't make a speech. I didn't turn it into a ritual. I just watched the small living thing do what it does best, be flame. When the wick leaned, I cupped my hand around it and made a windless room with my palm. Outside, the jacaranda shook more confetti free. Inside, the dog snored, a small piggish sound that would have made her defensive if she'd been awake to hear it. My phone buzzed on the bench. SIS: Weather in Karratha, windy as hell. Hold onto your skirt, woman. ME: Holding. I pictured my sister on her red-dirt street with her Rotti, the wind picking up, sand lifting into the kind of storm that rearranges everything and dares you to be precious. I imagined standing there beside her, our hair horizontal, the dogs pressing against our knees for ballast.

"Okay," I told the candle, the dog, the room that had watched me fall apart and then sit very still inside the ruins. "Okay." I knew what was coming next. The ocean had been calm for a handful of days. It wouldn't last. Grief is a weather system that refuses to be domesticated, and there is always a front gathering behind your back. Anger was building again, the clean, bright kind with edges. The kind that doesn't whimper or beg. The kind that aims. I could feel it in my hands, the way they started to want to throw, to smash, to put words where I'd once put apologies. I could feel it in my jaw, held tight like a door you brace with your shoulder. I could feel it in the way I looked at the sky and wanted to tell it the truth. Tomorrow, I thought. Or the day after. I would take the rage outside and let it hear itself. I would give the wind something to carry.

For now, I blew the candle out and watched the smoke rise, a ribbon, a signal, a sentence that didn't need words.

"Stay," I told myself in the dark, and I did.

In the next chapter, the air will split, the quiet house will hear me, and for the first time since the knock at the door, I will aim my voice upward and refuse to be polite. Let heaven be warned.

Chapter Eight

The hill behind the house is a small thing, scrub grass, an old fence post half-rotted at the base, a sky that drops down so hard it makes your jaw ache. I climb it because it gives me distance from rooms that remember too much. From the windows that replay arguments like re-runs, from the chairs that still know his weight. Up here, the town spreads like a tidy lie, roofs behaving themselves, and a road cutting a straight line through other people's stories. The air smells faintly of rust and sunburnt weeds. The wind tastes like metal. Clouds herd themselves east in slow bruised folds. I press my palms to my thighs and breathe until the shake turns into heat.

The grass hisses beneath me. A beetle clambers over my boot like it's scaling Everest. The earth feels solid enough to carry confession.

"I'm here," I say to the sky. "If you're listening."

Nothing answers, of course. The wind clicks the long grass like a thousand small tongues. Somewhere far below, a dog barks at a thing it can't control.

"Fine," I say. "I'll talk. You can be silent. That seems to be your specialty."

I've brought nothing with me, no phone, no water, no prayer I trust. Only the stubborn pulse in my throat and a fury that won't sit down when asked. I look up until my neck hurts.

"Why him?" The words come raw. "Why that night? Why the drink, the speed, the road with its mouth open like it had been practicing for him?"

Because consequences, the sky says, except it doesn't. I hear it anyway, a sentence in the same voice that told me to apologise when I was six, to be small when I was sixteen, to forgive a man who did not repent at twenty-six. It's my voice with a pious mask. It's every sermon I swallowed and called sustenance.

"Don't you dare," I whisper. "Don't you dare use me against me."

The wind gusts in response, lifting my hair, flattening the grass. I don't believe in the white-bearded judge, never have, but I believe in a listener. A presence. Something that feels the way a hand does on the small of your back when a crowd threatens to close. I used to call it God. On my worst days, I called it nothing. Today I call it Heaven because it gives me someone to fight.

"Say it," I demand. "Say it out loud. He chose it. Say it."

He chose it, the imagined voice concedes, soft as rain. But you were the storm in his head.

The hill tilts, and I bite my cheek until I taste iron. "I was the storm? I was the one who begged him to stop. I was the one who hid the bottles and sorted the lies by size. I was the one who learned to smile with a split lip and called it grace."

And you were the one who left the interview, who drank, who knocked on the door too late. You were the last face he saw before night. You knew he was a fuse.

I laugh, sharp and wrong. "There it is. The math I do at three a.m. You've stolen my chalk and started working the sums in the sky." I jab a finger upward. "Return what is mine."

Silence. The grass leans and comes back, the way bodies do in crowds. The silence becomes a mirror, and I hate what it shows.

"Say something real," I snap. "You demand honesty from us, don't you? From the living? Here's mine: If you are there, you did a wretched job. If you are not, then we are fools to be this tender with each other."

I am not a wall to throw your head against, Heaven says, except it doesn't. I am the space that keeps you from bruising on both sides.

"Spare me poetry," I hiss. "Be a fact."

You are a fact.

I am shaking now, not with fear but with the fury of a body that has run out of polite containers. "Then look," I say, opening my hands. "Look at me. Not the tidy version. The day-before and the day-after. The woman who thought surrender was a synonym for love. The woman who speaks to air because the one person she should be shouting at sits in a bottle on top of the bookshelf."

The wind lifts my hair like a blessing that forgot its purpose. I wait for lightning that never comes.

"Answer me," I say.

I am answering, the not-voice says. You are still standing.

"That isn't an answer," I spit. "That's a technicality."

It's a beginning.

"I don't want beginnings," I say, and hear the child in it. "I want reversal. I want a film reel I can wind back with my hands until he chooses the couch instead of the car, until I choose the truth instead of the drink, until every small cowardice I dignified as coping becomes a courage I can live with. Give me that."

I don't give time back, the sky says in the voice of the obvious.

"Then what good are you?" I whisper.

To keep you from leaving with him.

I close my eyes so hard the bright behind them fractures. To keep you from leaving with him. It lands like a sentence and like mercy. I hate it. I want to tear it up with my teeth. I also want to lie down in it and sleep.

"Why should I stay?" My throat is sand. "List it."

A pause I invent stretches between us. Because your daughter is in a dress she hasn't bought yet and wants you to say she looks like the sun. Because she will call at midnight from a car park and not say she is sad but mean it, and you will hear it and keep her from stepping into a river she can't see. Because there is a tree you haven't yet planted that will shade a stranger you will never meet. Because you will laugh again in the place where you are certain laughter can never cross.

"I don't want prophecy," I say. "I want him."

You want the version you were promised. He doesn't exist.

I drag my fingers through the dirt until crescent moons grow under my nails. "You're cruel."

I am not anything, the imagined voice says, and it's almost relief to hear it admit what I know. I am the name you give to what you cannot carry alone.

"Then carry it," I demand. "Carry this with me."

I am, right now, in the shape of your breath.

It's the kind of sentence I would have mocked before, the kind that looks pretty cross-stitched on the wall of a woman who's never seen a night like mine. And yet. And yet my ribs do move. And yet the wind does slip in and out of me like it's been practicing for years.

"Do you forgive me?" I ask. It is the first honest question.

For what is yours to own, I ask you to forgive yourself. For what is not, I ask you to put it down.

"Tell me which is which."

The drink, the ankle, the knock, you own those. The speed,

the road, the rage, you do not.

I am quiet. I don't agree. But the sentence sits down beside me and does not leave.

"Say his name," I whisper to the sky. "Say it so I know this is not theatre."

You say it, the sky replies, or maybe I do.

I do. It breaks me open and doesn't kill me.

I stand, pacing the small lip of the hill like a witness rehearsing testimony. "You want honesty? Here it is. I am furious with him for dying before we could change. I am furious with you for being nothing when I needed something. I am furious with myself for calling a house a home and a bruise love. I am furious that the world is still outrageously beautiful, and I can see it beyond the veil of this ache. I am furious because part of me is relieved."

The last one scorches my tongue. I wait for lightning; the sky does what it always does, pretends not to hear.

Relief is a door, the not-voice says, mild as a teacher. It does not make you wicked to walk through it. It makes you ready to live.

"Live what?" I demand. "A widow life? A half-life? A story told in apologies and casseroles?"

A true one.

I sit. The ground is hard; the ground is faithful. Ants negotiate around my boot like a busy committee. Somewhere a kookaburra laughs the way it always laughs at inappropriate times.

"Then let me rage," I say. "Let me rage and don't tidy me up."

Rage until the flame shows you what it's burning for.

"For him," I say, reflexive.

Look again.

I do, reluctantly, like someone peering into a mirror with the lights too bright. Under the red, there's a colder colour, a sharper need.

"For me," I say, almost ashamed.

For you, the not-voice agrees. For the girl you were before you learned to rehearse silence. For the woman you will become when you retire apology.

"Retire apology," I repeat, snorting. "You make it sound like a gold watch and a speech."

It will be both.

I don't want to smile. I do anyway, crooked as a paper cut. For a moment the hill is two places, a wild, wind-bitten pulpit where I indict the sky, and a small room where I sit across from myself and try to tell the truth like it's not dangerous.

"What do I do with the part that still wants to die?" I ask.

Feed it something other than endings.

"Like what?"

Bread. Sun. Your daughter's name. A list of things that did not abandon you. The ridiculousness of dogs. Clean sheets. Music at 2 a.m. because you can. A promise you make to the woman you will be in a year that you will bring her there alive.

"You sound like a fridge magnet," I mutter.

You came here for something you could carry down the hill in your hands. Sometimes wisdom travels light.

We are quiet then. Not the watchful quiet that follows a lie. The human quiet of two people who have said enough for one breath. The wind softens and falls away. The ants return to their parliament.

Down the slope, the roof of my house winks in and out of trees. Inside it are the rooms that have heard my worst. Inside it is the mirror that will not negotiate. Inside it are the dishes I abandoned and the cup with the ring of coffee that reads like a planet around absence.

"Walk with me," I say without meaning to.

I already am.

"Don't leave when I hit the bottom," I say.

I am the bottom.

"That's not comforting."

It's honest.

I start down, my knees remembering how steep feels. Halfway I stop, dizzy with sudden memory, the garden path lit like judgment, that flash of imagined skull and blood, the quiet that looked almost like relief. I have been carrying the picture like a talisman, as if horror could protect me from itself.

"I wanted that," I admit to the trees. "I wanted the simple of it."

You wanted rest. You can rest without ending.

"How?"

By not pretending your strength is infinite. By lying down when the living hurts. By letting others bring the kindness they insist on bringing. By asking for help in the simple language of hunger and thirst.

"Help," I say to the air, surprised at how the word pulls my shoulders down from my ears. "Help, help, help."

Yes, the sky says, through leaves, through breath, through the small mercy of gravity that delivers me to the flat ground without incident. Like that.

I push open the back gate and stand there stupidly, because the yard is the same shape it always was. The pegs on the line are miniature gallows in primary colours. The rosemary bush smells like Sundays I didn't deserve. The dog whips herself into a figure eight when she sees me and then checks my hands for treats, as if I might have hidden something for her in all that empty.

"Nothing today," I tell her, rubbing the warm spot behind her ear. "But thank you for asking."

In the kitchen, the cup still waits with its brown ring around the inside, a planet of dried intention. I run water and watch the circle loosen and slip under the surface. It feels obscene to call it baptism. It also feels exactly like that.

I leave the cup upside down to drip and lean my forehead against the cool of the cabinet. "You there?" I ask.

In the drip. In the ache. In the dog's ridiculous joy. In the way your feet have not quit their post.

"Don't go," I say.

I am a name you can change. I am not the leaving kind.

The dog settles with a sigh like a small accordion. A fly throws itself against the window, stubborn and stupid and somehow brave. I pull the chair out, sit, and put my hands flat on the table the way women do when they are about to plan their survival.

"Okay," I say to the air, to the version of Heaven that has agreed to be a sparring partner as long as I don't make it into an alibi. "Okay."

Okay, the not-voice answers, and I hear my own mouth in the shape of it.

There are a thousand things to do that do not care whether I am grieving: call the bank back; find the paperwork for the car; answer my daughter when she texts without punctuation but with need; cut the crusts off the sandwich because my hands remember how to love even when my brain insists on questions. I will fail at some of them. I will succeed at others. None of it will look like the holy art I was promised. All of it will count.

Before I make any calls, I write. A small list. The names I have for what will keep me here today, just today:

- Water.

- Toast.

- The sound the magpie makes at 4 p.m.

- The smell of clean on a pillowcase.

- A text to my sister that says only: still here.

- The dog's warm insistence.

- The sky, even when I am rude to it.

I put the list under a magnet shaped like a strawberry, the kind of cheerful lie that even now does not offend me. I stand, and for once, the standing is not a metaphor. It is precisely what it is, muscles, bones, and breath. It is everything Heaven promised and never delivered, and everything the body promised and somehow still does.

"Stay," I tell the air one more time.

I will if you will, the air says back, in my voice, in the voice of the woman who is not finished.

"I am not finished," I say aloud, to practice. "Not yet."

Outside, the hill keeps its secrets. The town continues its choreography. Somewhere a siren begins and fades. I put the kettle on and do not flinch when it screams. I answer it with a mug and a teabag and the knowledge that rage, handled with both hands, can burn without consuming. That I can argue with Heaven and still believe in mornings. That I can name a thing that doesn't answer and feel answered anyway.

When the water hits the leaves, steam rises like a soft unlearning. I hold my face over it and let my anger go on breathing.

It will be with me for a while. So will the quiet. I can stand between them. I can be the room where they meet and do not kill each other.

"Okay," I tell them both, gentler. "Okay. We'll do it this way."

And for the first time since the door closed, I do not feel like I am rehearsing a life. I am living one, raw, rude, unsupervised. The heavens do not clap. They don't need to. This is my applause: a mug warming my hands; the dog's sigh; the small, bright shock of realising I'm still here to pour the next cup.

Chapter Nine

Some nights the rage burned itself clean, and what remained wasn't peace, it was the quiet hum after lightning, the tremor that follows a scream. The kind of silence that holds its breath and waits to see what you'll do next.

The fire had burned itself low. It was no longer a raging thing that leapt and roared and demanded air, it was a heap of smouldering embers, a dull red glow under a skin of ash. And yet I sat before it as though it were alive, as though it held answers I could not pry from anyone else.

The lounge was dark except for the weak pulse of the coals. Shadows gathered at the edges of the room like spectators who knew better than to speak. The walls held the smell of smoke and the quiet hum of electricity, that low, steady sound of a house trying to remember it still exists.

I should have gone to bed, pulled the blanket over my shoulders, tried to wrestle my body into sleep. Instead, I folded myself down before the fireplace, knees to chest, staring into the residue of flame as if it were a mirror. The carpet scratched my skin through my leggings, the hearth breathed heat in tiny sighs, like the slow exhale of something still deciding if it wanted to live.

I stared at the fragments of heat, the way they pulsed faintly in the dark, and whispered into the smoke. "Is this it? Is this all that's left of me?"

The embers shifted, sighing a thin thread of warmth into the air. Their silence mocked me.

"Don't you dare play quiet with me," I said, my voice

cracking. "You used to roar. You used to be everything. And now look at you. You're pathetic. Just like me."

I leaned closer, so close my skin tingled from the warmth still trapped there. "I know you can hear me," I said, softer now. "I know you're not dead. Not really."

The ash crumbled inward, a little collapse, as though in reply.

Ashes are strange companions. They carry the memory of fire but not the flame itself. They hold heat without blaze, a past tense of passion. Sitting before them, I could almost believe they were listening.

"You remind me of him," I said bitterly. "Full of spark one moment, gone the next. Burned out and leaving me with the mess. Do you know what it's like to gather up remains with your bare hands? To sift through what's left and try to pretend it still means something?"

I pushed at the embers with the fire poker. Sparks leapt up like startled birds, a flare of life, brief and cruel.

"That's what grief feels like," I muttered. "One second you flare, tricking me into thinking the fire's back, that warmth is possible, that love could exist again. And then, nothing. Grey, empty, cold."

One spark clung stubbornly, refusing to die.

I laughed, the sound hollow. "Oh, you think you're clever, don't you? You think you're proof. Proof that something is left. Proof that I can't give up yet." My voice wavered. "But you're not. You're just a reminder of what I've lost."

I waited for the ember to answer, but it only pulsed, steady and small.

The room hummed faintly, the clock, the fridge, the breath of the house. Everything alive except the one person who should have been. The stillness became a mirror I didn't want to face.

The room smelled of smoke and regret. My clothes were marked with it, and my hair clung to its scent. It was inescapable, this reek of what had burned. I pressed my hands together, fingers blackened with soot, and held them out as though in prayer.

"Do you even know what you've done to me?" I asked the ashes. "You've stripped me down to nothing. Everything I thought I was, wife, woman, mother, believer , gone. All that's left is… this."

The embers glowed faintly, like a heartbeat under ash.

"Don't you dare pity me," I whispered. "Don't you dare."

A coal split open with a sound like a sigh, releasing a thin snake of orange. It reminded me of veins under skin, how something can glow even after the body is gone cold.

I thought about the vows. The broken promises. The nights I had clung to the illusion of forever, even when forever had already started to crumble.

"You know about vows, don't you?" I asked the firepit. "They're like you. Bright at first. Warm enough to make you believe. And then, over time, they fade. They leave only smoke and stains. And still, like a fool, I sit here breathing it in, choking myself on what used to be."

My eyes stung. I pressed my palms to them until the darkness spun. "I hate you," I whispered. "I hate that I can't stop watching you. I hate that you remind me of everything I lost."

The ember sparked again, flickering defiantly.

"No," I said quickly. "Don't you dare. Don't you dare give me hope. Not tonight."

But still it glowed.

Time blurred in front of the fire. I couldn't say if it was hours or minutes. My thoughts circled like moths too stupid to know the flame would kill them.

"You think this is funny?" I demanded. "That you can taunt me with your little glow, your tiny heartbeat, while I'm here falling apart?"

The ash hissed faintly.

"Answer me!" I screamed, slamming the poker down into the heap. Ash scattered, sparks flared, and for a heartbeat the fire was alive again, angry, chaotic, brilliant. I gasped, my breath sharp in my throat.

"See?" I said, my voice trembling. "That's what I want. That's what I miss. The fury, the life, the… the heat."

But almost as soon as it had flared, it collapsed. A few sparks fell silent into the ash.

And I sobbed.

"You're just like me," I whispered. "Burned down to nothing but fragments. But do you know the worst part?" I leaned close, so close I could taste the metallic tang of smoke. "The worst part is you still glow. You don't get to die clean. You don't get to vanish. You just linger, reminding me that I can't either."

I rocked back onto my heels, wrapping my arms around myself. "I should be grateful, shouldn't I? I should see you as hope. Proof that something survives the fire. But I don't. I see you as torment. You won't let me go. You keep me tethered to a life I want to walk away from."

The embers shifted, collapsing softly, and a new glow appeared where the ash had covered it.

I closed my eyes. "You're cruel," I said. "You're cruel, and I'm tired."

But exhaustion is not the same as surrender. It mimics it well, the same slack jaw, the same slumped shoulders, and the same hollow breath. But one is a pause, and the other a vanishing. And as I sat there, tears streaking my face, I realised the truth I didn't want, that I was not yet done. The fire inside me, battered as it was, still lived.

"You're not going to die, are you?" I asked the embers softly.

They glowed back at me, patient.

I laughed weakly. "I hate you for that."

Silence.

"…I love you for that."

The contradiction made me shake my head, made me smile even through the ache. It felt ridiculous, holy, human.

Somewhere in the quiet, memory stirred, uninvited, but insistent. Another night, another fire. His laughter then, deep, boyish, full of something I used to mistake for safety. He had thrown a log into the flames, the sparks catching on the air like gold dust. I remembered the way he'd looked at me, eyes soft, beer bottle dangling from his fingers. "You always stare at fire like it's telling secrets, "He'd said. I'd laughed and said, "Maybe it is." I'd thought that was intimacy, the way we could exist together in glow and shadow, pretending our love was the steady thing and not the smoke rising from it.

The fire that night had been bright. We'd talked about holidays we never took, about Poppy's future, about things that sounded like forever but were really rehearsals for goodbye. Later, when he'd reached for me, the heat of his skin had felt like confession. And even then, some small voice inside me had whispered that all this burning would end in ash.

Now, years later, sitting before this new heap of ghosts, I wanted to tell that younger version of myself to look closer, to see the way flame always trembles before it dies, to listen to the crackle that sounds too much like breaking. But she wouldn't have listened. She'd been too full of faith in sparks.

The rain outside grew heavier, a percussion against the roof, steady and cleansing. I watched the last coal pulse under its veil of grey. My mind drifted to the hospital room again, the white light, the cold tile, the sound of the clock that refused to stop. I had begged for something then, mercy, release, meaning, and gotten only breath. It had felt like betrayal at the time, being left alive.

But now, in this half-dark room with its soft ruin of heat, I wondered if survival had been its own strange grace, not mercy, but mandate. To keep tending what flickered. To stay near the ember, even when it hurt.

I pressed my palm to the hearth, the stone warm against my skin, and whispered, "I'm still here." It wasn't prayer. It wasn't victory. It was inventory, proof of pulse, proof of breath.

The embers answered with a small sigh, a final breath that rose and settled again.

At some point the night folded into morning. The clock on the wall muttered past midnight, then one, then two. My body ached from sitting cross-legged on the rug, but I couldn't leave. The embers were my jury and my priest, my tormentor and my companion.

The world outside shifted while I stayed still. A possum thumped across the roof. Rain began, thin at first, then harder, a percussion on the tin that almost drowned my thoughts. The smell of wet earth seeped in through the cracks. And still I stayed with the fire.

The rain did something merciful, it blurred the edges of the world. The sound filled the gaps where his voice used to be. It washed the silence clean.

I thought about how many times I had felt like this fire, used up, emptied out, good for nothing but smoke. There had been nights in the hospital, whispering for mercy while machines hummed their indifference. Nights in my marriage when I curled myself small, praying he would stop shouting, stop drinking, stop turning love into something jagged. Nights after the funeral, staring at the ceiling, daring the air to stop filling my lungs.

Each time I had thought, *this is it. This is the end.* And yet each time, like these coals, something in me glowed back. Stubborn. Infuriating. Alive.

"Why won't you let me quit?" I asked the embers. "Why won't you just let me die too?"

The embers pulsed, red through the ash, and I hated them for their patience.

I pressed my hand flat to the floor. The boards were warm beneath me, the ghost of the fire's reach. I thought of his hands, how they had once warmed me, then wounded me, then left. Everything burns in its own way.

I remembered a line I had once underlined in a book: *It is not the blaze that proves life, but the ember that refuses to die.*

At the time I hadn't understood. I wanted blaze. I wanted joy, laughter, full rooms, bright voices. I wanted a love that was cinematic, not stubborn. Now, sitting before the hush of coals, I began to understand.

The ember's job was not to dazzle. It was to endure.

Endurance is ugly. It doesn't parade. It doesn't inspire postcards or Instagram captions. Endurance crouches low, smoulders in silence, hides its brilliance under ash. It does not care if it is noticed. It simply lasts.

And maybe that was enough.

I thought about my own endurance, the mornings I still made coffee, the bills I still paid, the moments I still smiled when someone said something kind. Each act felt microscopic, but maybe that was the point. Life had shrunk to its essentials. I didn't need grandeur. I needed continuation.

I picked up a small twig from the basket beside the hearth and laid it gently across the embers. It caught, slowly, shyly. The fire exhaled, a faint crackle, a sigh, the smallest flame rising to meet its own shadow.

"You're still here," I said. "And so am I."

At last the sky lightened. The room shifted from black to grey to the faint suggestion of day. Birds began their sharp, insistent chorus outside. The dog barked once, as if to remind the dawn it had a job to do.

My throat was raw from whispering to things that could not answer. My cheeks were sticky with dried tears. My body felt ancient, every joint announcing its displeasure at grief's posture.

But the fire was still alive. Faint, but alive.

"I'm still here," I told the ashes. My voice rasped like a confession. "Do you hear me? I'm still here."

And though they said nothing, though they only glowed faintly in their ruin, I felt it, the smallest acknowledgment. A pulse in the air. A soft nod from the universe that hadn't completely turned its face away.

I leaned back against the couch, exhaustion settling over me like a blanket I didn't deserve. The first light of morning caught the ash and made it shimmer, tiny galaxies inside what had already died.

A reminder that even after fire, there can be warmth. Even

after ruin, there can be ember.

And maybe, just maybe, ember is enough to begin again.

I sat there until the room forgot how to be dark. Morning stretched its pale arms through the curtains, touching the ash with shy light.

The fire had done what it came to do, not to warm, not to destroy, but to reveal what refuses to die.

I reached for the cold cup beside me and took a sip anyway. It tasted of smoke and something else, faint, familiar, impossible. Hope, maybe, in its first awkward form.

The embers sighed once more, a low breath like gratitude, and I thought of all the small mercies still hidden under the rubble, a dog's warm flank against my leg, my sister's crooked laugh, and a text waiting to be answered, the sound of a world that kept going.

Love, I realised, doesn't disappear in the fire. It breaks apart and hides in the smallest places, a fragment here, an ember there - waiting for the day you're brave enough to touch it again.

And so began the slow search for what survived the burning.

Chapter Ten

Some mornings ask for courage, but this one asked for gentleness, gather what love left behind and see what can still belong to a life.

I kept the box under the bed because I couldn't bear to see it, and I couldn't bear to throw it away.

Cardboard, the wrong size for shoes, the right size for an aftermath. It smelled faintly of dust and fabric softener and something I didn't want to name. When I pulled it into the light, the corner snagged on the rug and a little rip opened along the seam, like even the box was tired of holding its breath.

"Alright," I said to nobody. "Let's do it."

If grief was an ocean, this box was the tidepool. Small enough to look harmless, deep enough to drown a fingertip. I lifted the lid.

Paper first. The kind of paper you don't think is important at the time, receipts curled like fish bones, napkins with a date and a time and a hastily drawn heart, a flyer for a midnight movie we left halfway through because we were young and in love and the theatre was colder than the car. I smoothed each slip flat on the duvet like they were prayer flags.

"Tell me something I forgot," I whispered to a receipt from a freeway roadhouse. It didn't answer, obviously, it only offered the evidence of two coffees and a Mars bar. That night came back, though, the ache behind the eyes, the rush of the highway, the silence that meant peace, not punishment. We'd laughed about nothing, shared the Mars bar the wrong way, taking turns instead of breaking it in half, because even sharing had been a little ritual then. He'd kissed the chocolate off my thumb at a red light. I remember thinking, *if this is forever, I could live here.*

"Isn't it wild," I told the receipt, "That a thing so small can hold a whole night?"

The receipt crinkled, held its shape. "Fine," I said. "Keep your secrets."

Underneath the paper were the heavier things. A keyring from a motel on the salt highway where the bed squeaked like an accusation, and we laughed so hard we had to bury our faces in the pillows. The stingray-shaped fridge magnet he bought me after we walked too far along the jetty, and I cried because the wind felt like a hand pushing me toward the drop. A strip of photographs from a booth that has since been ripped out of the shopping centre, four tiny squares of us trying not to blink at the countdown light. In the last one we're both blurred, mid-laugh. Once upon a time I would have thrown that strip away for being imperfect. Now it's my favourite, because it proves we were alive.

I held the magnet up to the bedside lamp. The stingray's cheap enamel shimmered. I heard the ocean without hearing it, the memory-sound you don't notice till it's gone. "You tried," I told the magnet. "You were in over your head, too."

The magnet's smile didn't change.

Deeper, then. The box asked for truth in layers. There was a T-shirt of his I used to sleep in when love felt like a fever I wanted to keep. Threadbare now, the collar giving up the ghost. I pressed it to my face and breathed in habit, not scent. The smell was long gone. But muscle memory is a strange perfumer, my body gave me what I asked for anyway. For one second it was him, newly showered, cheap soap and cheap deodorant and the skin-smell I could pick out of a crowded room.

"Where did you go?" I asked the shirt.

It didn't answer. It couldn't. That was the problem with artifacts, they held the shape of a person without the heat.

I folded the shirt and set it aside. My hands shook a little. Not panic, not quite. That hollowed-out tremor of someone who's been holding too much for too long.

"You don't have to be brave," I told my hands. "Just be here."

There were photographs in the box I'd avoided since the funeral. I had planned to burn them the night I couldn't stop seeing the crash in the darkness behind my eyes, but the lighter ran out and I took it as a commandment. Live with it. Learn from it. Don't erase what made you.

I had a theory as a girl that photographs stole time. That each one took a sliver you would never get back. If that was true, the box was a heist.

I slid the stack onto the bed. The first photo was the first summer, both of us on the bonnet of his beaten-up car, his arm thrown across the windshield like he could protect it from sunburn. My hair is pulled up in a lopsided knot atop my head, my smile is careless, the kind of smile you only make before you understand the price of smiling. He's looking at me, not the camera. I forgot that used to be his favourite direction, to look at me like he was memorising the moves.

"What did you see?" I asked the boy in the photograph. "Who did you think I was?"

The boy's mouth stayed open as if he was about to say something blasphemous or tender. Photographs are cruel that way, they trap you before the sentence lands.

I laid out more. The wedding, white dress that wasn't truly white, a shade off, as if the shop knew something I didn't. His hand at the small of my back, my laugh too loud. The day we painted the first house together, my hair threaded with cobwebs from the skirting boards, his cheek stamped with a perfect rectangle of off-white. Then the one where we're not touching at all. Same faces, different distance. There we are at somebody else's barbecue, standing two skewers apart. There we are at a Christmas that tastes like company eggshells, pretending. There we are on a sofa, facing forward, bodies parallel like twin roads that used to cross and don't anymore.

"I remember this," I told the gap between our shoulders. "This was when I learned to talk without saying anything."

Pieces. That's all it ever was when you stared hard enough. A life torn into salvageable squares.

"Alright," I said to the fragments. "Tell me the truth I hid from myself."

Silence, the honest kind.

I lay back on the floor beside the bed, the photos above me like ceiling tiles. If I softened my eyes, they almost connected into a mosaic. That's what I wanted, the illusion of seamlessness. But mosaics are mortared with something. Grout. Glue. Hope. Lies. I felt around inside myself for whatever I had used and came up with emptiness and habit.

"I loved you," I told the photos. "Even when I shouldn't have. Even when love was the wrong word for what we were doing."

A postcard slipped out from somewhere and floated down like a fallen leaf. Broome. A lake so blue it might as well have been a lie. He'd written on the back in that uneven lowercase print: Wish you were here. Miss you like mad. Back Friday. He'd been back Tuesday. I remembered now, the way relief became suspicion. The smell on his shirt that wasn't soap. The apology that didn't say the noun. We'd fought in the kitchen with our hands in our pockets, both of us pretending we wouldn't break the plates if we took them out.

"Why did you stay?" I asked the woman on the kitchen floor, years younger, equal parts steel and softness.

"Because I wanted the story to come true," she might have said, if paper could admit anything. "Because leaving is a kind of death, and I was already a ghost."

I put the postcard with the others. It felt like placing a sharp shell back on the sand. You can't carry them all, you can't leave them all behind.

In the bottom of the box was a smaller box. I knew what was inside without opening it, his wedding ring, two cufflinks, a pin with the clasp bent the wrong way, and his father's watch. The ring had been returned to me in an envelope I kept in my sock drawer for a week because I couldn't bring myself to touch metal that had touched him for so long. When I finally opened it, the ring was warmer than it should have been, as if it had kept a little heat from his skin. It sat in my palm now like a coin I hadn't earned.

"You didn't take it off," I said to the circle. "Not even when you should have."

It seemed important then to try it on. I slid it over the knuckle of my right-hand ring finger and felt the old indent it had left on my life, how the mind can feel marks the body can't see. Too loose. It would fall. I curled my hand into a fist and held it honey-tight.

"Look," I told the air. "I can carry the thing that broke me without letting it slip."

I sounded braver than I felt.

There were fragments you couldn't put in a box. The sound of a slammed door that didn't mean anger, just hurry. The weight of his hand on my knee under a table when the conversation went bored. The shove. The sick apology after. The laugh we shared when the toast burned the day we decided we were the kind of people who could do breakfast together forever. The silence we bought wholesale when we learned we weren't.

"Do you ever stop judging me?" I asked the invisible jury I'd installed in the corner of the room. "Do you ever quit replaying the worst pieces?"

The jury shrugged. They were all me, of course. Me in different masks, me with different gavels. We're our own harshest court.

I sat up. The photographs, the magnet, the shirt, the ring, these were the kind of fragments everyone recognised. Less easy to name were the slivers lodged under the skin. The way I flinched at a certain cough from the television because it sounded like his temper clearing its throat. The way I avoided the middle aisle at the bottle shop because that's where the brand of whiskey stood like a loaded word. The way I still reached for my phone to tell him about the dog doing something comical, then remembered there was no telling left to do.

"Okay," I told the unmet impulse. "You can sit beside me, but you don't drive."

It wasn't prayer and it wasn't affirmation; it was some new thing, a line I drew in sand inside my own head.

I made piles the way children do when they are serious about a game. Keep. Maybe. Burn. The keep pile surprised me by being small. The maybe pile swelled, and the burn pile glittered dangerously.

"What would burning do?" I asked the matches. "Would it free me or only perfume the house with what I already breathe?"

The matches kept their sulphurous secrets. I lit one anyway, watched the blue lick up into orange, held it close to the edge of a photograph of us grinning toothpaste-commercial grins. I waited until the heat tapped my fingers and then blew it out. A wisp of smoke wrote a line in the air and vanished on a word I didn't catch.

"Not yet," I told the ashes that could have been. "Not like this. Not out of spite."

There's a way to bury without fire. There's a way to honour without keeping. I was learning new verbs for love that didn't end with possession.

I put the ring back in the small box. The shirt, too, folded into a tighter square, as if making it compact could make it less loud. I tied the little ribbon that had been there once upon a wedding present. A reef knot. Something a sailor would trust. That made me smile. We had never been sailors, we had both been so very, very bad at weather.

"Thank you," I said to the shirt.

"For what?" the room asked me with his voice, or maybe my own.

"For teaching me how to recognise softness, even if it came late."

The room accepted the amendment.

I took a break, because honesty is a muscle and mine was cramping. Coffee, then. I made it the way I like it now, not the way we used to compromise, stronger, a little bitter, without the sugar that once convinced me I could swallow anything. I stood at the window and watched two magpies argue a fate with the lawn. When I came back to bed, the afternoon had sloped into that tender light that makes everything look like a memory even before it happens.

There were fragments that weren't about him at all. There was a notebook, for one, with my handwriting slashing diagonal across the lines. Lists of groceries, lists of grievances, lists of dreams written in the margin where the anger couldn't erase them. I'd written a page once about what I wanted from love. It was not complicated - respect, touch, a partner who could hold a silence without punishing me with it, someone who would see the room I walked into and make more space, not less.

"You could have left for this list alone," I told the woman who wrote it. "You could have left as soon as you knew you were bargaining with oxygen."

She didn't answer, because I hadn't given her the vocabulary yet. I forgive her for that now. It's hard to speak when someone else keeps stepping on your sentences.

On the very bottom of the box was an envelope I didn't recognise. No return address. My name on the front in a neat hand that wasn't his. I slid a finger under the flap and pulled out a single sheet of paper, a printout from a social media page I had forgotten existed. A photograph of me and him at a work function, the caption full of hearts. Underneath, a comment from a woman with a name I didn't know: *Lucky girl.*

I laughed. It wasn't a kind laugh.

I wanted to write under it now: Luck has nothing to do with this. Luck is a game I stopped playing when I realised I didn't have to win a man to win a life.

I set the printout in the burn pile. Some things deserved the small mercy of flame.

"What are you keeping?" I asked out loud, because the room had been kind enough to listen this long.

I sorted more than objects then. I sorted words. I held up "forever" and found it too heavy to keep carrying. I put "always" beside it and watched them both sulk at being returned. I kept "again." I kept "despite." I kept "meanwhile." I kept "yet." I kept "and."

"And" is the only word that ever saved me. He was cruel and he was tender. I was brave and I was afraid. We were beautiful and we were a mess. He died and I lived, and I broke, and I started. "And" holds all of that without choosing a favourite.

When the keep pile had become honest and small, I looked at the maybe pile one last time. That's when I found the smallest fragment in the entire box, a button. Off one of his shirts or my favourite dress from back when my favourite dress still made me feel like anything was possible, I couldn't tell. It was just a cheap plastic disc, off-white, two holes, a chip at the edge where impatience or a washing machine had taken a bite.

I held it up to the light and spoke to it like it was a saint.

"Do you remember when I could fasten a thing and it would stay?"

The button, holier than an icon for one slow second, caught a ray of sun and gave it back to me. I threaded it into my pocket and decided it could live there awhile. A small promise to myself that I can hold what's necessary in simple ways.

The night came in sidelong. I put the bigger box back under the bed, lighter now, the way a heart feels lighter when it puts some of what it carries back in the earth. I kept the small box on the bedside table. Not as an altar. As a ledger. A tally of what I owed and what I'd paid and what debt I no longer recognised as mine.

"Are we done?" I asked the room.

"For today," the room said, generous.

I turned off the lamp. Darkness poured into the corners like it had been waiting there all along. The house clicked, settled, whispered. I lay on my side and considered the way the body curls when it's protecting the middle. A small animal posture. A human one, too.

That's when I spoke to the fragments that couldn't be catalogued, the ones that live in the soft places and vibrate at odd hours. The memory of his laugh when it wasn't a weapon. The way his eyelashes looked when he slept through a storm. The rhythm of two bodies forgiving each other for a night. All the pieces that were worth keeping but not worth worshipping.

"Listen," I told them. "I won't build a shrine to you, and I won't pretend you're trash. You get a drawer in me. You get a label. You get to be part of the story without owning the ending."

A beat. A breath. That quiet again, this time not the watchful kind, but the kind that says, good.

Somewhere between that thought and sleep, I dreamed I was sweeping a beach after a party no one would confess to throwing. Bottle caps, ribbon, a child's sock, a single shoe. The sky was unashamedly beautiful, sun peeling itself up from the water, clouds staying in their lanes. I was barefoot. The sand was cold. Every time I bent to pick up a piece, the sea tried to take it back. We made a deal, the sea and I. You can have what you made, I'll keep what I can use.

When I woke, there was grit under my tongue like I'd been whispering to the shore all night. I laughed at the ceiling, and for once, the ceiling laughed back with a thin crack of morning light.

I made coffee and stood by the window again. The magpies were quiet now; the lawn was satisfied. In the reflection of the glass I caught myself, hair a foolish halo, eyes less haunted. Not cured. Not fixed. Just … more here.

Fragments of love. Not the kind I'd been taught to expect, photogenic, obedient, collected in albums. The real kind. The kind that cuts and heals at the same time. The kind that teaches you to bleed and bandage yourself in the same movement. The kind that makes mosaics you can stand on.

I pulled the small box toward me and opened it one more time, not for drama, not for pain, but for accuracy. The ring, the cufflinks, the bent pin, his father's watch. "You belonged to a life," I told them. "I'm building a different one. You're invited to sit quietly in a corner."

They behaved.

There is a moment in every rebuild where your hands stop shaking while they work. I felt it then, the steadiness. A quiet, stubborn craft taking hold. Not the glamour of transformation. The incremental mercy of it.

The house hummed. The kettle clicked off. A breeze slipped the curtain and touched my wrist like an old friend who remembered my name without asking for it.

"Okay," I said to the day. "Let's see what you can make from all this."

The day didn't answer. It opened.

And I walked into it holding a pocketful of buttons, a photograph where we're both blurred mid-laugh, a keyring from a motel that still owed us a good night's sleep, and a new grammar that started every sentence with and.

I stood there a moment longer, breathing in the ordinary air like it might agree to keep me. In, a count of four, out, a count of four. The smallest lesson, the oldest one. I didn't call it healing. I called it practice.

And that is how, with fragments in my pockets and the door open to morning, I began, quietly, and stubbornly, learning to breathe again.

Chapter Eleven

I came out of the fragments carrying one plain instruction like a warmed stone in my palm, begin with breath, even if it arrives late.

The first time I noticed it was gone, I panicked. Not his absence, that had already grown into a creature pacing the rooms, nosing the skirting boards, and curling on my chest at night, but my own breath. It had shrunk itself into a frantic flutter, a bird thrown against glass. Each inhale scraped. Each exhale evaporated before clearing my throat. I learned quickly that terror has its own choreography, hands on benchtop, knees unlocked, mouth open, and the body bargaining with air as if air were a reluctant god. The room didn't change to help me; I had to change inside the same room.

"Breathe," I said, fingers white on the benchtop. "Come on. Just…breathe." The word felt too big for the small pipe of me, it rattled, uncooperative, like a marble in a straw.

The air ignored me. My ribs locked, as if they'd signed a contract with grief and I hadn't read the fine print. Fine print always hides where the light is worst. Mine lived at the hinge of the sternum, thou shalt forget the easy things first. I tipped my forehead to the cool laminate. "Please," I whispered to the cage of my chest, "don't leave me too." The bench smelled faintly of lemon and old tea, I tried to breathe that gentleness in. It stalled, then thunked forward, a stubborn engine on a cold morning.

Silence. Then the drum of blood in my ears: you're here, you're here, you're here. The body is a blunt instrument, but sometimes bluntness is mercy. It counted for me when arithmetic failed.

Grief had stolen so much already, sleep, appetite, laughter, faith in mornings. But this felt like the cruellest theft, the simple ability to draw the world inside and not choke on it. I hadn't realised breath was a relationship until it ghosted me. Now I was the one waiting by the door, pretending not to listen for footsteps. The house seemed to agree. It breathed without me. Walls sighing, doors settling, the fridge with its patient hum, everything in rhythm, like a choir I'd been voted out of. I watched steam lift from the kettle and felt jealous of how confidently it rose. I envied the plants, too, how they trusted light, how they opened on schedule without apology. I put my hand over a basil leaf and copied its small courage, open, even if the day doesn't deserve it.

When I couldn't stand it, I faced the mirror. A stranger there, mouth parted just enough to beg, collarbones sharp as parentheses, and chest barely moving. "Why can't you just…do it?" I asked her. "Why can't you just be normal?" The stranger blinked like a lighthouse with a broken bulb, signal, darkness, signal. My job, apparently, was to keep turning the crank.

She didn't answer. My breath fogged her face into cloud. Proof I still existed. Thin, but proof. I drew a heart in the fog and wiped it away, embarrassed by the tenderness with myself.

The days blurred. I forgot to inhale until the room tilted. I woke at night gasping as if I'd been sleeping underwater. Panic lived under my skin like static. I didn't fear death anymore. I feared life, this relentless requirement to keep taking in air I didn't want. I learned the geography of tilt, which corner of the lounge steadied me, which chair lied, which window could be bribed open by a prayer I didn't believe in.

People said the lines you're supposed to say when you don't know what else to do. Time heals. Keep busy. Be strong. Words buffed smooth by overuse, tossed like coins, as if wishing could fix it. I stacked their sayings on the bench like coasters and set my shaking cup on top. They didn't stop the rings from forming, but they kept the table from staining worse. Time didn't heal. It lengthened. I woke to the same blade pressing my sternum. I fell asleep heavy as a stone, lungs unwilling. Length can be a kindness if it makes space, I told myself, it can be a cruelty if it only stretches the ache. Most days it did both.

And yet, every so often, breath arrived without being asked. A sharp inhale watching a magpie strut along the fence, arrogant as a monarch. A laugh I didn't authorise when my sister sent a spiral of emojis that made no sense and all the sense. A long sigh when the dog tucked himself against me, warm and oblivious, like a living hot-water bottle with a heartbeat. Those stowaway breaths slipped past the bouncer at my throat and got the party started without me. I resented them for their audacity, and I loved them for their nerve.

Those small breaths terrified me. Each one felt like betrayal. How dare I breathe when he no longer could? How dare I choose air when his last choices were speed and bottle and sky? Guilt has good aim and it shot each inhale on sight. Still, some survived, limping into my chest and setting up camp.

Because you're still here, something whispered, maddeningly calm. It sounded like the voice you use with frightened animals, low, shoulder turned, nonthreatening.

"I don't want to be," I said into the dark. The dark accepted my answer like a clerk accepts a form, noted, filed, no comment.

You are. Two words, no halo, no bargain. A stubborn fact

squatting on the mat.

"It should have been me." I was building a theology out of if onlys.

It wasn't. The sentence fell like a brick into water. No splash big enough to satisfy.

Sometimes I said the argument out loud and startled myself. "You don't get it. I don't want this air. Take it back." The ceiling, long-suffering, held.

But breath didn't negotiate. It kept coming, stubborn, relentless, filling me in ways I had not consented to. Consent would come later, like weather changing after weeks of sameness. Maybe that was lesson one, life doesn't always ask permission. Survival can be as offensive as it is miraculous. I wrote it on a sticky note and hid it under the salt, a little sacrilege to season the day.

In those first weeks, grief and breath hitched themselves to the same rope. When I sobbed, the air tore through me like weather. When I went carefully quiet, breath thinned to thread. My chest wrote Morse code, long, short, broken, frantic.

I tried to translate myself, SOS, stay, send help, send silence, send sleep. I tried to boss it. Sat cross-legged on the carpet, hands warm on my belly, counting like a child - four in, six out, four in, six out. I whispered the lullaby I wished someone would sing to me. In. Out. Stay. Sometimes it worked and I felt oxygen move like cool water, smoothing the inside edges. Then panic surged back with its messy stampede and I lost the count to sobbing. On good tries, the numbers were a pier. On bad ones, they were matchsticks on a tide.

Still, I kept at it. Not trying meant dying, and though I wanted that more often than I'd admit, a stubborn ember in me refused to let the match catch. I did not congratulate this ember. I tolerated it, the way you tolerate a neighbour who plays the radio too early but also waters your plants when you forget.

That ember carried me outside one morning. The sun was too gold for the weight inside me and I resented it, but I sat on the back step with my knees to my chest and listened to the world breathe. Leaves fussed. Bees made their soft industry in the lavender. Somewhere, a sprinkler ticked off its liturgy. Everything knew how to do the one thing I couldn't. I matched the sprinkler at first, tick, tock, in, out, a clock face I could rest my cheek against.

"Show me," I asked the yard. "Show me how to stay."

The yard answered by being ordinary, which is another word for faithful. The answer didn't come from the sky. It came from my ribs, small, irregular, like a little girl hiding there. Don't give up on me. She had my mother's stubborn jaw and my father's soft eyes; I could not refuse her.

"I don't know how to hold you," I said. I have broken nicer things with trying too hard.

You don't have to hold me. Just let me come. So simple I almost laughed. So hard I almost wept.

So I did. One inhale. One exhale. Not steady. Not pretty. Mine. Ownership is different from ease. I took the title anyway.

After that, I treated breath less like plumbing and more like a relationship, neglected, yes, but repairable. Each morning, I asked, "Will you stay?" Breath answered in the only way it knows how to, by arriving. Thin, but enough. I started saying thank you to the first yawn like you thank a bus that actually stops.

Some nights I still picked a fight with it. "Why are you still here? You should've left with him." Breath is not sentimental; it stayed because staying is its job.

Breath didn't leave. It waited, the kind of patient you can't buy. And the kind you can barely accept.

The kitchen became a chapel where the liturgy was ordinary, the kettle squealing its hymn, the dog's theatre of sighs on the mat, and the house exhaling when the day folded itself small. I practiced with dishwater on my wrists, and steam kissing my face. "In," I murmured. "Out." When panic rose, I planted my palms on the bench and told myself, "The ocean is in your chest, yeah, but you can float." The silence, kind for once, didn't argue. I floated half a minute. It counted. Half a minute is a raft. I named it after myself so I wouldn't lose it.

At the supermarket, I forgot how to be a person. Fluorescents buzzed like worry. Choices stacked to the ceiling. Strangers took whole breaths in front of me, casually, like thieves in daylight. I stared stupidly at milk. Breathe, I said, but the word snapped in half. A woman in a red coat stepped around me and smiled. Nothing dramatic, just human. Something in me unclenched. I inhaled. It hurt. I exhaled. It hurt less. I put the milk in my trolley as if I'd won a small, private war. That night I toasted victory with toast. Butter, nothing else. I ate it standing up as if sitting might jinx continuation.

At the cemetery, I hated the wind for how well it did what I could not. It moved where it wanted. It entered and exited without apology. It pressed my dress against my legs like it knew me. "Show-off," I muttered, and the leaves trembled in laughter. Four in, six out, like the therapist would suggest weeks later, but that day there was no therapist, just stones, names, and a breath learning from a leaf. I touched the cool top of his marker and let my lungs copy the breeze. I did not forgive the wind. I borrowed it.

Nights were worst. I would wake clawing the air, wild for a handle. "Help," I told nobody. The fridge answered with its steady hum. "Not you," I hissed. "Someone who loves me." Something in the quiet came closer, not rescue, but steadiness. In, it seemed to say. Out. I followed. Cursing, then crying, then quiet. By dawn's pale smear on the blinds, I'd made a thought that wasn't rage, survived. Survival is the ugliest beautiful word I know. I put it in my pocket anyway.

I learned to address breath like a skittish animal. "I won't chase you," I promised on the back step, feet on concrete still holding the night's cool. "I'll wait." It came near, retreated, came near again, curious at my collarbones. "You act like you're doing me a favour," I told it. Breath answered by being breath. Fine, I sighed. Stay then. But I get to be angry sometimes. Breath left me room to be angry, then came back when the anger spent itself and left the door on the latch. This was our treaty, I would not slam the door, and it would not vanish without knocking.

Grief taught my body a new alphabet. Shoulders spelled sorry. Jaw spelled stubborn. Spine spelled stay. Whole days spelled no. "We're not doing this," I told the morning. The light ignored me, slipped under the curtain and made galaxies out of dust. Show-off. Breath, undramatic, coaxed, in, out. On those days survival felt petty. Fine, I thought. I'll keep breathing just to spite the sky. Spite isn't noble, but it's efficient. I used what I had.

My sister called and filled the silence with emoji nonsense, shrimp, rocket, baby duck, until I snorted the kind of laugh that makes you ugly and alive. "There she is," she said softly, and I almost hung up because being seen stung worse than being alone. "Stay," she added before goodbye. The word stuck to the fridge like a new magnet. I resented it. I obeyed it. After the call, I breathed like a metronome on purpose, so the house would hear me and relax.

Sometimes shame arrived with the mail, a bill still bearing his name, a glossy brochure to Mr. & Mrs., or a sympathy card perfumed with certainty. "It gets better with time," the handwriting insisted. I pressed the paper to my face as if I could inhale years. I coughed instead. "Time doesn't know what it's doing," I told the bin, dropping the envelope. "We're teaching each other." The bin, like every object in my house, kept breathing. Even the toaster ticked after use, cooling itself, small breaths of metal. I copied that, too, exhale the heat you do not need.

On a Tuesday that tasted like metal, I drove past the last neat houses to where the city forgets itself. The salt flats opened like an empty page. The wind thumped my chest. "If you want me here," I shouted, "teach me how." A gull barked at the audacity. The horizon pretended to be shy. Breath arrived without announcement, rushing in so fast I coughed. "Don't sneak up on me," I said, and laughed because who else argues with oxygen? "Fine. You win." Breath did not gloat. It repeated its thesis, in, out. On the drive home I rolled every window down and let the car fill with air like a lung. We were ridiculous together and it helped.

I collected small rituals like talismans. A pinch of lavender crushed between fingers when the room tilted. The cold lip of the sink under my palms when my heart outpaced me. Heel, toe, in, out all the way to the letterbox. Neighbours watched with the tender caution reserved for people who have survived fires you can't see. "How are you?" they asked. "Breathing," I said, honest and annoying. Some looked relieved. Some flinched, as if honesty were contagious. I didn't blame them. I used to flinch at my own truth, too.

The mirror stopped being my enemy and became a witness. Most mornings I interrogated the woman there. "Still here?"

"Apparently." "Prove it." I exhaled until fog bloomed over her eyes. "There," I said. Childish. Victorious. Alive. On braver days, I spoke to the fog as it faded. "Come back," I asked the glass. It always did. Repetition is devotion in plain clothes.

Shame and gratitude traded rooms inside me, slamming doors. Shame hissed, You don't deserve this air. Gratitude, quieter, stubborn, answered, You are made of it. On shame nights I rationed inhales, superstitious and mean with myself. Mornings pried me open with the dog's warm insistence and coffee pretending to be a friend. Gratitude sat on the back step with its knees touching mine. No speeches. I breathed easier when it showed up, so I started inviting it even when I didn't feel it. "Sit," I told it. "Fine. Stay." It did. Sometimes I thanked the cup for being a cup. Objects cannot accept thanks, maybe that's why it felt safe to give it.

I practiced forgiving myself in the smallest unit I could manage, one breath. Not a future. Not a week. One inhale that didn't hate me. One exhale that didn't abandon me. Sometimes forgiveness looked like toast eaten standing up, butter collecting in the corners like tiny sunrises. Sometimes it was a shower, water drumming a beat my lungs could copy. Sometimes it was a drive with the windows down, hair tangling, anger loosening in the salted air. Forgiveness also looked like failing at noon and trying again at 12:07. I wrote that in the margins of a bill.

When panic dressed itself as prophecy, You will stop breathing, you will die, I surprised myself by answering, "Maybe. But not this minute." I watched the clock. The minute passed. I remained. See? breath said, smug without words. "Don't gloat," I warned, smiling anyway. The smile opened a door. Air walked through. I put a tiny tick beside that minute in my diary. Later the ticks would look like constellations.

Setbacks still knocked the wind out of me. A smell that belonged to a night I'd rather not remember. A bureaucrat who broke my life into bullet points over the phone. On those days breathing was labour, it was noisy, effortful. I crawled into bed furious with lungs that would not obey. In the morning, my body yawned on its own, a ridiculous, involuntary surrender to living. "Traitor," I told my mouth, and forgave it at once. There is a holiness in involuntary things. I am learning to bow to them without making a scene.

And then there was the sink, the place where the worst idea had once glinted like a solution, and the afternoon I stood there and realised I was breathing. Not counting. Not bargaining. Deep enough to be called living. The garden path lay under its grid of light like a promise, not a trap. No blood. Just sun.

"Thank you," I said. I wasn't sure who I meant, my lungs, the stubborn thread that kept saying stay, or the nameless quiet that showed up when I left a chair open for it. "Thank you." The window fogged, soft-blurred proof. I did not frame that proof.

I started treating breath like a friend I used to take for granted and now wanted to keep. "How are we?" I'd ask at red lights. Manageable, it answered by staying. "What do you need?" I'd ask before bed. Room, it answered by unclenching my jaw. "What now?" I'd ask when grief put me on my knees. Nothing heroic, it answered. Just in. Just out.

Learning to breathe again wasn't just air. It was recalibrating a body that had carried too much. It was forgiving myself for survival. It was choosing, moment by moment, to let life in even when it stung. Ordinary courage, the courage to fill my lungs while washing a plate, to laugh without yanking the sound back by the collar, to admit I wanted to know how autumn would smell when it got here, and to imagine a future measured not in years but in inhales I had yet to take.

Some nights I still stood at the window and told the dark the whole, graceless truth. "I didn't ask for this," I said. "I don't want it." The dark, older than argument, didn't reply. It pressed the world to sleep and left me to decide whether I would join it. Breath waited by the bed like a forgiven dog. "Come on," it panted in its wordless way. "Up you get." I lay down. I let the room breathe me to the edge of sleep. I let the room teach me how.

It wasn't graceful. It wasn't linear. But it was real. And maybe real was enough.

By afternoon, the light went soft and ordinary. I stood at the sink, the same place I'd once pictured my exit, and realised I was breathing without thinking about it. Not beautifully. Not bravely. Just enough. The garden path was bright but no longer cruel, the bricks held light instead of blood.

"Thank you," I said, to my lungs, to the thin stubborn thread inside me, and to the nameless stillness that kept saying stay. The words fogged the window. Proof.

That night the house breathed with me, the slow exhale of the fridge, the shy hiss of the kettle before it clicked off, and the dog's steady rhythm at my feet. Now and then panic rose again like a tide claiming its shore. Each time I followed breath back, in, out, stay. Not a cure. A way through.

And when the room went quiet enough, the visitors I'd been avoiding stepped from the hall and sat down, as if they'd been waiting politely for me to have air. The old ones first, Why didn't I leave sooner? Then the ones I feared most, Was his last thought of me? Did I kill him?

Breath didn't answer. It pulled up a chair beside me and said, we can sit with them together.

I turned off the light and lay in the dark, counting the distance between inhale and exhale. Between them, the questions gathered. In the morning, I told myself, I will name them out loud. I didn't promise to survive the naming. I only promised to try.

Chapter Twelve

I came out of the breath carrying its quiet instruction like a thread through the dark, the questions will come next.

By morning the questions had multiplied. They perched on the rim of my mug, smudged the mirror, hid under the day's errands. I wrote them on the back of receipts and the corner of an old bill as if the ink could tame them. What was the last thing he said? Where was the point of no return? If I had answered the phone, if I hadn't gone to the pub, if I'd loved him better…

"Enough," I told the page.

But questions are patient hunters. They circle back when your hands are full, when you're mid-sip or mid-sentence or halfway down the laundry line with a peg in your mouth. They do not care if you are doing your best. They do not accept casseroles.

I tried, at first, to answer like an adult. I put facts in neat rows. I made tidy piles of logic and lined them up under "Not My Fault." But logic is a poor carpenter. The house I built from it kept losing its roof in the night, and I woke inside rain.

In the afternoons I sat on the back step and let memory spool out without pulling it tight, the first time he smiled at me over a paint-peeled bar, the years we were certain a new suburb and a nicer couch would fix it, the sting of words thrown like cutlery, the night he stepped over me on the mat, and the next morning's knock.

Sometimes, when the quiet grew too loud, I asked the questions aloud, as if the air owed me an answer.

"Was your last thought of me?"

A long pause. Eucalyptus leaves gave their small applause. A magpie heckled. And in the hush between sounds I almost heard him say, It wasn't a thought, it was a blur. Not absolution. Not indictment. Just the terrible ordinariness of what happens at speed.

"Did I kill you?"

No voice answered that. The neighbour's sprinkler offered its timed yes/no/yes/no across the fence. Breath stood beside me like a friend who refuses drama. We'll sit with it, it said without words. We won't solve it today.

When I could breathe again, I gave the questions jobs: You - stand guard on the past. You - keep watch on the grief I keep trying to skip. You - tell me when memory turns to self-harm. Some obeyed. Some didn't. But delegating turned the mob into a council. Not friends, not yet, but something I could face without flinching.

I learned new places to ask them. In the car, engine off. In the queue at the post office. In the 02:00 corridor between the bedroom and the kitchen, where the floor knows every foot I've ever placed upon it. The answers, when they came, were rarely kind, but sometimes they were clean: You loved the best you could with what you knew then. He made his choice, and so did you. The truth is not a weapon unless you pick it up and swing it at yourself.

Still, one question would not leave, If I could join him, would I?

That one moved differently. It didn't sit; it hovered. It smelled like metal and rain. It waited at intersections, lingered near high places, followed me into rooms with bad light. When I looked at it square on, it stepped closer. When I pretended not to see, it whispered from behind my ear.

I started leaving the bedroom door ajar the way you do when

you're waiting for a late teenager to come home, and you've promised yourself you won't fall asleep. I wasn't waiting for him. I was waiting for the question to blink first.

It didn't. I did.

The night I finally said, "I want out," the room did not judge me. The dog lifted her head, considered my confession, and sighed as if to say, You're still here. Breath stayed. The ceiling held. The dark was only dark.

In the morning, I washed my face with cold water and wrote that sentence in thick, ugly letters at the top of a clean page. Beneath it, smaller, And I will stay anyway. Treason and truth at once.

That day the questions changed shape. They still haunted me, they always will. But now they had a corridor to walk down, a room where they could sleep, a door I could close when my lungs needed quiet.

***

Questions didn't arrive like thoughts; they arrived like weather. In the first weeks after the funeral they moved through the rooms of my house with a proprietary breeze, lifting papers, chilling my skin, and rattling doors that didn't lock anymore. I could ignore people, neighbours with casseroles and careful faces, and colleagues with sympathetic emails, by letting their messages pile neatly in the corner. Questions refused corners. Busy creatures, they rearranged the furniture of memory while I slept.

I woke to a kitchen that had turned itself into a courtroom. The laminate counter became a witness stand, the sink a soft-spoken stenographer capturing every slip of recollection. I learned the vocabulary of evidence, what I drank, what he said, which shoes I wore, the sound the ring made against the doorframe. I didn't choose to testify. My body did. Every time my fingers touched a cup or a doorknob, they remembered more than I'd asked them to.

The first question was always the simplest and most savage, *Why*. It came without punctuation, without mercy. It didn't want a story; it wanted a verdict. I tried to dress it in logic, statistics, psychology, all the words that had lived clean lives on my bookshelves when grief belonged to other people. Logic didn't survive in that airless kitchen. Images did, the pub's lonely light, the step I missed, his eyes swollen red, the gentle knock I made as if manners could hold the night together, the car reversing into black. I felt the question breathe at my neck, Why did you stop there? Why didn't you stop him? The more I answered, the more I learned that answers don't dissolve a question, they multiply it.

The morgue followed me home. It had the precision of arithmetic and the cruelty of a nursery rhyme. My mind refused to convert the body on steel into him. It slid away like oil. But the room's details kept returning, light that refused drama, cold spoken like a sentence, and my arms failing at the last task of love, touch, and that failure feeling like betrayal and mercy at once. Another question arrived on slower feet, Did he know I loved him at the end? The morgue allowed me only that one and then refused to answer.

Outside, the world continued with its insulting ordinariness. The postman whistled. The jacaranda rehearsed its purple chorus. A dog across the street laid its head on a windowsill and fell asleep, untroubled by blame. The sky wouldn't wear mourning. I started walking at dusk because that light was the only honest thing I could bear, nothing finished, nothing beginning, everything smudged. I learned the rhythm of my suburb by immersion, the same sedan reversing at the same time each day, the same boy on a scooter growing braver while my courage shrank, and the magpie with one feather crooked toward arrogance. I counted bins for comfort, dogs for mercy, porch lights for proof that people still chose to come home.

The questions liked dusk too. Quieter then, but craftier. They didn't accuse; they insinuated. They slipped inside ordinary sentences. What do you want for dinner? meant Do you deserve to eat? What time is your shift? meant How long can you pass for functioning? Will you sign here? meant Are you making choices, or are choices being made for you? I answered with a staircase of small motions, boil the kettle, butter the toast, feed the dog, water the plants, hoping repetition would grow into ritual, and ritual into something like faith.

Sleep grew clever in its evasions. When it came, it was shallow and mean, full of rooms I knew and doors I'd never seen. I woke hearing his car in the driveway and hurried to the window to watch taillights fade into imagination. On the worst nights my chest locked into refusal. Breath flattened into argument. I stood over the sink with my palms braced and talked to air like a child hiding under a table: Come on. You're safe. You can come out when you're ready. Eventually breath returned, sulky, suspicious, but present, and I coaxed it back to bed, slow as if it were a stray.

On my dresser lived an ugly notebook that had been a conference freebie, cheap logo, thin paper, perfect for unglamorous work. I titled pages with date and weather the way my grandmother did in her Bible, but mine were inventories.

What hurts: throat, behind the knees, the place humiliation

lives in a woman's back. What I can do: feet on grass, tea with lemon, open one window, put the phone in another room. Who will understand if I say nothing but still need to be heard: Eliza. What I know: grief is not linear; shame is not honest; the kettle obeys.

Most nights that was all, an audit of damage, and a list of small hinges on which the heavy door might swing. Questions behave better on paper. They like to be seen, it tames them. Left to roam, they turn to superstition. Written down, they become weather you can at least name, a southerly, a sudden change, and a heat that breaks at midnight.

Every few days I wrote a letter I never meant to send. Not to him. Not to God. To the version of me who spent decades studying the geometry of endurance. Dear you, I wrote, you are not a test. You do not have to pass or fail this. There is no grade, only breath. There is no winning, only choosing not to lose today. I filed the letters inside a cookbook I never used. It felt right, recipes I didn't trust, instructions I couldn't follow, and nourishment I would have to invent.

I learned the difference between helpful questions and cruel ones by the way they sat in my body. Helpful loosened my shoulders and made room in my ribs. Cruel tightened the base of my skull and fogged the mirror. Helpful: What small thing could I do now that wouldn't feel like betrayal? Cruel: Why weren't you enough? Why didn't you leave sooner? If I let the helpful speak first, answered with an apple, fresh sheets, and bare feet on cold lawn, the cruel sometimes lost their voice. Not forever. For the length of a cup of tea.

Some days the engine of self-inquiry sputtered and died, and on those days I didn't fix it. I let the questions pass me on the highway with superior headlights and smug destination faces. I watched them go and called after them, "Drive carefully." Those days I carried absence like a bowl filled to the brim and moved slowly enough not to spill.

I kept showing up at work in a way that wasn't martyrdom so much as muscle memory. My body had been trained to function in rooms that needed competence, and grief hadn't wiped the program. I learned which corridors would hold me when the questions leaned in and I had to lean back, unlit stairwells, a supply cupboard's cool privacy, and the car's driver seat where I could drop my forehead to the wheel and let my soul sweat without witnesses. The world didn't know what to do with me. I didn't demand it learn. I signed forms, nodded on cue, wrote emails like scaffolding, workmanlike, enough to hold the next hour.

Guilt, once a tidal wave, turned current, sly, strong, visible mostly by what it moved. When it tugged at my ankles I sometimes named it and planted my feet. This is the part where you decide if you caused the moon, I'd think, and the absurdity saved me. Other times it dragged and I went under, survival was old-fashioned, kick back to air, cough, and rest. Small mercies kept arriving, unadvertised. The neighbour who rolled my bin in without waving. The old woman at the pharmacy who pressed a peppermint into my palm like a sacrament. The way the dog fitted his head into the cradle of my knee with such mutual certainty I wondered if animals were the only creatures who fully understood grace. I recorded one mercy each evening, even when I hated the assignment. Today, magpie swagger, ridiculous. Today, five minutes thinking only of light because a bus-stop ad gave me a line of poetry I didn't hate. Today, the exact green of the lemon tree.

When his voice came, I let it. Not condemnation, not

apology, those belonged to history. What rose now was smaller, like a radio three rooms away playing a station I hadn't chosen. It said things that didn't require answers. You always kept the lists. Or, You kept breathing. Or, I didn't. Truths that landed the way dust does, everywhere at once, visible only when light slants correctly. Sometimes they hurt. Sometimes they were just true, and that, too, hurt.

I tried on explanations the way you try on dresses when the attendants leave you alone. Why did he die? Because he believed himself lucky, and luck has teeth. Why didn't I stop him? Because I didn't own him and never could. Why did I stay? Because hope is a muscle, and mine was overdeveloped. Why do I still love him sometimes? Because love doesn't read memos, it arrives on its own schedule and refuses the sign-in sheet. I didn't buy any answer outright. I rotated before the changing room mirror and watched how each sat on my bones. Some were too tight in the throat, and some fell off the shoulders. A few fit for an evening and then lost their shape. I learned not to be ashamed of returning them to the rack.

By late summer the house had a new arrangement, nothing dramatic, just the practical admissions of reality, the second pillow stacked in the wardrobe, the empty chair pushed back under the table without its place setting, and the toothbrush I tossed and then missed as if it had been a person. The questions adapted. They learned not to scream, partly because I'd stopped being a stage for them, partly because I'd learned to negotiate terms. Midnight interrogations surrendered knives and car keys. The shower was sanctuary. The mirror shared custody between inquiry and compassion. At red lights the car took my hand like it was a skittish animal until green.

In my better hours I felt a contract forming, not with him, not with heaven, not with the questions, but with my own life. It wasn't sentimental. It promised neither safety nor meaning on demand. It asked simple things, put your feet on the ground each morning, ask what hurts without making it a contest, refuse the cheap drama you once mistook for love, tell the truth faster, let joy in when it knocks, even if it has the wrong address, learn plant names, make public the names you whispered to yourself only in bathrooms, rest before you beg, eat the apple, open the window, and answer fewer questions.

When people asked how I was, I started saying, "It depends on the hour." The small accuracy widened the day. Inside that width, the worst questions became less athletic. They still came, but they no longer sprinted laps around me before tea. If they visited, they had to sit at the table and listen to birds for one minute before speaking.

I don't think the questions will ever leave. I'm no longer interested in evicting them. They're not devils to cast out or virtues to cultivate. They're proofs of life, signs that meaning still matters to me, even when meaning refuses to perform on command. The difference now is that I am not their habitat, I am their host. Hosts have rights. They can say, "Not tonight," and shut the door. They can say, "You may sit, but you may not shred the furniture." They can say, "One at a time."

On the evening that felt like a hinge, no holiday, no omen, just an inner click. I sat on the back step and watched the garden resist its own wildness. The lemon tree wore a rash of green fruit. Clover kept the lawn's secrets. Somewhere past the fence a child called a name and laughter answered. I wrote the day's mercy on the back of my hand with a dull pen, light insists. I waited to be interrogated. No one came. Air moved in and out of me the way it moves when you haven't frightened it. The night lowered itself without ceremony. I let it.

That is the only answer I trust now when the old chorus stirs, because I am still here. Not because I am innocent. Not because I am strong. Not because I passed a test. Because breath keeps choosing me, and I am learning to choose it back. The questions may never tire. I may never satisfy them. But I can walk with them to the end of the street and back and, when we return, I can open the door, turn off the porch light, and tell them, with an authority I didn't know I owned, enough for tonight.

In the quiet that follows, sometimes I hear him, not a lecture, not a plea, just a simple truth placed where I can reach it: You didn't kill me. And sometimes I can answer without flinching: I know. Right now, I know.

I switch off the lamp. The room holds. My ribs make space. Sleep gathers like weather, unpredictable, then suddenly everywhere. Morning waits on the other side, ungilded and undecorated, only the next page.

I turn it.

And when I woke, death was there too, not as threat, not as thief, but as company. Waiting at the edge of breath, polite as dawn."

Chapter Thirteen

Out of the long night of questions, another presence fell into step, close, patient, undeniable, death at my shoulder.

In the weeks and months after Marko's death, I came to know death not as an event but as a companion. He didn't pack up with the florists' vases or leave with the last condolence. He found a perch, the slope where neck meets shoulder, and stayed. At first I mistook him for a question I hadn't solved. But questions require language. This presence didn't. He spoke in tilts and edges, the imagined swerve of a steering wheel, the cold invitation of a high place, and the ordinary kitchen knife briefly lit like a door.

It would be easy, he breathed, not threatening, not tender, just factual. "Not yet," I told him, and my voice sounded older than me. He didn't argue. He didn't need to. Death is a long-game player, terribly punctual. He arrived every night just before sleep and every morning just after it and sits beside me while the kettle sighs. Even so, the more I named him, the less he owned me. He ceased to be a storm and became a weather report, chance of leaving, high likelihood of staying, periods of sudden clarity. I began to speak to him the way you speak to a difficult colleague you cannot fire. "You're here," I'd say. And in the small mercy of that sentence was the equally true one my breath kept offering back, "So am I."

He followed me into the car first. I buckled my seatbelt and there he was, leaning in from the passenger side, not a man, not a figure, just a pressure, a certainty, the suggestion of a hand on the wheel. The road unrolled its glinting ribbon. A truck thundered by, the vacuum tugging at the hatchback like a dare. It would be easy, he breathed. I drove like a sober penitent, both hands at ten and two, jaw set, eyes locked on the middle distance where safety pretends to live. "Not yet," I said aloud. "I have milk to buy." He reclined, amused. Milk, as if dairy were a spell that held the world in place. At the lights I caught my reflection in the rear-view mirror, the woman who talks to no one as if someone were there. Haunted, practical, the kind of person who could file a report while bleeding. The light turned green. The horn behind me sounded, reminding me that haunted or not, I was still part of a system that required motion.

I parked far from the supermarket entrance, a small self-kindness, distance to breathe. Death walked beside me across the asphalt, keeping pace. A trolley wheel squealed like pain. Inside, the first aisle ambushed me, cereal, a gallery of our arguments. His brand, still bright and grinning, lit like a history that didn't care how it ended. I stood there long enough for a staff member to ask if I needed help. "Yes," I wanted to say, "can you guide me through the rest of my life?" Instead, I shook my head. "Just looking." Death pressed his invisible chin to my shoulder and murmured, It would be easy to stop here. To let go in the cereal aisle. People would say, *She never recovered.* They'd nod knowingly, their hands resting on trolleys like lifebuoys. I put a plain box of oats in the trolley like a vow and moved on.

At home, he learned the map of my kitchen. He knew which drawer held the knives, which crack in the window sang when the wind came through, which spot on the benchtop I leaned on when breath went thin. He watched me cut tomatoes with exaggerated care, blade moving slow as a Sunday bus. "Don't get ideas," I told him. He tilted his head. I don't need ideas. I have time. Some afternoons I filled the sink and let hot water burn my wrists just enough to insist I was present. Steam rose and wrote its soft weather on my face. The dog patrolled the doorway, toenails clicking a domestic metronome. Death leaned in the frame like an uninvited guest who knew he'd never be thrown out. "You're nothing but a reminder," I told him. Of what? he asked. "That endings are trustworthy." He shrugged. So are beginnings. I hated that he could be right.

He liked the balcony best. A modest drop, barely two storeys, nothing cinematic. But tragedy doesn't need height, it needs only timing. I stood there once in the late afternoon as the street slipped toward evening, and watched kids on scooters, an old man whistling, and a woman dragging a bin with defiance. The air carried the kind of forgiveness that comes quietly after hard days. It would be easy, Death breathed. Easy like leaning. Easy like closing a book halfway through. He didn't add the rest - the neighbours' screaming, the headlines, the child who'd walk past tomorrow and learn something ugly about gravity and women. "Not yet," I said, stepping back inside. You say that like a prayer, he said. "Maybe it is."

He visited every night, precise as habit. He sat on the edge of the bed three minutes after lights out, two before sleep might take pity. I counted breaths, four in, six out, the math of persistence. Why not let go? he asked one night, voice fog and velvet. "Because Poppy has a test tomorrow," I said. "Because the dog only trusts me to cut her pills in half. Because I want to see what the jacaranda does this year." Petty, he said, but almost approving. "Petty keeps people alive," I told him. I laughed then, small and crooked. He looked at it like a collector inspecting a coin minted wrong. You'll lose that again. "I know," I said. "I'll also find it."

He followed me into the shower where grief does its private work. Steam sealed the room into a confessional. I leaned my forehead against the cold tile, water drumming the back of my neck where panic lives. It would be simple, he breathed. "So is turning the tap," I said, and did. The silence ballooned. The mirror, fogged and forgiving, made me look like a myth of myself, edges soft, eyes anonymous. I wrote one word in the mist, *stay*. By the time I dried my hair, it had vanished, work done.

There were days he left me alone. Those were the strangest. The air felt too light, the quiet too wide. I flinched at kindness. I mistrusted peace. I made a second cup of tea just to have a reason to move. When he returned, he didn't apologise. He doesn't do apology, he does math. "Welcome back," I'd say. You were fine without me, he'd reply. "I didn't say I wanted you." Wanting is over-praised, he said. Habit is stronger. He wasn't wrong.

He sat with me in the GP's office, legs crossed, polite as eternity. The waiting room hummed with coughs and scrolling thumbs. Posters promised miracles in bureaucratic fonts. I practiced my lines, dizzy, sleepless, panic like a feral cat. I didn't rehearse the one that began with *I want* and ended with *out*. When the doctor called my name, Death rose too. "Sit," I told him, like a dog. He followed anyway, listening while I described my symptoms as if they were weather from another country. The doctor nodded, offered referrals, numbers for when night goes mean. On the way out, Death read the pamphlets over my shoulder. He respects a plan. He respects any human who tries.

He watched me parent. When Poppy threw down her bag and said, "I can't do this," Death leaned forward, greedy for collapse. "Hey," I said to her, and to him, "we don't have to do this perfectly. Just the next ten minutes." "And then what?" she asked. "Then we renegotiate." Toast for dinner. A win. Later, after she slept, I stood in her doorway, feeling the fragile privilege of being the adult still present. Death waited in the hallway, courteous but close. You could leave, he breathed. "I could," I said. "I won't." He didn't praise, but he stepped back, and sometimes two inches is the distance between ruin and survival.

I hadn't meant to drive by the roadside memorial. A detour, a whim, maybe a test. Flowers wired to a pole, ribbons tired from wind, a sun-bleached teddy bear hugging nothing. The laminated poetic words warped by rain, words dissolving. Death stood beside me, both of us facing the same direction like two women waiting for a bus. We said nothing. A car hissed past. The air smelled of petrol and grass. "It would be easy," I said, surprising myself. "To let this be the story." Easier than beginning again, he said. I closed my eyes and saw him as he'd been, on the beach, with our daughter, on the day he chose not to stay. "Not yet," I said, to the toy, to the air, to myself. We walked back to the car. I drove home slowly, like someone who intends to arrive.

He came with me to therapy, standing in the corner while I sat on the couch with twitching hands. "I have a shadow," I told her. "Talk to it," she said. "I do. It says, 'It would be easy.' I say, 'Not yet.'" "Why not?" "Because I promised." I didn't know to whom, my daughter, my dog, my first self who once imagined me alive. We built a plan that wasn't dramatic, safety never is. Numbers in my phone. Alcohol gone from the house. One person I'd tell if the shadow grew loud. When I left, Death shook the counsellor's hand. On the footpath he whispered, I'll see you at midnight. "You're punctual," I said. He bowed. He appreciates form.

He followed me to work, auditing the milk levels in the fridge, hovering by the printer, sitting in meetings at the far end of the table. When someone made a joke, he watched my laugh like a rare stamp. When someone asked how I was, he tested my throat. "Depends on the hour," I said, and he eased. At lunch I sat with one shoulder in shadow, the other in sun. "You're fluent in pain," he said. "Why keep practicing?" "Because I'd like to be conversational in joy." Ambitious, he said, and approved.

In public bathrooms, he leaned over the sink while I washed my hands too slowly. "You're still here," I told my reflection. "For now," he said. "For now," I agreed, giving the moment its dignity.

On good days we walked like neighbours who no longer took offence at each other's hedges. I could feel him but not fear him, like a coat left hanging nearby. "You see this?" I asked as the lemon tree flaunted its fruit, as a boy mastered his scooter. "The small continuances?" He nodded, hands behind his back like a history teacher pleased with the timeline. At the corner where the wind repeated the street's name, I touched the warm brick of the wall, and he placed his hand beside mine. For a moment, the wall was an altar, and we were two species agreeing.

On bad days, he climbed into my mouth, weighted my tongue, turned sentences into shards. He made ceilings low, air heavy. The list on the fridge saved me: OPEN CURTAINS. SHOWER. TOAST. WALK DOG. TEXT ELIZA: "I'M HERE." The list made a stair I could climb. Death leaned on the banister, offering commentary. To his credit, he never took the stairs away.

At the beach he pretended to be the horizon. "You could walk," he breathed. "Let the water take the argument from your legs." "You forget I'm stubborn," I said. "Then salute it," he told me. I did.

He liked anniversaries and their cruel cousins, the almost-anniversaries. I baked a boxed cake and didn't pretend it meant anything. I ate standing up. "Blow out the candle," I said, and did, wishing only, 'let me still want tomorrow.'

Over time, he visited the mirror not as an enemy but as a witness. The woman there changed slowly, mercy softening the edges. "You're not leaving," I said, not meaning him. "No," he said. "Neither are you."

One afternoon, I told him, "You can come, but you can't drive." He smiled. Authority suits you, he said. "It's rented," I told him. Fair.

He watched me write lists, doctor, sunlight, clean food. He added one: *A place to bring panic where it can't harm you.* I wrote it down. He bowed. I contain multitudes, he said, and for once I believed him.

When I took the last boxes of his clothes to the op shop, the volunteer smiled kindly without asking. Death held the door. "You can look," I said to him in the car, "but you can't keep." The practice had become its own prayer.

He tried to seduce me with poetry. "You've got the wrong woman," I told him, folding towels. "I like prose. Sentences that carry groceries." "Everyone says that," he grinned, "until the verbs start rhyming." I flicked him with the dishcloth. "Not yet."

Some days he left long enough for me to forget. I'd hum, clean the sink, send a text without subtext. When he returned, he'd ask, Miss me? "No," I said, proud of the accuracy. He'd look at the small evidence of life and nod, as if we'd both accomplished something. We had.

Eventually, he grew bored of the obvious temptations, bridges, knives, balconies, and turned his attention to the long game, exhaustion, paperwork, and the thousand paper cuts of being human. I answered with smaller rebellions like water, sunlight, toast, and bed by nine. He sat by the window like a tired parent. "See you at three," he said. "Fine," I said, and meant it.

He can't stand laughter. I learned that when my sister sent a video of a toddler falling asleep mid-banana. My laugh startled the room into brightness. Death stepped out into the hall. "Oh," he said. "I forgot about that." "What?" "The loophole." I filed it away. *Loophole: laughter.*

He hates being ignored even more. So I practiced not denial but coexistence. I brushed my teeth as if the mundane were sacred. He paced, then settled. "You're getting good at this," he said. "I'm getting practiced," I replied. "Practice is better than good," he said. "Practice keeps showing up." "So do you." Touché, he said, and, for once, didn't sound like he was winning.

He became my teacher without meaning to. He taught me longing can be bridge or cliff, and that the body will try despite you. He taught me that the future is just a series of small rooms you enter one at a time. He taught me that *not yet* can hold an entire day. He taught me that the opposite of death isn't life. It's attention.

Death leaned his shoulder against mine, companionable. You're welcome, he said. "For what?" For keeping me unemployed. For another hour. I snorted. "You're on retainer." He smiled. I'm always on retainer. But even I respect a worker who shows up.

We stood there together, two faithful employees of the difficult job, watching the kettle think about boiling. Every so often panic rose again like a tide intent on reclaiming its shore. Each time I followed the breath back in - *in, out, stay.* Not a cure, just a way through. When the room went quiet enough, the old questions stepped in. Death nodded as if to say, this I can allow. I turned off the light and lay in the dark, counting the distance between each inhale and exhale. Between them, a decision formed quietly, tomorrow I would begin to choose life, not as argument, but as agreement with breath.

"I didn't promise to want it every hour," I whispered. "Just to try."

"Not yet?" Death asked, almost hopeful.

"Not yet," I said, and meant it like a vow.

He settled more lightly on my shoulder, as if relieved to be carried by someone who'd finally learned how to share the load. Morning waited, ungilded, unthreatening, only the next page. I turned it.

Chapter Fourteen

Some mornings don't announce themselves; they simply arrive and wait to see if you will. This was one of those mornings.

The morning began the same way as the others, thick with silence, and heavy with the stale scent of yesterday's grief, but something small nudged from the inside, like a seed shrugging off a husk. Maybe it was the light slipping across the wall, paler than usual, a thin gold that asked nothing. Maybe it was the ache in my chest that didn't feel like collapse for once but like insistence, as though my lungs themselves were tired of being negotiated with.

When I sat on the edge of the bed, I whispered the smallest command I could bear. "Choose." Not heal. Not forgive. Not move on. Just, choose. It sounded absurd. What was left to choose when so much had already been chosen for me? He was gone. The future I'd organised into tidy lists had been bulldozed. My life had a new shape I hadn't voted on. And yet the word stayed, stubborn as breath. "Choose," I said again, and the room didn't argue. I began with the kind of decision that wouldn't impress a soul. I called the doctor. The phone felt like a stone in my hand, heavy with all the conversations I didn't want to have. Tinny hold music thinned the air. The dog watched from her mat with the kind of concern that makes you perform bravery. When the receptionist answered, my voice arrived in pieces. "I… need an appointment. Just, check in."

"Tuesday at ten-thirty?"

"Tuesday," I repeated, as if I were agreeing to live until then. I wrote it on the calendar in ordinary ink that looked, to me, like defiance. A small square surrendered to living.

Then I cleaned the kitchen. Not a purge, not penitence - just plates and a mug and the gritty circle where coffee had dried into a small moon. "Just this plate," I told myself. "Just this corner." When the sink finally gleamed, a long breath left me like a permission slip signed by someone in charge.

I fed the dog. The drama with which she greeted kibble made me laugh against my will. I knelt on the lino and smoothed her velvet ears. "You're still here. I'm still here," I said, and her tail thumped the floor like applause.

I opened the curtains. Light shocked the room, then settled. It didn't heal anything. It made the air honest.

I boiled an egg. Sliced an apple. Buttered toast as if the knife were a pen and breakfast a sentence I wanted to finish. Preparing food felt like an act for someone who expected to survive long enough to digest it. I ate standing up, as if chairs were for people sure of themselves, and told my mouth, "This is not an apology. This is fuel."

And then, the bravest bit, I called a friend.

Her voice arrived like colour after grey. "Tell me where you are," she said, and didn't mean philosophy.

"In the kitchen," I said.

"What do you see?"

"Curtains open."

"Good."

We did that for thirty minutes - kettle, bench, dog, toast - locating me by nouns. When we hung up, the silence felt less like punishment and more like space.

None of it would look like recovery from a distance. Up close, the stitches showed, call, clean, feed, open, eat, reach. Tiny verbs binding a torn fabric.

I wanted applause, but I got quiet. Maybe that was better. Distraction had always been the costume I wore over desperation. Quiet required a different sort of courage.

I kept going, not because I believed in the plan, but because the plan believed in me. Three more small things before noon, I told myself, and wrote them on a torn envelope: shower, water plants, put shoes outside to dry. The list looked both ridiculous and also like a life.

After lunch I opened the blinds in the bedroom and stripped the bed. The fitted sheet and I conducted our usual fistfight; I won on a technicality. Fresh linen smelled like restraint and lemon. I stood there longer than the task required, because the sight of something in order felt like news my body needed to hear.

I tried a budget next. Nothing dramatic, just meeting the numbers like skittish animals. I opened the bank app and breathed through the first wave of nausea. Rent, electricity, phone, groceries, petrol. I added a line called "Mercies" and set aside the exact price of a bunch of supermarket tulips or a packet of gerbera seedlings from the nursery. A small bribe to the future. A line that said: *I expect to see you.*

By late afternoon, I had the first leaf of a routine. It didn't look like a routine. It looked like the kind of day you'd forget to tell anyone about. But the house knew. The house breathed easier. So did the dog. So, very slightly, did I.

The next morning, the word met me before my feet did. Choose.

"Fine," I muttered, and reached for the curtains.

If Act I of grief had been shock and Act II its interrogation, I decided Act III would need a scale I could carry. I named it in the margin of the ugly conference notebook I kept on the table: The Ordinary Plan. Below it I listed the day's architecture in bad capitals: BLOODS. SUNLIGHT. PROTEIN. WALK DOG. CALL SARAH. I drew a square beside each like a kindergarten teacher who liked boxes.

At the clinic the waiting room was a soft chorus of coughs and shoes. Death sat two chairs over reading a months-old magazine, performing civility. When the nurse called my name, I rolled up my sleeve and watched the vials fill. My blood looked ordinary, which felt like an insult and a kindness. The nurse taped cotton to the crook of my arm with the sort of firm tenderness you learn in jobs that face sorrow without saying its name.

"You okay with needles?" she asked.

"I'm learning to be okay with everything," I said, and surprised us both by not crying.

Back home I put laundry on the line and listened to it speak the language of wind. Socks made their damp confessions, and a T-shirt snapped at the sky like it was done being humble. The sun didn't vote on my survival; it just kept giving itself away. I stood in it and thought, this is not a metaphor, this is vitamin D. Maybe I am allowed both.

I ate an apple with attention. Called Eliza and let her talk about nothing, which is sometimes the most faithful subject. Walked the dog on the long loop and named what I saw aloud like a person learning a new town, lemon tree, fence cat, boy on a scooter, bins lining up for bin night like instruments waiting for their cue. The breath stayed. When panic tried to argue, I said, "Not now," and pointed at a sparrow daring the dog's tail.

That evening, the calendar above the kettle had more ink on it than fear. Tuesday - GP 10:30. Thursday - therapy 15:00. Friday

- Poppy's parent-teacher 18:00. The squares were small and unglamorous. They looked like footholds.

I tried cooking something that required two pans. The recipe promised comfort as if comfort were a spice I'd forgotten in the back of a cupboard. The onions softened and admitted they'd always been sweet. Oil took on the colour of the tomatoes the way grief takes on the colour of the room it's in. I burned the first batch of garlic because I flinched at nothing, then laughed because even mistakes smelled like a home. When Poppy said, "This is good," I accepted the compliment like medicine, no speech, just swallow.

"Thank you," I said, and meant it for the food, the mouths, the table that had seen more confessions than celebrations and kept its place anyway.

After dinner I paid two bills I'd been afraid of. The numbers didn't bite. Fear is expensive in its own currency, but I saved a little by opening the envelope. I set a reminder to check the meter and felt like a woman who knew where the fuse box lived.

Later I took the dog out and stood on the wet grass barefoot. The cold bit my soles, which is how I knew I was alive. Somewhere a neighbour's wind chime remembered a tune. A moth threw itself at the porch light because that is the story of moths. I whispered into the sky, "I'm choosing," and the sky, having heard wilder things, stayed.

The therapist's room had orange oil in the air and a clock that measured mercy in minutes. We made a plan that wasn't about nobility, but about rails instead. I stored numbers I hoped never to call. I promised to let one person know if the night went mean. I practiced the sentence I hated, "I need help," until my mouth could carry it without breaking.

"What do you want from this hour?" she asked.

"To learn how to choose without resenting the choice," I said.

"That's big," she said, and we made it smaller.

When I left, I bought myself a cheap bunch of tulips from the supermarket to spend the "Mercies" line I'd budgeted like a dare. They looked vulgar and perfect on the table. Death stood by the sink and pretended not to admire them.

"You hate colour," I told him.

He shrugged. "I hate waste," he breathed. He would have been an excellent accountant.

It wasn't all forward. Some afternoons I folded into the bedroom and let the ceiling lower itself onto my chest. I didn't choose anything then, instead, I negotiated with air. Those hours were long and unflattering. Afterwards I wrote, simply, *Survived*, and ticked the box. The box ticked me back.

I made a rule, when I couldn't manage a task, I would manage a surface. Wiping a bench is cheaper than despair and often as effective. The house taught me resilience. Clean one square foot and the room remembers itself.

I made another rule, eat something with colour by noon. Greens counted. Mandarin counted. Jelly snakes did not (I argued that, but the rule held). Drink water on purpose. Step outside for at least the time it takes to read the electricity meter. Five minutes became ten because the lemon tree was obscene with fruit and I wanted to be present for its audacity.

I got practical in ways that once would have bored me. I put the strong spirits on a high shelf and the tea on the counter. I moved the knives to a drawer that stuck and told myself it was annoying on purpose. I labelled a small box NIGHT and filled it with a lavender roller, a pen, a notebook, a chocolate I was allowed to eat without apology, and the numbers I'd saved. The box felt like a friend I could point to: Look, this is where the help lives.

I bought a cheap alarm clock and banished my phone from the bedroom, then smuggled it back the next night because I am a person, not a parable. On the third night I kept the banishment. On the fourth I fell asleep without noticing. Practice, not perfection. Rails, not wings.

On the bus one afternoon, I sat by the window and let the city pass with its unembarrassed life, tradies eating decent sandwiches in utes, teenagers daring each other to live louder, and a woman dragging her groceries with a grocery-dragger's dignity. I copied the rhythm. When the bus stopped, I didn't rush. I stood, checked I had my keys, thanked the driver because he had carried me and I wanted to honour that. Small courtesies felt like votes for the world I wanted to stay in.

At the pharmacy I bought vitamins, the kind that promise nothing spectacular, just the slow invisible work of not falling apart. "Anything else?" the chemist asked.

"Mercy," I wanted to say. "And a mouth that doesn't keep swallowing its own tongue."

"That's all," I said, which was also true.

At home I made a two-week board, a cheap whiteboard with squares that could hold hope without threatening me with forever. I wrote appointments and meals and the kind of reminders that keep despair from winning on technicalities: BINS. FEED DOG. CLEAN SHEETS. CALL MUM (SET TIMER: 12 MINS). I left one square blank and wrote REST in pencil on a post-it note so I could easily remove the command when I was too stubborn to obey it. Some days stubbornness was my saviour, and other days it made me a liar. Pencil forgives both.

I learned to like lists that ended with FUN? and tried to answer yes once a week. Sometimes "fun" was watching a bad movie while the dog judged my taste. Sometimes it was buying a $12.99 geranium and pretending I was a person who kept plants alive. Sometimes it was a drive to the salt flats with the windows down and the radio too loud for remembering. My hair came home in knots, and my chest came home looser.

I became suspicious of the idea that recovery has to feel like victory. Often it felt like paperwork. I returned calls I'd avoided. I sat on hold and breathed on purpose and did not apologise to the stranger who mispronounced my name and my grief. I kept a notebook near the phone to write down a single sentence after bureaucratic conversations: No one knows what to say and that's not my fault. It kept me from inventing cruelties and assigning them to the wrong people.

I got nosey about sleep. I layered it with little bribes, a fresh pillowcase, a podcast about nothing, and the dog allowed on the bed until lights out. I told death, "You can visit at three, but you can't bring poetry." He prefers poetry because it gives him better lines. He sneered and obeyed, and I slept four hours straight. We both pretended not to be impressed.

When shame tried to auction off my oxygen, I counterbid with ceremony. I lit a candle at dinner even when dinner was scrambled eggs and avocado on toast. I blessed the toast with butter, and the eggs and avocado with pepper, and the room with the kind of silence that has presence in it. Ritual is just habit with attention; I wrote in the margin. I gave myself permission to be religious about small, ordinary things.

I kept walking. My feet knew routes my heart was still learning. I counted porch lights and magpies and red cars. I talked out loud sometimes, which probably unsettled the fences but calmed me. "I'm choosing," I'd say to the lemon tree. "I'm choosing," to the post box. "I'm choosing," to the sky that kept not falling.

Choosing didn't mean I stopped wanting to stop. Some afternoons the door in my head flashed open and I could see the shorter road. It glimmered. It lied. "Not today," I told it, palms flat on the counter. "I have a GP at ten-thirty, a child who needs her PE notes signed, and a dog with a pill that only I can cut exactly in half." Petty things. They saved me more than sermons ever did.

When the shadow at my shoulder leaned in and breathed, It would be easy, I answered with chores. "Perhaps," I said, wiping the bench. "But I have bins to roll and shirts to hang and rice to soak." Death respects a list. He has one of his own. We both ticked boxes and stood back to admire the clean line.

Friends texted invitations. At first. I refused them like a reflex. Then I said yes to one coffee, then another, and learned that sitting across from kindness was its own exposure therapy. "How are you?" they'd ask. "Depends on the hour," I'd say, and the honesty widened the room. I watched people breathe easier because I wasn't trying to be inspirational, I was trying to be accurate. Accuracy is a relief disguised as plainness.

On a Sunday I went to the nursery and let the names talk me into hope, lavender for the door, parsley for the windowsill, and feverfew for headaches and history. The woman at the till said, "These are hardy," and I touched the leaves the way you touch the face of a baby you aren't allowed to pick up. Hardy. I wanted to recruit the word.

Back home I planted the seedlings and told them the truth. "I might forget you," I said. "Remind me loudly." They did, by wilting just enough to force me back outside with a watering can and the humbling knowledge that survival asks for attention, not genius.

The week filled. Not with triumph, just with presence. Tuesday's bloods. Thursday's therapy. Friday's parent-teacher. Saturday's laundry. Sunday's quiet. I stood at the sink one morning, same sink where I'd once rehearsed exit strategies, and realised I was breathing without thinking about it. Not beautifully. Not bravely. Just enough.

The garden path, stubborn as ever, held light instead of blood. "Thank you," I said, to my lungs, to the thin thread in me that refused to snap, and to the nameless stillness that kept saying stay.

After lunch I sat at the table and opened the notebook. I listed the day's ordinary victories like a stingy accountant who had learned to be generous: Doctor booked. Curtains open. Dog fed. Friend called. Budget drafted. Plants watered. My hand shook a little, not from panic but from the thrill of seeing ink commit to a narrative I could live with.

Then I wrote one more line, the one I had been avoiding because it sounded like a dare I might lose. Tomorrow: Name what haunts me.

I stared at the words until they blurred, waiting for my body to revolt. It didn't. It only adjusted its posture, like someone preparing for a conversation that cannot be postponed and might be the beginning of freedom.

I closed the notebook and pressed my palm flat to its cover as if sealing a letter. That night I slept without drama. I dreamt of walking through a field at dusk, the grass high, the sky drunk on its own colour. Death was there, as he always is, patient and punctual, a shadow one step behind. I didn't invite him closer, and I didn't ask him to leave. I kept walking. The path unrolled without asking for eloquence.

Morning came the honest way, no trumpets. The dog nudged my hand. The fridge breathed. The kettle considered boiling. I stood, a little steadier than yesterday, and spoke the plan aloud so the house could hold me to it.

"Choose," I said.

I opened the curtains. I made tea. I ate an apple. I rolled the bins. I laid the notebook on the table and uncapped the pen. The day didn't change its weather for me. It didn't need to. I had learned to set my own.

This is how it begins, not with fireworks or forgiveness, not with a vow spoken from a mountaintop, but with a woman putting her name on the day and letting the day put its name on her back. Call. Clean. Feed. Open. Eat. Reach. Repeat.

I looked at the blank page and felt the old haunt stir in the walls and the air and the pockets of my bones, shame, fear, violence, the faithful lies I had carried like heirlooms.

"I see you," I said to whatever listened.

Then I wrote the first name and let the ink lead me into the next work of naming the demons.

Chapter Fifteen

By morning, the promise I'd made the previous night had teeth, but I vowed to keep the appointment with the page.

The notebook sat where I had left it, closed on the kitchen table, plain and unassuming. But I could feel the weight of its words pressing through the cardboard cover, heavy enough to rattle my chest.

Tomorrow: Name what haunts me.

Well, tomorrow had come.

I stared at the words like they might bite. My hands hovered above them, then dropped, then hovered again. Fear curled in my stomach like smoke.

Because naming meant exposure. Naming meant no more running, no more pretending the shadows weren't mine. Naming meant dragging them into the light, one by one, and seeing if they still had teeth.

I wanted to slam the notebook shut forever. Instead, I forced it open. The pen trembled in my grip.

"All right," I whispered to no one, to the silence, to myself. "Let's meet them."

The first name came too easily.

Alcohol.

It had stalked me for years, dressed as comfort, disguised as a friend. The glass that sparkled, the bottle that whispered, Just one more and you'll be softer, calmer, better. Except I never was.

"Liar," I spat at the page, my pen gouging the paper with the word. "You never loved me. You just wanted my ruin."

The kitchen clock ticked, unimpressed, as if to say, *finally*.

The next came like a knife to the ribs.

Violence.

Not just his fists, though those had left their marks. It was the slammed doors, the spit in his words, the way silence was used as a weapon sharp enough to cut.

"You didn't just bruise skin," I hissed at the word. "You bruised the air I breathed. You turned my own house into a battlefield."

The dog shifted at my feet, restless, as though even she could smell the anger rising.

Then came Lies.

A short word, too small for the weight it carried. Lies wrapped in charm. Lies that let me believe I was chosen, wanted, needed. Lies that kept me anchored to a story that was never mine.

"You hollowed me out," I wrote. "You made me distrust my own reflection. You made me apologise for truths you couldn't handle."

I pressed so hard the pen nearly tore the page.

And then: Shame.

This one nearly broke me. Not because it was unfamiliar, but because it was mine. Not something he had done to me, but something I had swallowed, nurtured, carried like a parasite.

"Why did I keep you?" I whispered aloud. "Why did I feed you every time I looked in the mirror? Why did I let you crawl into bed with me every night?"

My throat burned. Shame didn't answer, but its silence was heavy enough to feel like confession.

The list grew. Infidelity. Betrayal. Family with barbed wire tongues. Fear. Self-loathing. Loneliness. The mask I wore. The silence I kept.

Each word scratched onto the page like a wound opening. Each one dragged into daylight whether it wanted to be or not.

When my hand cramped, I shook it out and kept writing. I would not stop mid-exorcism.

At some point, I realised I was speaking the words aloud, as though reading them to an invisible jury. "Violence - guilty. Alcohol - guilty. Shame - guilty. Loneliness - guilty. Fear - guilty."

The house echoed with the accusations. The dog barked once, sharp, like she agreed.

But naming wasn't enough. The demons sneered at the ink on the page, daring me to think a word could undo years of damage.

So I went further. I spoke to them directly.

"You don't own me anymore."

The silence snapped, like static in the air.

"I said, you don't own me. You had your time. You took your pound of flesh. But I am not your home anymore."

I expected no reply. But in my mind's eye, I saw their faces - shifting, grotesque, sometimes his, sometimes mine. They hissed, they laughed, they tried to remind me of the nights I'd begged, the mornings I'd hidden bruises, and the lies I'd swallowed whole.

Still, I wrote the final word: No.

No more silence. No more surrender. No more pretending their power was infinite.

I closed the notebook to breathe, but the air tasted like metal. Sitting wasn't enough. My body wanted the names out where I could see them. I rummaged through a drawer until I found a pack of post-its and a half-dried marker.

On the first square: ALCOHOL. On the second:

VIOLENCE. On the third: LIES. The marker bled, thick and ugly. Good. Let them look how they felt.

I stood and pressed each square to the wall above the table. Then more: SHAME. SELF-BLAME. MINIMISING. PEOPLE-PLEASING. SILENCE. HIDING. DENIAL. FORGIVE TOO FAST. RETURN TO THE FIRE. APOLOGISE FOR EXISTING.

I kept going until the wall looked like a fever chart. The dog had moved to the doorway, watching as if a stranger had entered the house. In a way, one had. Me, but with a spine.

I stepped back. It was an awful mural. It was also a map.

"Old tools," I said, and uncapped the marker again. On a fresh post-it I wrote the new heading and stuck it above the rest. The moment I named them tools, something shifted. They weren't demons dropped out of the sky to torment me anymore, they were implements I had picked up once because I needed them to survive. People-pleasing to diffuse bombs. Minimising to keep the peace. Silence to end arguments that fists would continue. I had been a craftsman of endurance. No one had shown me anything else.

"You helped me once," I said to the wall. "I owe you that. But we're not building that house anymore."

I began grouping them the way you group cutlery after washing - like with like. Under COMPLIANCE I set: PEOPLE-PLEASING, MINIMISING, FORGIVE TOO FAST. Under NUMBING: ALCOHOL, OVERWORK, SCROLLING. Under PROTECTIVE LIES: I'M FINE, IT'S NOT THAT BAD, HE'S BETTER NOW. Under SELF-HARM: SHAME, APOLOGISE FOR EXISTING, STARVE/SLEEP/STARVE. Under ISOLATION: SILENCE, HIDING, AVOID FRIENDS. Under

FALSE HOPE: RETURN TO THE FIRE, THE NEXT TIME WILL BE THE LAST TIME.

It looked tidier, which almost made me laugh. As if you could file demons and call it healing. But the grouping did something practical, it let me see patterns, not failures. My body had been building an architecture to survive inside a collapsing house. The architecture had worked. I was here. That was not nothing.

"Thank you," I said, shocking myself.

The wall didn't answer. The refrigerator clicked. Somewhere outside a neighbour's wind chimes wrote a line of mercy and then forgot it.

I pulled a chair close and climbed up until my face was eye-level with SHAME. "You first," I told it. I peeled it off the wall and held the thin square between my fingers. It stuck to my skin like a bad habit.

"What were you saving me from?"

The answer arrived as an old sensation, not a sentence, the aftertaste of a slammed night, the way my shoulders crawled when he sighed that particular sigh, the calculation, how small can I make myself to get through this. Shame had been the tax I paid to live through evenings that might have ended worse.

"You did your job," I said. "But you're making me pay when no one is billing me anymore."

I breathed in, breathed out, and, surprising myself, pressed SHAME not back on the wall, but into a small ceramic bowl I used for olives. It made a soft sound, that paper landing. The sound of something put down.

One by one, I lifted other squares and asked them the same question.

PEOPLE-PLEASING. "What were you saving me from?"

From the rage that erupted when I had needs. From the way love turned contingent if I made a request. "You helped me avoid earthquakes," I told it, and set it in the bowl beside SHAME.

MINIMISING. "From what?" From the embarrassment of my own pain. From being the woman who makes a scene. Into the bowl.

FORGIVE TOO FAST. My hands trembled with that one. "You promised me a shortcut to peace," I said. "But you handed me a leash." Into the bowl.

ALCOHOL. I didn't take that one down. I left it pinned like a warning sign on a cliff: DO NOT APPROACH ALONE. "You're not a tool," I said. "You're a trap." I drew a black square around it with the marker and wrote, in smaller letters beneath: TELL SOMEONE WHEN TEMPTED. Then I wrote a name under that: Eliza. Another: Dr. Morison - Tuesday 10:30. It was a spell I trusted, names make things less likely to win.

SELF-BLAME. I could barely touch it. When I peeled it free, it came in two pieces, as if it had been there so long the paper had fused to the paint. I held both halves and found, beneath my scorn, a seam of gratitude. Self-blame had given me the illusion of control, if it was my fault, it meant the world wasn't random. "You tried to give the chaos a handle," I said. "But you broke my back."

Into the bowl. The bowl was not big, but it held.

I worked until my calves ached from standing on the chair and my fingers were smudged yellow. Some squares went to the bowl. Some I hung lower on the wall under another new heading: SKILLS I'LL KEEP, BUT DIFFERENT. BOUNDARIES lived there. SOFT VOICE, HARD LINE. PAUSE. ASK FOR CLARITY. WALK AWAY. I had never considered that I could keep the parts of me that were good at care, just aim them better.

When I finally climbed down, the wall was reorganised into three small kingdoms: OLD TOOLS (RETIRED), SKILLS I'LL KEEP, BUT DIFFERENT, and DANGER - TELL SOMEONE. The third section had only two squares: ALCOHOL and ISOLATE. I added a third: LIE TO THERAPIST. I underlined it twice and felt sick, because I knew exactly what that one could cost me.

The dog whuffed and came to lean her warm body against my shin. It steadied me. I made tea. I watched the kettle shiver and hiss and tried not to narrate it like grief, like a body that kept finding its boil. When the water ran into the cup, I breathed in the steam and told my lungs, "Look, a cloud you can eat."

Tea in hand, I took the chair to the opposite wall. I needed a second map. Above the clean plaster I wrote, in block letters, MEDICINE. Then, in smaller squares, I wrote the pairings that had risen in me while naming the demons.

ALCOHOL → BREATH. I pressed it to the wall and stood with my palm over it as if it were a small heartbeat.

VIOLENCE → PEACE (IN MY BODY FIRST). I added, almost without thinking: TAKE A WALK BEFORE YOU TEXT.

LIES → TRUTH. Underneath, I wrote: TELL IT FASTER.

SHAME → WORTH. Then: LOOK AT HER - DON'T LOOK AWAY. I glanced at the mirror, which had watched all of this without offering the worst. I nodded to it, a truce.

PEOPLE-PLEASING → HONOUR (ME + THEM). I printed: YOU'RE NOT A VENDING MACHINE.

MINIMISING → SAY IT PLAIN. I added a line I could hear my grandmother saying: YOU CAN BE KIND AND STILL BE CLEAR.

SILENCE → VOICE. I wrote: DON'T SING FOR YOUR SUPPER. SPEAK FOR YOURSELF.

HIDING → COMMUNITY. Two names: Sarah (lunch). Eliza (text tonight).

SELF-BLAME → RESPONSIBILITY WITH BOUNDARIES. I added: SIT WHAT IS YOURS IN YOUR LAP. HAND BACK WHAT ISN'T.

RETURN TO THE FIRE → DOOR STAYS LOCKED. I underlined it and felt a clean, hard sorrow. Some answers were brutal because they were simple.

When I finished, my kitchen looked like a detective's office in a film, names and lines, a woman's handwriting all over the walls as if the house had told me secrets and I didn't trust my head to hold them. It wasn't pretty. It was honest. That would have to be enough.

I took a photo with my phone, not because I needed proof but because grief makes you forget even the things you swear you won't. And I suspected there would be days when I needed to see the wall even if I couldn't stand to face it.

The phone pinged with a message from Eliza: Thinking of you. No need to respond. Love you xxx

I typed and erased three drafts before sending: Doing a weird thing with post-its. Naming stuff. Feels like I'm building a courtroom and a garden at the same time.

Her dots appeared, then disappeared, then reappeared. Finally: That's exactly what healing looks like from here. Save me a seat on the jury. And a trowel.

I laughed, ugly and sudden, and the sound punched a hole in the solemn air.

Afternoon sagged into the room like a tired aunt. I ate an

apple over the sink, juice sticky on my wrist, and stared at the square that read SHAME → WORTH. My eyes burned. "I don't know how to do that one," I told the wall. "The worth part."

The wall declined to advise me. So I tried something unscientific. I stood in front of the mirror and said to my own face, "You are not a project. You are a person." It felt like lying at first. I could see all the ways I had failed at being human, at being woman, mother, wife, believer, even dog-owner on the days I forgot to buy food. I pressed my hand to the glass until the heat of my palm fogged a circle around my mouth, and then I said it again. "You are not a project. You are a person." The second time it felt less false, the way a new shoe still hurts but no longer rubs skin off.

Back at the table, I opened the notebook to a clean page and made two columns. LEFT: OLD SURVIVAL SKILLS. RIGHT: HOW I'LL THANK THEM / HOW I'LL PUT THEM DOWN.

People-pleasing. Thank you for buying me time in rooms with weather I couldn't predict. I'll put you down by asking, "What do I want?" before I ask, "What will they think?"

Minimising. Thank you for letting me survive conversations where truth would have been punished. I'll put you down by saying, "That hurt," and letting the sentence stand.

Silence. Thank you for saving my teeth. I'll put you down by choosing my moments and my witnesses.

Forgive too fast. Thank you for helping me cross dangerous nights. I'll put you down by letting consequences be their own kind of mercy.

Return to the fire. Thank you for trying to get me what I thought I wanted, and love that stayed. I'll put you down by refusing to re-enter burning rooms.

Self-blame. Thank you for giving me the illusion of a lever. I'll put you down by holding only my end of the rope.

I worked until my neck cramped. When I lifted my head, dusk had painted a thin bruise across the window. The dog bumped my knee with her nose, time.

We walked the block, the two of us an unremarkable procession, a woman who looked like she was learning to count again, and a dog who forgave any pace. I repeated the pairs under my breath as if they were a new alphabet. Alcohol → Breath. Lies → Truth. Shame → Worth. My footsteps kept the beat.

At the last corner before home, a magpie landed on the curb and strutted like a ridiculous priest. I laughed and felt instantly disloyal, as if the wall might hear and strike my name from the list of people taking this seriously. "I'm allowed," I told the street. "I'm allowed to laugh and still be in the middle of this." The wind moved. It didn't object.

Back home, I made dinner without bargaining with myself. Nothing elaborate, just pasta with garlic and olive oil, and too much pepper because that's just how I like it. I ate at the table with the herbs kissing the open window and the post-its staring over my shoulder like curious children. Between bites I read them aloud, softly, as if I were tutoring my own mouth to say new things.

When the plate was empty, I washed it and felt the clean weight of finishing something ordinary. That feeling was new too. For months, I had abandoned half-done tasks like breadcrumbs in a forest I refused to navigate. Tonight, I stacked the plate to dry and wiped the bench. The cloth moved in simple arcs. The house responded by being a little less sticky, a little less sad. The smallest mercies are often domestic.

I knew I should sleep. I also knew sleep was a negotiator with no ethics. Instead, I made a nest on the floor beneath the wall and leaned my back against the cupboard until the wood learned my shape. The dog resettled with her spine to my thigh, a guard in reverse. I stared at the square that read APOLOGISE FOR EXISTING and felt, inexplicably, angry.

"Who taught you that?" I asked myself.

Memory obliged. A primary school classroom where a teacher with damp breath praised girls who didn't take up space. A church hall where women were thanked for their quiet. A living room where the loudest person got what he wanted. A bedroom where sorry was a currency I spent even when I had done nothing wrong.

"I'm done," I said to the wall, to the past, to the curated gods of compliance. "I'm done apologising for having a pulse." I peeled the square down, crumpled it, satisfying, that sound, and fed it into the little bowl. It felt like an altar and a bin at once.

Sometime after ten, my phone lit with a photo from Eliza: a badly iced cake with "YOU'RE STILL HERE" scrawled in blue. No caption. Just sugar and defiance. I sent back a picture of my wall. Her reply was almost immediate: I love your brain. Also, please don't sleep under a rain of post-its.

I didn't trust sleep anyway. I sat, and I let the quiet move through the room on its clean feet. Every so often I would stand, touch a square, shift it two inches. This is how you prune a plant you love, you cut so it can live. Compassionate pruning. I hadn't known I could be gentle and decisive at once. No one had ever told me that was allowed.

Near midnight, I lit a candle. Not to be spiritual, there were no hymns in me tonight, but because the house needed a softer kind of light. The flame made a little theatre of the wall, each square's shadow a second opinion. My breath fell into rhythm with the flicker. I realised, not for the first time, that breath is the only thing I can do without being taught. It keeps choosing me even when I forget its name.

The candle burned low. I blew it out. Smoke wrote a brief script above the wick and then translated itself into nothing.

Sleeplessness performed its old tricks, but they didn't land. I was busy. I had a job, keep sitting, keep noticing, keep not lying. When the first pale slice of morning slid between the blinds, I felt the soft ache of a muscle I had used for the first time in years. Honesty. It had weight. It also had relief.

That day I kept the wall as it was. I didn't need to win the whole war by noon. I showered. I put on clean clothes that did not pretend to be a new personality. I drove to the GP and sat in a waiting room that smelled of disinfectant and people trying. The magazine on the table had a cover model with an airbrushed soul. I turned the pages as if they were made of glass. When my name was called, my body stood before my mind could argue.

In the room I did not soften the facts. "My husband died in a crash. He had been drinking. I have been drinking too much since. I don't want to." I did not apologise for taking up the doctor's time. I watched his face for the flinch that would confirm all my old stories about being too much. It didn't come. He nodded, factual, human. We made a plan. It had numbers in it, and also compassion. He said the sentence I hadn't known I needed: "None of this makes you weak, it makes you a person."

I bought bread on the way home, the good kind, the one that feels like a small weight in a paper bag. In the car I said out loud, "I told the truth." My voice sounded like a woman's. It sounded like mine.

Back in the kitchen, I texted Eliza a photo of the DANGER-TELL SOMEONE section with the new additions circled and the GP appointment card tucked in the frame. She sent back a heart and then: Proud of your ruthless kindness.

Ruthless kindness. The phrase fit like a garment I could live in.

Evening came, and with it the old sensation that the house and I were the only two people left in the world. I made toast. I buttered it like a person who believes she will still be here in an hour. I ate standing up, not as punishment but as proof that I could choose where to put my body.

When the plate was clean, I opened the notebook again. The pages had begun to curl at the corners with the humidity of breath and kitchen. I read what I had written earlier, then added the thing I hadn't known yet: These patterns were not sins. They were strategies. Useful once. Useless now. Thank them. Retire them. Build something else.

I drew a small box in the margin and wrote inside it: Space. It looked silly in ink, but I felt it in my chest, a little widening where shame lived yesterday. I took the bowl of retired post-its to the bedroom and set it on the floor beside the wardrobe where years of compromises had gone to sleep. I didn't need a bonfire. I needed a place to put things down.

The night gathered its hem and lowered itself over the house. I made tea. I washed the cup. I turned off lights and left the one over the stove glowing like a small moon. The wall breathed with me. That is how it felt, like we had agreed, the wall and I, to stop pretending that rooms don't remember.

I sat back and read the page aloud, each word like a stone set down: Alcohol. Violence. Shame. Fear.

Not poetry. Not prophecy. Just the things that haunted me, written in my hand so they could no longer pretend to be fog. I drew a line beneath them and waited for the room to change. It didn't. The kettle didn't bow. The air didn't brighten. But something inside me unclenched, a small click of truth into place.

If naming is a door, I had finally found the handle.

I turned the page. White space stared back, wide and terrifying. At the very top, with a pen that trembled anyway, I wrote one word I wasn't sure I believed in: Prayer.

Then I closed the notebook softly, like putting a sleeping child down.

Tomorrow, I thought. Tomorrow I'll ask for a language bigger than lists, prayers for a broken woman.

Chapter Sixteen

By first light, the page I'd labelled last night waited like a held breath. Prayer.

Morning found the notebook where I left it, the word Prayer hovering on the next page like a dare. I wasn't ready to speak into that space yet. So I chose smaller verbs, ones my body still trusted.

I opened a window.

I made tea and finished the cup.

I stepped outside barefoot and let the cold bite my soles until my lungs remembered how to move.

Becoming wasn't a revelation; it was a sequence of unglamorous mercies. I watered the pot plant that never judged me for forgetting it. I fed the dog first instead of last. I replied to one message with eight honest words: I'm here. Not okay. But here. Love you. None of it fixed the ache. All of it kept me from disappearing.

I didn't try to be new. I tried to be present, ten minutes at a time. One load of washing. One slow walk to the letterbox. One call booked for next week with the GP, because next week is a kind of faith too. When my mind lunged toward the abyss, I gave it a task: *"Fold this towel. Breathe out. Now the next towel."*

By afternoon the house had put its noise back on, the old fridge clearing its throat, a magpie heckling the fence, and the dog's claws ticking the kitchen tiles like a metronome. Small life going on. I wiped the bench because lint had stuck to a ring of tea, because the cloth was in my hand, because motion is kinder than stillness sometimes. When the surface shone, nothing in my life was solved. But the bench was clean, and my hands had stayed.

I sat, pulled the notebook close, and let my thumb worry the rough edge of yesterday's page. The ink hadn't dried clean, the words bled at the edges, as though even the paper couldn't hold them without bruising. Alcohol. Violence. Shame. Fear. I ran my palm over each one like you might press a bruise to prove it's still there. Naming had helped, like throwing the lights on in a room where something skulked. The shapes were still ugly, but they weren't invisible.

If I left it there, though, they'd find their way back. They always did.

I turned the page.

My hand hovered. The pen was heavier than it had any right to be. I wrote, in letters thinner than I intended: Prayer.

Not because I knew how. Not because I believed in the polished way people in pews did. I wrote it because something in me knew I needed to answer my demons with something bigger than ink. And maybe prayer wasn't about knowing what to say. Maybe it was just about speaking anyway.

At first, it came out clumsy. "God? Spirit? Universe? Whoever's listening? Hell, even if it's just me listening to myself…"

The words scattered into the silence. The fridge hummed like a choir with no conviction. My throat tightened.

"I don't know what I'm doing," I whispered. "I don't even know if you're real. If you are, you haven't exactly done me many favours."

The silence didn't argue. So I kept going.

"I'm angry. You hear me? Furious. At him. At myself. At you. At everything. I don't want to wake up like this every morning. I don't want to carry this weight. I don't want to breathe when he can't. I don't want to survive if surviving means dragging all this through every day of my life."

The words shook out of me like broken glass. My chest heaved. Tears slid, hot and constant. "But here I am. Still here. Still breathing. And I don't know why."

I slammed the pen down and let the words spill from my mouth instead. "If you're out there, then damn it, show me. Don't send me verses, don't send me sermons. Show me in something I can hold. Show me in the air I keep forgetting to breathe. Show me in the way my dog curls up beside me when I'm breaking. Show me in the stupid laugh my sister sends me at midnight when she knows I'm awake. Show me in something real."

The silence thickened, listening.

"I'm not asking for miracles. I don't even know if I'd believe one if it slapped me across the face. I'm just asking for... enough. Enough strength to get out of bed. Enough calm to eat a meal without gagging on guilt. Enough light to see past this hour. Enough."

Saying it surprised me. The words weren't polished. They weren't holy. But they were mine. And in the saying, I realised prayer didn't need to be anything more than honesty. It didn't need incense or robes or even certainty. It needed only truth.

So I told more. "I'm terrified. I'm lonely. I'm so goddamn angry. I miss him even though he destroyed me. I hate myself for missing him. I hate myself for surviving when he didn't. And I don't know how to carry any of it."

The silence pressed close. And though it didn't answer, something in me loosened. Maybe prayer wasn't about getting an answer. Maybe it was about not having to hold the questions alone.

After that, I kept going, badly, faithfully. Not neat, not

ritualised. Sometimes I muttered in the car, gripping the steering wheel like a rosary I didn't believe in. Sometimes I screamed into the shower so the water could carry the words down the drain. Sometimes I sat on the edge of the bed and whispered one sentence: "Don't let me go."

Other nights it was the opposite: "Fine. Let me go. If you're real, take me. If you're not, then at least I've said it out loud."

And still, every morning, I woke. Breath in my chest. Feet on the floor. It felt like betrayal and mercy at the same time.

The prayers became locations as much as sentences. In the supermarket queue, I practiced a private liturgy, hands against the cool of the trolley handle, eyes on the rows of gum and batteries and impulse promises, and a whisper no louder than a thought, *Keep me steady*. Between the bread and the milk, a stranger's perfume could still yank me back to nights I wished were rumours. When it did, I'd touch the shopping list like it was an anchor. "Right here," I'd tell myself, out loud if I had to. "We're right here."

On the footpath outside school pickup, all those mothers in their bright leggings and brave voices, How are you, love?, and me, with a smile that never knew if it was lying. *"Help me be honest without spilling,"* I'd ask the air. Then: *"Two sentences. That's enough."* And I'd say to them: "It's hard. I'm getting through." Which was true, and which felt like prayer because it asked for the smallest possible mercy, let me speak without breaking open.

At night, when the house went soft and loose around the edges, the prayers got blunt. "Don't let me text him," I'd tell the ceiling. "Don't let me rewrite history at midnight. Don't let me believe the sweet version. I know how that film ends."

Some evenings I wrote them down, not to explain them but to get them out of my body. I kept the notebook open on the table so I had to walk past it and decide, again and again, whether to speak or swallow. Most days I spoke. On the not-speaking days I tried not to punish myself, silence is its own kind of weather. Even then I'd drag the pen across the margin and write a single word - Stay - so the page wouldn't feel abandoned.

The prayers I could live by were small. "Give me wisdom" became "help me shut my mouth for ten minutes when I'm angry." "Make me patient" became "let me count to five before I speak." "Heal me" became "help me eat without hating myself today." I didn't know if the Universe answered those. I only knew I could.

I learned to set them like timers. In the car at a red light: Keep me gentle. In the chemist, standing too long in front of the sleep aids: Keep me honest. In the bathroom with the mirror, the mouth I didn't recognise: Be kind to her. In bed at two a.m., when thought turned into weather and all of it violent: Don't let the tide take me.

One night, after a day that nearly broke me, I paced the backyard while the stars pretended not to care. "Where the hell were you?" I shouted. "When he hit me, when he lied, when he drank, when he died? Where were you when I begged for help? Where are you now? Why give me a life like this if you're not going to show up in it?"

The garden swallowed my rage and handed me back the wind. Not an answer. Not a miracle. Just a cool brush across my face, almost like a hand. I hated how much comfort it gave me.

"Don't you dare," I hissed at the sky. "Don't you dare make me hope again."

But hope crept in anyway, sly, and stubborn. Not the trumpet-blast kind. The quieter kind, like a breath I didn't notice until it had already filled me. It came when Poppy laughed at a bad joke I made, when the jacaranda spilled its reckless purple across the path, when I slept three hours straight without waking to the horror movie in my head. Each time, I whispered, "Thank you." Sometimes sarcastic. Sometimes desperate. Sometimes real.

Prayer shifted then from demand to rhythm. It wasn't Our Father or Hail Mary. It was:

"I need help."

"I'm breaking."

"Stay with me."

"Don't let me drown."

"Thank you for not letting me die tonight."

Sometimes it was nothing more than a sigh. Sometimes it was a rant that lasted an hour and left me hoarse. But it was still prayer, because it was still conversation, me refusing to shut up even when heaven stayed silent.

There came a night when sleep wouldn't have me, when the walls leaned in and whispered all the old names of the demons I'd written down. I pressed the pillow over my ears and shouted into the dark, "Do you want me or not? If you want me, take me. If you don't, then give me something worth staying for."

The silence that followed was unbearable. And then, from the other room, Poppy stirred in her sleep and mumbled my name.

I broke. Fell to my knees. Whispered, "All right. I'll stay."

The staying didn't feel noble. It felt like a bargain struck in the ruins; I'll keep breathing if the day keeps handing me one honest thing to hold.

In the weeks that followed, I started writing the prayers down. Not to make them pretty. To make them real. Little fragments I slid between recipe books and receipts:

- Don't let me lose myself today.

- Help me find my breath again.

- Keep me angry enough to live, but not angry enough to destroy myself.

- Show me how to love without breaking apart.

Some days I tore the pages out and burned them over the sink, watching the smoke curl upward like a delivery service I didn't fully trust. Other days I left them where they fell and stepped around them like islands in a messy sea.

The strangest thing was feeling less alone, not because a stained-glass God suddenly sat at my table, but because every prayer proved there was still a voice inside me. Still a spark. Still someone who refused to stop talking to the dark. If I could pray, then I was not finished.

I began keeping a list of "household prayers," because lofty ones evaporated and left me hungrier. These stayed:

- Give me clean words.

- Give me strong no's and soft yes's.

- Keep my hands busy when my head is dangerous.

- Help me apologise quickly and forgive slowly, in the right order.

- Let me rest before I break.

- Let laughter find me without me chasing it down.

I taped the list inside a cupboard door, above the tea, where I'd have to touch it to reach the tin. Touch became part of the prayer, fingers brushing paper, and paper reminding skin, you asked for help. Keep asking.

Sometimes the prayers arrived as an argument I didn't want to lose. In the chemist a woman ahead of me sighed at the price of something and said to the clerk, "Well, grief is expensive." I felt my whole body prepare a lecture. Instead, I said, "Keep me tender," and paid for Panadol and a cheap bottle of nail polish the colour of bruised plums. That night I painted my toes like a teenager. "Make me ridiculous," I said, and meant it as worship of survival.

On a Tuesday I sat in the GP's waiting room and performed the prayer of being a person, name the symptoms, tell the truth, and say yes to help. "I don't need fixing," I told him, voice steady. "I need scaffolding." He nodded. We built something small and practical together, a check-in date, a number to call, a line in my file that said the word alcohol without flinching. In the car afterwards I held the steering wheel and said, "Thank you," to nothing I could prove and everything that had kept me from lying.

The prayers did not domesticate my grief. I still had days when rage burned the edges of everything, days when the dog's water bowl felt like a personal affront, and days when the supermarket's fluorescent lights accused me of pretending to be human. On those days the prayers were stripped down to one syllable: "Help." Sometimes "Stay." Sometimes "No."

I failed at them often. I asked for a gentle mouth and still snapped. I asked for patience and still slammed a drawer. I asked to be unselfish and still measured who texted first. On those nights, I practiced a prayer I'd never been taught, forgiveness that began with me. "You tried," I said to the mirror, and winced at how trite it sounded. "You're tired," I corrected. "Start there." Then I drank a glass of water slowly, like penance and permission at once.

Now and then I heard Marko's voice the way you hear an old song float out of a car window at the lights, tidy phrases that life had taught him too late. You kept breathing, he'd say, almost matter-of-factly. Or I didn't. The sentences didn't absolve him, and they didn't accuse me. They sat down on the step beside my shoes and looked at the night. Sometimes I answered. "I'm angry," I'd say. "I know," the air would reply. "I loved you," I'd add. "I know," it would say again. It wasn't theology. It was the practice of speaking without pretending.

I learned to pray with my body. Knees in dirt while I attacked the garden bed that had gone feral, hands in suds while I rinsed the day off plates, feet on bitumen, lap after lap around the block, counting letterboxes as if they were beads. Breath became the oldest prayer, the one my ancestors must have prayed without language, in, out, in. Some mornings I'd put my palm to my sternum and ask, "Are we safe?" and my ribs would answer by opening.

I began to notice the shape of answers, not thunderclaps, but alignment. When I asked for wisdom, my phone stayed in my pocket. When I asked for courage, my "no" landed without my voice shaking. When I asked for gentleness, I stroked the dog's ears for a full minute before picking up my keys. None of it would impress a prophet. All of it was saving me.

There were relapses. A Friday I almost drowned myself in a bottle and stopped because the dog knocked it with her tail, and a splash on my toes felt like someone tapping my shoulder. "Don't," the cold said. "Not like this." I put the glass in the sink and prayed the ugliest prayer I know, "Please don't let me be my own enemy." I didn't sleep well, but I woke. Which counted.

There was a Sunday I lost my temper and burned a bridge in a text I couldn't unsend. I spent three hours on the floor pretending the tiles were a raft. "Fix it," I begged the ceiling. "Or fix me so I don't need it fixed." The next day I walked the apology to the post box like a parcel I didn't trust to survive on its own. "Let my mouth be better than my pride," I said to the red metal.

The box made no promises. The letter left my hand. I breathed.

Slowly, the entries changed their texture. There was still rage, but it learned to share space. Between "Why did you let this happen?" and "How could you?" there were thin blades of gratitude:

- For the nurse who said my name softly.

- For the neighbour who mowed my verge without asking.

- For the way grief has a rhythm and today I can dance half a step.

Gratitude didn't cancel fury. They stood, awkward but side by side, and I learned to let them. Faith, if that's what this was, could hold both.

One afternoon, stuck at a red light, I spoke to the windscreen like it was a confessional. "I don't know who I am without suffering," I said. "I don't know how to be a person who isn't carrying a wreck." A beat. "Teach me." The light changed. I drove on. No choir sang. But I noticed I wasn't holding my breath.

Not long after, I tried something that felt dangerous, I asked for joy. Not the big cinematic kind. The household kind. "Let my laughter return," I wrote. "Let me be ridiculous without apology." The request felt almost obscene, like ordering dessert at a funeral. It also felt necessary. If joy couldn't live in a house like mine, whose house could it live in?

That night I burned the page, not out of shame, but as a way of saying, I meant it. The ash lifted and disappeared into the dark. I stood in the kitchen with the window cracked open and the dog leaning against my calf and felt, for a breath, like the room and I were the same size.

By then, prayer had become muscle memory. I could reach for it without performing. Sometimes it was nothing but my hand on my chest, tapping a rhythm my heart could follow. Sometimes it was a single sentence repeated under my breath at the supermarket, between the cereal and the tinned tomatoes, "Keep me gentle." It worked badly and beautifully. I snapped at a stranger in the car park and apologised before the guilt did its full lap. I used my soft voice with Poppy and didn't punish myself later for wanting to scream.

The notebook thickened. Its spine learned to lie flat. The pages kept their bruised edges, evidence of a woman who had pressed too hard, who was learning not to. On the inside back cover, without thinking, I wrote a line and underlined it twice: I will not be silent. Silence was what almost killed me. Speaking, even when it was messy, furious, unfinished, was what kept me alive.

Hope didn't arrive with trumpets. It arrived as a ridiculous video Poppy shoved under my nose of a bulldog skidding across a kitchen floor in tiny socks, legs working harder than physics should allow. I laughed. It split me open. I clapped a hand over my mouth like I'd sinned. Poppy grinned. "There she is," she said, as if my laughter were a person coming up the drive. I cried and laughed at the same time, a sound like tearing fabric and letting light through.

After that I paid attention. Joy came disguised. A lemon fallen from the tree, warm as a palm. A stranger at the servo calling me "love" without making a claim on me. The exact way the late sun turned the dog's fur into something holy. Each time, a small prayer - "More of that" - and then the work of letting it land, of not arguing with it, and of not asking whether I deserved it.

On a rain-heavy Thursday, I did something I'd promised myself I'd do, I wrote prayers not to the sky, but to my own future. Dear Tomorrow Me, I began, please be gentle with my bones. Please remember to eat. Please remember that anger is not a personality, it's weather. Please, when someone offers you kindness, take it like bread. I signed it, Love, The One Who Lived Through Today. I tucked the note behind the sugar. The next morning, reaching for a teaspoon, I found my own handwriting and cried into my coffee because it felt like being mothered by a stranger who was only me.

I learned, finally, to aim my stubbornness in a better direction. The same iron that kept me in a bad story could keep me in a good one. "Stay," I told myself when it would have been easy to shut down. "Stay with the discomfort. Stay with the tenderness. Don't bail on the moment because it's not symmetrical." It was a prayer in disguise, really, asking the animal of me to trust the human of me long enough not to run.

At dusk the house exhaled and so did I. I wiped the bench clean, not because a clean bench saves anyone, but because it gave my hands a reason to stay. Then I pulled the notebook close, turned to the waiting page, and uncapped the pen. If becoming was the work of my hands, what came next would have to be the work of my mouth.

"Okay," I whispered, almost to myself. "Speak."

And the words came, not elegant, not profound, but true enough to stand on:

- Keep me honest when I want to perform.

- Keep me soft when hardness feels safer.

- Keep me fierce where boundaries are needed.

- Keep me laughing when shame says hush.

- Keep me kind to the woman in the mirror.

- Keep me faithful to breath.

The dog huffed as if to agree. Somewhere outside a child called a name and laughter answered. I wrote until the page filled, then another, then stopped because I was tired and, for once, tired felt like permission instead of failure.

I closed the notebook and let my palm rest on its cover. The house breathed with me, the shy hiss of the kettle before it clicked off, the slow exhale of the fridge, the ordinary hush that comes when a day has said what it needed to say.

Every so often panic rose again like a tide intent on reclaiming its shore. Each time I followed the breath back in: in, out, stay. Not a cure, just a way through.

And then a day arrived that did not ask permission to be gentle. Poppy tripped over the dog and swore, then looked at me, horrified, and we both burst out laughing, the wild, inelegant kind you can't pretty up. I didn't cover my mouth. I didn't negotiate with the past before accepting the moment. I laughed until my sides hurt and the dog barked just to keep up. When it settled, I caught my breath and said the simplest prayer I know.

"Thank you."

No thunder. No halo. Just the sound of our house carrying laughter again like it remembered how.

I left the notebook on the table as I washed the mugs and turned out the lights. Tomorrow would have its own weather, its own small verbs, its own arguments with the dark. I didn't promise triumph. I promised participation.

"Stay," I told the room.

"Stay," the room told me back.

And in that soft call-and-response, a new word took my hand - becoming - and led me toward the next page.

Chapter Seventeen

Before I called it healing, I called it noticing.

I never meant to pray. I never meant to write the words that bled into that notebook. But once I did, once the prayers spilled into the silence, something shifted. Not everything, not even most things, but enough. Enough to notice.

Maybe that was the beginning of becoming, not a grand declaration, not some lightning-strike transformation, but the simple act of noticing.

The mornings were still brutal. I woke with my stomach in knots, my throat dry, my body heavy with the same grief I had fallen asleep in. But now I had something to say to it. "Stay with me," I would whisper into the air before I even sat up. Sometimes it came out as a plea, sometimes as a dare. Either way, it anchored me. The day couldn't swallow me whole until I'd spoken it aloud.

I started small. One morning, instead of letting the weight keep me in bed, I stood. My knees shook, my head spun, but I stood. "See?" I muttered to the quiet. "I can still do this." I shuffled to the kitchen, made tea I didn't want, and drank it anyway. Steam curled from the mug like a tiny prayer of its own. Later, I stepped onto the back step and let the sunlight find my face. It burned my eyelids red. For the first time in months, I didn't flinch from it. "You're still here," I whispered to the light. "And so am I."

Morning found the notebook where I'd left it. The dog nosed my ankle, tail thudding the doorjamb like a metronome. I scratched the slope of her head and felt, with a kind of shock, the ordinary blessing of warm fur under my palm.

I didn't try to be new, I just tried to be present, ten minutes at a time. One load of washing. One slow walk to the letterbox. One call booked for next week with the GP, because next week is a kind of faith too. When my thoughts began to slip, I anchored them to the small. One breath. One ordinary task. Then the next.

Some days I slid backward so hard I thought everything I'd gathered spilled out behind me. There were mornings I pressed my face into the pillow and screamed until my throat shredded. Nights I poured a drink I had promised I wouldn't, just to remember what numbness felt like. When guilt came, heavy and merciless, I wrote it down: I failed today. Then I wrote another line: But I am still here. That became the rhythm, fall, write, rise, repeat.

The mirror turned into a battlefield. I hated her, the woman staring back. Her hair limp, her skin dull, her eyes hollow. One morning, after a night of prayers that had turned into a shouting match with heaven, I stood there and whispered, "Who even are you anymore?"

She didn't answer. So I answered for her. "You're me. And we're not done."

The defiance startled me. It didn't feel like courage - it felt older, like the ember that refused to go out was finally daring to flare. I tapped the glass once with my knuckle, as if to knock on my own door. "Come back," I said to my reflection. "I'm trying."

Becoming showed up in strange places. Like the day I finally packed his clothes into boxes. For months I'd walked past that wardrobe like it was a grave I wasn't ready to disturb. But one afternoon, with the sunlight too golden to ignore, I opened both doors and let the fabric fall heavy in my hands. His shirts still held the faintest echo of him, though time had blurred the edges somewhat, the ghost of cologne, the memory of rain. I pressed one to my face, and the memories cut and comforted in the same breath. Then I folded it. And another. And another. I cried over every button, every collar. By evening, the wardrobe was empty. My tears had soaked the cardboard flaps, but the boxes closed just the same. "Goodbye," I whispered into the dust. The room felt strange, hollow and echoing, but under the hollowness was a tiny declaration, I am still here. I am still moving.

Sometimes I felt him in the house. Not like before, not death at my shoulder, not the haunting absence. More like a memory caught in the air, faint, watchful, but not heavy. One night, when the silence pressed too close, I spoke into the dark. "You broke me," I said. "But I'm not staying broken." The words surprised me with their steadiness. They didn't feel borrowed or brave. They felt mine. Saying them showed me that becoming wasn't about erasing him, it was about reclaiming me.

Poppy noticed before I did. "Mum, you're laughing again," Poppy said one evening, half amazed, half relieved. I agreed with her. I hadn't realised a sound had escaped me that wasn't a sob or a sigh. It felt like a small animal, startled and bright, darting from a bush. Their words became their own kind of prayer, proof that becoming was visible, that healing wasn't just something I felt, but that it was also something that reached the people I loved.

I made a list no one else saw:

- No more skipping meals.

- Two walks a week, even if I cry the whole time.

- Call the GP. Keep the appointment.

- Text one friend back, even if it's just a heart emoji.

- Open the curtains.

- Eat a green thing.

The list wasn't heroic. That was the point. Heroics had

broken me; small faithful acts began to knit me back together.

On a Tuesday, I sat in the doctor's office, hands cold, feet in shoes that pinched. I told the truth, badly. The GP didn't try to fix my soul, he adjusted my meds, ordered bloods, and then told me to eat protein in the morning. It felt almost indecent to be handed an instruction I could actually obey. I bought eggs on the way home and cried over a frying pan. The crying didn't ruin the eggs.

On Wednesdays I walked the dog around the block where the jacarandas trimmed the sky with purple. I timed my steps to the rhythm of my breath, four counts in, six counts out, until the panic in my chest loosened its grip. An old man watered his roses and nodded like I was part of the street again. I nodded back and felt, inexplicably, like I'd returned from a far country only I had known I'd visited.

I started answering the phone. Not always. Enough that my name didn't look like an unanswered question when it flashed on someone else's screen. When my sister rang, her hello was too gentle for the jokes we usually used to cushion seriousness. "I'm making spaghetti," I said, and the mundane sentence was astonishingly hard to say without crying. "Good," she said. "Eat two bowls." I ate one and a half and called it obedience.

At the op-shop I tried on a dress that didn't belong to any of my old lives. It was simple and soft, not the kind I used to wear to make myself presentable, not the kind he would have chosen, but something my skin liked. I bought it for seven dollars and wore it home with sneakers and a cardigan that had lost a button. In the mirror I didn't look transformed. I looked like a woman who had chosen herself. It was enough.

I deleted numbers that had become doorways to old harm. I blocked one. I sat on the edge of my bed, phone warm in my hand,

and waited for regret to pounce. It didn't. In its place was a strange quiet, a clearing where air could move.

I planted gerberas in a pot by the back step, pink, because they look like happy faces even when you're not. The soil crumbled between my fingers, and the roots took hold. For weeks they looked like mistakes, a stunted cluster of leaves pretending to be brave. Then one morning a bud turned itself inside out and declared itself a flower. "Show-off," I said, smiling despite myself. I understood the impulse.

On a Friday, I took the car to be serviced, sat in the plastic waiting room with stale magazines, and paid the bill without apologising to the man behind the counter for taking up space on earth. It's a ridiculous thing to admit, how apologies had soaked through my life until even my breath felt like an intrusion. I drove home listening to a radio station that played songs I knew the words to. When a lyric cracked me open, I let it, and then I turned the volume down and kept driving.

I kept an appointment with a counsellor and told the truth more cleanly than I ever had before. How the nights still tried to pull me under, and how some parts of me wanted to go. She said, "What helps you remember yourself?" I said, "Hot showers. Clean sheets. Poppy's laughter. Dogs. The smell of toast. The exact colour of the sky at 5:42 a.m." She said, "Do those like medicine."

There were setbacks. An anniversary ambushed me in the supermarket cereal aisle, and I left a full trolley to hide in the car and shake. A song pressed an old bruise, and I cried so hard I scared the dog. On those days death sat close again, whispering, It would be easier if you stopped fighting. I answered out loud, "Not yet. You don't get me yet." It wasn't strength, it was stubbornness. But stubbornness counts.

I made a budget that didn't humiliate me. I cooked simple food and ate it at the table with a fork like a person. I changed a lightbulb I'd been avoiding for months and no one cheered, so I cheered for myself, quietly, washing my hands under warm water, watching the dirt leave my fingers and circle the drain.

One evening I lit a candle, not for ritual, not for ceremony, just for light. The flame flickered, fragile and steady, and I stared until my eyes watered. "That's me," I whispered. "Not gone. Not yet. Still burning." The dog sighed at my feet like an old lady, as if to say, Obviously. I laughed, caught myself laughing, and didn't apologise to the empty room.

I began to mark my days not by what shattered but by what held. The mug that didn't break when I knocked it, the appointment I kept, the boundary that stood even when guilt rattled it like a thief at a window. On a good afternoon I sat on the back step with a pen and wrote a different kind of list:

What held today:

- My breath, through the whole cup of tea.

- My voice, when I said "no."

- The sky, stubbornly blue when it could've been cruel.

- Me.

The house learned my new rhythms. The kettle's shy hiss before it clicked off. The dog's nails ticking the tiles. The steady heartbeat of the fridge. There was a time I'd called those sounds loneliness. Now they felt like evidence. Each noise said, in its own language, You're in a life.

I practiced standing with myself in rooms that used to make me disappear. The chemist, with its aisle of sleep and calm and shut-it-off. The bank, where numbers once made me feel like a child. The school gate, with its cluster of bright mothers and agile talk. I didn't dominate those spaces. I didn't need to. I stood. I stayed. I let my shoulders belong to me.

There were tiny, invisible graduations. The day I left the house without checking the locks three times. The afternoon I took a nap on the couch because my body asked, and I let it, and the world kept turning without my vigilance. The night I watched a film with a love story in it and didn't look away when they kissed. I didn't believe in their happy ending, not yet. But I didn't punish myself for watching it happen to someone else.

If becoming had a sound, it was the clink of cutlery returning clean to the drawer. It was my own voice saying enough and meaning enough for tonight, which is enough. It was the dog's collar jingling as we walked past the house where the lemon tree throws shade over the fence like generosity. It was Poppy's laughter, thin at first, then richer, and sometimes she practised a joke she hoped would land. Sometimes it didn't. We laughed anyway.

I started noticing the difference between relief and restoration. Wine gave relief. Sleep gave restoration. Scrolling gave relief. Talking to a friend under a sky that wouldn't mind if I cried gave restoration. Anger gave relief. A boundary gave restoration. I began to choose accordingly, not because I was holy, but because I was tired of waking up emptier.

On a Saturday I went to the beach alone. I sat where the shore could reach my ankles and let the foam lace my feet. The horizon did that trick it does where it pretends to be both line and invitation. A boy nearby buried his sister's sandals and pretended he didn't know where they'd gone. She screamed like she was being murdered, and then she laughed. I thought, the luxury of that kind of drama. The gulls argued about a chip. The wind salted my mouth. I didn't cry. I didn't make a speech. I just sat in a body that was learning, slowly, stupidly, and beautifully, to be a home.

I taught myself a small practice my counsellor called re-entry. When coming back from hard places, like the supermarket, the cemetery, or a bad memory, I stood in the doorway and named five ordinary things I could see. The spoon on the bench. The smear of sunlight across the rug. The plant leaning toward the window like desire. The mug with a chip that looks like a country. The calendar with its honest little squares. Sometimes that was enough to keep me from drifting out of myself.

There were days I almost picked a fight with the past just to feel hot and certain again. Instead, I scrubbed the grout. I took the dog for a longer walk. I sent an apology I owed someone from months ago, two clean sentences and a full stop that felt like a stitch pulled through fabric. It held.

I wrote promises small enough to keep:

- I will drink water before coffee.

- I will not text ghosts after 9 p.m.

- I will let the sun touch my face for five minutes a day.

- I will speak to myself as if I loved me.

- I will ask for help when the floor tilts.

They didn't make me a hero. They made me a person. Sometimes becoming looked like grief getting clever and trying on new costumes. Loneliness would arrive wearing competence: Look how well you do it all by yourself. Shame would borrow tenderness's clothes: You're soft, which means you're weak, which means you'll be hurt again. I learned their tricks. I learned to answer softly and refuse the premise. "I am not a performance," I said to the bathroom mirror. "I am a body that stayed."

Poppy and I invented rituals because rituals give chaos

corners. Friday night pasta, too much parmesan, one terrible movie and one good one. Tuesday morning toast with jam in the car if we were running late, I called it "automotive breakfast" and pretended it was chic. We lit a cheap candle on the first day of every month and said one thing we wanted, even if it was as small as more naps or a good pen that doesn't scratch. We didn't call any of it healing. We just did it, and it helped.

There was a day I unrolled the rug and found a stain I couldn't remember making. Old me would have spun a story from it, some metaphor about damage. New me scrubbed it and, when it faded but didn't vanish, put the coffee table back on top and moved on. Not everything has to mean everything, I wrote in the notebook. Some things are just rug.

I started to like my own company in a way that felt suspicious and then, slowly, trustworthy. I took myself to a café with a book. The first fifteen minutes I watched couples and planned fake lives for them and nearly went home. Then the coffee arrived. Then the dog two tables over sneezed and everyone laughed. Then my shoulders dropped. I read one paragraph three times and enjoyed all three readings for different reasons. When I paid, the barista said, "See you next time?" and I said, "Yes," and meant it.

If you'd asked me then what becoming was, I would have said, a thousand quiet pivots. The moment I choose the walk over the scroll. The minute I put my phone in a drawer and let my hands remember how to be hands. The way I reach for the good cup because I am not saving nice things for a future where I am tidier, calmer, better. The way I put the second pillow back on the bed, not for someone else, for me.

There were apologies to make to myself. For the years I starved my own joy out of loyalty to someone else's comfort. For the times I told my body to hush when it begged me to leave. For mistaking chaos for love and endurance for virtue. I wrote them down like receipts and didn't ask for reimbursement. I just promised not to overspend my life the same way again.

On the first cool night of the new season, I opened every window and let the house trade its air. The curtains breathed. Somewhere a neighbour practised piano, just the left hand, hesitant, then certain, then hesitant again. I stood in the hallway listening to the wrong notes grow steadier and thought, that's me. Not the song. The willingness to keep playing it badly until it starts to sound like living.

The notebook kept widening inside. Less pleading, more participating. Less why me, more what now. I wrote a sentence I didn't see coming: I will stand with myself in every room I enter. Under it I added, Start with the smallest rooms. The kitchen. The car. The doctor's office. My own head.

I practised. In the kitchen, I cooked food my body could use. In the car, I drove myself to places that weren't emergencies. In the doctor's office, I let my voice be ordinary, not apologetic. In my own head, when the spiral began, I put down salt, little truths to help me find my way back. You are breathing. You are fed. You are loved by at least two people and a dog. The sky is doing something beautiful somewhere even if you can't see it from here.

A Sunday evening brought a test dressed as a kindness, an invitation I would once have said yes to because saying yes was how I mattered. I looked at the text and waited for the old reflex to grab the phone out of my hand. It didn't. "I can't," I typed, and put the phone face down and went to water the gerberas. When guilt came sniffing at the back door, I didn't let it in. I stood among flowers I'd kept alive and nodded at myself like a woman who recognises good work.

I kept track of my own beginnings. The first time I hummed in the shower again. The first time a song found me and I didn't change it. The first time my laugh arrived early to a joke and brought me with it. The first time I slept, not like a stone, but like a person who trusted the night to return her safely.

There are parts of the story that will never be tidy. The past doesn't owe me symmetry. But becoming gave me new math. I didn't need closure to move. I didn't need forgiveness to eat breakfast. I didn't need certainty to book the dentist. I needed breath, and a pen, and the next small verb.

At dusk the house exhaled and so did I. I wiped the bench clean, not because a clean bench saves anyone, but because it gave my hands a reason to stay. Then I pulled the notebook close, already open to a waiting page, and then I uncapped the pen and lowered the point to the paper. I didn't write a creed. I didn't write a plan. I wrote a promise small enough to keep: I will begin again tomorrow. The night gathered at the windows. Somewhere, a neighbour laughed. Far off, a siren went looking for someone else's emergency. I pressed my palm flat to the page, feeling the texture of paper, the stubborn presence of my own hand. "We're not done," I said, out loud this time, to the woman I was, to the ember I kept tending, to the life I was learning to live without apology.

The prayers had cracked something open. The becoming had given me breath, laughter, and space. But now came the hardest test, the test to stand alone, not against the world, but within it. To move through my days without leaning on death, on memory, or even on prayer as a prop. To carry myself into the daylight and hold, with both hands, the quiet fact of being here.

Tomorrow, I decided, I would practise. Fix one small thing

in the house that had waited for me. Book the dentist. Say yes to the walk, no to the obligation that made my chest tighten. Plant another gerbera just because. Not huge things. Proof-of-life things.

I closed the notebook, then left it open, the way you leave a door on the latch when you're expecting someone. The someone, I realised, was me.

And with that, I turned off the kitchen light, crossed the dim hallway, and stood for a second in the doorway of my own room, steady enough to enter as the woman I was becoming.

The next chapter would ask more of me. It always does. But tonight I could say it without flinching. I can stand. I can stand alone. And in the standing, I am not alone at all.

In the morning, I will take my first deliberate step into learning to stand alone.

Chapter Eighteen

Before I could grow, I had to test the ground under my own feet and see where it held, where it wobbled, and where it wanted roots.

Prayer didn't change the world around me overnight, but it helped to change my posture inside it. The day after I wrote I will not be silent, I tested what that meant at ground level. I made two phone calls I'd been dodging, the clinic to book bloods and the bank to face numbers I'd rather pretend were friendly. I opened the curtains before the guilt could close them again. I said out loud to the empty room, "We're staying," and for once my feet believed me.

The sentence didn't ring like triumph; it landed like furniture set properly on its legs. I could move around it without bracing.

Small declarations. Small actions. The scaffolding of a life that could hold my weight while I learned the rest.

I wrote the phrase in the margin of my notebook and underlined, Hold my weight. That was the assignment now, not perfection, not performance, just load-bearing.

Standing alone is not something you decide once. It's not a declaration shouted into the air that magically rearranges your days. It's smaller than that. Sharper. More ordinary. It's the way you steady yourself at the sink when there's no one left to hand you a towel. It's the way you lift the groceries even though your arms tremble. It's the way you answer the phone, make the appointment, sign the papers with only your name at the bottom. At first it felt like punishment, You wanted independence? Here, have it all at once. Slowly, painfully, it began to feel like practice. Practice meant repetitions. Repetitions meant a rhythm. And rhythm, unromantic as a metronome, kept me from bolting.

The first test came in the cereal aisle. Grief lives in supermarkets, and every shelf is a memory arranged by brand. For years I'd reached automatically for the box he liked, even when it wasn't mine. Now the cardboard stared me down, daring me to repeat the old choreography. My hands shook on the trolley handle. People drifted past with their own small lives and I said, barely above a breath, *"You don't live here anymore."* I left the box on the shelf and pushed on. It was a tiny rebellion, but my chest lifted as if I'd put down something heavier than wheat.

I picked a plain muesli and added dried apricots just because I could. A small, edible vote for myself.

Another day, a drip started in the laundry, patient, maddening, a metronome for the past. He had always promised to fix things 'on the weekend.' Weekends came and went and the house learned to live with the leakage. I Googled how to fix a leaking tap, watched a woman with neat nails unscrew a thing I didn't know had a name, and tried to copy her. The pliers' bit, my knuckle split, and the dog slunk away from my swearing. When the drip finally stopped, the silence sounded like applause. "Look at you," I told my mirror that night, grinning at my bandaged finger. "You stopped a drip. Maybe two."

In the hush that followed, I heard another sound, my own regard, unflinching for once.

Standing alone did not mean standing steady. There were collapses. I sobbed on the kitchen floor because the Wi-Fi wouldn't reset and I felt stupid for not knowing which button mattered. I screamed at the tax forms, crumpled them into a snowball of numbers and shame, then smoothed them out again like a scolded child. Each time, I noticed the same thing, I was the one who picked me up. No cavalry. No rescue. Just my own two shaking hands. It was humiliating, yes, but also, quietly, empowering. If I could survive broken Wi-Fi and bureaucracy, perhaps I could survive bigger things too.

I started keeping a tiny ledger on the fridge: "Fell apart / Stood up." Both columns collected ticks. Both counted.

Nights were the worst. The bed was a battlefield. I stuffed pillows into the empty shape, stacked books like barricades, let the dog sleep diagonally across the sheets as if he were a living sandbag against memory. The gap still yawned. I started talking aloud just to put a voice in the room.

Words kept the dark from inventing its own.

"You're doing it," I told the dark. "Badly, messily, but you are."

It became ritual, a sentence spoken before sleep like a spell to hold me through until morning.

Friends tried to help. Invites arrived for coffee, dinners, movie nights. At first I declined all of them. The thought of being the lone widow at a table of couples felt like being placed under a bell jar, their good intentions fogging the glass. Eventually I said yes to one. I sat across from a friend in a café that smelled of hot milk and cinnamon and realised I had come alone and that this was a fact, not a wound. The first sip tasted like defiance. I realised I didn't need a chaperone for my own life. I needed a chair and the price of a coffee.

"I'm proud of you," she said, squeezing my hand.

"Don't be," I started, out of old habit.

"I am," she said again, firmer.

I didn't cry. I didn't collapse. I stirred my coffee and let myself believe her.

Belief didn't roar; it just nodded quietly and stayed seated.

Standing alone also meant learning not to apologise for existing. I had spent years rounding my edges, filing down my opinions, making myself smaller to soothe a storm that could not be soothed. Now, with no one to appease, my voice returned with a rasp at first, then with tone.

Edges reappeared like coastline at low tide.

At the bank, when the clerk spoke to me as if I'd left my brain in the glovebox, I straightened. "Explain it properly, please," I said, not loud, just clean. "Or I'll take my business elsewhere."

At home, when Poppy asked what was for dinner, I said, "Whatever I make, or you can make your own," and did not rush to rescue her from the microwave.

These weren't speeches. They were reminders. To them and to me, that I was here, and that I take up space.

And space, once claimed, stops apologising for its borders.

I tested the edges of my solitude. I went to the movies by myself, sat in the back row with a popcorn the size of my head, laughed out loud when the scene earned it. The empty seat beside me pinched for the first twenty minutes, then loosened until it felt like freedom. I walked home under streetlights, humming, then wrote that night in my notebook: I am beginning to like my own company. The sentence scared me. It also thrilled me.

It read like contraband, and it felt like permission.

Of course, there were ghosts. Every time I managed something new, his old voice slithered up from habit: You'll never make it without me. I had an answer now.

"Watch me."

Sometimes I whispered it. Sometimes I said it out loud to the hallway because the house needed to hear it too.

The walls did not object.

The mirror softened. She was still tired, that woman, but a new line had etched itself beside her mouth, not sorrow but resolve. "You're standing," I told her one morning, touching the glass. "Not tall. Not straight. But up." She didn't answer. She didn't need to. Up was enough.

Standing alone didn't mean rejecting help, it meant choosing it. When my neighbour offered to mow the jungle my lawn had become, I said yes and baked him a loaf that collapsed in the middle but tasted like thanks. When another offered to fix the gutter, I said no. I wanted to try. It was a dance, leaning sometimes and planting my feet at other times. Strength, I learned, wasn't isolation. It was agency. And agency, I learned, is a muscle you only build by using.

An errand needed doing. The kind that turns the stomach for no good reason. I went anyway, waited my turn beneath fluorescent lights that made everyone look slightly unwell, and sat with my hands folded so I wouldn't fidget. When it was my turn, I listened, nodded, signed where they pointed, and paid without offering an explanation for existing. Outside, the radio caught me mid-step, a song I knew too well. One line still found the soft part of me. I turned the volume down and kept going. I filed the lyric under "tenderness tolerated." Progress.

At the clinic, I nearly didn't go in. The smell of antiseptic tugged a thread that connected directly to the part of me that wanted to run. "Just the bloods today," the nurse said with brisk kindness. "Vitamin D, B12, iron." Practical magic. I nodded and watched my own blood ribbon into the vial, evidence that my body was still a story being written, not a full stop.

On the way out I booked the follow-up before courage could leak.

I made a budget that didn't humiliate me. I cancelled two subscriptions I'd been too tired to notice were gnawing at my account like mice. I opened a savings account with a name that made me smile - Sunlight Fund - and moved twenty dollars into it. "It's nothing," the shame hissed. "It's a start," I answered, and the start was the point.

Every deposit said: I expect a future.

In the middle of one raw week, I took a free community workshop in basic home maintenance. Half the class were retirees who could build a shed blindfolded, and the other half were women like me, nursing the same embarrassed determination. The instructor placed a drill in my hands. It whirred like a small animal. "Steady," he said. "Let the tool do the work." My arms shook and the screw went in crooked, but it held. "Looks good," the woman next to me said. "Looks like progress," I said back, and we both grinned like thieves.

I went home and hung a picture without asking the past for permission.

I began to repair other small things around the house, like the wobbly kitchen chair, and the loose hinge on the cupboard that had been complaining for months. Every fix made a sound only I could hear, a click inside, a piece sliding into place. The house started to feel less like a museum of what had been and more like a workshop of what might be.

Hope, it turns out, loves a Phillips-head.

I bought a second-hand dresser and painted it the colour of the sea I grew up beside. The first coat looked like a mistake but by the third, it looked like a decision. I replaced the old handles with ones that fit my palm. At night, when I passed it on the way to brush my teeth, it felt like a conversation with the girl I had been before I learned to disappear.

She answered by staying.

I learned to eat like I was on my own side, early eggs, late apples, bread thick enough to hold butter and vegemite without apology. I sat at the table and ate with a fork, not over the sink with guilt. I opened the window while the kettle boiled and let air do what air does best, remind a room it's not a cave.

Even the curtains seemed relieved.

One Friday I took myself to the coast. The water wore its winter face, steel and honest. I stood on the sand and let the wind thread my hair into knots, then unthread them. People walked dogs, and children shrieked with the particular joy of not being cold yet. I said to the sea what I'd been saying to the mirror. "I'm still here." The sea did what the sea always does when faced with declarations. It kept arriving.

So I matched it, breath for wave, wave for breath.

On a Monday I went to the nursery and bought a trowel, potting mix, and packets of seeds I wasn't sure I deserved, gerberas (pink, because they look like they're trying), parsley, and snapdragons. The woman at checkout told me not to overwater them. "People drown them with love," she said, as if we both knew something else about that.

I promised the seedlings mercy measured, not mercy flooded.

Back home, I cleared a patch by the back fence. The ground was stubborn, but so was I. I turned the soil, finding bottle tops, a nail, and the small green marble Poppy had lost as a child. I set the marble on the windowsill. I pressed my palms into the earth and inhaled a smell older than any of us. "Teach me," I said to the dirt. "Teach me how to hold and let go at the same time."

The lesson came as patience, which is the same as saying slowness with purpose.

In the park, late afternoon, the light did that soft thing that looks like forgiveness even if it isn't. I felt the old presence at my shoulder, familiar now, like a shadow I knew by name. I turned as if to face him. "You don't get to drive," I said, not angry, just done. "You can follow. I'm walking." I headed down the path, leaves breaking under my boots like thin stained glass. My breath fogged in the air. Proof of life.

The path did not shorten for my declaration, but it welcomed my feet anyway.

By the end of that season, I could feel it in my bones, that I wasn't just surviving, I was learning. Learning how to pay bills without panicking. Learning how to carry grief without drowning in it. Learning how to laugh without apology. Learning how to breathe without asking permission. Learning to stand.

Learning, I wrote, is a form of love.

There was a day, I can't say exactly when, when the house sounded different. Not quieter, not louder. Just more mine. The chair didn't groan at the same place, and the floorboard that used to complain under his step was still, as if it had decided it could stop bracing for impact. I poured tea, leaned against the counter, and realised I was steady without holding on. Steady has a temperature, and I was learning it.

I wrote a list titled What held today and added:

- My breath, through the whole cup of tea.
- My boundary, when guilt rattled it and I didn't open the

door.

- My voice, even at the bank.

- My feet, through the long aisle where I left his cereal behind.

- My hands, steady enough to fix a drip and plant a seed.

I stuck the list to the fridge and every time I reached for milk I read it again, letting the verbs weigh more than the doubts. Verbs, I decided, are anchors with handles.

Standing alone became less about defiance and more about rhythm. The morning, I woke before my alarm and didn't dread the hours. The afternoon I napped because I could. The evening, I said yes to a walk and no to an obligation that tightened my chest. I started calling these choices proof-of-life, the small decisions plants make every day to turn toward light, to take what you need, and to keep growing even if last night was cold.

And when the night was cold again, I kept a blanket at the end of the bed and a list at the end of the day.

One late Sunday, rain shouldered in across the suburb and the gutters finally remembered their job. I stood under the eaves breathing petrichor and felt a simple, accurate thought, *I can look after this house.* It wasn't a boast. It was a pact with four walls and a roof, and the woman who lived under them.

We signed it with a dry towel and a swept step.

The next morning, I woke to the kind of sky that makes promises. I opened the back door and stepped onto the path I had swept the night before. The soil in my small patch was dark, ready. The packets of seed waited like quiet daredevils on the table. I knelt, pressed a line into the earth, and began.

Beginning, I've learned, is a plural. You do it more than once.

This was the exit I hadn't known I was walking toward, the

garden as metaphor made literal. Readiness to plant. Readiness to root. Readiness to believe that what I put into the ground with my own hands might answer me back in colour.

A reckless, necessary hope.

I wasn't fearless. I was willing.

I covered the seeds, watered lightly, don't drown them with love, and sat on the step with dirt under my nails and a dog leaning against my calf. The yard looked exactly the same as it had an hour earlier. The world did not break into applause. But something in me unclenched, the smallest click of truth into place.

The quiet said: Now we wait.

I could stand. I could stand alone. And because I could stand, I could plant.

Tomorrow would bring its errands and its ghosts. But today there was a narrow bed of newly turned soil and a woman who had taught herself how to walk through a house without apologising to the furniture. The first true work of standing had been done.

The rest would bloom in its own time.

And when the first green nub lifts the crust of earth like a soft shoulder, I will call it by its real name, proof that standing makes room for bloom.

Chapter Nineteen

Before the first colour returned to my life, there was a pause, a thin hush where the world seemed to hold its breath and wait to see if I would, too.

It began quietly, as most resurrections do. Not with fireworks or choirs or any single turning point. It began with something smaller, something I almost missed, a geranium blooming in a pot I had forgotten to water.

I almost stepped past it, the way you step past your own reflection in a window at night, aware of a presence, unsure you want to meet it.

I found it one morning on the back step, petals pressed open to the sun, bright and unapologetic. It shouldn't have survived. I had left it dry for weeks, too lost in my own drought to notice its thirst. Yet there it was, crimson against the pale clay, announcing, life will have its way.

The declaration didn't argue with my grief, it simply just refused to ask permission.

For a long moment I just stared, mug of cold coffee trembling in my hand. Then I laughed. Not because it was funny, because it was outrageous. This tiny plant, against all my neglect, had decided to bloom anyway.

Outrage has its own kind of mercy, the ability to wake the sleeping parts and makes them look.

"Show-off," I said, and touched the petal with one fingertip as if I might startle it back into hiding.

The petal held. So, unexpectedly, did I. Maybe I could

bloom, too. Not as spectacle. As insistence. Not as a performance to convince the world, just a private agreement with breath.

At first, blooming felt suspicious. Dangerous, even. As if joy were an uninvited guest barging into a house still draped in black. I would feel it creep up, a laugh at a ridiculous meme my sister sent, a sigh when the dog pressed her warm weight against my calves at night and immediately scold myself. How dare you?

Rituals of caution are hard to break, and I began by loosening them a single knot at a time.

But life doesn't ask for permission. It sneaks in through hairline cracks, lays down a rug in rooms you were sure were condemned, and then makes a home in soil you were sure was barren. I caught myself humming while folding laundry. I opened the curtains just to watch the sky change its mind from grey to blue. I lingered in the grocery store flower aisle, fingertips grazing stems like a woman choosing her future.

All modest acts, each one a petal. Together, a beginning.

Grief kept its seat, sharp as broken glass under bare feet. Blooming didn't replace it, blooming learned to step beside it. Dark and light, woven.

The loom was ordinary time, and the thread, stubborn breath.

One morning I wrote a list in my journal. It wasn't profound: bread, petrol, dog food. At the bottom, almost without thinking, I added: Find something beautiful today.

Beauty, I discovered, answers to invitations written in small handwriting.

I didn't know what I meant until later, walking to the letterbox, when I noticed the jacaranda spilling purple confetti over the street. The colour clung to my shoes, staining them. For the first time in months, I didn't curse the mess. I stood under the rain of blossoms, arms loose at my sides, eyes closed, letting them fall across my hair, my shoulders, my broken pieces.

Some ceremonies choose you, and your only job is to stand inside them.

Here it is, I thought. Something beautiful.

The words felt like cool water on a fevered tongue.

The tears came soft, a salt gloss sliding into a reluctant smile.

Reluctant, yes, but it arrived.

Blooming didn't mean I was healed. Far from it. Nights still clawed at me with their old nails. Silence still pressed its heavy hands against my chest. Some mornings I woke convinced I had stumbled back into the pit.

What changed was the compass, this time, I knew which way was out.

What changed was this, even in the pit, I could smell flowers. Memory of scent is sometimes stronger than the bloom itself.

At first, it was subtle, the way sunlight pooled in corners like honey, the way birds dared to sing when my world was ash. Then, gradually, I participated. I bought a new pillow and didn't feel guilty. I cooked on purpose, seasoning for pleasure and not survival. I played music in the kitchen, songs with a pulse that made my hips sway before my mind could scold me.

Participation is the opposite of disappearance.

One evening I caught myself in the oven door, hair undone, and cheeks flushed from dancing badly with the dog, and instead of recoiling, I smiled. Not the old smile. Crooked, imperfect, alive.

It fit my face like something I'd finally grown into.

"Okay," I told the stranger-me, "I see you."

Naming is the first kindness.

My family noticed, because family always do.

They're the weathervanes of a house.

"Something's different about you," Poppy said one afternoon, squinting at me over the rim of her juice glass.

"What do you mean?" I asked, wary.

She shrugged, searching for words too big for her age. "You don't look… as sad. You still look sad, but also… lighter."

Her honesty pierced me. Children don't lie about this sort of thing.

"I'm trying," I said, and my voice cracked. "I'm trying to be here with you. Really here."

She climbed into my lap and pressed her forehead to mine. "I know," she whispered.

Every stubborn breath I'd fought for felt worth it.

And worth, I realised, is measured in presence.

I began planting again. Herbs on the kitchen windowsill, basil, mint, and parsley. Then flowers in the garden bed that had gone feral while I stopped caring. I dug my fingers into soil, dirt blackening the crescents of my nails, sweat at the nape of my neck, and felt a pulse of something primal answer back.

It was not eloquent. It was real.

"You're still alive," I told the earth. "And so am I."

The ground kept my secret and returned it as green.

The garden answered in its own time, shoots pushing through, colours daring to exist. Each sprout felt like a conversation between me and whatever keeps the world turning. Each bloom a small promise that there is still life left to live. And slowly, I began to believe it.

Promises are light things until you hold them, and then they weigh you to the world in the best way.

One Saturday at the farmers' market I caught myself bargaining with a woman over peaches, both of us laughing when the bag grew too heavy for the price. She slipped an extra fruit into my hand as if I'd passed a private test. "You look like you need sweetness," she said, and I did not argue. I walked to the car with the peaches perfuming the air and thought, *So this is what returning feels like*, sticky and ordinary and a little unbelievable.

I licked juice from my wrist and let the day forgive me for enjoying it.

Of course, blooming brought guilt. How could I laugh while others still cried for him? How could I plant roses when his body lay in the ground? How could I dare to live fully when his choice had ended his life so abruptly?

Guilt is a fervent priest, and it wants sacrifice, not ceremony.

One night the guilt pressed so hard I sat on the shower floor, sobbing into the steam. "I'm sorry," I told the tiled walls. "I'm sorry I get to be here when you're not. I'm sorry I keep breathing, keep eating, keep laughing. I'm sorry for the life in me."

I let the apology run until it emptied itself.

The water hissed louder, white noise, or answer. In that rush I heard his voice the way mercy sometimes sounds, not like a memory exactly, but like a reprieve.

Stop apologising. You don't owe me your silence. You don't owe me your suffering. Live. If you can, live.

Was it real? Does it matter? I chose to believe it. Belief is sometimes the handrail you install yourself.

Handrails save ankles and afternoons, and I gripped this one with both hands.

Blooming was not linear. Some days the petals closed tight. Some days I felt wilted, crushed under a heat I couldn't bear. But even then, the memory of colour lingered. Even then, the knowledge remained. I have bloomed before. I can bloom again.

Resilience is repetition with hope inside it.

Flowers are fragile, they bruise, bend, and wither. They are also relentless, season after season insisting that beauty is worth the risk. Maybe that was becoming my truth, too.

Fragile and relentless, both, an accurate diagnosis.

I started keeping tiny rituals like talismans. A spoon of honey stirred into tea with patience instead of hurry. A long inhale at the back door before the day could climb me like ivy. A ten-minute amble around the block with no destination, just a promise to notice one kind thing, a mailman whistling, a dog leaning its whole belief system against a fence, and a pair of elderly hands folding napkins in a kitchen window. My body learned these were safe instructions. This is how we inhabit a day, the rituals said. Not grandly. Faithfully.

Faithful is a verb.

On a Tuesday I took the long road home and stopped at the nursery, just to look. A row of gerberas held themselves like small suns, each face in a different shade of glad. I didn't buy any. I stood and let them look at me. Perhaps it's ridiculous to feel seen by a flower. Then again, perhaps it's the point.

Recognition doesn't always require words.

One morning I faced the mirror and, for the first time, did not search it for a ghost. The woman staring back wasn't the one who begged for breath, who raged at silence, who courted the shadow at her shoulder. She was new. Tender. Scarred. Blooming.

"Keep going," I mouthed. She didn't flinch.

"You're still here," I whispered.

For once, the voice inside me didn't argue.

Agreement, it turned out, is a kind of grace.

Life became a patchwork of contradictions: grief and laughter, memory and hope, tears and music, ashes and blossoms. Instead of tearing me apart, the contradictions stitched me back together. Blooming wasn't erasing the past. It was weaving it into the present and carrying the ashes in one hand, and the flowers in the other. Living not in spite of loss but alongside it.

Two hands. That's what I have. That's what I'll use.

I painted the hallway a colour I'd never had the nerve to choose before, soft green, like a held breath. The first coat looked wrong, and suspicious, like a bad idea. The second settled itself, and by the third the house exhaled as if relieved I'd finally asked it to be something other than faithful witness. I hammered a small nail into the wall and hung a frame with nothing in it yet. Not because I had something to display. Because I believed I would.

Sometimes the future needs a hook.

By spring the garden was riotous. Bees wove drunken paths. Butterflies hovered like floating prayers. Colours clashed and collided in unapologetic abundance. I stood in the centre of it, dirt embedded in my fingerprints, and the scene blurred into watercolour. Not sad tears, grateful ones.

Gratitude watered places I'd been afraid to touch.

This was mine. This blooming, fragile, resilient life. Mine to waste or to treasure.

For the first time, I wanted to treasure it.

Wanting is a threshold and I stepped over it.

I started buying flowers when there was no occasion. Not to celebrate, not to apologise, and not to decorate. Just because. I'd cut their stems, slide them into a jar, and set them where I would trip over their colour.

"Make a nuisance of yourselves," I told them. "Don't let me forget."

"That's right," I'd tell them, half-teasing, half-serious. "Show me how it's done."

They did. A cosmos leaning toward light. A daisy refusing symmetry. A ranunculus unspooling like a secret. Lessons I could hold in water.

I became a willing student.

The world, of course, still contained its sharp edges. Paperwork in stiff envelopes. A scent that ambushed me in a crowd, and his cologne on a stranger. The way dusk sometimes reopened rooms I had already locked. On those days I returned to the small practices that steadied me, open a window, finish the cup of tea, step outside barefoot and let the air say my name.

When in doubt: air and light.

"Stay," I told myself. "Just today, stay."

And most days, I did.

Staying, I learned, is a skill.

I began to say yes to invitations that once felt like tests. A friend took me to a Sunday market on the river. We ate dumplings and sat on splintered steps watching a busker play a violin that sounded like a conversation between weather fronts.

"You're glowing," she said, and I rolled my eyes, but I could feel it too, some low light turned on inside me, not for display, just for navigation.

It was enough to see by.

Another afternoon I took myself to lunch with a book and no plan for where to put my hands. Eating alone once felt like evidence of failure and now it felt like proof of trust. I ordered exactly what I wanted and stayed long enough to watch the table next to me first flirt, then bicker, then laugh again. I didn't envy them. I blessed them, quietly, for being alive in public.

Blessing others, I found, made more room inside me.

I painted my toenails with a colour called peony and left two smudges on the bathmat because grace doesn't always dry before we walk on it. I bought sunblock because I planned to have a future to wrinkle in. I opened the wardrobe and gave away a dress that had always been a costume. When the charity shop volunteer asked if I wanted a receipt, I thought, For what? For letting go? I shook my head and walked out lighter.

Letting go, I decided, was its own proof of purchase.

The garden taught me the rest. That roots grow in darkness long before anyone sees green. That pruning is kindness, and that deadheading is not cruelty but invitation. That some seeds sleep a year before they decide it's safe to break open.

So I gave myself a year, and then another if needed.

I walked the beds at dusk, fingers light on leaves, listening. Plants don't speak, but they have a way of answering.

"Keep going," the geranium seemed to say, the original survivor nodding at me from its clay cup. "You think you're fragile. You are also built to bloom."

I touched the warm terracotta. "Thank you for waiting," I said. "I didn't know how to meet you here."

The breeze lifted the edges of my shirt like a small benediction.

Some blessings don't require names.

Sometimes I still felt the old shadow step close, a death at my shoulder, patient as ever. "Not today," I would murmur, not unkindly. "You can walk behind me if you like. But I'm busy."

Busy watering. Busy laughing at nothing with the dog. Busy

choosing peaches because they smelled like Augusts from another life. Busy texting my sister made it through the afternoon. Busy standing in the doorway, watching evening pool in the garden like ink, and letting the quiet fill without swallowing me.

It turns out you can be busy with staying.

And staying is sometimes the bravest job.

I learned that joy is not a mood, it's a practice. I failed at it often. But failure, too, became part of the ritual, like the way a rose drops its head and is still unmistakably a rose. On days I couldn't manage delight, I tried for gentleness. On days I couldn't manage gentleness, I tried for neutrality. On the worst days, I tried for a nap.

Naps, I discovered, resurrect small kingdoms.

When Poppy brought home a school project, a seed in a wet cotton ball pressed into a jar, I treated it like a relic. We watched it split and wriggle free, the shy thrust of root searching for a foothold. "It's doing it!" she said, thrilled. I nodded and tried not to cry. "It is," I whispered. "It is."

Beginnings are embarrassing and holy. We applauded anyway.

In the kitchen I hung a string across the window and clipped photos and recipe cards and one square of paper that simply read: Find one kind thing. Under it I tucked a picture of Poppy and I at the beach, hair punished by wind, eyes punishing nothing. When I made mistakes, the string held steady, as if to say: You will not fall far. There is structure here.

I added a second square: Remember softness.

By late spring I could feel a new question forming, less like an interrogation, and more like an invitation. Blooming had made the room airy, but shadows still crouched in corners, old fears with new masks, and unspoken stories whispering from the baseboards. Survival had given me breath. Becoming had given me spine. Blooming had given me appetite. Now something else asked to be named.

It pressed the way a story presses before it chooses its first line.

One afternoon, rain rehearsed on the roof and the dog elected to become a rug at my feet. I took a pen and sat at the back step while the geranium kept its crimson counsel. "What story am I telling about myself?" I asked the wet air. The question landed with a weight that didn't crush. For once, it felt like I had time to answer.

Time, for once, felt like company rather than judge.

The house breathed with me, the kettle's shy hiss, the fridge's patient hum, the gutter's sudden confidence as water remembered the path it had always known. I watched the lemon tree collect drops like beads and the lawn pretend it had not flirted with yellow a week ago. The garden was full of small liars and faithful truths.

I decided I could be faithful, too.

"Okay," I told the sky, the dirt, the stubborn life that keeps kneading itself into the day. "Okay."

Consent, whispered to the world and to myself.

I went inside and rinsed the soil from my hands. I wiped the bench because lint had stuck to a ring of tea, because motion is kinder than stillness sometimes, and because tending the surface makes room for what lives underneath. Then I pulled out the notebook I'd been avoiding, the one with pages that knew too much. On a blank sheet I wrote: Find one kind thing. Beneath it I wrote, smaller: Tell the truth faster.

Truth, I'd learned, blooms best in uncluttered rooms.

I stood at the back door before bed and looked out at the dark that wasn't empty. The geranium watched me from its pot, outrageous as ever. Somewhere a neighbour laughed. Somewhere a siren asked the night to move aside. I closed the door softly, as if the house were a body asleep and I loved it enough to keep quiet.

Love, as it turns out, is often quiet.

Tomorrow would come with its envelopes and errands, its surprises and traps, its good coffee if I went looking, its stubbed toes if I didn't pay attention. I would forget and remember and forget again. I would make something edible and burn something else. I would stand up and sit down and, if I could manage it, lie down before midnight like a person who trusts morning to return.

That trust was new. I chose it anyway.

I turned off the last light and felt the room hold. Breath went in and out without asking me to sign for it. Somewhere in that patient movement, a decision set, blooming had not been an accident. It was an agreement.

Agreements can be renewed. I planned to renew mine daily.

Tomorrow, I thought, I will face what still haunts me.

And before I face it, I will ask, gently, and without apology, What story am I telling about myself? If it's too small, I'll plant a bigger one.

Then, in the quiet that follows, I will name it.

And after I name it, I will begin to tell it, the first bright thread in the story of a girl.

Chapter Twenty

I was woven together in the secret of my mother's womb.

Long before anyone spoke my name, I had already been named by the universe, by love itself. I was seen, known, and cherished even before my first cry. I was held by something bigger than words, before I even knew what it meant to hold myself.

And years later, I felt that same knowing when I carried my daughter.

Before I ever spoke Poppy's name aloud, before she learned air, she too had already been named, by love, by something ancient and watchful. I knew it in my body. I knew it in the quiet certainty that settled over me when she moved. She was seen. She was known. She was cherished.

But life has a way of covering that first truth with layers of weather: a long winter here, a bad harvest there, an early frost nobody could have predicted. The bright beginning did not disappear. It was simply buried for a while.

The girl I became was not the glossy figure from magazine covers. I was messy, imperfect, and startlingly human. My hair tangled easily, my nails chipped, and my feet bore the stains of dirt roads and barefoot wandering. Sometimes I wore the same clothes for days, too tired to care. I was clumsy in my movements, awkward in my laughter, and often out of step with the world's rhythm. I loved the wrong songs too loudly and the right people too hard. I cried at advertisements and kept the tags from birthday presents as if they were wedding rings.

When I opened a magazine, I saw the opposite of myself -

women polished to a shine, smiling with an ease I didn't recognise. My reflection told another story, a story that consisted of knobbly knees, freckled arms, and scars scattered like constellations across my skin. A body shaped by survival, not by perfection. A face that carried weather maps of where I'd been.

And yet, I was good enough.

Good enough for the One who strung stars where night needed company. Good enough for the One who painted oceans and asked them to keep breathing. Good enough for the ordinary miracle that kept my heart beating even when I begged it to stop.

I was never too much. I was never not enough. I was exactly what I was meant to be.

But people didn't always see me that way. Some days the world felt like a chorus that only knew one song, and it was not mine. They taunted me, rejected me, and misnamed me. They mocked the very things that set me apart , my laugh that startled birds, my love that arrived like a flood, and my difference that refused camouflage. My heart, too soft to withstand cruelty, cracked under the weight. I carried scars, not just on my skin, but deep inside of me as well, delicate fractures that light would later find.

Forgiveness, then, felt impossible. My love soured into bitterness. Sarcasm became armour. Sharp words became a habit that masqueraded as safety. I learned to cut first before anyone could cut me. I stood in doorways with folded arms and dared people to enter. I told myself I didn't need anyone, and at night I wept because I did.

Still, some small part of me, stubborn as a weed in concrete, longed to be known.

One night, staring at my own reflection in the mirror,

freckles, tears, scars, I whispered, "Forgive them." The words tasted like broken glass. "Forgive them for the way they treated me. Forgive them for not seeing me. Forgive them, because I don't have the strength to."

The night gave no applause. No dove descended, and no sky tore open. But in the quiet that followed, something unknotted by a fraction. Not lightning. Dawn. A light inching through cracks, a softness testing the locked door.

After that, forgiveness did not come as a river. It came as a cup of water carried carefully down a hallway that tilted. I spilled most of it, but I kept walking anyway.

Each time I stumbled forward, reaching for a hand stronger than my own, even when the only hand nearby was my own, broken pieces of me began to fall away. Beneath the shards, something new emerged. My stubbornness, once a wall, learned how to become a backbone. My anger, once a wildfire, became a small, steady flame for justice. My sarcasm softened into wit that sparked laughter instead of harm. My scars learned a second language. They began to whisper to other people's scars; *you're not alone.*

I was still clumsy. Still scarred. Still imperfect. But perfection was never the point. Wholeness was. And wholeness doesn't come from denying the cracks, it comes from letting the light shine through them, from learning which fractures are fault lines, and which are skylights.

I was no longer the girl who mistook weeds for flowers. I was no longer the girl who thought I had to wear a mask to be loved.

Now, I am a woman in bloom, fierce, tender, complicated, and free. I can dance barefoot in the rain and let the cold kiss my shins without apologising. I can laugh until tears streak my face. I can cry without shame, rage without apology, and love without a leash. I am both broken and whole. Both ashes and fire.

And now I am a mother.

The story of the girl is my story, but it is also Poppy's inheritance. It belongs to every girl who ever believed she was too messy, too scarred, and too different to be worthy. Every girl who folded herself into polite shapes to fit spaces never meant for her. Every girl who carried shame in her body and silenced her joy because someone flinched at its volume.

In telling it, I give her, and them, permission to unfold.

My story became their story. And in telling it, I began to understand that this telling mattered, not just for me, but for the girls who would come after me. Including my own.

But stories rarely move in straight lines. They are more like rivers, curving, doubling back, and gathering silt and sweetness along the way.

I grew from that girl into a woman who doubted herself often, who looked into mirrors and sometimes saw only damage. On those days I turned away from my own face like it was a room where a fight had just happened. Yet there were other days when I saw strength in the set of my jaw, resilience in the way I kept standing when gravity campaigned against me.

I remembered the names I had been called, ugly, useless, crazy, weak. Words that cut canals through me. But I also remembered the names whispered in quieter moments, brave, kind, strong, needed. Those canals, it turned out, were not only for pain. They could conduct light, too.

It wasn't a fairytale transformation. I didn't wake one morning radiant, healed, and untouchable. No. Healing came like wildflowers through cracked pavement, slow, stubborn, and surprising. It arrived disguised as small mercies like an unexpected laugh at a joke that wasn't that good, a full night's sleep that didn't hold knives, the ability to sit with silence and not shatter, and the defiance of breathing when every cell screamed don't.

I became the kind of woman who could carry contradictions easily: grief and joy, fragility and ferocity, past and present, tenderness and teeth. I stopped demanding that the pieces fit neatly together. Instead, I let them stand side by side, imperfect but whole, like mismatched chairs around a table that nonetheless held dinner.

On Tuesdays I wrote lists that would never impress anyone and saved my life anyway: bread, bin out, ring the dentist, text back, water the plant. On Thursdays I forgot the list and survived that, too. I learned the shape of my own permission. I learned where to place a no so that a yes down the road could breathe.

Sometimes I bought myself flowers for no other reason but colour. Sometimes I left dishes in the sink because I was tired and chose to be a person instead of a martyr. Sometimes I returned to the old puddles and didn't jump in. Sometimes I did, and then laughed at the mess.

I did not become a saint. I became honest.

There was a night under a sky thick with stars when I decided not to ask for anything. I lay on the grass and let the earth take some of my weight. The dog snored softly at my feet, and a plane stitched a white scar through the dark. I whispered, not to be heard, but to be real, *"Thank you for making me me. For the freckles. For the scars. For the stubbornness that kept me alive. For the laugh that sometimes embarrasses me. Thank you for it all. Because it makes me who I am. And who I am... is enough."*

The stars said nothing, as stars do. Their steadiness was answer enough.

That night, I slept like a person who had chosen her own company.

In the days that followed, that quiet stayed with me, not loud or triumphant, just present. It settled into my body and made space for remembering without breaking.

There are pictures I keep in a shoebox at the back of the wardrobe. In one, I'm five in a yellow dress, gap-toothed, hair in a reckless halo the brush surrendered to. My knees are dirty. I'm holding a snail like it's a precious jewel. I look straight into the camera with unedited trust.

When I found that photo after the funeral, I sat on the floor and cried for the small person I had once been, and for the ways I had left her waiting. "I'm coming," I told her. "I'm late, but I'm coming."

The girl in the picture doesn't roll her eyes. She believes people when they say they're on their way.

These days I'm learning to keep my word to her. And to the girl who lives under my roof now. I buy the good crayons. I let singing happen even when the words are wrong. I take Poppy for ice cream on days that don't deserve it, because she does. Because we do.

Once, at a roadside café, I watched two teenage girls trying to fold themselves into smaller versions of themselves under the gaze of someone impatient. They weren't loud. The world just makes even small sounds look big when they come from girls. When the impatient voice went to the counter, one of them rested her head on the other's shoulder and exhaled like she'd been holding her breath since Tuesday.

I wanted to hand them a sentence like a sandwich: *You are allowed to take up space.* Instead, I left a note on their table, three words that used to be the whole of my hunger: *You are enough.*

Driving away, I felt ridiculous and brave in equal measure. Maybe that's what growing up is, doing the thing that helps a stranger and heals your younger self at the same time. Doing it quietly, without applause.

Becoming myself has required a thousand ungorgeous choices. I started with food that loved me back. I answered messages with honest brevity: Can't talk today. Thinking of you. I drew boundaries that made no sound but changed the air. I said no and the world did not collapse. I said yes to things that scared me and discovered the fear had exaggerated its own height.

On good afternoons I write lists titled *What Held Today* and stick them on the fridge with a magnet:

- My breath, through the whole cup of tea.

- My voice, when I asked for clarity at the bank.

- The sky, stubbornly blue when it could've been cruel.

- Me.

On bad afternoons I write different lists titled *What Needs Kindness*:

- My body (feed it).

- My brain (rest it).

- My heart (tell it the truth, then tuck it in).

Sometimes the lists are the only proof I have that I exist. Sometimes they're a flag on a hill I've already climbed.

Forgiveness keeps circling back like a stray. Some days I welcome it with a saucer of milk, and on other days I hiss and shut the door. People think forgiveness means pretending it didn't matter. For me, it means saying it mattered, and choosing to stop carrying what isn't mine. I forgave slowly, out of order, and badly. I forgave the easy things too soon and the hard things too late. I forgave myself last. When I finally did, the house inside me changed its lock.

There are setbacks. There always are. A smell in a supermarket aisle can crack me open. A word in a song can become a small, sharp blade. In those moments the old instincts return, the urge to disappear, to apologise for existing, and to mistake numbness for peace. I've learned to pause at the sink, hands braced, and say out loud, "Stay." The word itself has become a porch light I can find from the street.

I used to think strength looked like stainless steel. It turns out it looks like a garden hose, flexible and ordinary, and making green things possible. It looks like a woman who goes to the dentist and keeps the appointment. Like unclenching my jaw before opening the door. Like catching myself mid-apology and turning the sentence into a statement. Like laughing and not checking the room for permission.

The garden taught me that progress hides. Roots work in the dark. Buds form while you're busy believing nothing is happening. I planted herbs on the windowsill and gerberas by the back step, pink as good gossip. When the first flower turned itself inside out, I saluted it with my coffee. "Show-off," I said, and meant thank you.

I practise meeting my reflection like a friend I'm still getting to know. We have a ritual now. "Good morning," I tell her. I name three things we've survived together, then one thing we might enjoy. *Survive, enjoy.* Not the same verb, and that's the point.

I stopped waging war against my face and started hosting it. I moisturise not to reverse time, but to be kind to the skin that kept the rain out. I wear lipstick on Tuesdays because why should Friday have all the fun? When a stranger catches me reapplying in the car and smiles, I smile back, not because I seek approval, but because joy is a contagion I don't mind spreading. I keep a jar of glitter nail polish for no occasion at all.

You should know I am still learning. I still trip the same wires some days. I still want to call the wrong person when the night gets tall. I still make bargains with the past and cancel them at dawn. I still sometimes mistake martyrdom for love. But I recognise the costume faster now. I change back into myself more quickly.

On a day that could have gone either way, I drove to the coast alone. The water wore its winter face, steel, and honest. I let the wind thread my hair into knots, and then unthread them. I walked to the edge where sand forgets it's sand and becomes willingness. "I'm still here," I told the sea. It didn't clap. It kept arriving. Somehow, that was better.

I ate hot chips with too much vinegar and didn't apologise to my tongue. I watched three teenage boys dare each other to jump from the rocks and thought about how close courage and foolishness often sit on the same bench. I thought of the girl I had been. The mother I am. The woman I am becoming. I drove home with the windows down and the radio up and let the afternoon make of me what it wanted, a person, unremarkable and alive.

Sometimes people ask me what changed, like there was a switch I can point to, a sentence I can hand them that will do the work. I wish there were. But this is the truest answer I have, Nothing changed. And yet everything did.

No miracle arrived with fanfare. No letter came stamped *Permission Granted*. What changed was the accumulation of small, stubborn choices, the next right thing, the next right breath, the next kind word to the girl I used to be. And to the girl watching me now.

What changed was how I narrated my life to myself. I stopped telling the story where I was the villain or the ghost. I wrote a truer script: I am a woman who is learning. I am allowed to take up space. I do not owe anyone my vanishing.

What changed was the direction of my looking. Less backward for proof. More inward for permission. More outward for colour.

I look at myself now, still scarred, still imperfect, still learning, and I see both the girl I was and the woman I am becoming. I am no longer weeds pretending to be flowers. I am no longer a mask pretending to be a face. I am no longer silence pretending to be peace.

I am bloom and thorn. I am laughter and scar. I am unfinished…and enough.

My story isn't finished. But I understand something now that I didn't before, and that is that I don't have to become someone else to be loved. I only have to become myself. And that is more than enough.

In learning to love the girl I had been, I began to dream of the woman I could become, not a copy of someone else's idea of goodness or beauty, but my own. Strong. Graceful. Unapologetic. Alive. Not a woman without history, but a woman who can carry hers without it dislocating her shoulder.

If you ask me where the girl went, I'll tell you the secret I'm only just brave enough to say out loud, and that is, she didn't go anywhere. She grew. She made room. She learned to stay.

And on days when I forget, I pull down the shoebox, look the five-year-old in the yellow dress straight in the eyes, and say,

"Look at us. We made it this far." She grins that gap-toothed grin like she never doubted it. She never did. She was waiting for me to catch up all along.

I'm still catching up. I think that's what living is.

Some nights I step outside and the sky is a deep, impossible blue, the kind that makes you believe in tomorrow without evidence. The dog sniffs something very important by the fence. A neighbour's laughter slips over the hedge. I tip my head back, breathe in the ordinary miracle of oxygen, and whisper, to the girl, to the woman, to my daughter, to whatever is listening and whatever is not: "Thank you for making me me. For all of it."

Then I go back inside and do the next small, sacred thing like, wash a cup, text a friend, water a plant, or set an alarm I intend to keep. The life I am building isn't glamorous. It is real. It is mine.

And the girl, the one who once thought she had to be someone else to be loved, gets to live here with me now.

Chapter Twenty-One

I was never meant to stay a girl forever.

The girl who counted freckles like constellations and wore scabs like medals, the girl who hid her laughter in her sleeves and learned to read a room before she could read a clock, she carried me as far as she could. I owe her that. But every scar I earned, every laugh I fought to keep, every breath I clawed back from the edge was shaping me into something larger than girlhood. Into womanhood. Not the paper-doll version that tears at the seams, but the kind that grows roots, quiet, stubborn, and real.

And now, when I look at Poppy, I see it beginning again. That same fierce becoming. That same tenderness trying to survive a world that would rather tame it.

We were never born just to be pretty. We were never born just to be pleasing. We were born to be women, whole, wild, resilient, and uncontainable.

From the time we're small, the world hands us a script in fine print that reads, be quiet, be sweet, be agreeable, be desirable. Don't be too loud. Don't be too angry. Don't take up too much space. Measure your worth by mirrors and milestones, by rings and recipes, by how easily you smooth a man's rough day and how quickly you swallow your own. Smile. Soften. Stay.

But the truth runs deeper than any script.

Womanhood is not a costume to wear; it is a capacity to hold. It is strength without spectacle, the kind that rises after nights that should have broken us. It is tenderness without apology, the kind that cradles children, or strangers, or the shivering animal of our own hearts. It is the fierce instinct to protect, to nurture, and to speak when silence would be easier. It is grace, not as politeness, but as dignity. Not a performance, but a presence.

I think of the women who made me possible.

My mother, whose hands still remember the shape of my fevered forehead. My grandmother, who measured life in teaspoons and hymns and survived by laughing too loudly in kitchens. And behind them, a line of women I will never meet, women who birthed babies in storms, who stitched the same skirt three times because money was air and always running out, who stood in doorways and said no with their bodies when no one else would.

They were not flawless. They were not polished. They were stubborn and contradictory and messy and good.

They carried me here inside their unfinishedness. And whether they know it or not, they are carrying Poppy too.

They taught me, without speeches, that womanhood is a symphony, not a solo. That a woman can carry grief in one hand and laughter in the other. That truth spoken gently can still shake a house. That tenderness is not the opposite of power, but that it is a kind of power. That endurance is not the point. Resurrection is.

For years, I forgot.

I shrank myself to fit inside his weather. I made myself smaller to soothe storms I did not cause. I kept the peace by swallowing my own. I measured my value by whether or not a man stayed, as if love were a test and I was always on the verge of failing.

I thought being a woman meant endurance at any cost.

But standing here now, scarred, imperfect, alive, and with my daughter watching how I stand, I know better.

Being a woman is not about how well we endure harm. It is about how fiercely we rise after it. It is about reclaiming our own names, our own laughter, and our own voices. It is about inhabiting both softness and strength. It is about the alchemy of turning brokenness into wisdom, survival into story, and silence into song. It is about the quiet revolution of staying kind in a world that keeps trying to make us hard.

There was a day, after the casseroles stopped arriving and the calls thinned to polite check-ins, when I stood in a hardware store under a ceiling made of light and choices and didn't cry. I picked out a trowel with a grip that fit my hand and potting mix that smelled older than heartbreak. A woman in a green apron showed me which screws wouldn't strip on a cupboard hinge. We talked about weather and gerberas and nothing sacred-and yet it felt sacred, because I did it.

A small errand. A small transaction. And no one rescued me.

I didn't apologise for asking questions. I didn't apologise for existing.

I paid, carried the bag to my car, and drove home with the feeling that I had just declared something wordless to myself, and to the future I'm shaping for my daughter.

I am capable. I am here. I am a woman doing her own life.

The women we were born to be are not fragile ornaments.

We are oak trees, rooted deep, bending in storms, cracked sometimes, but never uprooted. We are rivers, making new paths through rock, patient and relentless. We are fire, consuming what would destroy us and offering light to those who come after.

And we are also quiet hands making tea. Steady arms rocking children. Soft shoulders where grief can lay its entire history down without being rushed.

Our power isn't only in the dramatic. It lives in the ordinary mercies: the daily choice to keep loving, keep showing up, keep laughing, and to keep living, especially on the days when it would be easier not to.

This is the woman I am becoming. This is the woman I hope Poppy learns she is allowed to be.

I try on my old names sometimes, out of habit. Too much. Too loud. Too tender. Too stubborn. They don't fit anymore.

My laughter, once called too much, has become a gift, a flare lit on days that pretend to be dull. My tenderness, once called weakness, is the muscle that has kept me human. My stubbornness, once dangerous to my safety, is now directed, toward healing, toward justice, and toward the quiet, sacred task of growing a life from the inside out. Not just my own, but the one I am raising, watching, and loving into herself.

I keep a picture of me as a child, knees dirty, hair wild, and face upturned to a sky I was sure belonged to me, tucked inside a box, and I look at it sometimes. When I do, I study her for a long time. She did not yet know how to make herself palatable. She did not yet know how to shrink. She had no idea what would be asked of her, and still, in that photo, I can see a woman already gathering inside the girl, already practising her future, the tilt of defiance in the chin, and the softness in her eyes that refuses to shut.

When I look at Poppy, I see that same gathering beginning again.

We were never meant to be one thing. We were meant to be many, and true.

A friend said once over coffee, "I don't know how to be a woman without performing." We were in a café that smelled like burnt sugar and new beginnings. She traced a ring mark on the table with her thumb. "Half the time I'm being a Cool Girl. The other half I'm being a Good Girl. Neither one is me."

"Maybe being a woman isn't a role," I said slowly, careful with the newness of the thought. "Maybe it's a house you live in. Some rooms are soft. Some rooms are burning. Some are messy and yours."

She smiled, the kind of smile that knows we've said something we'll need later. "A house," she repeated. "I could live with that."

At home, I considered my own houses. The literal one, bricks, mortar, and a front door I lock because the world is sometimes unkind. And the other one, my body, my voice, my history, and my possibility.

I started rearranging both.

Not a makeover. A reclaiming.

The harsh lights came down. Softer lamps went up. I thinned my wardrobe to clothes that feel like a language I actually speak. I painted a dresser the colour of the sea and put the good cups where I could reach them on ordinary days. I learned to sit at the table alone and eat with a fork and not apologise to the chairs that remain empty.

It is a radical act to stop performing and still be loved, especially by yourself. It is an even braver one to let your child see you do it.

The world will ask you to choose: strong or soft, mother or maker, saint or delight, leader or listener. The women I admire have stopped choosing. They arrive as themselves, which is to say, as both.

A colleague who runs meetings like a river, direct, and steady, and texts me soup recipes when the weather turns bleak. A neighbour who can change a tyre and cry at a music video in the same hour. A friend who sits with me at midnight through a panic storm and the next day sends a meme so stupid I laugh until I remember my ribs are good for laughter.

They are not trying to be men. They are not trying to be angels. They are trying to be honest.

Being the women we were born to be is not about declaring, I don't need anyone. It's about being allowed to need ourselves first, our breath, our boundaries, our medicine, our joy.

It's about choosing help without surrendering agency. It's about asking: What loves my life? and arranging a day around the answer as best we can.

Some days what loves my life is action, phone calls, laundry, and lists that bloom with ticks like a garden. Some days it is stillness, hands around a warm cup, chin to chest, and the dog's heartbeat thudding against my shin. Some days it is saying no like a sentence with a full stop that doesn't apologise. Some days it is saying yes to the kind of invitation that feels like opening a window.

I think of a morning not long ago.

Poppy was practising her speech for school, words tripping over nerves. "I can't," she said, cheeks flushed, hands tight at her sides.

"You can," I answered without theatre. "And you don't have to be perfect to be brave."

We practised breathing on the back step, four counts in, six counts out, watching a line of ants do their good work in the cracks. I told her about the first time I spoke in front of a room full of people, and how my hands shook like leaves but the words still came.

"You don't have to be the best at it, love," I said. "You just have to be you while you do it."

She smiled, small, and certain, and I realised this is the inheritance I want to pass down. Not the myth of flawlessness, but the habit of returning to who you are. The willingness to be visible. The courage to be kind.

The women we were born to be raise girls who do not have to unlearn as much.

Not every lesson is a speech. Some are posture.

On a Tuesday afternoon, I carry my own groceries to the car, arms aching, refusing the old instinct to wait for someone else to notice. In the bank, when the clerk explains my account like he's translating for a small child, I ask him to try again, clearly, and do not shrink. At the clinic, I sit in the bright chair and let the nurse find a vein, and when she says, "You're brave," I answer, "I'm here," because sometimes that is the braver truth.

On a Saturday, I go to the movies alone and take up one seat's worth of space like a person who belongs to herself. The empty chair beside me hums for a while like a missing tooth. Then it quiets. I laugh when the scene earns it, cry when it earns that too, and walk home under streetlights without performing a version of safety for anyone but me.

On a Sunday morning, I don't go to church. I do my own liturgy, open the window, make the bed, pour a cup, and write a thank-you in the notebook without specifying to whom.

If there is God in that, He can find me. If there is not, I have still practised gratitude, and that, I have learned, is its own kind of holiness.

People ask me, gently, what I believe now, about womanhood, about grace, about this life that keeps refusing to leave me. My answer changes depending on the weather of my heart, but the bones stay the same.

I believe in women who pay their own bills and also accept casseroles without hysteria. Women who step into high places and low places and call both sacred. Women with loud laughs and quiet rooms. Women who leave when leaving is salvation and women who stay when staying is honest. Women who say me too and mean it. Women who do not look at another woman's face to find a map to their own.

I believe in women who make things, bread, poems, playlists, budgets, babies, gardens, safe homes, exit plans, dinner reservations, and policy. I believe in women who rest as a protest. Women who take naps because no one ever gave them permission to as children. Women who wear soft clothes and shoes that allow them to run, toward joy or away from danger. Women who do not ask their thighs to be small in a world that asks their voices to be smaller.

I believe in women who are learning the difference between gentleness and surrender, between peacekeeping and peacemaking, between keeping quiet and being quiet. I believe in women who keep a toolkit beside the kettle and a red lipstick in the glovebox. Women who rage without burning down their own houses. Women who burn down the right things.

And I believe in men who cheer for these women and do not feel erased by our wholeness, because a true thing about womanhood makes the world more human, not less.

The day I began to feel it in my bones, the shift from girl to woman, didn't come with fanfare. It was afternoon. I was on my knees in the garden, brushing soil from the tender neck of a seedling, when the truth slid into me like a key, I am not trying to become someone else. I am trying to return to the person I have always been, minus the costumes, plus the courage.

I stood, rubbed earth between my palms, and looked at the house. It was not a magazine spread, but it was mine. It held the echo of old fights and the thrum of new songs and the dog's biography written in scratches on the back door. It held my daughter's laughter and my own name spoken in my own voice. It smelled like garlic and clean sheets and eucalyptus oil in the mop bucket. It held room for grief and for dancing badly while the pasta boiled.

It held us.

I walked inside and faced the mirror, no makeup, hair in the kind of bun bobby pins would be embarrassed to claim. I saw the girl I had been and the woman I was. The freckles didn't ask for permission. The scars didn't apologise. The eyes didn't flinch at their own kindness.

"You are not just surviving anymore," I whispered to her. "You are becoming."

And for the first time, I didn't see only the girl who had been broken. I saw the woman I was born to be, and the mother my daughter is watching me practise how to be.

She is not a fixed picture. She is a practice.

She is the way I answer a knock at midnight, first with caution, then with care. She is the way I choose my words in a world that spends them cheaply. She is the way I hold a friend's secret and my own boundaries at the same time. She is the way I choose to be seen by the people who have earned the right to see me and unseen by the ones who haven't.

She is the way I say I don't know without shame, I was wrong without collapse, and I forgive you without forgetting what I survived.

She is also delight.

She wears earrings on a Monday and eats dessert first sometimes. She buys yellow flowers for no reason but joy. She laughs with her whole back. She allows softness in her voice and steel in her spine. She knows how to make soup and how to say no and how to be bored without destroying her life. She owns a drill and a diary and her decisions.

The women we were born to be are not copies. We are constellations, different shapes, same sky.

We carry different stories and share a single note, dignity. The kind that is not given by the world and cannot be taken by it. The kind that notices another woman's crown is crooked and adjusts it without expecting a parade. The kind that does not need the room to be small for her to be big.

If the story of a girl was a map of my origins and ruins, then this is the bridge, planked with truth and ordinary courage, toward the next shore. I told her story in third person because it felt safer for a while. Now the pronouns shift in my mouth like a rite of passage.

I is a word I can wear without apology.

I am the woman I was born to be, unfinished, yes, but recognisable to myself. I am rooted and in motion. I am scarred and soft. I am louder than I used to be and quieter where it counts. I am still learning, which is to say, I am still alive.

And because I am alive, another chapter waits.

Not a pedestal. Not a prize. A practice.

The woman I'd like to be is already here in pieces, on the back step with dirt under her nails, at the sink with sleeves pushed up, and in the mirror with a gaze that does not flinch. She asks me for small, faithful things: Water the plant. Send the text. Keep the appointment. Open the window. Tell the truth. Let the laugh out. Rest before you beg. Choose the green thing. Say no without a story. Say yes like a door.

Tomorrow, I will gather more of her.

Tonight, I lay my hand over my own heartbeat and promise, as simply as I can: I won't go back to the girl who had to disappear to survive. I will go forward as the woman who knows how to stay, and still be free.

Chapter Twenty-Two

There are days I stand in front of the mirror and wonder: who even is this woman?

The glass keeps my secrets and gives some back. I see someone who has walked through fire and is still standing, a survivor, yes, a fighter, yes, but I also see the gaps, the places still tender, the habits I want to release, the strength I long to claim. I touch the edge of the basin like a rail on a moving bus and breathe until my breath doesn't sound surprised to be here.

This chapter of my life is not only about surviving loss but about becoming. Becoming is not a lightning strike, it's an intention, renewed daily, like water you have to remember to drink. I don't want to drift into the next version of me. I want to shape her, not a perfect woman or anyone else's ideal, but a woman I can meet with respect every morning and sleep beside in peace every night.

So I make a quiet vow, I will practice being the woman I'd like to be, on ordinary days, with ordinary tools, where no one claps.

I want to be patient.

Impatience has shadowed me as faithfully as my own silhouette, quick to act, quick to speak, and quick to assume. Grief sharpened it until it cut me coming and going. But patience is the soil where peace grows. The woman I'd like to be pauses. She breathes before she bites. She listens for the click inside that says wait.

I practice in small ways. At a red light when I am late, I

unclench my jaw and let the minute be a minute. In the grocery line, I put my phone away and study the faces around me, this one tired, this one soft, and this one trying. I let someone merge in front of me and feel the edge round off my impatience like sea on stone. I do not become patient all at once. I become patient one held breath at a time.

I want to be wise.

Wisdom is a way of seeing that makes room for both tenderness and consequence. It isn't a library, it's a lantern. I ask for it, sometimes to God, sometimes to the Universe, sometimes to Angels, and sometimes to the quiet core that has survived everything with me, to guide my daughter, to help me know when to fight, when to hold, and when to let go. Wisdom often answers by handing me a question. Does this choice love your tomorrow? When the answer is yes, I follow. When the answer is no, I try again.

I want to be at home in my own skin.

For too long, mirrors and makeup dictated my worth. I worked at my reflection like it was a problem set. The woman I'd like to be doesn't require external proof to take up space. She walks tall, not because she believes she is flawless, but because she knows she is enough. Some mornings I still wince at the mirror out of habit, and then I meet my own eyes and say, "Good morning."

I want to be mindful of my words.

I have cut with my tongue more than once, spoken fast and repented slowly. The woman I'd like to be speaks with intention. She builds bridges where others build bonfires. She can say the hard thing without hardening herself. I practice this at home, in the thick of real life. When my daughter pushes every button I own, I count to five before I reply. Your feelings are allowed. My boundaries are too. When a friend asks how I am and I want to lie, I say, "I'm here. Not okay, but here." When I am wrong, I apologise without a closing argument.

I want to be stubborn for the right reasons.

I know my fire. It has saved me and scorched me. I want it aligned with truth, not pride, obedient not to rules, but to what is good. Fierce for justice, soft for love, steady for compassion. I practice by holding one boundary no one else can see, the one where I do not volunteer for my own diminishment. I send the text that says I can't this week and do not explain. I decline the invitation that would empty me for someone else's comfort and water my plants instead.

I want to love without fear.

Love has broken me, and it has mended me. It is both the wound and the salve. The woman I'd like to be carries so much love that it spills where it is needed, into family, friendships, and the lives of strangers who may never know the intention behind the small mercy. I practice by noticing things, the weary cashier whose shoulders collapse when I say, 'take your time,' the elderly neighbour whose bin I roll back without a speech, and the friend who needs soup more than advice. I practice by loving myself like I'm someone I'm responsible for.

I want to laugh more.

There was a season when laughter felt like treason. Then, shyly, it returned, a snort at a dog in sunglasses, and the ridiculous emoji chain my sister sends when she knows I'm awake. Laughter is rebellion against despair. The woman I'd like to be laughs often, openly, and so freely that people wonder what secret joy she is hiding. The secret is not joy. The secret is permission.

I want to be unselfish.

Not a doormat, unselfish. To give without keeping score. To serve without wearing martyrdom like perfume. I practice by washing a cup I didn't dirty and not announcing it. By leaving the last piece of cake and not resenting the person who takes it. By giving time to those I love and also refusing the kind of giving that is really disguised self-abandonment.

I want to be humble.

Not the false humility of self-erasure, but the groundedness that comes from truth. The woman I'd like to be asks each morning, what is mine to do today, and how can I carry it with grace? Some days what's mine to do is big and public, most days it is small and faithful, answer the email, fold the towel, keep the appointment, and reset without drama. Humility keeps a short account with reality, I am not the centre, and I am also not nothing.

I want to be gentle.

I have called myself clumsy, loud, and a little too sharp at the corners. But gentleness is not weakness, it is strength dressed in kindness. It makes room for people to exhale. I start with the person closest at hand, me. I place a hand on my own chest when panic rises and tap a rhythm my heart can follow. In. Out. We're safe. I choose the softer voice with my daughter and the cleaner boundary with myself. When I fail, I begin again without the theatre of self-loathing.

There are ancient lines I once could not bear, like she is clothed with strength and dignity, and she can laugh at the days to come. They used to feel like an indictment, a costume I would never fit. Slowly, painfully, my prayers have changed that, not the polished prayers of pews, but the plain ones said over dishes and traffic lights, the whispered ones to God, to the Universe, to Angels, and to the part of me that refuses to die.

I pray for patience when my feelings stampede. For wisdom so my daughter can see something steadier than pain when she looks at me. For confidence that has nothing to do with mascara. For humility when pride and stubbornness push me into battles that do not matter. I pray to laugh again - really laugh, loud and unpretty. I pray to be generous in ways that don't make me disappear. To become gentle without losing my fire. To be beautiful in the way that love makes a face luminous from the inside.

I don't want to be a perfect woman.

I want to be a whole woman.

The woman who rises after she falls. The woman who chooses love over bitterness. The woman who can laugh at the days to come and mean it.

So I practice her in small, unspectacular ways. I call the doctor, then keep the appointment. I make the bed even when no one will see it because order steadies me. I choose the true sentence over the tidy lie and accept the cost. I set one boundary and keep it even when my hands shake. I say no to what empties me and yes to the quiet that gives me back my breath. I put flowers in the house for no reason but beauty. I apologise without the word but. I forgive myself before bed and wake lighter. Sometimes I fail, often I fail. But the woman I'd like to be keeps going. Becoming isn't a single leap, it's a string of ordinary choices, remade on the days that no one is watching.

There are scenes that teach me faster than any list.

At the chemist I wait behind a man who argues about a price. The line grows. People sigh. I feel the old impatience fizz in my bones. The woman I'd like to be puts her hand on the counter when it's her turn and says with a smile, "Rough day?" The pharmacist's shoulders drop. Mine do too.

On a Tuesday, I take myself to a café with a book. The first ten minutes, the empty chair pinches like a shoe. Then I notice the sun on the table, the clink of cups, and the blossom tree rehearsing spring out the window. I eat the whole muffin without checking the room for permission. On the way out, I catch my reflection in the glass, woman alone, upright, and enough.

At home, the tap begins its metronome of drip. Once, I would have waited, complained, hoped. Now I fetch the wrench and YouTube a fix. I curse. I bleed. The drip relents. I grin at my bandaged finger in the mirror. "Look at you," I say. "Stopping leaks, two kinds."

When shame arrives dressed as self-improvement, I give it a job. You may remind me to be kind. You may not rewrite history. When fear knocks at midnight, I sit up and drink water, then tell it the truth, "You can sit. You're not driving."

When a friend cancels plans I was counting on, I feel the old loneliness open its mouth. I take myself for a drive to the coast. The sea wears her honest face and keeps arriving. I let the wind knot my hair and do not apologise to anyone for how it looks.

I keep a list titled What Held Today on the fridge:

- My breath, through the whole cup of tea.

- My boundary, when I said, "I can't."

- My joy, long enough to grow roots.

- My mouth, when silence was kinder.

- Me.

And beneath it now, a second list, its twin, its echo, What Needs Practice:

- Slowing down when I've already decided.

- Asking for help before I'm on fire.

- Letting compliments land.

- Eating breakfast like I am on my own side.

- Leaving a room without explaining why.

These lists have become more than reminders; they are the bridge between my old survival and my new becoming. I see them each morning as I pour milk into coffee, and I whisper, *"We're still learning."* The woman I'd like to be leaves small notes for me where I will trip over them: Drink water. Stretch your jaw. Step outside for three breaths. Call your GP. Open the blinds even if your heart is heavy. Choose the green thing. These are not commandments. They are invitations, tiny prayers disguised as to-dos, ways of saying, 'you're still here, keep tending yourself.'

I try on new rituals like dresses from the op-shop. There's the Sunday Reset: change the sheets, water the plants, put fresh fruit where you can see it, sweep the kitchen floor, choose a podcast that reminds you you're not alone. There's the Evening Unknot: a lamp instead of the ceiling light, a cup of peppermint tea, phone on the charger in another room, ten minutes with a book that is not about self-improvement, just a door into someone else's weather. There's the Morning Permission: open the window, make the bed, say aloud, 'we are not hurrying grief or joy today. We are just living.'

These rituals aren't decoration. They are scaffolding. They remind me that becoming the woman I'd like to be isn't about grandeur, it's about rhythm, the steady heartbeat of ordinary acts done with presence.

I plan a tiny solo trip, two nights in a coastal town where the bakery knows what salt is for. I book a small room with a window that faces west. The first night I feel strange eating alone, but the second night I bring my journal to dinner and write between bites.

The waiter asks if I'm waiting for someone. "I was," I say, smiling. "She arrived." On the train home, I catch sight of my reflection in the carriage glass and see a woman travelling alone with a tote full of sand, a book, and a loaf of bread. I think, *'This is what competence looks like in my language.'*

I am learning that standing alone is not the same as standing against the world. It is standing within it, grounded, porous, and ready.

The woman I'd like to be keeps her promises to herself. Not all of them, not perfectly. But enough that trust grows. I say I will walk twice this week and walk twice. I say I will drink water before coffee and do it four mornings out of seven, which is four more than before. I say I will not text the person who confuses me, and when loneliness prowls, I light a candle and watch the flame do what it does, burn anyway.

I learn my own tells. When the house feels suddenly too loud, I haven't eaten. When everyone irritates me, I need water. When I am contemptuous of strangers, I need sleep. When I want to burn it all down, I need to cry.

I allow myself rituals of celebration that don't depend on occasion, like fresh flowers in a jar, a nice pen for a free afternoon of writing, clean pyjamas on an ordinary Tuesday, or a walk at dusk to watch the streetlights decide. These small, quiet gestures are how I stay tethered to myself when the world tries to pull me back into forgetting.

One cool night I sit beneath a sky freckled with stars and speak my vow into the dark, "The woman I'd like to be is already here in pieces. Tomorrow I will gather more of her." The night answers the way it always has, silent, steady, and listening, and something anchors inside me, a softness that is also steel.

And in that settling, another truth arrives, quiet and certain, my life does not need to orbit around a man to be radiant. I can be whole, joyful, and wildly alive in my singleness. Not waiting room living. Not the understudy version. A full, laughter-bright, dignified life that belongs to me.

If love comes someday, let it be additive, not oxygen. Let it be two whole people walking side by side, not one dragging the other, not one shrinking to fit the other's shadow. Let it be a good guest, not a landlord. Let it marvel at the house I have built and offer to sweep the floor sometimes. Let it leave the windows open.

And if love does not come, I will still set the table for two, me and my life, and eat the meal I made without apology.

The woman I'd like to be is not a fantasy. She is a daily practice, a posture I can feel in my bones when I am doing it right, shoulders dropped, jaw easy, breath like a tide, and eyes that look for light without pretending the dark isn't there.

In the mornings, I meet her in the mirror. Let's try again, we agree. At noon, I meet her at the sink with sleeves rolled and music on. In the evening, I meet her at the notebook and tell her what held and what needs kindness. Some nights I am close to her, and some nights I am far. We keep walking toward each other anyway.

Tomorrow I will do one brave ordinary thing for her, book the dentist, turn off the phone at nine, choose the green thing, say I need help, or say no. I will water the plant and myself. I will be gentle and firm. I will laugh on purpose. I will make my bed and lie in it with gratitude. I will forgive myself before sleep and wake ready to practice again.

The woman I'd like to be is not waiting at the finish line. She is here, in the lit kitchen, in the soft lamplight, in the small mercy I offer a stranger, in the boundary I keep, and in the breath I choose. She lives in the patience that steadies my hands when the world shakes, in the laughter that refuses extinction, in the silence that hums with peace instead of punishment. She is here each time I say, I am enough, unfinished, but enough, and then live like I believe it.

And in living like I believe it, I become her. Not suddenly, not spectacularly, but quietly, through every ordinary act of staying. Through every breath I choose instead of abandon. Through every truth I tell myself even when it stings.

Tomorrow I will rise again, not as a new woman, but as the same one, truer. Steadier. Softer.

And somewhere between the first sip of tea and the soft ache of evening, I will remember that the woman I'd like to be has never been a stranger to me at all. She has been waiting here all along, beneath the noise, beneath the fear, beneath the version of me that forgot her name, patient, luminous, and already home.

But home isn't only a feeling.

Sometimes it's a road.

Sometimes it's a wheel in your hands on a wet day when you don't feel brave and you go anyway.

And when the next chapter arrived, it didn't come as romance, or rescue, or revelation.

It came as weather.

And a car.

And the quiet decision to drive.

Chapter Twenty-Three

The next chapter arrived exactly like I'd promised myself it would, not as a feeling, but as a road.

The first thing I did when we got home was rinse the grime out of the wheel wells. Not red-dust-from-the-north grime, the kind you collect on a wet day when the city is all spray and sump-water and road film. It came away in spirals, thin ribbons sliding down the driveway and fanning across the concrete like a map of everywhere we'd been in a day we hadn't wanted but had done anyway. The little Mazda ticked as it cooled, a tired animal after the effort. Poppy sat on the curb, chin in her hands, doing that half-squint she does when she's thinking hard. The hose hissed in my palm. Every now and then a clot of grit let go and tumbled out with a soft thud, not evidence of some grand expedition, just proof that the road had asked for more courage than it looked like it should.

"Does it feel better?" Poppy asked.

I looked at the arch of the wheel, the little scuff at the edge that hadn't been there last week. "I think we both do," I said, and rinsed until the water ran clear.

In the laundry I peeled off the day in layers, clothes, tired shoes, and a jacket that still held the faint smell of rain and city air. I turned my pockets inside out and shook loose the crumpled receipts, then lined them up on the bench like a timeline and laughed, one short, breathless sound that wasn't disbelief so much as relief.

We were home.

The silence of the house didn't punish me this time. It held us. Poppy dozed on the couch with the dog's head on her ankle, a soft, ridiculous weight. I made tea with both hands wrapped around the mug, not because it was cold but because I needed to feel something simple and loyal. Then I stood at the kitchen window and watched the last streaks of dirty water run off the driveway and vanish into the street.

I hadn't realised until that moment that I'd been bracing all day, not just for the drive, the waiting, the road slick with warning, but for the appointment itself, the words we might hear, the way a single sentence can change the architecture of a life. But it didn't. We went in. We did the thing. We came back out. Poppy was still beside me.

We made it.

People asked for the story in the days that followed, and I learned to tell it without flinching, not because it was dramatic, but because it had been real. How we left early under a sky that already had sharp edges, grey and heavy like a thought you can't shake. How the woman at the servo eyed the little car and asked, not unkindly, "You heading into town in this?" as if the weather had opinions and could veto our plans.

"We've got an appointment," I said, and heard how steady my voice sounded, as if steadiness were something you could manufacture with enough will.

How the first flooded patch lay across the road like a sheet of hammered glass and I actually whispered, "No one's going to believe how much this is making me sweat," to the empty air between us. How the cars ahead turned around at the causeway one by one, their brake lights speaking in a language of caution my body understood too well. How I pulled into the bay and sat with my hands on the wheel, knuckles drained, while the rain kept talking to the roof.

I told them about the waiting, how it can be its own kind of crossing. How we ate muesli bars from the glovebox like they were rations and tried to talk about nothing while fear tried to talk about everything. How a council truck pushed through first, water curling around its tyres like it wanted to prove a point, and the level dropped inch by grudging inch, as if the road were negotiating.

How a stranger in a higher car rolled down his window and said, "Follow me close. Don't stop," and my stomach dropped at the authority in his voice, not because I didn't trust him, but because it meant we were doing it.

And how we did.

How the Mazda lifted its skirts and waded, how my eyes stayed glued to the far bank the way you keep your gaze on a doorway when you're moving through smoke, how the water pushed at the tyres and hissed like a warning, and then, suddenly, we were on the other side, and the relief hit so fast it made me laugh like a person half-mad with gratitude.

I told them the city, too, the way the streets look after rain, all shine and hurry, how the buildings hold themselves like they've never been afraid of anything in their lives. I told them about the parking meters that blink their little demands, the waiting room smell of disinfectant and old magazines, the sound of Poppy's breath when she tried to keep it even.

I told them how she made a joke so bad it looped around into brilliance, just to keep my nerves from chewing holes in the air.

I told them how, when her name was called, my whole body stood up inside itself.

I told them how we walked back out again and the sky had not fallen.

The appointment hadn't swallowed us.

The day hadn't turned into a verdict.

It was just a day, hard, wet, expensive in energy, and we had lived through it.

I left certain parts out, not because they were secrets but because they were mine, like the private words I said under my breath in the car that weren't for anyone else, the moment on the causeway when I felt Marko as clearly as if he'd put his hand over mine on the wheel and steadied the tremor. He didn't speak. He didn't have to. The steadiness was enough.

The after, though, that I learned to describe in ordinary detail, because that was where the relief lived.

The first rain after we got back came at three in the morning. I jerked awake, soaked in adrenaline before the storm even found its voice. The roof began its old percussion, the gutters thudded, and the downpipes took up the rhythm. My body remembered the causeway and flooded me with the wrong chemicals for a bedroom. My mouth went cotton-dry. The room went tight.

"Stay," I said to myself in the solid tone I used with Poppy when she was small and trying to bolt from a vaccination. "It's a roof. It's not a river."

I got up and made tea, just the kettle's patient hum and the light over the sink, nothing dramatic, nothing cinematic, and waited for my body to catch up to the truth. It did, in increments; panic is stubborn, but so am I.

When the storm softened, I opened the back door and let the smell of wet dirt kiss my face. The backyard was only a backyard again, not a test. I stood in it barefoot and said hello to the lemon tree like it had held the fence for me while I was away.

The next day, I drove to the carwash. The queue of utes and SUVs was long and impatient. The little Mazda and I waited our turn like a kid among adults. When the foam cannons burst, Poppy clapped her hands in mock applause. We watched the windows blur into white then blue then clear.

It felt superstitious, indulgent, and unnecessary, and yet like ritual.

The dirty water had been part of the story.

It didn't need to live on the paint.

At home, I spread the day's paperwork across the table the way I used to spread his bills, back when I mistook financial avoidance for romance. I sorted receipts into neat, unembarrassed piles, wrote numbers in clean columns, and named the total out loud.

"We can afford the consequence of the choice," I said to the room that had once heard me hiss numbers through my teeth like curses.

The room did not answer.

It didn't need to.

Later, Poppy breezed into the kitchen and leaned her hip against the bench.

"I pretended to sleep," she said, not quite looking at me.

"When?" My chest tightened.

"In the car, after," she said. "I thought if I acted calm, you'd stay calm."

I swallowed and nodded.

"It helped," I said, because it had. "You helped."

She exhaled and let her head fall against my shoulder like she hadn't done in a long time.

"We're good, Mum," she said into my shirt. "Even when it's bad."

I held her there a second longer than either of us needed, then pulled back, cupped her face, and smiled.

"Even when it's bad," I agreed.

The week after, the day stayed in my muscles, not as fear, but as memory. It showed up in small places. In the way my hands didn't shake as much when the paperwork piled up. In the way I didn't postpone the phone call I didn't want to make. In the way I looked at a problem and thought, *Okay. We're doing this.*

When the first bill came with Marko's name on it again, as if the system couldn't remember what the world had done to us, I didn't put it in the drawer to deal with next month. I called them.

"You're sending bills to ghosts," I said to the man on the line who had a practised condolence in his voice. "Please send them to the living."

He corrected the account. I hung up and laughed, the kind of laugh that comes from a place past anger.

I didn't erase Marko in doing these things. I just stopped letting the mess follow me into every room.

Poppy told me, "When the water covered the road, I tried to imagine the asphalt underneath as if my eyes were on the ground. It helped."

I nodded, pleased, proud, and humbled by her practical theology.

"Keep doing that," I said. "With everything."

She made a face like I was being annoyingly wise.

"You know you can just say 'be brave,' right?"

I laughed. "Okay. Be brave. And bring snacks."

When the next storm found the house and the windows

flinched under the wind, I stood in the hallway and listened to the old timbers talk to each other.

"We've held before," I said to them, and to myself. "We'll hold now."

The roof obeyed.

The walls didn't cave.

The day had taught me that holding isn't always dramatic. Sometimes it's just staying where you are and letting the weather pass through.

Friends tell the story differently. They gasp at the part where the water came up. They repeat the stranger's line, "Follow me close. Don't stop," like a benediction. They shake their heads at the waiting, at the appointment, at the way a woman and her daughter in a small car refused to stay small.

I don't correct them.

Every story needs its dramatic beats.

But when I tell it to myself, the turning point happens after the wet road: the carwash, the receipts, the first storm, the next drive, and the leaky tap.

Not because those things are poetic.

Because those things are real.

Poppy says she doesn't remember falling asleep with her mouth open on the way home.

I do.

I remember looking at her tilted head and seeing the child who used to sleep hot and heavy on my chest and the almost-woman who could sit up straight in a waiting room and pretend calm so that I could borrow it.

I remember thinking, not for the first time and certainly not for the last, that we had saved each other that day.

Eliza dropped off a container of soup for two on Thursday and left a note on the lid: "For the road that still runs inside the two of you."

Poppy and I heated it at lunchtime and ate it at the table with clean spoons.

I texted my sister a photo of the empty bowls and wrote, "Arrived."

She sent back three pink hearts and the word "Always."

After that, the words *road home* lived in my mouth as shorthand, a private code. When work paperwork snarled up like fishing line and I sat too long at the computer feeling my spine turn to gravel, I said it: *road home.* And my hands remembered to stay with the wheel, pick the lane, and watch the far bank.

When Poppy hyperventilated over a math assignment and insisted she couldn't possibly do it, I said it out loud to her, and we both laughed because it had become our in-joke.

"Fine," she said, rolling her eyes at me with love. "We'll follow us close, and we won't stop."

I used to think the point of a hard story was the lesson you wring out of it like water from a rag.

I think now the point might be smaller and kinder.

A hard day shows you what you can do.

It doesn't fix your life.

It just proves you can keep going in it.

A week later, I found one last clue of that day in the lip of the hatch when I lifted it to put in groceries. It crumbled in my fingers, grit, silt, and the aftertaste of rain, and fell to the driveway with a small tap.

I didn't keep it.

I don't want relics that require altars.

I want the ordinary that keeps me alive: eggs, a green thing, bread thick enough to hold butter and vegemite, Poppy's laughter spilling from down the hall, and the dog sneezing because the sun found his ridiculous nose.

I set the bags on the bench and looked out at the yard.

The gerberas we planted before the wet week had staged a quiet coup while we were gone, pink faces turned toward the sun, shameless and practical. I wiped my hands on a tea towel and went out to touch each bloom, one by one, the way a person touches the shoulders of friends at a table to signal hello without interrupting their conversation.

"Still here," I told them, and they, being flowers, said nothing.

They didn't need to.

Presence is eloquent all by itself.

That night, Poppy fell asleep long before me, finally letting the last of her vigilance go. I stood in the hallway and watched her chest rise and fall and felt a calm that didn't need proving.

The house breathed its old, faithful music, the fridge's low exhale, the hedges rubbing their leaves together in the wind like old women gossiping.

I went back to the kitchen and wrote one more line for the chapter I knew this day had given me: *We can do hard things.*

And then, because I am the kind of woman who likes clean exits, I turned off the light, walked down the hall, and went to bed without looking for water under the door.

The road home wasn't a way back to who I was. It was practice for who I am.

And when I turned the key in the front door that night, I realised something quietly radical, the world hadn't changed. I had.

Chapter Twenty-Four

Becoming her didn't arrive with a dramatic moment.

It arrived in the aftermath, in the quiet competence of ordinary days, in the way I started trusting my own hands again, in the way the world stopped feeling like something I had to survive and began to feel like something I could live inside.

It wasn't a cinematic morning where I stood at the mirror, chin lifted, and declared, Today I'll become the woman I always wanted to be. No trumpet. No switch flipped. No sudden radiance. It was slower, stranger, and more ordinary than that, like shedding a skin I'd worn for decades and discovering that underneath there wasn't a brand-new creature, just a truer one who'd been waiting patiently for air.

The woman I used to be was quick-tempered and quicker with words. My humour had barbs. I laughed too loud, drank past the point where feelings blur, swore when I stubbed my toe, and also when I didn't. I carried my pain like armour and then acted surprised when no one could get close enough to touch the softness beneath. Strangers got my prickles, friends got my impatience, and kindness made me suspicious. I mistook vigilance for wisdom. I mistook survival for identity. Loss is efficient at finding the hairline fractures in a life. Grief seeped into mine and widened them until the wall I'd built to hold myself together could no longer pretend to be good architecture. I was left looking at the raw, trembling version of me I'd kept hidden even from myself.

For a while, I thought becoming her meant becoming someone else entirely, the perfect widow, the saintly mother who never snapped, the gracious friend who never declined, the woman so soft-spoken and perpetually forgiving that candles bowed when she entered a room. That fantasy lasted exactly as long as it took the kettle to boil. Because I don't want to be someone else. I want to be the truest version of myself, the woman who existed before fear taught me to shrink, before shame taught me to decorate my silence, before compromise taught me to call exhaustion love.

The first hints of her showed up in unremarkable places, the steady warmth that moved through me when I said a clean no and refused to add an essay of apologies after it, the way my shoulders lowered on a midnight drive as Poppy told a joke so bad it circled around and became brilliant, the moment I cried hard and did not hide in the bathroom to do it, the soft voice I used on myself afterward, and the same tone I used once on a feverish child, saying, 'You're safe. We're safe. Stay.' Becoming her was as much unlearning as it was learning. I unlearned the old economy where a man's attention was currency, and I was always waiting to be cashed in. I unlearned the lie that beauty is something painted on rather than something lived into. I unlearned that love is proven by the pain you can endure without complaint. It isn't. It never was.

Sometimes, without my chaos, I didn't know who I was. Without the theatre of endurance, without the familiar roles, wife, long-suffering partner, the woman who forgives until she disappears, would there be anything left? The answer arrived not as revelation but as repetition, the pleasure of finishing a cup of coffee while it was still hot, the click of the front door when I locked it behind me and felt like I was shelter, not a person hiding, and the rhythm of my feet on the pavement at 6:10 a.m., body remembering itself as an animal that moves toward light. The truth was simple and embarrassing in its obviousness, becoming her wasn't replacement. It was reclamation.

Of course the old self fought back. She had seniority and a habit of talking over everyone. She arrived as shame, as the late-night voice that listed my faults alphabetically, as the daytime voice that insisted love is a prize and I had dropped the ticket, as the hand that reached for a drink when what I needed was water and a nap. Each time, I had a choice, I could obey or I could keep walking. I chose walking, badly at first, then with something like rhythm. Becoming her meant deciding I was worthy of love even when no one was around to offer it. It meant believing I could raise my child without apologising for the days I was learning in public. It meant honouring my body for the roads it had carried me over, the flood-brown ones and the quiet kitchen tiles, not for the way it performed under strip-mall lights.

There's a tenderness to this becoming. It isn't loud. It doesn't pose. It doesn't get applause. It's the tenderness of folding warm laundry slowly, of leaving the last slice of toast for Poppy and then making another without resentment, of speaking softly to the part of me that still thinks the worst is a form of preparation. I used to pray for transformation to be sudden, as if virtue were a switch hidden behind the fridge that I could flick if only I were tall enough. Now I understand, becoming her is an unfolding. Daily. Hourly. A long obedience in the direction of my own life.

A quiet day taught me what the new normal could feel like. I woke before the alarm to a house that had already exhaled its night, the fridge humming, a galah heckling the morning with comic certainty, and the dog snoring in soft consonants. I lay for a minute and let my ribs widen without permission, then stood, glad I could. The kettle did its good work. I cracked two eggs into a pan and didn't insult them with apology. Poppy shuffled in, hair wild, mouth forming a complaint before her brain had fully connected. I put a plate in front of her and kissed the top of her head. "You're cross," I said cheerfully, "and beloved." She rolled her eyes and grinned because both could be true.

By eight I had booked the dentist, answered the email I'd been avoiding, and texted Eliza with a plan for Friday that didn't require either of us to dress up as people with energy. Her reply came quick: "Tracksuits and cake, church." I watered the gerberas by the back step and told them to keep showing off. They obliged. On the way to work I drove the way the new version of me drives, hands loose, shoulders down, and music at a humane volume. At a red light I watched a man in the next lane hit his steering wheel at nothing and felt, not superiority, but the quiet relief of not being possessed by the same ghosts. I used to collect other people's anger the way my grandmother collected teaspoons, an absurd habit with sharp edges. I don't anymore. I keep my palms for the wheel and the faces of people I love.

At work I did the next necessary thing until it added up to a day. I didn't audition for competence, I used it. I took my lunch break, the whole thing, at a park bench where two ibises strutted like men in bad suits. I laughed out loud and didn't pretend to be on the phone to justify the sound. On the way back, a woman in the lobby complimented my dress. "Op-shop," I said, proud as if I'd sewn it from sunlight. "Seven dollars." "You look like you mean it," she said, and I carried that sentence like a secret until home.

At three, a call I didn't want came through, an old number that used to summon dread into my throat. I declined it. Then, because I am the kind of woman who keeps her own promises, I put the number on the blocked list. The relief after was clean, not performative. Boundaries have a sound when they click in, and you can hear it if you're quiet.

The evening chores were the same as always, chopping onions, killing the recipe half a dozen times and bringing it back to life with salt, standing barefoot on cool tile while the dog stared at me as if I were the only entertainment left in the known universe, folding towels into blunt, honest rectangles, and picking Poppy up from practice and listening to her narrate her day in a tone that swung between operatic outrage and tender awe. The difference was me, the woman moving through them. My patience didn't strain like old elastic. My voice didn't have to travel through barbed wire to reach gentleness. I didn't make a speech about being tired. I was a person, not a martyr. It felt… solid.

After dinner, Poppy sprawled on the rug with homework and a groan that suggested algebra was a conspiracy. "Talk me through the first step," I said, and she did, and the second step arrived because that's what steps always do. We lit a candle because we like the way the room looks at itself when there's flame. When she went to shower, I wiped the bench, not as penance for eating but as gratitude for having. The cloth moved in small circles until the surface shone the way it does in magazines, except this wasn't a photograph, it was real life.

At nine, when the house was quiet, I opened the notebook that had once been full of prayers like broken glass and now held sentences that were neither rehearsed nor desperate. I wrote: Today I held. I listed what had held: my boundary on the phone; my voice at the bank, my breath through the length of a cup of tea, my humour when the ibis looked like a man named Trevor complaining about rates, my body in the car when the old panic tried to crawl back in through the air vent. I wrote, without drama: the inside of me is less sharp. I closed the notebook and put my palm on the cover as if to bless the girl I had once been. She, too, had tried her best with the tools she had. Becoming her did not require hating who I'd been. It required telling the truth faster and more kindly.

It would have been easy to end the day there, to call it a good story and make a neat exit. Instead, I did one more ordinary thing, I laid out the tools for morning, keys in their bowl, shoes by the door, and the letter that needed posting tucked into my bag where I couldn't pretend I'd forgotten it. I'm learning that the woman I'm becoming leaves ladders for the woman she will be. It is a surprisingly tender act.

I used to wear my edge like jewellery, it glittered and cut, and I mistook that sparkle for power. Becoming her hasn't removed my edge, it has redirected it. My stubbornness now plants itself in service of life instead of spite. My temper has learned the difference between righteous and recreational. My sarcasm, oh, she's still here, alive and well , but most days she chooses wit that warms instead of wit that scorches. There is a way to be quick and still be kind. I am practising.

There are failures, and I want to tell you, for accuracy, about them. I snapped at a stranger who pushed past me in a queue, and my face burned afterward with old shame. I apologised, to her and to myself, and the day didn't collapse. I drank too much at Eliza's birthday because I forgot that tiredness doesn't love gin as much as my mouth promises it does. The next morning I made eggs, drank water, and didn't spend an entire day turning my body into a courtroom. I missed a deadline, owned it, and renegotiated without turning self-forgiveness into theatre. I told Poppy I'd be at her thing and then my brain betrayed me and I wasn't. I told the truth, and we both survived it. Perfection is brittle. I am choosing durable.

There is also joy that doesn't apologise for arriving uninvited. At the garden centre I bought seeds with names that sound like charms, snapdragon, cosmos, and sweet pea. The woman at the counter said, "Don't drown them with love," and we smiled like we both knew that advice was bigger than planting. I drove home with a cardboard tray of possibility humming in the passenger seat like a friend singing along to the radio. Later, I pressed each seed into soil and promised to keep my hands gentle.

A neighbour knocked with lemons from a tree that should be famous. I gave him a jar of marmalade I'd made in a fit of domestic optimism and warned him it might be more enthusiasm than technique. He returned the jar a week later empty and grinning, which felt like a benediction. I went to the movies alone and cried at a scene that wasn't written to be sad, it was just honest. I walked out into the night and didn't rush to wipe my face as if to hide the evidence that I'm alive. On the way home I stopped at the servo and bought jelly snakes. The attendant said, "Long night?" and I said, "Good one," and he said, "Nice," and that was enough human contact to count as community.

On a Wednesday I blocked a number that had learned to perform concern while practising control. My thumb hovered a second, then pressed. The quiet afterward felt like a room aired for the first time in years. On a Thursday I stood over the sink and said out loud, without performance, "Marko, I will always wish the story had ended differently. But I won't live inside the wish." The sentence didn't make me saintly. It made me honest. I have room now for both love and boundary in the same rib cage, and it turns out they are not opposites but neighbours. On a Friday I sent a message I used to think would be the end of me: *No.* No explanation. No sugar around the edges. The person wrote back, unbothered: "No worries." I laughed at how expensive I had made simple things.

You might be waiting for the pivot , the moment where I claim I am fully arrived, that I have become her at last, certificate stamped, future certain. But becoming is not a station, it is track underfoot. What I can tell you is this, I am steady enough today to walk back toward the past without letting it pull me under. The human ghosts can be faced without the room caving. The letter can be written. The door can be shut without slam. This, more than any dramatic triumph, is what the new normal looks like, a quiet day that holds. A woman who holds with it.

Poppy notices the difference. She doesn't use adult words for it, and she shouldn't have to. She says, "You laugh more, Mum," or "You don't go quiet the same way," or, after a hard conversation we had to have about something ordinary and teenage and hot with feeling, she said, "Thanks for being… like this," and waved her hands as if to press the shape of it into the air. I nodded and said, "Me too," because gratitude goes both directions. Sometimes, late, when the house has settled into its old timber and I'm the last person awake, I stand in the dark kitchen and practise liking myself. It's a skill like any other. I think of the girl I was, the mother I am, and the woman I am becoming, and I choose gentleness for all three. I no longer mistake that gentleness for weakness. It takes strength to be soft after the world has taught you hardness as armour.

There is a story I used to tell about myself, that I was the kind of woman things happened to, floods, fights, loss, love, sharp turns. I know now I am also the kind of woman who happens to things. I am the person who calls the bank and says, "Explain that properly." I am the person who drives through water and then teaches her hands to rest on the wheel. I am the person who waters gerberas, who buys the flowers when there's no occasion, who lights a candle because flame makes a room tell the truth. I am not finished. I don't want to be. Finished things are for shelves. I plan to be used.

Tomorrow, I will do the next plain act of becoming. I will fix something small and unglamorous. I will call the dentist again and actually go. I will say yes to the walk and no to the obligation that tightens my chest. I will eat a green thing. I will send the letter that closes a chapter without ceremony. I will put money in the Sunlight Fund, even if it's only twenty dollars. I will tell Eliza the truth about how I'm doing and accept her cake whether it falls in the middle or not. I will leave the porch light on for Poppy because she loves the way the house looks when it's expecting her.

And when the past knocks, as it will, polite or not, I will open the door only as far as I decide. I will say what is true without decorating it. I will not audition. I will not apologise for taking up space in my own life. Then I will close the door cleanly. Not a slam. Not a flinch. A click that sounds like a boundary doing exactly what it was made to do. Becoming her is not a costume. It is capacity. It is how much truth I can carry without spilling it on other people. It is how much joy I can hold without insisting it earn its keep. It is how much sorrow I can sit beside without turning the chair into a stage. It is, in the end, the ability to be at home in my own company.

The last thing I do at the end of the night before sleep is mundane, that is, I set out the morning, mug under the machine, spoon in the sugar, shoes by the door, and keys in the bowl. The woman I was would have called this fussing. The woman I am calls it care. The woman I am becoming lays out tomorrow like a welcome mat for her own feet. I switch off the lamp and the room holds. Outside, the wind threads itself through the lemon tree and the leaves answer back with gentle applause that sounds like grace, if grace had a sound. I think, not as a wish but as a fact I can live inside, that I am becoming her. Not all at once. Not even beautifully, some days. But truly. And I am steady enough now to turn toward what still needs saying, to the human ghosts who once wrote their names across my life, and speak plainly. Which is to say, I'm ready for the next chapter.

Chapter Twenty-Five

Love after loss is not a gentle country to wander into, it is a borderland with no map, its ground still hot from the fire that took everything before it. The first steps feel like trespassing, as if every move forward crushes something sacred. When Marko died, I thought all possibility of love died with him. Not because our marriage had been a fairytale that could never be repeated, far from it, but because our bond had been layered, knotted, and ancient. Two decades of chaos and laughter, cruelty and tenderness, betrayal and forgiveness, addiction and the small everyday mercies that keep a family upright, those years left roots that did not loosen because a body stopped breathing. His absence felt like a void that would bend my life into orbit around it. For months even the idea of another man's eyes on me felt obscene, like dancing at a funeral while the casket was still in view.

And then, nights folded in. The house grew quiet in its own language. The dog's breathing slowed, and the refrigerator hummed like a distant congregation. Alone in the dark, my body had its own language of memory. It remembered what it felt like to be held, to be wanted, to be laughed with in the arms of someone who saw you, not only the faults, not only the failure, but the whole folded, ridiculous bundle you carried. The ache I felt was not only grief, it was also hunger. Not for food, but for the most human of longings, to belong again, to feel the warmth of another shoulder beneath my head, and to have my laugh answered.

I would catch myself tracing the empty side of the bed as if memory could be summoned back through touch. Sometimes I dreamt of warmth, just the weight of an arm, or the whisper of breath against my neck, and woke with my palms open, the ache of absence flooding them. It was not desire that startled me most, but how easily the body remembered what the mind tried to forbid.

At first, I punished myself for those thoughts. Desire felt disloyal. I told myself longing for touch was erasure of the dead man's memory, a theft. Widowhood seemed to demand chastity from me, a vow I had not consented to but felt pressured into because other people's discomfort needed a proper outlet. People asked, with polite curiosity or sharp-edged judgment, "Are you seeing anyone yet?" as if romance were a checkbox on some cruel timeline. Their questions landed like stones. It felt as though there were no right answers, wait too long and someone would spit pity, and move too fast and someone would brand you ungrateful or worse. I learned that people prefer widows solemn and tidy, grief folded neatly like linen. They do not know what to do with a woman still pulsing with life.

I read, at one point, about a widow whose new romance was announced weeks after her husband's funeral. Journalists called it scandalous. Panellists debated whether she had betrayed sacred mourning, while a few others said, with something like understanding, that they'd seen that pattern before, that grief and desire cohabiting in a body like unwilling roommates. She said, starkly, "We were both in turmoil. We needed each other. We made love. We couldn't help ourselves." People called her disgraceful. I read the article and thought, brave. Brave to admit that two truths can live in the same chest, that sorrow and hunger do not annul each other, sometimes they are simply two harried, human impulses trying to be tended. I closed the magazine and sat in the half-light of the kitchen for a long time, the words breathing through me like confession.

Widowhood, I learned, is identity theft. One night you are a wife, and the next morning you wake as something else entirely. Your world changes and people measure you differently. Forms at the doctor's become torture boxes of "Married / Divorced / Widowed / Single," which one will hold you? Which box can hold the truth that you still set out two forks at dinner more from habit than hope? Which term captures the way you continue to pick up a hand that will never again be there? No label seemed adequate.

So I told myself I didn't need another person. I would pour my life into Poppy, into work, and into the small scaffold of routine that kept me from dissolving. I declared independence like a mantra. Yet at night the bed yawned open. The house cleared its throat like an old friend about to speak. There was a hollowness that was not absence of love but absence of touch, laughter, someone to meet my eyes across the coffee table and see a woman who was not simply surviving but was still, stubbornly, alive. And I hated myself for wanting it.

The first time a man smiled at me in a way that was not merely civil, my throat closed. It was not a theatrical smile; it was the gentle ease of a stranger being kind. But it pierced the fog. I went home and sat in the kitchen shaking, a heat flushing up my chest as if I had committed an indignity. My mind screamed betrayal, but my body whispered, alive. That whisper stayed. It followed me into sleep and morning, the small hum of life asking, quietly, to be let back in.

Grief and desire do not divorce easily. They live side by side, awkward roommates who never quite like each other but both have rights to inhabit the space. You can love the man who is gone and still want someone present. You can mourn and still crave touch; these truths sound tidy in theory but are messy in practice. The thing that surprised me most was how often memory softened the dead into saints. In the hard glare of hindsight, Marko's worst edges sometimes dimmed, and my mind, protective, rewired the record. Memory can be a tender, cruel thing, making ghosts easier to love than living humans who arrive with real fingerprints. Sometimes the ghost wins. Sometimes a living person's warmth cuts right through the cold nights that memory cannot touch.

So what does loving after loss look like? It is not substitution. No new person can replace the weight and shape of the years you had with someone else. Love after loss is expansion. The heart is a vessel designed to stretch, and grief cracks it open and, if you allow it, something else may be invited in. That invitation does not deny the past. It honours it by refusing to fossilise your life into a single, unchanging monument.

Guilt came in waves. The first time I imagined kissing someone new, my stomach rebelled and I vomited. My body seemed to register the act as kin to betrayal. The first time a message thread went beyond casual, I lay awake, whispering apologies into the ceiling as if the dark would swallow them. How could I laugh without expecting to hear judgement? How could I accept tenderness without picturing a thousand eyes accusing me? But another part of me whispered questions back: If I am still breathing, do I not deserve to live?

And there is the public theatre of it. People love a black-and-white narrative. Grief has been packaged into rituals; a funeral, a period of mourning, and a public hush. When someone exits that script, the audience clucks and throws labels like confetti. They do not see the private calculus. They do not see a widow calculating whether her daughter will forgive her, whether her grandmother will drop her from the will, whether her friends will whisper. They do not see the nights when the idea of forever silence is worse than the scandal of an affair. From the outside, decisions are shallow, from the inside, they are heavy with moral and practical consequence.

I began, in small ways, to re-ask myself what it meant to love. I remember standing in the bathroom, looking at the woman in the mirror who had learned to look smaller to survive. I asked: Can you love again and still mourn? The answer, which came like a slow drip of water in a sink you don't notice until you stare, was yes. You can. You must invent new language, new etiquette, and new grace. You must be brave enough to keep a ghost's chair in the room without making it all-consuming.

Love after loss asks for enormous generosity, not just toward new partners but toward oneself. You must allow yourself scandals of tenderness because living without joy looks like punishment. You must allow a prospective partner the dignity of being real, of having flaws, of being unintimidated by the dead, of not expecting to be a teacher of life-lessons you should have been the author of. Any man who wanted me had to understand that my heart came as a parcel already labelled: Handle with memory. There would be times he would hear me talk about Marko and feel a hot sickness. There would be times he would have to stand aside so that I could kneel and remember, or sing, or grieve.

Sometimes I would imagine sitting across the table from the man I had loved in my past life, if only for a brief, impossible conversation. "I loved you," I would tell Marko, pulling the sentence over me like a blanket. "I fought for you, for our family, for a life that existed in pieces. You were full of contradictions. And now you are gone. I will not bury myself alive in your absence.

If love calls me again, I will not refuse it, not to replace you, but to honour the fact that you are gone and I am not." Saying that out loud felt like blasphemy once, and now it feels like devotion to the living.

There are practicalities, too, that the romantic stories do not show. Dating, after loss, is an ethical negotiation. How quickly do you tell someone you were married? How much of the lover's mantle is taken up by grief? If I met someone now, would I have to negotiate favourite songs with a ghost? Would I have to rehearse boundaries that keep the past from swallowing the present? These questions are gritty. They are not answered by clichés.

A man came into my life once in the form of a message. Nothing dramatic, a username blinking into being on my screen, a recollection of a lecture we'd both attended years before. He was careful, not eager, curious but not invasive. We wrote for weeks about small things like the city's best coffee, an old film that made us both cry, and the way his mother said certain words. He asked about my daughter with gentleness. He listened in a way people rarely did. He asked to meet, not in the rush of a bar but for coffee. I said yes.

The first date was a minefield I navigated in a decent dress and hands that trembled. There were moments I felt absurdly alive, his laugh folding into mine like a soft echo, and there were times when the memory of Marko would set like a weight in my chest and I'd excuse myself to the bathroom to breathe. I came back steady. He did not ask for explanations he could not understand; he simply sat with my sorrow as if it were an extra person at the table. There is no truer test of tenderness than showing your fragility and watching someone choose to stay.

When you love again, you give someone access to a map

marked with the ruins of another city. It requires a person who will not try to bulldoze those ruins, who will walk among them respectfully, who will sometimes pick up a stone and say something quiet: "You are still here." It requires someone who can say, "I will hold the line for you when you cannot," without fantasies of being a hero.

Not every man was suited for that role. I met men who wanted to fix me, they used the language of saviours and spent conversation trying to rewrite what I owed them. I met men who wanted to be trophies, to parade a widow as proof of their magnanimity, and I came to despise the kind of performative compassion that is actually containment in a pretty wrapper. I met men who were terrified of grief because they did not know how to be present with it. And yes, a few intoxicated engagements sprang like weeds then flamed out. Each encounter taught me something about what I would accept and what I would not.

There were moments, too, when I felt ashamed for the small, illicit happiness I allowed myself. Poppy, my daughter, once surprised me laughing at her own terrible joke and said, half puzzled, "Mum, you're smiling like you used to." I almost apologised for it, then I didn't. Poppy deserved to see her mother alive, not a monument to the past. If loving again meant that my laughter returned here and there, it would be a gift to both of us.

You learn that the right kind of lover is not a rescuer but a companion. He must be capable of the small daily work of intimacy, showing up to the school concert without grand gestures, offering a hand at exactly the right moment, and making tea on a night when you cannot. He must accept that grief will sometimes take holidays from him without explanation. He will have to be patient when anniversaries arrive like unannounced guests. He must be generous enough to be less jealous of memory and more curious about how we can make new memories that honour the old.

There is also an internal reckoning that takes place. You must forgive yourself for the relief that sometimes comes in the arms of someone new. Relief does not mean you loved less, it means your remaining life is being tended, and survival is a worthy task. Many people cannot see this. They mistake moving forward for moving on, as if life were a series you press pause on and resume later. But moving forward means carrying your history differently, not erasing it. And sometimes you must be honest in the hardest ways. There were times I realised I loved the idea of being loved more than I loved any particular suitor. That was a dangerous admission that required stepping back from people who wanted to be loved into, rather than loved by. I had to learn the difference between being rescued and being chosen.

One of the cruellest myths about widowhood is that it closes the book on romance, that mourning permanently alters a person into a brittle figure who cannot love again. The more dangerous myth is the opposite, that new love will be simple balm. Neither is true. Love after loss is both harder and softer. Harder because you carry history, softer because everything is seasoned with the fragility of knowing how quickly things can be taken.

There are practical decisions, too, that tug at the heartstrings. If I were to invite someone into the house, how would I explain Poppy's room? How would I navigate Christmas? How would I introduce a new voice into family rhythms already carved by a lost life? Those are boring questions in a way, but they're real. Loving again is not always cinematic, sometimes it is logistical, coordinating calendars, asking the new person to understand a child's mobile schedule, and negotiating whether the ghost's framed photograph stays on the mantel.

And then there is time. Time is not a judge that decrees who has suffered enough, it is only a dimension that keeps teaching you that grief loses some edges and keeps others. There is no correct timeline. There is only a person's readiness, and the kindness of people around them who do not insist on an answer.

If no one arrives, if I spend the rest of my days preferred in my own company, weaving my garden into a riot of gerberas and basil, that is a life. It is not second-best. I would still be mother, friend, writer, woman. I would still light candles at dusk and dance badly with the dog and laugh too loud at my own jokes. I would still go to the sea and let its boundary dissolve my smallness. Loving myself must always be worthy of applause.

In the end, love after loss is not a betrayal of the past. It is a tribute to it. If I chose to accept tenderness again, it would be because living fully honours the memory of the life that once was. If I chose not to, that too would be an honest choice. The only failure would be to live in constant penance, to let grief fossilise into identity until everything else rots.

One evening, long after the funeral wreaths had gone brittle and the house had learned new rhythms, I sat on the back step with Poppy asleep inside the open window, the garden alive with crickets and the scent of damp potting mix. I whispered into the dark: If love calls, I'll answer clearly. If it doesn't, I'll still be here. The stars overhead were small, indifferent pinpricks. They offered no pronouncements. But their quiet persistence felt like agreement.

The night air was cool, smelling faintly of earth and rain. Somewhere a neighbour's wind chime sang its uneven song, and I thought: this is what peace sounds like, not the absence of longing, but its gentler shape. I pressed my hand against my heart, feeling the steady pulse beneath my ribs, the insistence of life continuing. There is courage in opening again, and there is courage in staying closed. Both demand honesty. Both require you to love yourself enough to choose. And whatever I choose, whether love finds me, whether I find it in the quiet of my own life, whether I hold the hand of another or hold my own, I promised to answer clearly. Not out of duty to anyone else, but out of duty to the life that stubbornly continues to beat inside me.

And perhaps that is what love becomes, after all, the quiet agreement between the living and the lost, that to go on loving, in any form, is to keep the light alive.

Chapter Twenty-Six

Some people never really leave you.

Twenty-eight years had passed, yet all it took was one email, one subject line glowing in my inbox, and suddenly he was back.

It arrived on an ordinary afternoon, the kind that doesn't announce itself. The house was quiet in that mid-day way, the pause between school hours and evening noise. I had opened my laptop to do something forgettable, pay a bill, clear spam, or chase a form that had already chased me twice. My inbox was a clutter of the living: newsletters I never read, reminders I resented, and promotions promising a better version of myself if I would only click.

And then there was his name.

Not disguised. Not tentative. Just there. As if it had never left.

For a moment I thought it must be a coincidence, another man with the same name, a mistake, a cruel algorithm dredging old data from some forgotten corner of the internet. But my body knew before my mind caught up. That familiar tightening behind the ribs. The way heat rose without warning. The way memory has weight.

I didn't open it straight away.

I sat back in my chair and stared at the screen, as if the words might rearrange themselves into something safer if I waited long enough. Somewhere in the distance a car passed. The fridge clicked on. The ordinary world kept happening, oblivious to the fact that time had just folded in on itself.

I wondered, absurdly, how he'd found me.

Later, I would piece it together in fragments, a mutual friend I hadn't spoken to in years, a name mentioned in passing, a late-night search driven by nostalgia or loneliness or both. Maybe he'd typed my name into the dark and waited to see what answered. Maybe he'd been carrying me quietly all this time, the way people carry places they once loved and never revisited.

At the time, none of that mattered.

What mattered was the subject line.

No fireworks. No explanation. No careful easing back into existence. Just: *Hey gorgeous… stop breaking my heart.*

It didn't read like an introduction. It read like a continuation. As if we'd only been interrupted, not separated. As if the space between us hadn't been filled with entire lives, marriages and children, betrayals and funerals, healing and rebuilding. As if twenty-eight years were nothing more than a long breath taken before finishing a sentence.

I opened the email.

The words were brief, almost careless. A greeting. A joke. A line that could be dismissed as flirtation if you didn't know better. If you hadn't stood with him once in the Blue Mountains, eucalyptus thick in the air, believing with the arrogance of youth that some things were permanent simply because they felt true.

The ache rose instantly, like an old weather system waking beneath the skin. The room seemed to thin, the air less cooperative, as if my lungs had to relearn how to breathe in a climate I'd once called home.

My fingers hovered over the keys, useless.

I hadn't heard from him in over two decades. Not a message. Not a rumour. Not a trace. And yet there he was, not knocking, not asking permission, just stepping back into my life through a screen, as if the door had never really closed.

Twenty-eight years collapsed into that moment.

All the versions of me, the girl I was, the woman I became, and the widow I survived being, crowded close, listening.

And I knew, even before I replied, that this wasn't about rekindling something simple.

It was about unfinished music.

Suddenly I wasn't the widow, the mother, the scarred survivor of too many battles. I was the girl who had once stood with him on a cliff in the Blue Mountains, hair whipped by wind, laughing at something we didn't need to explain. His name had once been a song in my mouth. I had locked it away for years, telling myself that chapter had ended. And yet here he was, uninvited, impossible, and inevitable.

I opened the email and read it again. *Stop breaking my heart.* The words shouldn't have mattered. But they did. They threaded a needle through the fabric of now and then and pulled the years tight until the seams touched; they dragged the scent of eucalypt and cold sandstone into my warm kitchen; they reminded my bones that they had once known a different rhythm and had not forgotten it.

The thing about people like him is that they carve their initials into you without even meaning to. You go on with your life, layering new stories over the old, telling yourself it's finished. But some loves are unfinished by nature. They linger like a refrain you can't shake.

He wrote of regret, his words spilling out too easily, as if they had been waiting for years behind clenched teeth. He told me he had quit his job after our last encounter, that he'd been "knocked for a six" when I left. He admitted he had never found the words he wished he'd said. And then, in a line that caught my breath, he wrote: *Life has kept going and boom, there you are. Just hope you're okay and enjoying whatever it is you're doing.*

It should have been simple, two old friends catching up after too many years. But nothing about grief, or memory, or the messy geography of desire is ever simple. Time pretends to be linear until a sentence like that folds it into a paper crane, and then you're holding something delicate and impossible that flutters in your palms.

I typed back before I could talk myself out of it. Honest, maybe too honest.

Wow, I was only just thinking of you this week. Something came up about Sydney, and Sydney always reminds me of you. While I'm moving forward, you're still a memory in my heart.

The emails turned into a dance, playful and dangerous. His words slipped past my guard. He reminded me of a concert we'd been to, the surf competitions we'd watched, and the nights we had stayed up talking until the sky softened into dawn. His affection was reckless, almost boyish. At first I laughed, shook my head, told myself it was nostalgia playing tricks. But somewhere beneath the laughter, my pulse betrayed me.

It's ridiculous, I wrote to him once. *You've been a ghost for over a quarter of a century. Why now?*

Because, he replied within minutes, *I have never stopped loving you.*

The words hit like a fist and a caress all at once. I stared at the screen until my eyes blurred. Twenty-eight years of silence, and he typed it out as if no time had passed. The world around me continued with its ordinary commitments, the kettle clicked off, a postie's bike whirred by, and a magpie scolded the fence, but my inner weather changed, clouds gathered, light moved, and I was raining and lit at the same time.

Sometimes I still dream of that first summer in the Blue Mountains. The air was thin and wild, the sky bleeding into mist, the two of us walking along a trail that smelled of wet rock and freedom. I can still hear his laugh ricocheting off the cliffs, his jacket tied around his waist, my hands stuffed into the pockets of my shorts because I didn't know what to do with them. He had kissed me at the lookout, not a practiced kiss, but a breathless, crooked one, the kind you fall into rather than plan. When I pulled away, he said, half laughing, "That's going to ruin me." And maybe it did.

Years later, the dream feels almost too vivid, like a film reel that never faded. That was the memory his email cracked open, not gently, but all at once, the smell of rain on gum leaves, the way his hands had trembled when he touched my face, the way my heart had argued with my head even then.

Desire is oxygen to a starved heart. When you have been invisible for too long, when your body has lived only as caretaker, widow, mother, survivor, being seen again is almost unbearable. His words made me feel like a woman, not a relic. They made me laugh. They made me ache.

But memory has sharp edges. His life was complicated, tangled. Mine too. We both knew the cost of reckless love, of stepping into a story already scarred. I told him plainly: *I have no desire to try and pick up the past. No hidden agendas, no bullshit. I am tired now. I have lived enough complication to last a lifetime.*

He replied with silence that stretched into hours. Then: *I hear you. But I'm still madly in love with you.*

The words sat between us like a lit candle. I wanted to blow it out, and at the same time I wanted to cup my hands around it and keep it alive. What do you do with a declaration like that, after years of burying yourself alive in grief? Part of me wanted to believe it, to throw myself into the fantasy of what might have been if timing had been kinder. Another part of me bristled, fierce with self-preservation.

I thought of Marko, my husband, my ghost. Our two decades together had been brutal and tender in equal measure. He had been my tormentor and my companion, and he had also been my undoing and my anchor. Loving again after him felt like desecration. And yet, sitting in the kitchen with my laptop glowing like an open wound, I knew it wasn't betrayal I was feeling. It was hunger.

Grief and desire live uneasily in the same body, but they both have a right to stay.

The first time we spoke on the phone, his voice startled me. Older, yes, but still carrying that low rasp that had once undone me. He laughed nervously, and for a moment I felt seventeen again.

We talked about nothing, about weather, work, children, music, but the undercurrent ran thick. When he said my name, I had to grip the table. The syllables had weight, as if each one came stamped with places and hours and a version of myself I hadn't dared invite back into the room.

Outside, rain had begun to fall. It drummed softly against the kitchen window. I turned off the light so I could listen better, as if the dark could protect me from what I was feeling.

There was a pause on the line, that dangerous, fragile silence between two people who know they should stop but don't.

"I miss the way you used to look at me," he said.

I swallowed hard. "You used to make it easy to look."

He laughed, quietly. "You still do."

I closed my eyes, let the words fill the room. They felt like a hand reaching across time.

We arranged to meet, cautiously, like conspirators. Not in public, not yet. A walk by the river, where strangers passed without knowing the history that hummed between us. The sun was low, the air damp with the kind of sweetness that comes before rain. When his hand brushed mine, the world tilted. Twenty-eight years of distance dissolved into a single electric point of contact. It wasn't a kiss. It wasn't even a held hand. Just a brush of skin, accidental or deliberate, I couldn't say. But it ignited something in me that I thought had died.

I went home shaken, exhilarated, and ashamed. That night I stood in the shower until the water went cold, trying to wash away the sense that I had stepped across a line. Yet even as I dried myself, the warmth on my skin wasn't the water's doing, it was his echo.

The next morning, my phone lit up with his message: *I can still feel you.* My mouth curved into a smile I couldn't stop. The smile was dangerous, the kind that belongs to women who know better and don't care.

The days that followed blurred. Emails, calls, stolen hours carved from ordinary life. We talked about the Blue Mountains, about the way the mist had swallowed us whole that day, making us feel like we were the only two people left in the world. We talked about music, about the songs that had been soundtracks to our separate lives, the ones that still made us think of each other. He sent me lyrics at midnight. I wrote back with confessions I hadn't dared put into words before.

I'm sorry, I told him one night. *For hurting you. For running. For not knowing how to love you back then.*

He didn't hesitate. *Shut up. I'm still madly in love with you.*

The words lodged in my chest like a thorn and a balm at the same time.

The next time we met, it was under the excuse of coffee. Public, safe, daylight. I told myself it was innocent, a conversation between two old friends. But when I walked into the café and saw him at the back table, my body betrayed me again. His eyes found mine and lit, and in that split second the years vanished.

We talked for hours, sipping lukewarm cups as the staff stacked chairs around us. He asked about Poppy, about my writing, and about how I was coping since Marko's death. His concern wasn't performative, it was heavy with sincerity, with history. At one point his hand covered mine on the table. It wasn't romantic, it was steadying, grounding, the kind of touch that says, I see you, all of you, even the broken parts.

And yet it was also dangerous. Because I leaned into that steadiness like a woman starved.

When I left, the sky outside was bruised purple, and the air thick with coming rain. I sat in my car whispering out loud, "Don't do this. Don't." But even as I said it, my phone buzzed. *God, you're still beautiful.*

The tears came hot. Not because of the compliment itself, but because of what it unearthed. I had forgotten what it felt like to be adored, to be looked at without pity or judgment. For so long I had been widow, mother, survivor. With him, I was simply woman.

That night, sleep didn't come easily. I lay awake listening to the sound of rain against the tin roof, the rhythm of it familiar and strange. It took me back to that mountain night, the two of us huddled under a shared jacket, rain soaking through our jeans, laughing at how hopeless we were at being practical. He'd kissed me then too, clumsy and urgent, and I'd pulled away only to laugh again. "We're going to get pneumonia," I'd said.

"Worth it," he'd replied, and meant it.

Now, twenty-eight years later, I caught myself smiling at the memory. The ache it brought was exquisite.

Days blurred into stolen moments. A walk by the harbour, shoulders brushing. A drive through back streets, music loud, windows down like teenagers. Words whispered as though they were too fragile to speak at full volume. Once, on a street corner, our hands brushed and stayed, rooted together while the world spun around us. Another time he pulled me into a quiet lane, kissed me with the ferocity of someone making up for twenty-eight lost years.

When we broke apart, breathless, I laughed nervously. "We're ridiculous."

"Maybe," he said, grinning. "But we're real."

Desire rewrote the rules I thought I'd mastered. I had sworn off complication, told myself never again. And yet here I was, sneaking away to see him, my heart galloping like a teenager's, my body burning with a hunger that I thought had died along with Marko.

One evening we drove to the coast, to a lookout where waves smashed themselves against cliffs. The salt wind tangled my hair, while the horizon bruised with fading light. He wrapped his arm around me and pulled me close. For the first time in years, I leaned without apology.

"I wanted your life," he murmured. "Because I didn't have

one of my own."

His words landed like glass in my chest, confession and indictment in one. Proof of his longing, evidence of his emptiness. I held them carefully, unsure whether to treasure or fear them. In his reflection on the car window, I saw a man both yearning and lost, the kind of man who could break you not because he wanted to, but because he didn't know how to stop needing.

I told myself it was temporary. A detour. A reminder that I was still alive. But each time I walked away, it hurt as if I had left something vital behind.

At home, Poppy noticed. "You're smiling more, Mum," she said, suspicious.

"Nothing," I replied too quickly. "Just… life."

But she was right. Something inside me had been rekindled, though not because of him alone. He had reminded me of myself, the part that was still fire, still woman, and still capable of stirring and being stirred.

Of course, there were complications. Women who thought they owned him. Ghosts he hadn't faced. Stories untold. I saw the mess and knew, deep down, that to step fully into it would swallow me. And yet, the longing was undeniable.

Sometimes we met in secret, parked in quiet streets, his lips brushing my wrist like it was holy. I rested my head on his shoulder and let myself imagine, for a heartbeat, what life might have been if we had chosen each other all those years ago. But imagination is a dangerous drug. It shows you what might have been without promising what will be.

One night, after a stolen rendezvous, I drove home shaking. My lips swollen from his kiss, my heart raw with contradictions. I sat in the dark kitchen and whispered, "This isn't love. This is resurrection." And maybe that was enough. Because what he gave me was not a future, but a reminder. A reminder that I was still capable of longing, of laughter, of feeling alive in my skin. A reminder that my life could still carry brightness that didn't have to apologise to the dark.

Our messages continued, sometimes sweet, sometimes sharp. He told me I was the only one he had ever truly loved. I told him not to say things he couldn't stand by. He swore he meant it. I doubted him and believed him all at once. The contradiction exhausted me.

And so, slowly, I began to step back.

Not with speeches. Not with ultimatums. Just with the quiet discipline of a woman listening to her own pulse and deciding not to gamble it away.

The last time we spoke, there was no fight. No dramatic goodbye. Just a shared understanding that whatever we were doing could not last. Too many ghosts. Too much history tugging us in opposite directions.

But even in that ending, there was tenderness.

"You'll always be my girl," he said softly.

I smiled through tears. "And you'll always be my unfinished song."

That night, I lay awake listening to the hum of the house. I thought about how some loves aren't meant to be lived out loud. They exist in memory, in whispers, in the space between words. Sydney Boy was never mine to keep, but he was mine to feel. And feeling him reminded me of something essential.

I was still a woman. Not just a widow. Not just a mother. Not just a survivor. A woman with desire. With fire. With the capacity to be stirred and to stir. That knowing settled in me like a lamp turned low, steady, warm, and unshowy. Enough to see by.

Weeks later, Poppy and I went walking at dusk. She kicked at pebbles and told me about a boy at school who'd annoyed her, and I listened with half a smile. The sky streaked itself violet above us. The world felt wide again, like a place where stories could keep unfolding. I thought of him then, not with longing, but with gratitude. He had been a door I walked through, not into a new life, but back into my own.

Love after loss is never clean. It's crowded with ghosts, tangled with questions, and heavy with memory. But it is also proof of life. Proof that the heart still beats. Proof that longing can survive the ashes.

Sydney Boy was not my future. But he reminded me that I had one.

Sometimes, late at night, when the house is quiet and Poppy is asleep, I still hear his voice. I still feel the echo of his touch. And instead of shaming myself, I let it be. I let it remind me that love doesn't always have to stay. Sometimes it only has to pass through.

One night, sitting alone on the back step beneath the stars, I whispered, "Thank you. For reminding me." The stars said nothing. But the night pressed close, like an answer. The jacaranda scattered its purple confetti across the paving, and I thought: some seasons arrive without trumpet, just colour, quiet, and the certainty that something has returned.

Some people never really leave you. Not because they are meant to stay forever, but because they carve their way into your song. Sydney Boy was a verse in mine, unfinished, yes, but unforgettable.

The echo doesn't ask me to go back. It asks me to keep going.

And in the hush that followed him, I learned this: Resurrection isn't about returning to what was lost. It's about remembering that the heart can rise again, even from its own ashes. Love doesn't vanish. It changes shape. And when I look back now, I see that he was never meant to stay. He was the flicker that reminded me of my own light.

Because in the end, resurrection was never about him.

It was about me, still here, still breathing, and still brave enough to feel.

Chapter Twenty-Seven

Grief does strange things to people. It exposes fault lines you never knew existed , racks in families, in friendships, in love itself. Sometimes, it draws people closer. More often, it tears them apart. I learned that lesson in the ugliest way.

Even after death, Marko's shadow loomed large. He had been my husband for twenty-two years, the father of my daughter, my greatest love, and my deepest wound. No matter what anyone said, no one could erase that history. But not everyone saw it that way.

The woman who had lived in the margins of our marriage, Caren, could not let go.

The first time she intruded, it wasn't even in person. It was a text, a message that arrived out of nowhere one late night, when the house was quiet and the only light came from the phone in my hand.

"You think you can rewrite history?" she wrote. "You were nothing but a liar. He hated you."

The number was unfamiliar, but I knew the venom instantly. I should have ignored it. I told myself I would. But grief has a way of stirring up everything you've tried to bury.

I poured another glass of wine, the cheap kind that bites the back of the throat and sat at the kitchen table staring at her words until they blurred. The digital glow painted my hands an eerie blue. I could see the fine lines, the tiny tremor of fatigue in my knuckles, the small betrayals of age. Somewhere down the hall, the dog shifted in her sleep. A pipe groaned. The world carried on, utterly unaware that a battle line had just been drawn between the living and the dead.

The silence of the house was its own kind of witness. Every creak of timber, and every hum of the refrigerator seemed to echo back her words, liar, hated, get over yourself. The language of cruelty has a strange way of filling a room.

My fingers trembled as I began to type. I wasn't writing to her, not really, I was writing to everything she represented. The audacity, the revision, the smallness of people who try to own pieces of you they never earned.

"I was Marko's wife for twenty-two years. The mother of his daughter. We shared an unbreakable bond. We still share that bond, even in death. You had barely two years with him. Two years of jealousy, insecurity, chaos. You were a disappointment to him. You left his home a filthy mess, you disrespected his family at the hospital, and you made his life smaller. I had a lifetime with him, not you. You were a blip. And thank God that blip is now over."

When I pressed send, I felt a rush of something close to victory. My hands shook, my chest burned, but for the first time in months I felt awake. Alive.

Then came the waiting. That small, excruciating gap before a reply appears, the dots pulsing like a heartbeat. I could almost feel her, somewhere across the void, vibrating with fury.

Her reply came quickly, venomous, feral.

"Bitch, he hated you. You lied, cheated, made his life miserable. Go get fucked and get over yourself."

She went on about letters, promises, vasectomy reversals, fragments of imagined intimacy she clutched like relics. The kind of things only someone desperate for proof would cling to. She called me a liar, and a crazy bitch. Each sentence more grotesque than the last, designed to wound.

And yes, it did sting. Not because I believed her, but because I hated being dragged into the mud of it all. There's something degrading about standing in the ashes of a shared life and arguing over who owned the fire.

I put the phone down and walked to the window. Outside, the night pressed close, thick and humid. The lemon tree swayed. The reflection in the glass startled me, my own face, drawn and tired, eyes rimmed red. For a split second, I saw Caren's sneer in the reflection overlaying mine, and the thought chilled me, grief can make monsters of us all if we let it.

For a good hour I avoided looking at my phone. But grief and anger are sisters, one silent, one loud, and both demand attention. I couldn't stay away. Eventually, late into the night, I typed again.

"He told you whatever he had to, Caren, to keep your delusions quiet. It was easier for him to let you believe he hated me than to deal with your rage. I know the truth. Marko knows the truth. You can scream all you want, but it doesn't change anything. You were never his future. You were his mistake."

The message sent. The bubble turned blue. And that was it, the silence after the storm. I put my phone down on the table and stared at it until the screen dimmed. I sat there in the dark, heart hammering like I'd been in a fistfight.

Somewhere in the distance, a storm was building. The first faint roll of thunder trembled through the air. It felt fitting, like the sky itself was cracking open under the weight of unfinished business.

That night, I dreamed of the hospital.

Marko was lying there on life support, the steady rhythm of

machines counting what his heart could no longer manage on its own. His face wasn't thin or grey, it was round and still, with that same furrow in his brow he'd always worn when something troubled him. I remember brushing my fingers over that furrow, smoothing it the way I used to when he couldn't sleep. I kissed his forehead, whispering something only he would understand. The smell of antiseptic clung to everything, the sheets, the air, the memory itself.

Caren was there too. She stood at the foot of the bed in a too-bright dress, her arms folded tight, her chin lifted like she was guarding territory. Her eyes burned with a kind of ownership that didn't belong to love, only obsession.

In the dream, I turned to her and said, softly, "We both lost him. But you're still fighting for the corpse."

She looked at me, her mouth twisting. "He loved me," she hissed. "You ruined him."

But when I looked back at the bed, Marko's eyes were open. He looked at me with that familiar, half-sorry expression, the one he'd worn in life after every fight, after every promise he broke and tried to fix with tenderness. Then the machines went quiet.

I woke gasping. The room was dark and still. My pillow was damp. For a moment I thought I could smell him, that faint mix of cedarwood and cigarettes, but it vanished as soon as I sat up.

The next morning, I moved through the house like someone underwater. The tiles were cold. The silence thick. My phone lay on the counter where I'd left it, face down, glowing once with a new message I refused to read.

It wasn't about Caren anymore. It was about the wars women fight over men, men who, half the time, aren't worth the bullets. We tear each other apart, clawing and spitting, while the real problem escapes unscathed.

Marko was gone. Caren was clinging to a fantasy. And I was left in the wreckage, trying to shield my daughter from the shards.

One night, another message arrived. Just a single line: "You'll never be rid of me."

I stared at it for the longest time. Then, calmly, I deleted it.

Later that night, I went outside, barefoot on the cool grass. The lemon tree rustled in the dark, the scent sharp and alive. I looked up at the sky. wide and ink-black, and whispered, "You're wrong."

The air shifted, soft as breath against my cheek. Somewhere deep down, I felt him, not as comfort, not as guilt, but as presence. And for the first time since his death, I wasn't afraid.

Because I knew the truth, and that was that no one ever wins these wars.

Caren could scream her version. I could scream mine. But neither of us could bring him back. Neither of us could rewrite the story. We were both women haunted by the same man, different ghosts, same grave.

And I was done letting the dead speak louder than the living.

In the days that followed, I expected silence to feel like peace. It didn't. It was a heavy quiet, the kind that hums in your blood, vibrating with something unfinished. The house seemed to exhale differently. The air carried that stillness unique to places where grief has settled, where words have been spoken too harshly, and where the ghosts of old arguments still hang from the rafters. I tried to fill it, turning on the radio, leaving the television muttering in the background, but every sound felt false, like a stranger in my home. Even the refrigerator hummed louder, the clock ticked more insistently, and the dog's sigh from the hallway sounded almost human. Silence was not peace; it was a haunting with manners.

I went through the motions of life same way I always did, laundry, dinner, bills, Poppy's homework, and the slow choreography of ordinary days. I folded towels that smelled faintly of the lavender softener Marko used to mock. I scrolled through bank statements, paid overdue notices, and cleaned cupboards that didn't need cleaning. At the supermarket, I stopped in front of the coffee aisle and stared too long at the brand he used to buy. My throat tightened. I pushed the trolley away quickly, pretending to check my phone so no one could see the way my eyes had glassed over. At home, I found one of his old shirts folded neatly in the back of a drawer. I held it to my face and gently breathed him in, the faint trace of cologne, and the dust of years, and then folded it again, slower this time, as though I were tucking a heartbeat back into the fabric.

Grief doesn't end when you stop crying. It lingers in the body, in the way you grip a cup too tightly, the way your jaw locks when someone mentions his name, or the way your voice trembles when you think no one's listening. It's in the pauses between sentences, and it's in the way you glance at the passenger seat while driving and forget, for half a second, that it's empty. Mine had found a new shape, not tears, not yearning, just ache. A quiet, pulsing ache that settled behind my ribs like an unwelcome tenant.

One evening, when the ache became unbearable, I grabbed my keys and drove. The sky was bruised, that in-between shade of violet and smoke, the hour where day holds its breath before surrendering to night. The roads were nearly empty, and the wind through the cracked window carried the damp scent of rain. I didn't plan the destination; the car seemed to choose for me. Only when the weathered cemetery sign appeared in my headlights did I realise where I was going. I hadn't been back since the funeral.

The parking lot was empty except for one old ute, its bonnet shining wet under the streetlight. I sat there for a while, the engine ticking cool. My reflection in the rearview mirror startled me, pale, tired, a woman still half-made of shadow. I took a deep breath, then stepped out into the night.

The air was cool and heavy, full of eucalyptus and damp soil. My shoes sank slightly into the earth as I followed the narrow path. The headstones stretched out like a quiet congregation, each name carved into permanence. I passed tiny offerings, plastic flowers, children's toys, notes tucked into jars. Life distilled into tokens of remembrance.

When I reached his grave, my chest tightened. The grass had grown wild around the edges. A few rain-spotted blooms leaned toward the earth, their petals beginning to curl. I knelt, brushed the leaves away, and for a long time I just stared.

"I don't know what you'd think of me now," I said quietly. "Maybe you'd laugh. Maybe you'd be angry. Maybe both."

The words surprised me, how easily they came, how natural it felt to speak into the open air. "She's still fighting you, you know. Still fighting me, too. You would've hated that." I smiled, small and broken. "You never liked women at war."

A magpie called somewhere in the distance, its song mournful and bright. The wind rustled through the gums with a sound like applause. I laid my palm against the cool stone. "I loved you," I whispered. "But I can't keep bleeding for your ghosts."

The wind lifted again, soft and steady, and for a heartbeat it felt like a reply, not forgiveness, not condemnation, just acknowledgment.

I sat there until the sky deepened to indigo. Streetlights flickered on one by one, casting halos across the wet path. A faint drizzle began, speckling my arms and hair, and instead of running for shelter, I tilted my face up to it. The rain was cool and cleansing. It traced down my cheeks and tasted like release.

When I finally drove home, the smell of wet earth followed me. I rolled the window down and let the air wash through the car, fresh, raw, and alive. Somewhere between the cemetery and my driveway, something loosened. Anger, grief, guilt, they all began to unspool, thread by stubborn thread.

Because the truth is, ghost wars don't end when one side wins. They end when you realise you no longer need the battle to feel alive.

Caren kept sending messages for a while, small provocations, little jabs meant to draw me back in. *"You'll regret this." "He told me everything about you." "You were the reason he drank."* Her words slid across my screen like venom, but I didn't take the bait. I let the messages pile up like dead leaves, unopened, until even the phone stopped buzzing. Eventually, they ceased. Or maybe they didn't, maybe I just simply stopped looking. Either way, silence took root again, and this time, it grew something gentler inside me.

I started sleeping again, dreamless and deep. I began to eat properly, lighting a candle at dinner, not out of ritual but reverence. I wrote again, scraps at first, then pages that began to sound like truth.

One morning, I caught myself humming while washing dishes. A silly tune from years ago, something Marko used to play while fixing the car. The sound startled me. I nearly dropped the plate. It felt foreign and miraculous to hear music inside myself again.

Sometimes, at night, I'd wake to rain on the tin roof and think of him, not with bitterness or longing, but with compassion. Marko had been many things, flawed and fragile, loving and cruel, and impossible and necessary. A man who tried, failed, and tried again. Maybe that's what love really is at the end, two imperfect people doing their best in the dark.

One night I dreamed of him again, but this time there was no hospital, no sterile light. We were back in the old house, sitting on the verandah while the storm rolled in. He looked younger, barefoot, hair damp from rain. He smiled that half-smile that had always undone me. In the dream, I said what I'd never been able to say in life: "I forgive you."

He nodded once, silent and certain, and the dream dissolved into gold light.

When I woke, the morning sun slipped through the blinds in long, honeyed stripes. I sat up and smiled. It was the first time I'd ever woken from a dream of him without crying.

That day, I deleted the last message thread from my phone. Not out of anger, out of mercy. There's a kind of peace that only comes when you stop trying to edit the past.

Later, I went out to the garden. The lemon tree was flowering again, tiny white blossoms like stars scattered among the green. I pressed one between my fingers, breathed in its sharp sweetness, and thought, *this is how it happens*. Life doesn't return all at once. It tiptoes back in, through scent, through song, and through the small bravery of mornings that don't ache as much as they used to.

Because in the end, resurrection was never about him.

It was about me, still here, still breathing, and still brave enough to feel. Still woman enough to stop fighting ghosts and start tending the living.

I will always carry him somewhere, not as a wound, but as a scar that glints when the light hits it right. And when the old pain stirs, I let it. I let it remind me that I survived.

Caren can keep her ghosts. I have none left to feed.

And if I ever see her name flash across my phone again, I know what I'll do, I'll smile, set the phone down, and step outside into the daylight. The world will go on humming its indifferent, miraculous song.

Because the war is over.

And I've already won by walking away.

Sometimes healing doesn't roar its arrival.

It comes quietly on ordinary mornings when the kettle hums and the air smells like rain. It comes when you realise you've gone a whole day without checking your phone for ghosts, when laughter escapes your mouth uninvited, when forgiveness stops feeling like surrender and starts feeling like freedom.

The past doesn't vanish; it softens.

The dead stay where they belong, loved, remembered, but no longer steering the living. The heart learns to beat differently, not harder, not faster, just steady.

And maybe that's what resurrection really is.

Not the blaze of miracles, but the gentle act of staying, staying kind, staying open, and staying alive despite it all.

I am still here.

Still breathing.

Still brave enough to love what remains.

Chapter Twenty-Eight

Sometimes the heart speaks in stories that aren't entirely our own.

The morning came softly, like a whisper through gauze curtains. Sunlight spilled across the sheets in thin gold rivers, and for the first time in what felt like years, I didn't flinch from the light. I lay there for a moment, listening, to the hum of the kettle, to the magpies calling to one another across rooftops, and to the slow creak of a world waking. The house breathed around me. The day waited, gentle and unassuming.

I used to hate mornings. The way they exposed everything, the unmade bed, the silence beside me, the proof of another night survived. Now, the light felt like forgiveness.

I swung my legs over the edge of the bed, my toes meeting the cool wood of the floor. That small sensation, cool against warm, felt almost sacred. For months, I'd lived as if my body were separate from me, a ghost of routine moving through familiar motions. That morning, I felt myself fully, skin, breath, weight. Presence.

In the kitchen, I boiled water and waited for the kettle's click, a sound that once meant nothing, now meant everything. I spooned loose peppermint tea into a mug and poured, watching the pale green bloom unfurl through the water. The scent rose sharp and clean, waking something in me. In the window above the sink, I caught my reflection, hair still wild from sleep, eyes softer than they had been. There was something almost new in my face.

I stepped outside into the garden, barefoot, the grass slick with dew. The lemon tree was in bloom again, its blossoms pale and insistent against the green. I touched one, fragile, fragrant, and alive. A year ago, I'd threatened to pull the tree out. Too tangled. Too stubborn. It had refused to die. So had I.

The world unfolded slowly around me, bees bumbling, the distant hiss of sprinklers, and the pulse of a neighbourhood entirely unconcerned with my history. The ordinariness steadied me. Healing, I was learning, wasn't made of grand gestures. It was built from these near-invisible acts: watering a tree, checking the mailbox, and folding the laundry while the radio murmured on.

I scribbled a small grocery list - lemons, bread, candles - and beneath it, without thinking, I wrote a single word: sea.

I didn't question it.

The sea had been calling me for months. I'd ignored it, afraid of what might rise in me if I stood there again, in that salt air where I'd once whispered my goodbyes. But now the fear felt smaller than the pull.

From the hallway, I heard Poppy's door creak open.

She padded into the kitchen in mismatched socks, hair tangled into sleep, rubbing her eyes with the heel of her hand. She paused when she saw me at the bench, as if surprised to find me already awake, already somewhere else.

"Morning," she said, her voice still rough around the edges.

"Morning, love."

She poured herself cereal, stood at the counter instead of sitting, crunching thoughtfully. After a moment, she looked at my list.

"What's 'sea'?" she asked.

I smiled. "I think it's an idea."

She considered that. "Like… now?"

The simplicity of it caught me off guard. No hesitation. No weight. Just possibility.

"If you want," I said. "We don't have to stay long."

Poppy shrugged, already halfway convinced. "Okay. Can we get hot chips?"

"Obviously."

We were in the car less than an hour later, windows down, the air cool and salted even before we reached the coast. Poppy kicked off her shoes as soon as we parked, slinging her backpack over one shoulder, already moving ahead of me down the path like she knew exactly where she was going.

The sea opened itself to us in wide, breathing sheets of blue. The horizon was clean and sharp, the kind of clarity that feels like a promise. Gulls cried overhead. Wind threaded through our hair.

Poppy ran straight for the water, jeans rolled clumsily, and squealing with delight when the cold caught her ankles.

"It's freezing!" she laughed.

"It always is," I said. "That's how you know it's real."

She glanced back at me, eyebrow raised. "That's weird, Mum."

"Most true things are."

We walked the shoreline together, not talking much. Poppy collected shells and showed me the best ones as if presenting evidence. I watched her, the easy swing of her arms, and the way she belonged to her body without apology. I felt something loosen in my chest that I hadn't realised was still tight.

At one point she took my hand, not out of need, just habit. Her fingers were warm and certain in mine. The tide crept close, licked our feet, and then retreated.

"You okay?" she asked, casual but perceptive.

I nodded. "Yeah. I really am."

She accepted that without interrogation, turned back to the water, skipping a stone that bounced twice before sinking.

We sat on the sand and shared hot chips wrapped in paper, the vinegar stinging the air. Poppy talked about school, about a friend who'd annoyed her, about a song she liked but pretended not to. I listened, truly listened, the way I hadn't always been able to.

The sea kept breathing beside us, steady and unconcerned.

For the first time, I understood something clearly, this wasn't the place of my goodbyes anymore. It was a place of return. Not to what had been, but to what was still possible.

When we finally stood to leave, Poppy brushed sand from her hands and said, almost offhand, "We should do this more."

"Yes," I said, without hesitation. "We should."

As we turned to face the path, the wind at our backs, I felt the quiet truth of it settle in me.

Healing doesn't always happen alone. Sometimes it happens beside a child kicking water and laughing at the cold. Sometimes it happens when you realise you are no longer walking back into grief, but forward, together.

And the sea, generous and ancient, let us go without asking for anything in return.

I walked along the shoreline with the lemon blossom still cupped in my hand. The world smelled of salt and eucalyptus, that clean, clarifying scent that feels like both beginning and ending at once. The tide rolled in patiently, unconcerned with my history.

My thoughts drifted to Marko, not the man in the hospital bed, not the silence he left behind, but the boy who once had carried me laughing into the shallows, both of us soaked and young and convinced we had life figured out.

"Look at you, Lenny," he used to say, teasing. "Always trying to make sense of the sea."

I smiled at the memory, at the nickname no one else ever used.

There were other echoes, too, Sydney Boy's reckless grin, the kiss that had felt like defiance rather than promise. Loves that had come and gone, not to stay, but to wake something in me. I understood now that love wasn't a single melody you get right or wrong. It was a rhythm, sometimes steady and sometimes breaking, that teaches you how to listen to yourself.

The lemon blossom trembled between my fingers. I crouched at the edge of the tide and set it gently on the water.

"Go," I whispered.

It wasn't a farewell. It was permission.

The tide caught the blossom and carried it outward. I watched until it became a pale dot swallowed by distance. The wind lifted my hair, light and insistent. Beneath it all, I felt my own heartbeat syncing with the waves, that old, universal metronome reminding me I was still here.

Behind me, Poppy laughed, bright and unselfconscious, racing the water as it chased her ankles. A sound so alive it stitched something back together inside me. I turned and watched her for a moment, the way she belonged to her body, to the day, to the future. Not a spectator. A participant.

I closed my eyes. The sun pressed warm against my face. In the dark behind my eyelids, that familiar glow appeared, soft, steady, unmistakably mine.

The soul song.

It wasn't coming from anyone else now. It never had been.

When I opened my eyes again, the horizon shimmered gold. The tide had crept closer, brushing my toes like a reminder.

"Thank you," I whispered, to the sea, to the ghosts, to the life that kept finding me no matter how often I tried to outrun it.

As we turned back toward the car, Poppy slipped her hand into mine without thinking. And for the first time, the world didn't feel like something I had to brace against.

It felt like something I could walk into.

At home, the faint chaos of life greeted us, shoes kicked off in a heap, Poppy's half-finished art project spread across the dining table, a candle burned low beside a forgotten mug of tea. These things used to ache like proof of absence. Now they looked like evidence of persistence.

Music drifted from the living room, something poppy and off-key. Poppy was singing along, twirling in socks, utterly unconcerned with grace. I leaned on the doorframe and watched her, tears pricking my eyes at the ordinary miracle of it.

We ate cereal for dinner, champions' food, side by side on the couch, a sitcom murmuring in the background. Between mouthfuls, Poppy leaned her head on my shoulder. The warmth of her undid me.

"You okay, Mum?" she asked quietly.

"I think so," I said. "For the first time in a long time... I really think I am."

"You look lighter."

"Maybe," I said, brushing a curl from her face, "I finally stopped fighting the ghosts."

"Dad?"

"Among others."

She studied me for a moment, then smiled. "I like this version of you better."

Later, after the house settled and the stars began to scatter across the sky, I sat on the verandah with my notebook open. The blank page no longer frightened me. It felt like invitation.

I wrote about renewal. About the quiet bravery of ordinary days. About burnt toast and lemon blossoms and laughter that arrives unannounced. About how love doesn't disappear, it changes shape until it fits inside you again.

I titled it *The Soul Song*.

Because that's what it was.

Not something I'd lost. Something I'd remembered.

The next morning came softly. Magpies, mist, and the kettle humming. Poppy asked what I was humming.

"I didn't realise I was," I said.

"It's pretty," she smiled. "You should write it down."

"Maybe I already have."

I went outside. The garden was damp, fragrant with earth. The lemon tree gleamed, each blossom bright as a star. I reached out, ran my hand along one branch, and felt its pulse of life, slow, strong, and familiar.

It struck me then; I was no longer surviving my story. I was living it.

I thought of the night at the sea, of the blossom I'd set adrift, and of how it must have broken apart somewhere out there, not lost, just transformed. Maybe that's all any of us are doing, breaking apart, changing shape, and finding new ways to belong to the world.

The kettle hummed inside. A bird landed on the fence, shaking off rain. The day stretched open, wide and waiting.

Sometimes healing doesn't roar its arrival.

It arrives without ceremony, woven into the fabric of ordinary days, the kettle humming, damp air drifting through an open window. You notice it only afterward, in the quiet victories: a day that passes without summoning the dead through a screen, a laugh that escapes before you can stop it, and the moment forgiveness loosens its grip and feels less like loss and more like release.

The past doesn't vanish; it softens, its sharpest edges worn down by time and repetition.

The dead remain, loved, carried, folded into the fabric of who we are, but they no longer set the direction of our days.

The heart learns a different rhythm. Not urgent. Not fragile. Just present.

Maybe resurrection isn't about rising at all, but about staying, inhabiting the life that's still here without apology.

I stand at the threshold of the day and let it be what it is.

I am here.

Breathing.

Learning how to live forward.

Chapter Twenty-Nine

For a long time, I thought it was his voice that undid me.

It didn't seem to matter how much time had passed, how far apart we lived, or how final our endings had appeared, whenever certain words found me again, it was as though my chest had cracked open and something ancient had remembered itself. Not memory in the ordinary sense, like pulling a photograph from a drawer, but remembrance in the bones, in the marrow, in that hidden place where recognition lives.

It wasn't just familiarity. It felt inevitable, like a melody that had played quietly beneath my life for years, waiting for me to finally hear it. We had never crossed paths again in the way people imagine when they speak of fate, and yet whenever that old resonance stirred, it felt less like discovery and more like remembering. As if somewhere beyond this life, in the space's that grief opens, love had already left its fingerprint.

There were days I told myself I was foolish, that I had turned longing into myth simply because loss had hollowed me out. But then a word would land just right, or a memory would surface, and the whole universe would tilt again. It was never only about the person attached to it; it was about the way those echoes felt. Like home. Like déjà vu. Like a song I hadn't realised I knew until I found myself humming along.

And yet, wasn't that the cruel part of the song? To call me closer only to remain unfinished. To haunt me with a promise never fully fulfilled. We were always almost. Almost brave enough. Almost free enough. Almost ready at the same time.

Those messages were fire and comfort. That familiar tone, when I dared to hear it, wrapped around me like smoke and starlight. But it was always somewhere else. With another life attached. Existing in a way I could not step into without betraying my own. I wrestled with it, with memory, with myself. The push and pull of longing and loss. The reality of boundaries, the impossibility of a love that could exist everywhere except here, in flesh and time.

There were nights I hated it for that. Mornings I hated myself more, for answering, for hoping, for letting the galaxy spin me around again when I knew the ground would not hold. But the truth remained, that echo was part of my soul-song. Its note, though jagged and unresolved, belonged to my melody.

Sometimes I wondered if it was less a person and more a mirror, a reflection of what I had buried, of the longing I'd been too afraid to name. It reminded me of the woman I'd been before the world bruised her, the one who had once loved wildly, laughed too loud, danced barefoot in the kitchen, and believed in miracles. Maybe that's why it sounded like music, because it woke something I thought had died.

It taught me that sometimes love's purpose isn't permanence. Sometimes love arrives not to stay but to awaken, to break, to burn, to build you again in the light of what you've survived.

I think now about galaxies, how stars are born in collapse, not in perfection but in implosions. That was it. Collapsing, burning, and scattering across the sky of my life. And in that scattering, something luminous was created inside me.

When I think of it now, I no longer ache for what wasn't. I bow to what was. It was a constellation I traced with trembling fingers, proof that I could still feel, still long, and still sing. Maybe that was the lesson all along, not that it was the answer, but that I was never lost to myself. Because in the end, love doesn't always finish the song for you. Sometimes it hands you back your own voice.

Sometimes I still hear it, in dreams, in laughter, in the echo of music through an open window. It doesn't hurt anymore. It hums softly, like memory turned gentle. The song remains unfinished, but I do not. My melody, my ember, my pulse, my truth, is mine to carry forward.

The heart, I've learned, never forgets its own rhythm. It might stumble, fracture, or lose its place in the score, but given time, it finds its way back to tempo. Healing isn't the absence of ache. It's learning to dance with it.

One morning, months after the last time that echo stirred, I woke before dawn. The air was cool, silver with early light. The kettle hummed softly as I watched the first bird cut across the sky. That's when I realised I hadn't thought about it in days, not with pain, not with longing. Just with gratitude. I whispered it into the quiet, Thank you.

It wasn't forgiveness I was offering. It was release.

I dressed and drove to the coast. The sea was calm, a vast sheet of glass broken only by the slow breath of waves. I took off my shoes and stepped into the surf, the water cold and clean around my ankles. I thought of all the names I'd carried, widow, wife, mother, survivor, and felt them lift like fog off water.

I wasn't defined by what had been taken from me, or by who had walked away. I was defined by the way I kept returning - again and again, to life.

The sky bruised pink as the sun broke through. I reached

into my pocket and pulled out a small lemon blossom, freshly fallen from the tree that had outlived so much, outlived our ghosts. I placed it on the water, watched it drift toward the horizon until it vanished into light.

It wasn't ceremony. It was simply truth, a truth that I am still here.

As I stood there, the wind shifted, soft and familiar, brushing my cheek like breath. I closed my eyes and for a heartbeat felt them all, the dead, the lost, the ones who had loved me and the ones who had not known how. They were part of the same song.

And somewhere inside that wind, or maybe just inside me, a voice whispered, *Sing.*

That night, I came home and lit a single candle on the kitchen bench. I hadn't planned a ritual, but the flame's small persistence filled the room like forgiveness. The light trembled against the walls, steady but soft, a heartbeat I hadn't realised I'd missed. Maybe healing begins like that, a flicker that refuses to go out, even when no one's watching.

Days unfolded gently, the way waves pull back after a storm. I started living again, not pretending to, not performing wellness for the world, just living. Music crept back into the house on Sunday mornings. The smell of toast and peppermint tea replaced the silence that had once hung like fog. Poppy's laughter travelled down the hall, bright and untamed. Life, imperfect and glorious, had returned.

Grief didn't leave; it simply changed its posture. Some days it brushed past me like a friendly ghost, others it lingered just long enough to remind me of its shape. But it no longer defined me. It no longer demanded a seat at every table.

Poppy was growing into herself, bold, opinionated, and

unafraid. Sometimes she caught me watching her and grinned.

"Mum, stop being sentimental," she'd tease, flicking her hair in mock defiance.

"I'm just… proud," I'd say.

"Of what?"

"Of surviving."

She'd roll her eyes, but I'd catch the smile hiding at the corner of her mouth.

One afternoon she found an old photograph, me and Marko, salt-haired and laughing, sunburned at some forgotten beach. "You were happy," she said quietly.

"I was," I told her. "And then I wasn't. But that doesn't mean it wasn't real."

She studied me, then shrugged. "You're happy now, too. Just… different."

"Different is good," I said, and meant it.

Later that night, after she'd gone to bed, I stepped out onto the verandah. The lemon tree shimmered under the moonlight, its branches heavy with new fruit. The air smelled of citrus and damp earth, clean, honest, and alive. I stood there barefoot, with the boards cool beneath my feet, and I let the night wrap around me.

Something inside me had shifted. I no longer felt like I was waiting, for permission, for closure, or for someone to come back and make it right. I had become my own rescue.

Writing returned quietly, like breath after grief. At first, just small fragments, half-poems on scraps of paper, lines scribbled on receipts, confessions left unfinished. But soon the rhythm came back. I wrote about ghosts and love, and about the way sorrow rearranges the furniture of your soul. I wrote until the world outside blurred and the words began to hum, that same old soul-song, only this time, it belonged entirely to me.

One night I wrote about that echo, not as an ache, not as a myth, but as a presence that helped me remember. The words didn't taste of pain anymore. They tasted like release. When I read them aloud, they didn't echo with loss. They rang with truth.

And that was when I realised that the story was never about the men who left or the ones who stayed. It was about the woman who kept standing. The one who walked through ruin and came out radiant.

Time softened around me. The days began to blur in a way that felt kind, no longer a countdown, but a continuation. The house aged with me. The grief in its corners grew gentle, like dust that caught the morning light.

Sometimes I'd take my coffee to the garden and sit barefoot in the grass, the sun sliding slow and golden through the clouds. The magpies would start their song, that tumbling, joyous music that always sounded like hope. And in those moments, I'd whisper thank you, to no one, to everyone, and to the universe itself.

Marko was still there, in the quiet. Not as a wound, not as regret, but as presence. Like the shadow of a tree you once sat under, you don't see it always, but you know it's shaped your shade. I felt him in the hum of the kettle, in Poppy's grin, and in the lemon tree that kept flowering long after he was gone.

Sometimes, I even thought of Caren. I hoped she'd found peace too. Maybe she was somewhere learning the same truth I had, that love, once fractured, doesn't vanish, it transforms. That forgiveness isn't a surrender to weakness, but a refusal to carry another person's chaos any further.

One day Poppy handed me her school project - *Write about someone who inspires you.* Her words were simple, but the last line undid me: *My mum taught me that you can be broken and still be brave.*

I laughed, blinking back tears. "You're impossible."

"You love it," she said, smirking.

And she was right. I did. Because it meant she had seen me, not as a tragedy, but as proof.

That night I sat at my desk and wrote one final sentence in my notebook: *Sometimes the song doesn't end, it just changes key.*

When I put the pen down, I knew the story had come full circle.

Years passed, quietly. No dramatic rebirth, no sudden epiphany, just the soft persistence of living. Work, friends, sunsets. The small, holy rhythm of survival turned into joy.

Every now and then, I'd dream , a laugh, a voice, a fragment of song drifting through sleep. It never hurt. It never asked for more. It simply reminded me that love, in its purest form, doesn't vanish, it echoes.

One morning, as dawn broke pink across the horizon, I walked out to the garden. The lemon tree was in bloom again. Dew clung to the petals like tears that had finally found their purpose. I reached up, touched one of the blossoms, and smiled.

I was still here. Still breathing. Still brave enough to love what remained.

The wind rose softly through the branches, carrying the faint scent of citrus and earth, a melody older than words.

And for the first time, I realised I didn't need anyone else to finish the song.

Because I was the song.

Inside, the kettle began to hum. Magpies called. Poppy laughed from down the hall. The woman who had once drowned in grief stood quietly in the doorway, light spilling across her face.

She smiled.

Because resurrection had never been about the ones who left. It had always been about the one who stayed.

Her.

Still here.

Still breathing.

Still brave enough to love what remains.

The melody went on, unfinished, yes, but infinite. And in that endless song, she was finally, beautifully, free.

Epilogue

Every story has its dark night.

Mine was long, brutal, and unyielding. There were days I mistook breath for defeat, nights when silence pressed on my chest until I wondered if the ember inside me had finally gone out.

I was wrong.

Grief stripped me bare. Abuse broke me down. Betrayal hollowed me. I thought the Tower of my life had collapsed for good, that the wreckage was all I would ever be. But rock bottom wasn't my ending; it was the foundation I hadn't chosen and somehow needed. When the dust cleared, I was still standing, shaking, scarred, and alive.

For years I measured my worth by other people's verdicts, the men who stayed or left, the rooms I kept together with my body, the names thrown at me across kitchens and car parks. I wore masks, good wife, brave widow, tireless mother. When I finally stopped performing for rescue and turned inward, I heard a voice I'd been drowning out for years. Call it God, call it Spirit, call it the marrow of my own soul, what we name it matters less than this, it was mine, and it told the truth.

You are more than what hurt you.

You are not the lies spoken over you.

You are worthy of love, of peace, of joy.

The Dark Night did not destroy me, it carved space. Ashes became ember, ember found breath, and breath became flame.

I think of the night I shook my fists at the sky certain my song had ended. Looking back, I see that was the first note. From the shattering news, through the country of exile where days smeared into each other, through the long walk back to my own body, the melody kept threading itself through the ruin. Even the unfinished loves, the ghost-songs that brushed past my shoulder and moved on, were part of it. They reminded me I could still feel. They did not define me. I define me.

To the woman I was, frightened, brilliant with survival, and begging the heavens for relief, thank you. You kept breathing long enough for me to arrive here.

To the woman I am becoming, fierce, radiant, and tender, keep going. Keep burning. Keep telling the truth faster. Keep laughing loud.

And to you, holding these pages, if you have lost yourself in the dark, if shame has taught you to make yourself small, if the mirror has felt like an argument you cannot win, know this, your story is not finished. The night is not the whole sky. Meaning can be stubborn, and so can you.

There is life after loss. There is love after heartbreak. There is light after darkness. Not as a slogan, as a practice, one breath, one yes, one boundary, one small mercy at a time. The soul-song was never about who sings beside you, it has always been about remembering you were born to sing.

Some days my voice is a whisper. Some days it is a shout. Both are proof I am still here.

If love comes again, it will find me standing, not waiting-room quiet, not half-alive, but whole in my own light. And if it doesn't, I will still set the table, still plant the gerberas, still dance in the kitchen with the dog watching like an unimpressed critic. I will still be a home to myself.

The Tower fell. The mask broke. The floor gave way and

then became ground.

What endured, what endures, is the ember.

I carry it forward. So do you.

Author's Note

If you've walked with this story this far, thank you.

Thank you for holding these pages, for carrying Lena's world in your hands, and for allowing her broken places to brush up against your own.

This was never a story written for pain's sake. But I believe now that no story is ever truly wasted. If even one moment in these pages lit a spark of recognition , if even one line reminded you that you are not alone, not too broken, not beyond hope, then this telling has done its work.

There are no neat answers here. Only the ongoing work of becoming. Of fumbling forward. Of learning, again and again, how to live inside a life that has been changed.

What I know, and what this story holds, is this: we were never meant to walk only in darkness. There is always an ember waiting beneath the ash. And sometimes, it is through stories, told, shared, and received, that we learn how to breathe it back to life.

So to you, wherever you are as you close this book: keep going.
Your song matters.
Your ember matters.
And you are already enough.

With love,
Mals x

About The Author

MAL STEVENS - THE AUTHOR was born in the small, country town of Geraldton, Western Australia, and at the very tender age of three - after discovering a love for reading whilst sitting at her Pops feet whilst he read in his library, decided that she would someday become an Author. Often her family and friends thought her weird because no matter where she was, she could always be found with her nose in a book…and if her nose wasn't in a book because of reading it, then it could be found in one of her many hundreds of journal notebooks filled with fanciful made up stories, and vivid descriptions about her life in general, and poetry.

Today, I am a Registered Nurse by trade, a Mum 24/7, a Mining and Construction Site Medic by day, and a writer by night. I rarely sleep. I find writing therapeutic, and I happily and passionately lose myself to it on a daily basis.

Shine, Shine, Shine.
With Lots of Love xxx

An Excerpt From 'A Star To Remember'

per ardua ad astra

Chapter One

"Good on ya, Indi!" Mollie and Aliviya sang in unison, before Aliviya added, "You need to start getting out there and doing things for you!"

"I know, I know. But that doesn't stop me worrying about the life I already have here now does it?"

I smiled at my housemates and best friends, two out of the three dearest people to me in this world, and I let myself wonder exactly what this brand-new life could possibly mean for me now. I had worked so hard to get to where I was today, and I couldn't help but feel a bubbling excitement for all the opportunities that now lay ahead.

A bachelor's degree had been quite the achievement for a young woman going through a traumatic life event at the very same time. I stared at the framed certificate hanging proudly on the living-room wall, a Bachelor of Science in Nursing, and suddenly I was overwhelmed by memories of how much work it had taken to reach that dream, and ultimately, what it had cost me in the end. I wondered, would my excitement always be tainted with tinges of sadness?

I remembered the criticisms so clearly, as though they were only yesterday. Sharp little pricks, aimed at my pride in an attempt to derail me. In hindsight, pricking my pride hadn't been hard to do, I was a proud young woman. I always had been, and I suspected I always would be. Back then, the criticisms were aimed at the life changes I had chosen to make for myself. Words spoken in the heat of arguments, things that never should have been said. The silly things you say but don't truly mean when you just want to hurt someone. I felt myself begin to crumble inside, just a little. But almost immediately, I caught myself. I can't let these thoughts detract from me anymore.

Deep down, I knew my guiding star was leading me toward bigger things, toward my destiny. I could feel it, an unshakable force pulling at me, one I couldn't resist even if I'd wanted to. I was being led, and I knew I was in trusted hands, the trusted hands of the universe. I walked over to the back door and stepped outside. Looking up into the pitch-black sky, I let my eyes roam over the stars. I knew one of them was mine. And I would let it lead me to where I was most meant to be in this world.

Not everyone had agreed with my choices back then. In fact, I don't think anyone had agreed with any of my choices at all. But that was okay. It hadn't been okay at the time, but it was now. I was old enough now to dance to the beat of my own drum. I didn't need anyone's approval anymore. Nor did I want it. My loved ones and my career made me feel happier than I had been in years. They gave me purpose and direction. Without them, I reckoned I would have just curled up and died. It was time to stop dwelling on the past. Five long years I had dwelled. Today had to be the day the dwelling stopped, and my new life began.

I walked back into the house, still caught up in my thoughts. After finishing my degree, I'd completed my graduate year, followed by a year on a busy surgical ward in one of Perth's large hospitals. It was just enough time and experience to give me the courage to join a nursing agency. I'd joined at first in the hope that working across different hospitals would boost my confidence. God only knew how low my confidence had been, buried down in my pink nursing sneakers, and it needed all the help it could get. Over time, I consolidated my learning, and I knew I needed to establish myself within my career. It was time to crawl out from under the rock I had been living beneath and step out into the big wide world that everyone kept telling me actually did exist out there.

The agency helped me in more ways than I had ever imagined it could. I had succeeded in stepping out from under my rock and, more importantly, stepping outside of my comfort zone. I had now worked in almost every hospital across Perth, in both general and mental health.

After Lionel's accident, I had resigned from my full-time nursing position, and the security it had afforded me, and with nothing but trust and a massive amount of faith in my heart, I chose to work exclusively with the agency. These days, I worked full-time hours as a casual registered nurse, and I danced, at least to some degree, to the beat of my own drum. And I loved it. I loved that I could choose where I worked, how much, and when. The new, improved, confident, unstoppable me had even branched further into remote area nursing, working in some of the most rugged, untouched regions of northern Western Australia. Sometimes, I hardly even recognised myself anymore.

"Wow," I whispered, almost in disbelief. "Who even is this?" Occasionally, pangs of guilt still came to me, especially when I thought of carving out a new life for myself beyond Perth. But my family and friends had always stepped in and supported me when I needed it the most, knowing exactly what to say, and when to say it. They were my greatest strength, my supports, and my daily reminder of all that was good in this world.

I had just completed an eight-week contract in Geraldton before taking a little time off to spend some much-needed girl time with my friends back in Perth. Next on my agenda, a twelve-week remote nursing contract in a fairly isolated part of northern Western Australia.

First, the hospital in Port Hedland for two weeks' of mandatory training and refreshers. Then, ten weeks' as the sole nurse in a remote Indigenous community east of Karijini National Park. Seventeen hours' drive north of Perth.

Back toward all the memories and everything I had once shared with Lionel. This wasn't the life I had dreamed of, but it was the life destiny had dreamed up for me. These days, I chose to see everything as either completely perfect, or as an opportunity for growth and learning. I just had to keep putting one foot in front of the other. That's what I kept telling myself anyway.

***

"Anyone up for pasta?" Mollie bounced into the kitchen, her voice bubbling with the same enthusiasm.

The mood in the house had been slipping toward sullen, weighed down by both my thoughts, and by Aliviya's recount of her day. She animatedly described the unprofessionalism of her coworker Hannah, whilst Mollie and I both listened intently. Mollie busied herself with making a start on dinner, while I opened a bottle of wine, before launching into an almost lecture-like conversation of my own about the importance of being true to yourself, and for standing up for what you believe in. I turned the stereo on and blasted AC/DC's *Whole Lotta Rosie'* just as Luna joined us in the kitchen. It wasn't long before dinner was well and truly underway and the atmosphere in the house had lifted considerably.

My eyes shifted toward the larger-than-life canvas of Lionel that hung on the living-room wall, pride of place in the house. I raised my glass toward it and gently whispered, "Cheers, Lionel." A small smile tugged at my lips as hidden tears threatened to escape my eyes. Random, funny little memories began flooding in, alongside the irritating ones, and the frustrating ones too. They were memories that had made some of the days since Lionel's passing easier to bear, and others almost unbearable. I let them linger briefly before gently tucking them back away again.

Sometimes, when the grief pressed hard, I'd reach inside my wallet and touch the edge of his old driver's license card. It had been there so long now that the plastic was worn smooth. It reminded me that love could keep moving, even when a life couldn't.

***

Mollie, Aliviya, Luna, and I had all found ourselves living in Perth at the same time, and we had jumped at the chance to rent a house together. Our only requirement was that it had to be close to public transport and the city. The four of us had first met back in grade seven of primary school, and right from the very beginning we'd known that we would be friends for life. Fifteen years had come and gone, and our bond had only deepened. School, university, family dramas, relationships that started and ended, happy times, hardships, births, deaths, and holidays, we had seen it all, side by side. We had laughed together, cried together, and leaned on each other through it all. Over the years, friends had come and gone, drifting interstate or overseas, but the four of us had remained strong. Even when busy schedules meant we could only catch up with each other every few months, we somehow always managed to find our way back to each other. It was hard sometimes, but it was also what defined to us who was truly a friend for life, and who had only been a friend of convenience.

Mollie was now an architect working in a global studio that specialised in sustainable design and urbanism. Aliviya worked as a dietitian at one of the major city hospitals. And Luna, our daily dose of Zen, was our Environmental Scientist, and the one who kept us grounded. She was the voice that reminded us to "get over ourselves" when we became too highly strung, and her sunrise Pilates on the verandah was standing-room only.

***

After dinner, Luna and Aliviya cleared away the dishes, Mollie returned to her laptop to finalise tomorrow's deadlines, and I finished packing the last of my things into my suitcase, mentally rehearsing the long journey north that lay ahead.

I had given myself two days for the drive to Port Hedland. If I left at 06:00, I could stop in Geraldton to see Mum and Dad for a quick coffee and toilet break before pushing on to Carnarvon. With luck, I'd arrive before dark. That stretch of road was notorious at sunrise and sunset, with kangaroos, cattle, and even the occasional donkey littering the highways. I'd already booked a room at the Gascoyne Hotel. A solid night's sleep there, then back on the road by 07:00 the next morning for the final leg to Port Hedland.

As I packed, a heaviness pressed on me. Anxiety? Nerves? Maybe both. The last time I had stayed at the Gassy had been with Lionel. I hadn't set foot in the north since his accident. My heart belonged there, though. It yearned for the red dirt, the rocky ranges, the peaceful silence. The north was very spiritual to me. And I knew that Lionel would always be right beside me. Still, the thought of the journey made me falter.

"What the friggin' hell am I doing?" I muttered out loud without realising.

"Indi, you need to do this," Aliviya said from the doorway, her voice steady and reassuring. "Everything's sweet. Hit us up if you ever need us, legit only just a phone call away."

"Stop worrying, Indi! Geeeeez!" Mollie called from across the room, her tone a mixture of exasperation and affection.

Just then, my phone sprang to life, the familiar strains of Lenny Kravitz's "Again" spilling out and striking me right in the heart. I had left it as my ringtone since Lionel, but now it felt like another thing I needed to let go of. Change was coming, and change meant that song had to go.

"Mole," I said into the phone, smiling at the name flashing on the screen.

"Hey, Mole," Kat replied.

Kat and I had met through the nursing agency, and we had clicked instantly. I didn't do well driving across Perth, so I mostly filled shifts close to home. Kat lived an hour away in the hills, but we often ended up at the same hospital, giving us the chance to catch up.

"You working South tonight?" she asked.

"No, Mole. I'm packing for Hedland in the morning. I need a break from here."

"Good for you, Mole! It's always the same there. I worked last night, Jack's half-hour break turned into an hour and a half. He waltzes back in at 06:00, and I'd been dealing with patients on my own the whole time. Then he disappears into the office to write his notes, leaving me to do the 06:00 checks. Meanwhile, I'm running cups through the dishwasher and trying to get vital signs on room sixteen done. Honestly, I'm sick of working with these lazy cunts."

I laughed because I knew exactly what she meant. I'd experienced the same frustrations myself more times than I could count. Her rant only confirmed that I truly did need this break. The people I worked with had grown too comfortable around me, too lax, and I had started judging them in my frustration. A change of scenery was exactly what I needed.

"Yeah, Mole, I'm hearing you," I replied. "I get dumped with the checks too, fifteens, half-hourlies, and the routines. Hard to get anything else done when you're the only one doing them."

She went on, animated and fiery as always, describing Jack's avoidance, the chaos of the smoking area, useless handovers, and her slow slide from mini breakdown to major breakdown. Her words came fast, peppered with curses, making me laugh even as she vented.

By the time she finished, I felt drained but grateful. Kat was the only person I knew who could use the "C" word and somehow not make it sound completely vile. She helped keep me sane in this crazy job.

We said our goodbyes, and I returned to my suitcase. My mind lingered on the call. The hospital wasn't all bad, I loved my job, and I loved nursing, but sometimes it was overwhelming. Sometimes you just needed space to breathe.

I zipped my suitcase closed without even realising I had finished packing. My thoughts were still spinning. Feeling heavy and tired, I decided on a quick shower to wash away the residue of old hurts. As I lathered soap over my skin, a sobering truth hit me, erasing Lionel from my heart would be far harder than I had ever imagined.

***

Mollie was still awake, her laptop glowing in the dim light as she finalised a design project. Something about an "office building space inspired by Karijini National Park," she muttered. All double-dutch to me, honestly.

"My boss just emailed, told me not to drive in tired, to take a taxi. He knows me too well. Knows I'll be up all-night finishing this."

"Then get some sleep, Mollie," I said firmly. "No point staying up all night and turning up exhausted. What's that going to achieve?"

I knew I sounded like a broken record, and I was sure she was rolling her eyes at me, but that was what best friends did right, nag when needed.

She changed the subject. "You haven't packed your Homer Simpsons, have you, Indi?"

I laughed. "No. Maybe. Yes."

She groaned. "I'll be glad when those finally fall apart."

Those pyjama bottoms were my favourite, bright yellow, Homer's grinning face plastered all over them. My housemates teased me constantly, insisting the street would know me by them, but I didn't care. Comfort mattered more.

I hugged each of my friends tightly. "Goodnight, besties. I love you very much." Tomorrow was going to be a big day.

An Excerpt from 'Atreia Rising - Book One' 'Life-of-Life Series'

alea jacta est

Chapter One

Leaning out from over the Karijini National Park gorge's edge, Leena closed her eyes, stretched, and then unfolded her wings as far and as high as she could, and slowly turned in a full circle as she absorbed all the sights, and the smells and sounds that Karijini afforded her. The waterfall, the crystal-clear waterway leading to the green-coloured pool of water that lay at the bottom, and the stripes of red, brown, and bluish black of the gorge's rock wall in-between, that spread for as far and as wide as her eyes could see. The brilliant blue sky of a Pilbara dry season that encased her like a mother's overwhelming love and made her feel safe. She listened to the sounds of water trickling its very own journey, of gentle breezes, of trees gently creaking their appreciation of spiritual wonder, and of sounds that just had no names to her.

Hawks circled above her head, and their haunting cries began to intertwine with her own until she no longer knew where they ended, and hers began. As the sunlight gently touched her face, Leena inhaled deeply and leaned into the gentle breeze and let it slowly lift her off her feet and off out over the top of the gorge's edge. She beat down hard with her wings, and as she did, she felt the air lift her up higher and higher, her blonde hair flailing wildly around her. She moved in circles, slowly at first, higher and higher, then increasing in speed with her sheer desperation to fly through the clear blue sky towards the Sun. Away from the pain, and away from the cold injustices of life, and into the warmth of that Sun. 'No one can hurt me here, this is where I am free.' Leena flew for what seemed far too short a time, but had in fact been quite a few hours, wishing that she could stay here forever, and never again return to her waking life. For some reason, that life depressed her, it lay upon her shoulders like a heavy burden, even though those that surrounded her loved her very much.

***

I opened my eyes and turned my head and looked to the bedside clock, 04:57, another few minutes and the alarm would have gone off and woken me up anyway. Most times I am a morning person and I love to get up with the Sun, but these days it takes all my energy just to drag myself out of bed. I rolled over in bed and lay on my back and stared into the blackness of my bedroom up into the direction of the ceiling. My mind was full of thoughts about anything and everything and nothing.

I consciously willed myself to remember my dream. I remembered flying. For as long as I could remember I had been able to fly in my dreams. A lot of things I did I assumed everyone else could do. The more people I spoke to though, the more I realised this not to be the case.

I could still vividly remember my very first memory of flying in my dreams. The day had been a very profound day because it had also involved Andy. I knew that day that I was about to embark on a very significant journey. The voices on the wind had tried to speak to me, whispering to my mind their gentle secrets. Secrets that at the time I had been unable to grasp, and so they had slipped easily from my mind. Then that first night… my dreams had taken me far away from home, I had been to the stars. Sometimes I wished I could just go to sleep and wake up in five, or ten, or twenty years' time, and at other times I wished to just not wake up at all.

'I wish I never had to wake up,' I whispered quietly, knowing all the while that it was a very silly thing to wish for, and then I started to feel all my burdens return to me.

The bedside clock alarm sounded. I reached over and switched on the bedside lamp first before turning the alarm off. I caught a glimpse of my eldest boy Bandit as he walked past my bedroom door, heading in the direction of his younger brother Zander's room.

Zander was only ten years old and always sick, and we had been kept up half the night from his coughing. I felt like I had been hit by a bus! Sleep for me these days was never restful. Slowly I dragged myself out of bed and joined Bandit in Zander's room.

Bandit was fourteen years old and every bit his father's son. He was already a full head taller than me in height. His thick, silky hair, the colour of rich chocolate that fell in soft waves to his shoulders, and dark-lashed golden-brown eyes the colour of good Jamaican coffee, with the depth of a bottomless well. Both of my boys had inherited their fathers' brown eyes. I could see the dark-red rings around Zander's eyes, and I wondered to myself if he would ever get better. When Zander was well, he was dashing, his hair the same crisp blonde colour as mine. It fell in waves around his shoulders too, though at the moment it looked ratty and dirty; it had lost its sparkle, and so had he.

Zander's bedroom was the smallest of the three. Our house was old but very much in line with the era for when it was built and for where we lived. It was built in the Pilbara in the 1970s. The window from Zander's room was the only bedroom window in the house that looked out over our back yard. It had a fairly large window that was draped in brightly coloured 'kiddie' curtains. He had asked me on more than one occasion to change them for him to something more 'suitable', seeing as now he was 'grown' up. In front of the window lay his most prized possession, his beloved DW custom-built drum kit that had once belonged to his dad. Above his bed hung model planes, planets, and a life-like replica of the solar system, and his ceiling was covered in stars that glowed when the lights were out. The floor was covered in a run-of-the-mill everyday carpet that was littered with floor rugs, and two of his bedroom walls were covered in shelves for all his bits and pieces. One day Zander hoped to be an astronaut and visit the stars.

My eyes were on Zander as I entered the room and walked to his bed. 'Hey, Buddy!' I lovingly brushed Bandit's shoulder as I walked past him to sit down on the side of Zander's bed. 'Didn't sleep well, huh? How are you feeling now?'

'Not good, Mum! I feel all light-headed and short of breath and I can't stop coughing. I'm sick of coughing!' Zander managed to say all this before another one of his coughing fits started.

'Morning, Mum,' Bandit interrupted.

'Morning, darl.' I turned and smiled to Bandit. 'Sleep well?'

'Mmm, not really! Zander coughed a lot last night.' Bandit headed towards the door, then glanced back to me to say, 'I will make him some breakfast, Mum,' before disappearing off into the direction of the kitchen.

'Thanks, darl,' I called after him as he exited the bedroom.

I focused my attention back to Zander as I spoke. 'I will make another doctor's appointment for you this morning as soon as the doctor's surgery opens, sweet. I love you.' I ran my fingers through Zander's hair as he lay in his bed looking back up at me.

We were both silent for what felt like the longest moment. I searched his eyes. What else could I do for him? How could I make things better? I sighed before leaning down and drawing him in close to me for a quick hug before standing. 'Is there anything else I can get for you, sweet?' I asked before leaving his room to join Bandit in the kitchen.

'Just something to eat and drink thanks, Mum. I'm starving!' Zander gave me his cheeky boy grin.

Zander's cheeky boy grin was the only thing I would ever need in this world to make my life complete. Bandit and Zander, and the bond and love we all shared as a family and nothing more. We were the three amigos! That was us!

'Right, my ole soldier. I shall check on how Bandit is doing in the kitchen then, shall I?' I smiled softly to myself as I left his bedroom.

***

Bandit had breakfast for both he and Zander well under way by the time I entered the kitchen, four Weet-Bix with milk, and a cold Milo!

I put the kettle on. 'I just wish I could do something more for him.'

Bandit stopped what he was doing to look at me as he spoke. 'Yeah, I know, Mum, don't worry, he'll be fine, you'll see.'

I smiled at his effort of breakfast. 'I'm going to ring the doctor's surgery as soon as they open at 08:30 this morning and make another appointment for him, hopefully for today,' Bandit scooped a hearty spoonful of the cereal into his mouth as I continued, 'and if they don't have any available appointments for today, then I will try for a cancellation instead and see how we go. Do you want me to drive you to school today, honey?'

'No, Mum, I'm all good thanks.' Bandit shovelled another mouthful of cereal into his mouth before he picked up Zander's breakfast. 'I'm meeting up with some of the other guys and we are all going to ride our bikes to school today.' And with that, Bandit turned and walked off to take Zander's breakfast to him.

I eyed off the fruit bowl sitting on top of the kitchen bench, overflowing with a whole pineapple and several oranges, apples, pears, and bananas. I picked up a single banana, and rather than cut up a bowl of fresh fruit for breakfast this morning as was my usual morning ritual, I decided instead to do a quick smoothie before going off to shower and get my day started. I measured out the almond milk and poured it into the blender, I then added some flaxseed, oat bran, my broken up banana pieces, and a handful of frozen blueberries, blitzing it all for about ten seconds. I poured it into a cup and then downed it all in one swift gulp. I filled the kitchen sink with warm soapy water to soak the dishes and then headed off to take a shower.

***

The shower today was gloriously hot. I stood beneath the massaging warmth of its spray and as I washed myself, my thoughts returned to my scattered, fragmented memories of last night's dream. I could remember feeling a 'presence' beside me in my dream, that I had not been alone. I had turned to look but had seen nothing, and then suddenly the words *Leena, my Life*' had rung through my mind. I smiled to myself as I remembered the feeling from those few words, gentle and loving and nothing to fear. There was something very familiar to me about them. I wondered also about the name Leena. There was something very familiar to me about that too. Leena from Atreia and Michelle from Earth were one… but not the same. The first night that I had flown in my dreams I had been with others, but I remembered nothing of them, except the whispers of a promise. I flew as I had done many times before, but this time something was unusual and different, about the 'presence' that is, I could feel it stronger this time than at any time ever before. Yes, I had felt it before, but I had always passed it off as just my imagination, but this time it was almost a touch, '*see me*' it seemed to say to me. I turned around at the time but had seen nothing other than the blue sky that surrounded me.

'Oh well,' I hung up the shower sponge, 'something to ponder on until the next time I dreamed.' I turned off the shower and hopped out, pulling the towel around myself, and drying quickly as I went. I got dressed. Trying to pull my knickers up over wet legs was no easy feat. 'Should have just dried myself properly to begin with!' I mumbled quietly to myself, frustrated, as I continued to strategically hop and manoeuvre myself around the tiny little bathroom, trying to fix my damn knickers into place.

I mindlessly finished dressing myself, then hurried with some makeup, catching glimpses of someone I did not recognise in the bathroom mirror. I wound my hair up in a loose bun atop my head, and then I paused for a moment to stare deeply into the bathroom mirror, only to see the dull eyes of unhappiness staring right back at me.

All I could see was the battered soul. The effervescent woman whom I put on display for the entire world to see was not at all whom I appeared to be. This had become my daily routine, for as long as I could remember.

I hid them very well! My scars! Performing beautifully, day after day so as not to reveal any part of the depths of my soul that I had desperately tried to keep hidden for all these years.

***

Loud banging on the front door startled me back to the present now. I glanced quickly at the bedroom clock as I hurried past on my way towards the front door. *'It's 06:30 in the morning, no one ever knocks on my front door at this time of the morning!'* My initial reaction was to panic. But that panic immediately turned to giant elephants stomping around inside my stomach as soon as I opened the front door, to find Andy Russo standing there. HOOOOOLY CRAAAAAAAAP! My heart pounded so deeply that I was positive he could see it jumping around inside my chest like crazy just beneath my shirt, and if he couldn't see it, then I was positive he sure as damn well hell could hear it. 'I think I'm going to be sick!'

Andy Russo was knocking on my front door at this time of the morning and turning my world completely on its head for what felt like the umpteenth time in just as many years. Actually, it was ten whole years to be exact! But I certainly wasn't counting! Andy Russo was definitely not who I had expected to see standing on my front porch when I opened my front door this morning that's for sure. Tall, clean-shaven, gelled back dark-brown hair, those soul penetrating blue eyes, and smelling oh-so-good. I traced my tongue slowly over my bottom lip before biting it. He was leaning to one side against the front verandah of my house, in an unforgettable way to me that only Andy Russo could deliver. He really was master and king of not only his own universe, but according to him, everyone else's as well.

'Miiicheeeeeeeelle,' his voice purred, 'what have I told you about biting that lip!' He looked me up and down, and then raised both shoulders as he lifted his hands slightly upward and away from his side as if to gesture an embrace.

'Andy.' I squinted at him. 'It's barely light.'

'I know,' he added, more serious now, 'but a 200-tonne crane went over just before dawn. Regulator's on site at nine. I need help.'

His voice intoxicated me, and momentarily I was drunk with him. Our paths had crossed on and off briefly over the last ten years on more than one occasion. Each time leaving me filled with feelings I couldn't explain. Feelings that felt so right, yet the timing never seemed to be. I could feel it instantly the moment I opened my front door. That undeniable pull between the two of us was still there! It permeated every cell of my entire being like sizzling thunder. Rising within me, and then paralysing me briefly for a moment until I was able to regain some composure. I prayed with everything I had in me that he didn't see the effect that he had on me.

'Andy! Well, aren't you just a …' I stopped myself, sight for sore eyes was what I was going to say, but that would have just meant that I was actually very pleased to see him, and at this point in time I was in no way ready to admit that yet. Actually, at this point in time I don't think that had even registered in my brain yet, '…vision of loveliness!' I quickly followed this up with a forced smile across my lips and a raise of the eyebrows. I spoke as calmly and as controlled as I could. I steeled myself against him with everything I was made of all the while desperately pushing away feelings that were invading my body, and memories that were flooding my mind about Andy Russo, and of the last time that our paths had crossed. The Pilbara dry heat, the wilderness against our naked bodies, and the taste of salt from his golden tanned skin. 'And to what do I owe this pleasure, Andy?'

'Cuppa tea'd be nice.' A cheeky smile passed over his lips as he nodded his head up and down in a 'yes' fashion. He then raised his eyebrows up and down once as he gently tapped a finger on the belt buckle of his jeans. Then there was just silence. His expression turned more serious as he again began to speak, breaking the awkward silence that had begun building between us. 'Work, actually. Word on the grapevine is that you could be interested?'

'Work!' I repeated, the warmth of his body having an intoxicating effect on me. 'You're here to talk to me, about work, on my doorstep at dawn?'

'If it could wait, I'd have called,' he said, lowering his voice. 'We'll be shut down if I don't front with a credible plan by midday.'

Andy Russo was head of mining safety operations at Hampton Industries in the Pilbara, Western Australia. He was their main man. Any concern about safety standards within the mining operations was a responsibility that lay squarely on his broad shoulders. Andy was first and foremost, always passionately motivated about his work; he held the reputation as the 'go-to' man within the industry. He had a proven track record that had taken him twenty solid years to build up. I did feel extremely flattered that he was standing on my front verandah wanting to talk to me about 'work'. I had my own share of successes within the mining industry as a site safety advisor though. I prided myself on maintaining a company's 'Zero Harm' policy, and I worked tirelessly every day to maintain work environment's that supported the health and safety of its own people, whilst at the same time minimising any impact that the company may have on the environment.

A smile slowly formed across his lips as he watched me, and the tingles started to run furiously throughout every cell of my being. Andy Russo was well and truly aware of the things his smiles did to me, and right now he was all in with both guns blazing. I refused to let my guard down.

Taking a deep breath in, I stepped aside and gestured with my hand for him to come in. I was interested to hear what he had to say, but I held up a palm as he passed. 'Ground rule, Andy, work is work. If I say yes, that's the hat we both wear.'

'Fair,' he said, nodding once. 'As you are aware Michelle, Hampton Industries is in the process of the construction of the new $15 billion mine right here in the North, and the project is now almost 77 per cent complete.' He eyeballed first, then sat down on my lone, beaten-up, old couch that sat against the far wall in the small family room area of my home, just inside my front door. 'In the last couple of months, I have been inundated with safety issues at the mine. Bloody head office has received several notices from the Western Australian Department of Mines, with the last of the notices that I received being issued earlier this month and relating to elevated work platforms and working at heights.' He reached into his satchel and produced a manila folder that was overflowing with paperwork. 'I need to re-assess the site policies before we kick into the next stage. Your background in heights work-permit systems, EWP, and crane lifts fits the hole I've got to fill today.'

He passed me the folder. I pulled over a kitchen chair and sat as far away from him as I could without looking obvious, as opposed to right next to him on the couch. 'So, what's in all this for me, Andy?'

'Apart from another opportunity to work closely beside me?'

I rolled my eyes. He kept it business. 'There's no denying this contract will look impressive on your resume. And as far as I am aware, at the present moment you are 'between' employment, are you not? And I think you will agree the salary on this contract is a hell of a lot better than any salary you might've previously earned. Also, regulator wants to see corrective actions by noon. Help me steady this, and I'll back your framework across the project.'

'You've had a lot of press about safety lately,' I said, refusing to be dazzled.

'We've earned some and copped some,' he admitted. 'But audits last month still called our overarching approach "excellent." We've had a couple of serious incidents, cranes, EWPs, and I need your head in the room to close the gaps before they close us.'

With Andy's business with me done, he stood in preparation to leave. 'Do we have a deal, Michelle?'

I took a breath, felt the pull, and kept my footing. 'If I say yes, I'm saying yes to the job, not…anything else.'

'Understood,' he said, softer.

He extended his hand to me, and I shook it without a second thought.

'We have a deal, Andy.'

As I shook Andy's hand, I couldn't help but feel like I was doing a deal with the actual devil himself. I saw Andy off, and then finished the morning routine before Bandit and his mates left for school. I checked the time. Still half an hour until the doctor's surgery opened for the day. Poor Zander, he will have to miss yet another day of school.

I smiled to myself as my thoughts then returned to my dream.